JOSEPH KEATINGE
CO-CREATOR / WRITER

WOOK JIN CLARK
CO-CREATOR / ARTIST

TAMRA BONVILLAIN
COLORIST

FERNANDO ARGÜELLO
FLATTING ASSISTANT

ARIANA MAHER
LETTERER

ALI BOUZARI
CULINARY CONSULTANT

RICH TOMMASO
LOGO DESIGN

SHANNA MATUSZAK
TRADE DESIGN

SPECIAL THANKS TO DOUG O'LOUGHLIN

FLAVOR. First printing. November 2018. Published by Image Comics, Inc. Office of publication: 2701 NW Vaughn St., Suite 780, Portland, OR 97210. Copyright © 2018 Joseph Keatinge & Wook Jin Clark. All rights reserved. Contains material originally published in single magazine form as Flavor #1–6. "Flavor," its logos, and the likenesses of all characters herein are trademarks of Joseph Keatinge & Wook Jin Clark, unless otherwise noted. "Image" and the Image Comics logos are registered trademarks of Image Comics, Inc. No part of this publication may be reproduced or transmitted, in any form or by any means (except for short excerpts for journalistic or review purposes), without the express written permission of Joseph Keatinge & Wook Jin Clark, or Image Comics, Inc. All names, characters, events, and locales in this publication are entirely fictional. Any resemblance to actual persons (living or dead), events, or places, without satirical intent, is coincidental. Printed in the USA. For information regarding the CPSIA on this printed material call: 203–595–3636 and provide reference #RICH–820359. For international rights, contact: foreignlicensing@imagecomics.com. ISBN: 978–1–5343–0882–4

Chief Operating Officer **Robert Kirkman**
Chief Financial Officer **Erik Larsen**
President **Todd McFarlane**
Chief Executive Officer **Marc Silvestri**
Vice President **Jim Valentino**
Publisher / Chief Creative Officer **Eric Stephenson**
Director of Sales **Corey Hart**
IMAGE COMICS, INC.

Jeff Boison Director of Publishing Planning & Book Trade Sales
Chris Ross Director of Digital Sales
Jeff Stang Director of Specialty Sales
Kat Salazar Director of PR & Marketing
Drew Gill Art Director
Heather Doornink Production Director
Nicole Lapalme Controller
IMAGECOMICS.COM

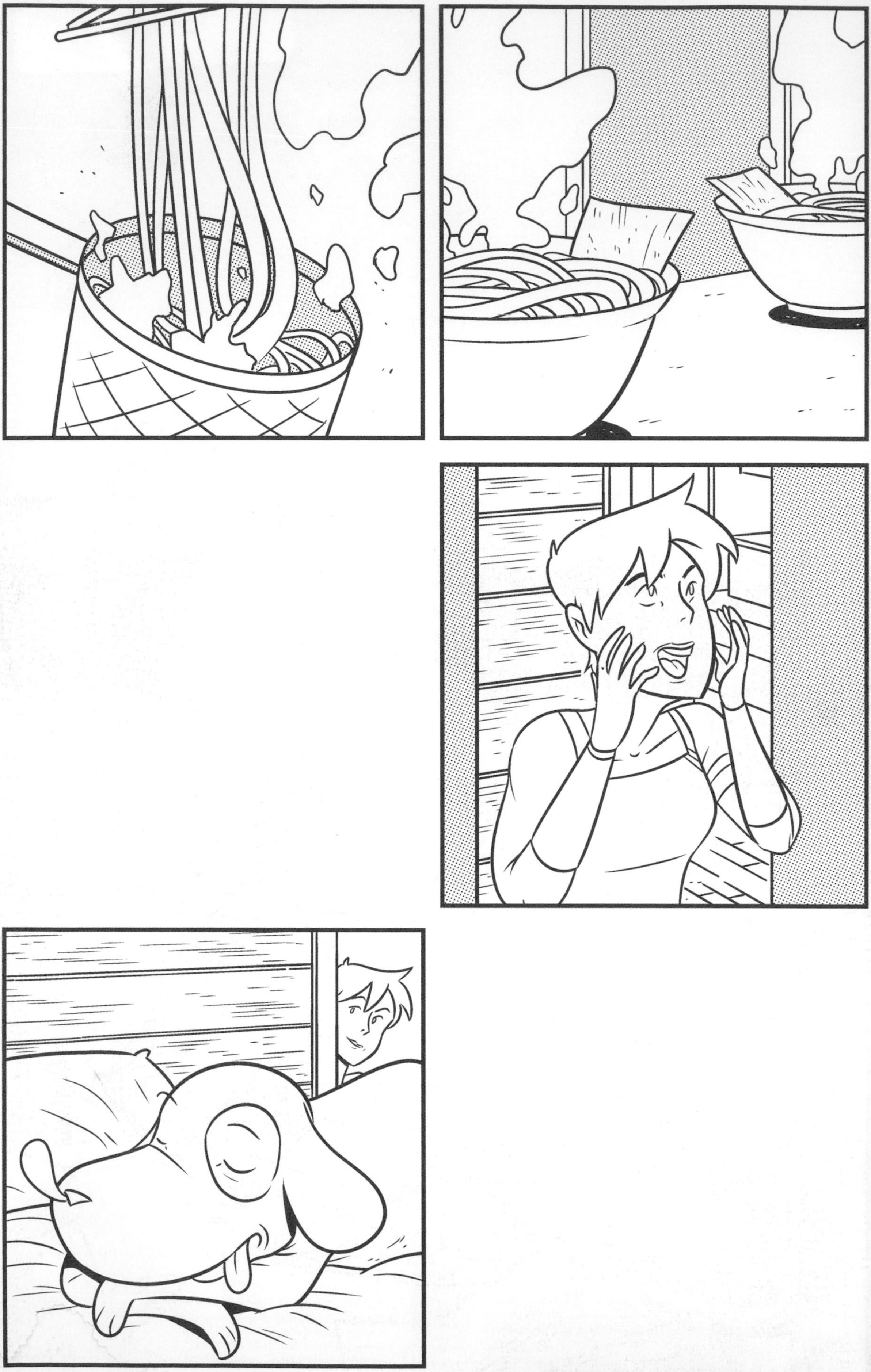

1

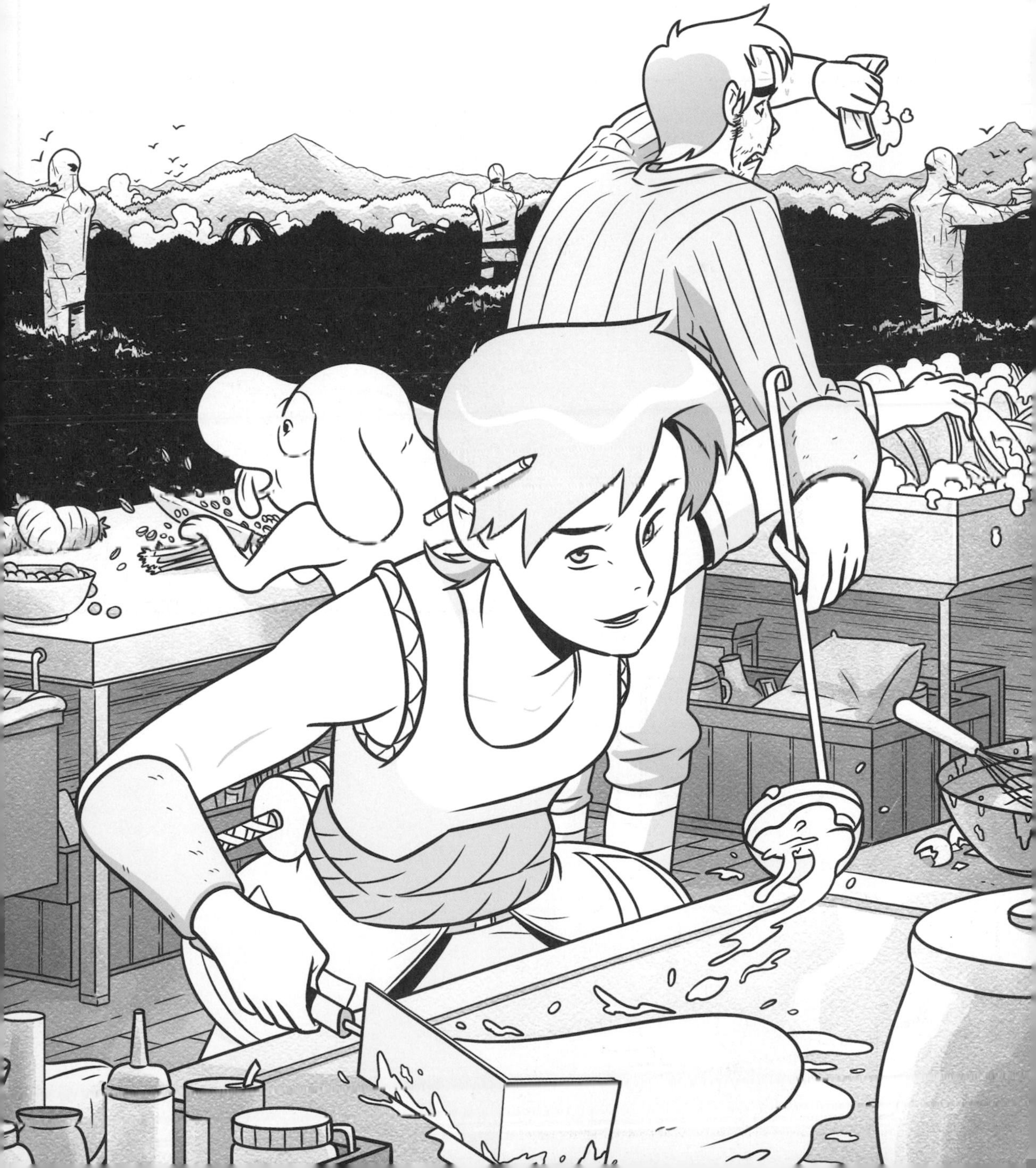

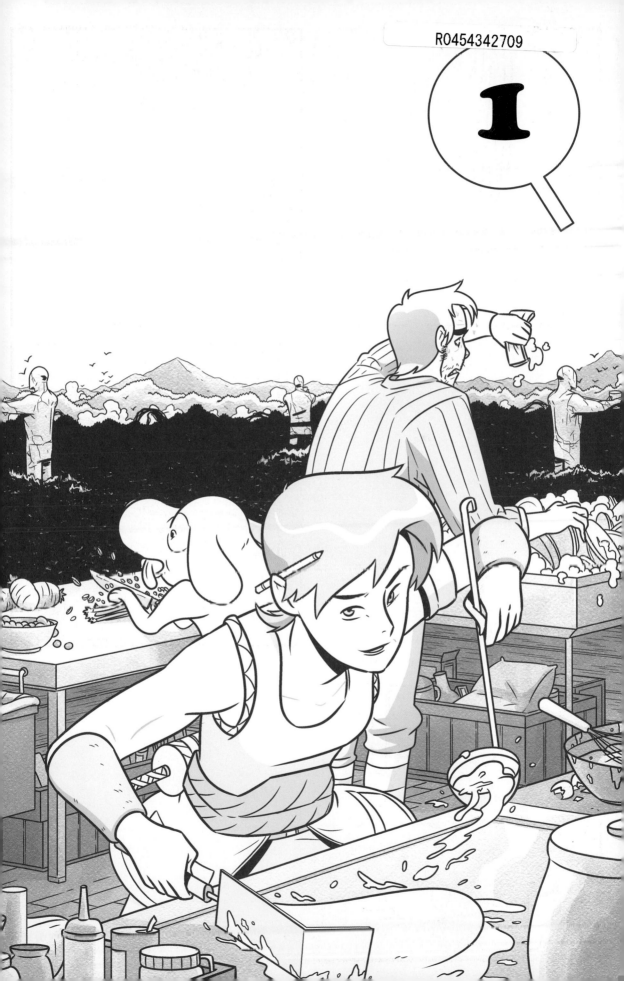

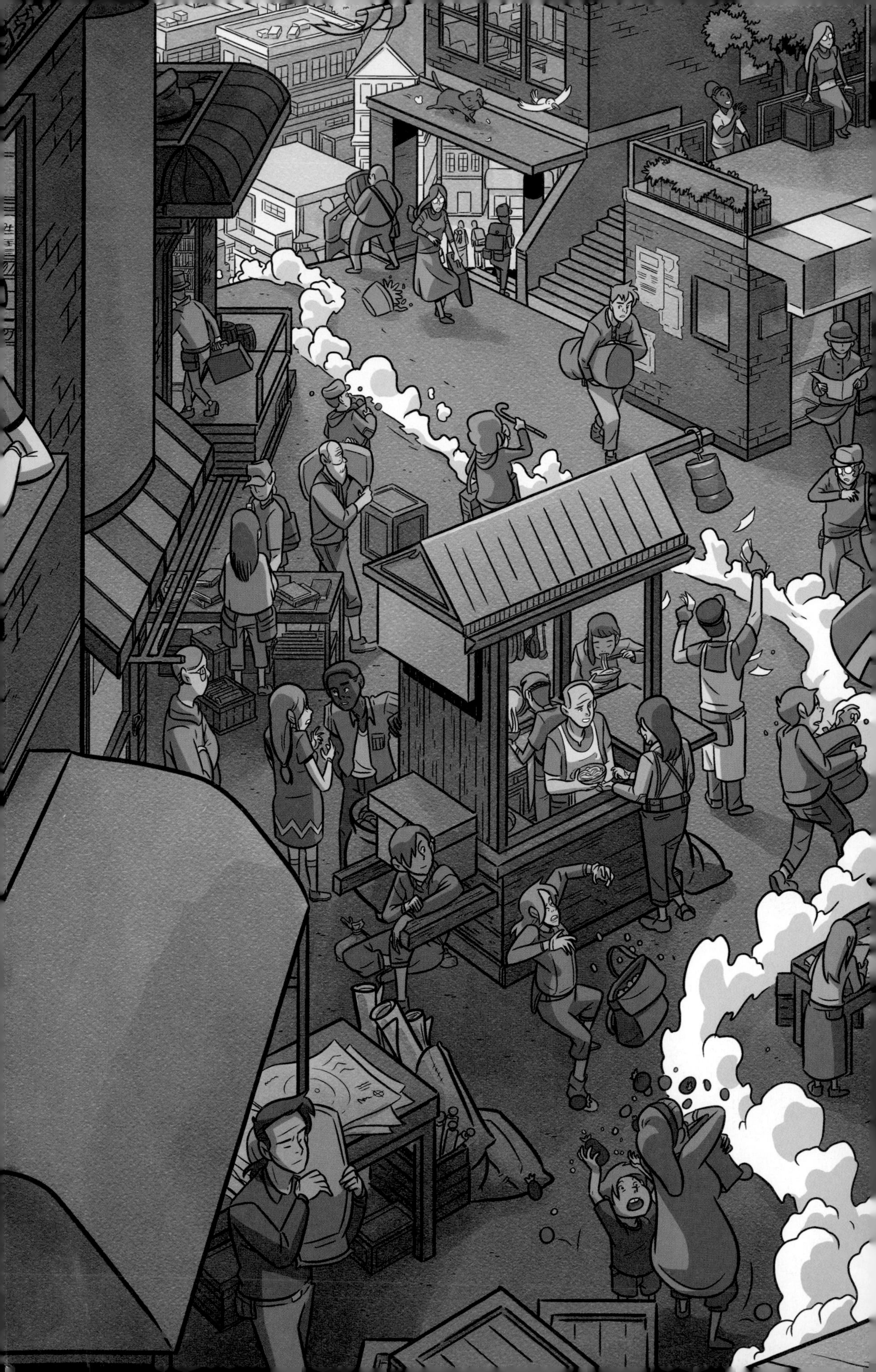

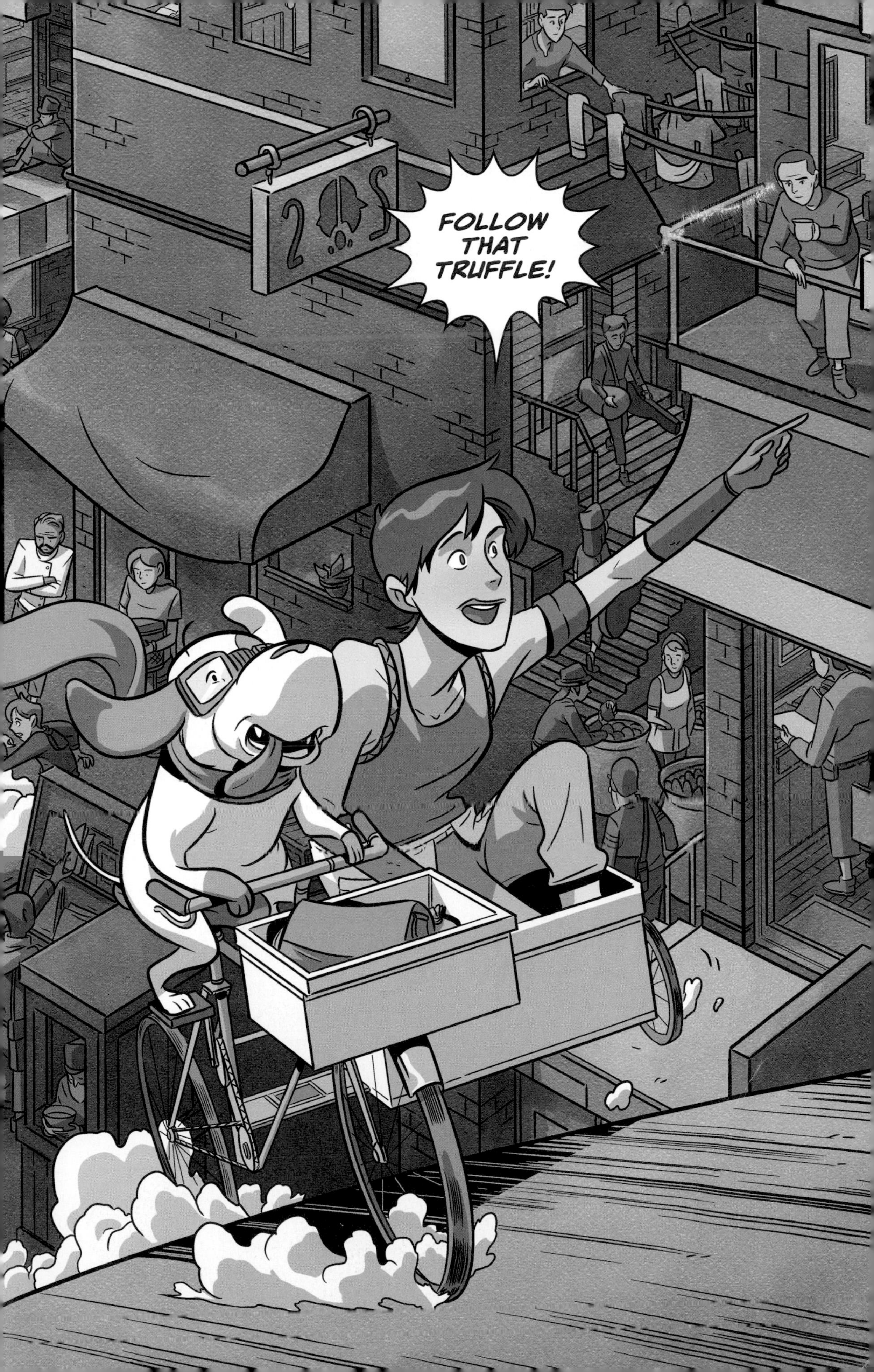
FOLLOW THAT TRUFFLE!

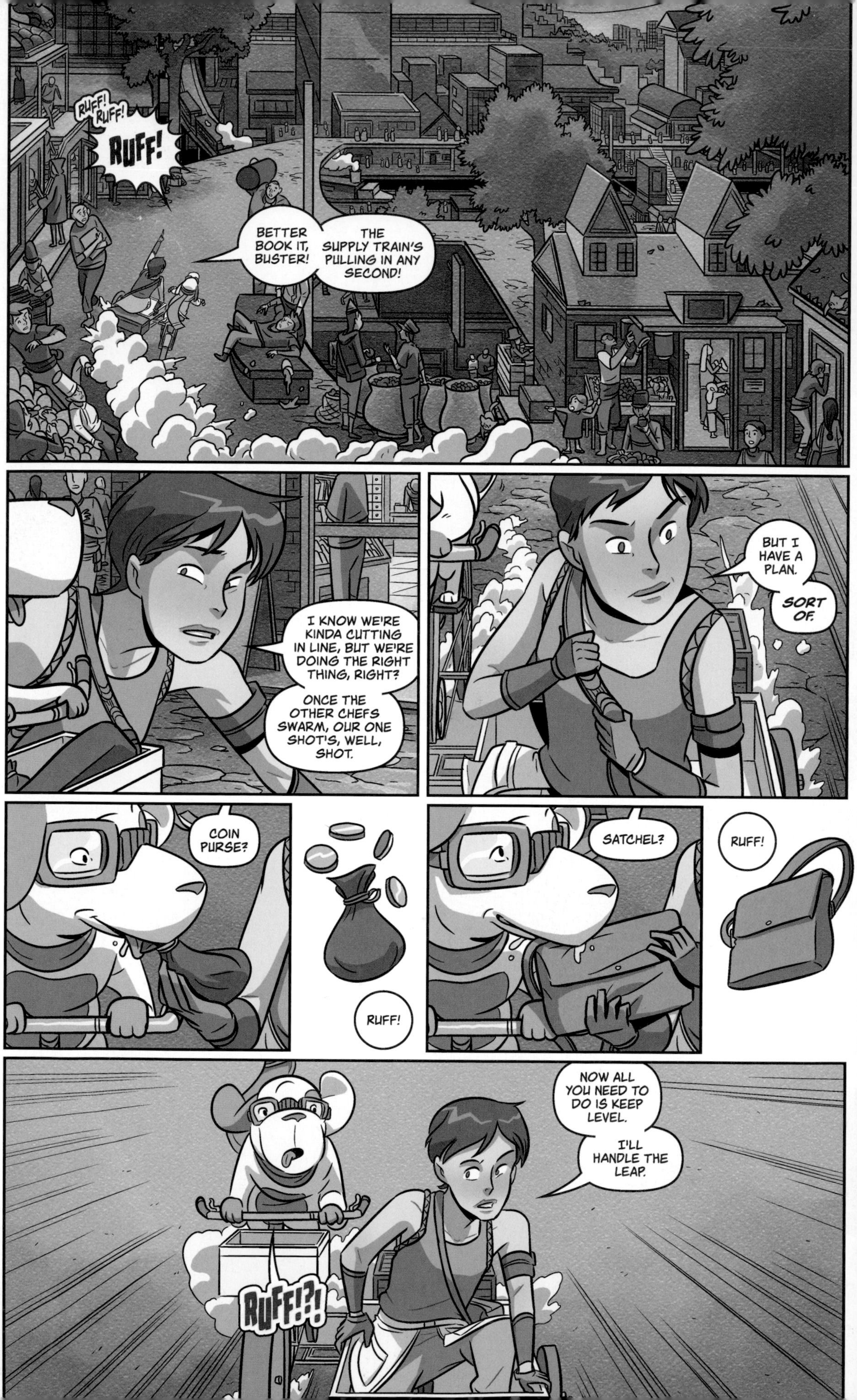
RUFF! RUFF!
RUFF!
BETTER BOOK IT, BUSTER!
THE SUPPLY TRAIN'S PULLING IN ANY SECOND!
I KNOW WE'RE KINDA CUTTING IN LINE, BUT WE'RE DOING THE RIGHT THING, RIGHT?
ONCE THE OTHER CHEFS SWARM, OUR ONE SHOT'S, WELL, SHOT.
BUT I HAVE A PLAN.
SORT OF.
COIN PURSE?
RUFF!
SATCHEL?
RUFF!
NOW ALL YOU NEED TO DO IS KEEP LEVEL.
I'LL HANDLE THE LEAP.
RUFF!?!

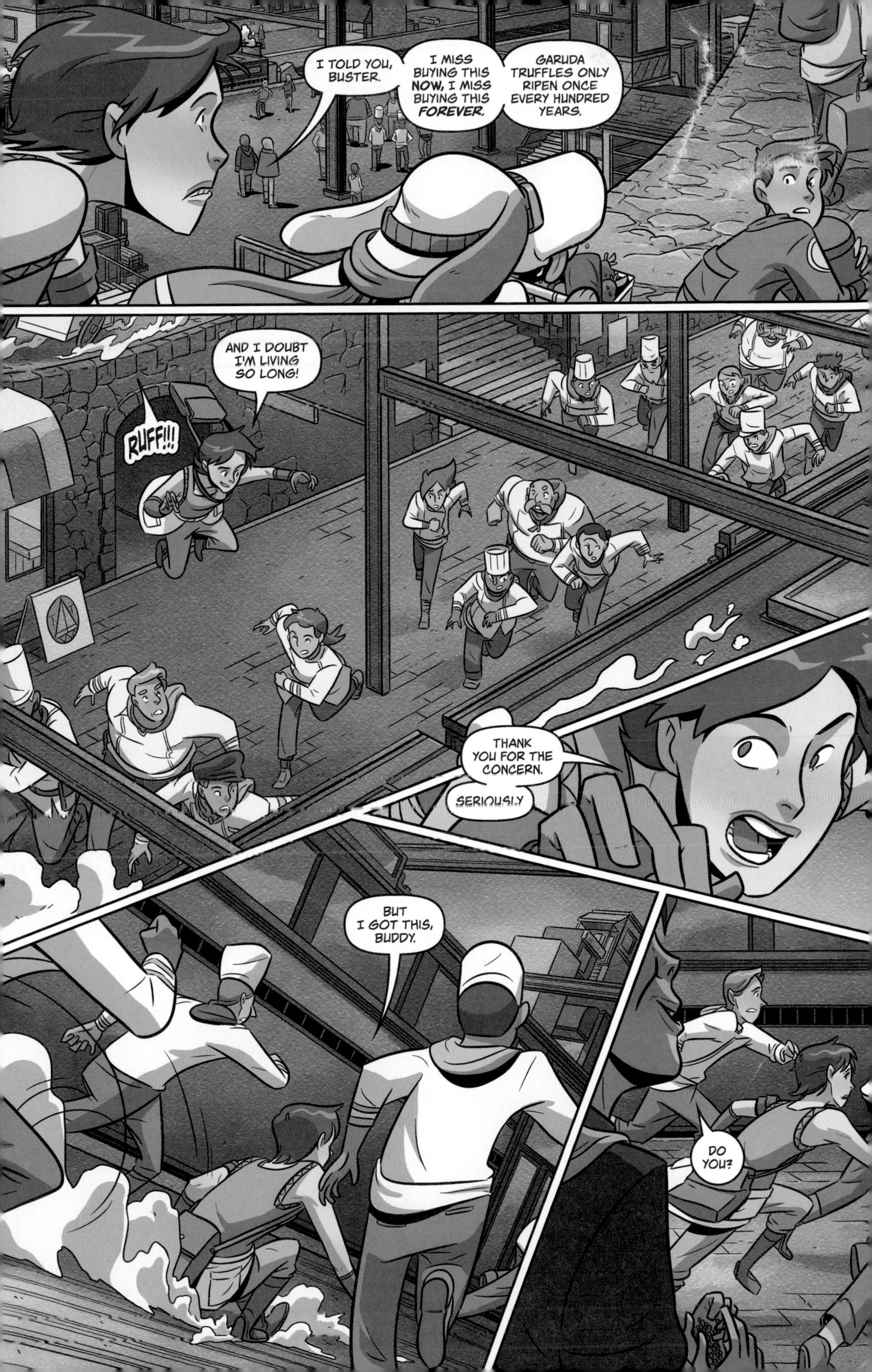
I TOLD YOU, BUSTER.
I MISS BUYING THIS NOW, I MISS BUYING THIS FOREVER.
GARUDA TRUFFLES ONLY RIPEN ONCE EVERY HUNDRED YEARS.
AND I DOUBT I'M LIVING SO LONG!
RUFF!!!
THANK YOU FOR THE CONCERN.
SERIOUSLY.
BUT I GOT THIS, BUDDY.
DO YOU?

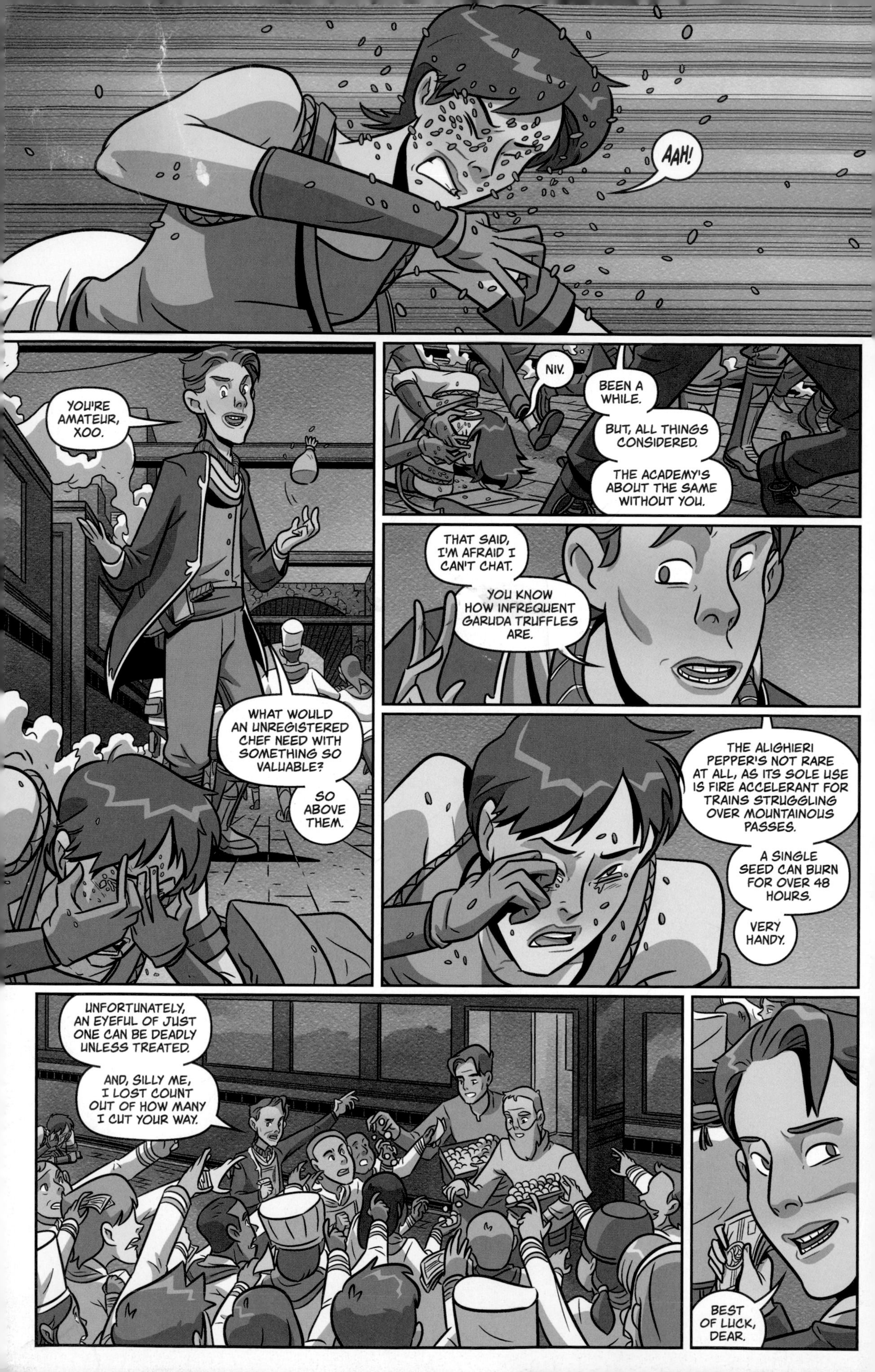
AAH!
YOU'RE AMATEUR, XOO.
WHAT WOULD AN UNREGISTERED CHEF NEED WITH SOMETHING SO VALUABLE?
SO ABOVE THEM.
NIV.
BEEN A WHILE.
BUT, ALL THINGS CONSIDERED.
THE ACADEMY'S ABOUT THE SAME WITHOUT YOU.
THAT SAID, I'M AFRAID I CAN'T CHAT.
YOU KNOW HOW INFREQUENT GARUDA TRUFFLES ARE.
THE ALIGHIERI PEPPER'S NOT RARE AT ALL, AS ITS SOLE USE IS FIRE ACCELERANT FOR TRAINS STRUGGLING OVER MOUNTAINOUS PASSES.
A SINGLE SEED CAN BURN FOR OVER 48 HOURS.
VERY HANDY.
UNFORTUNATELY, AN EYEFUL OF JUST ONE CAN BE DEADLY UNLESS TREATED.
AND, SILLY ME, I LOST COUNT OUT OF HOW MANY I CUT YOUR WAY.
BEST OF LUCK, DEAR.

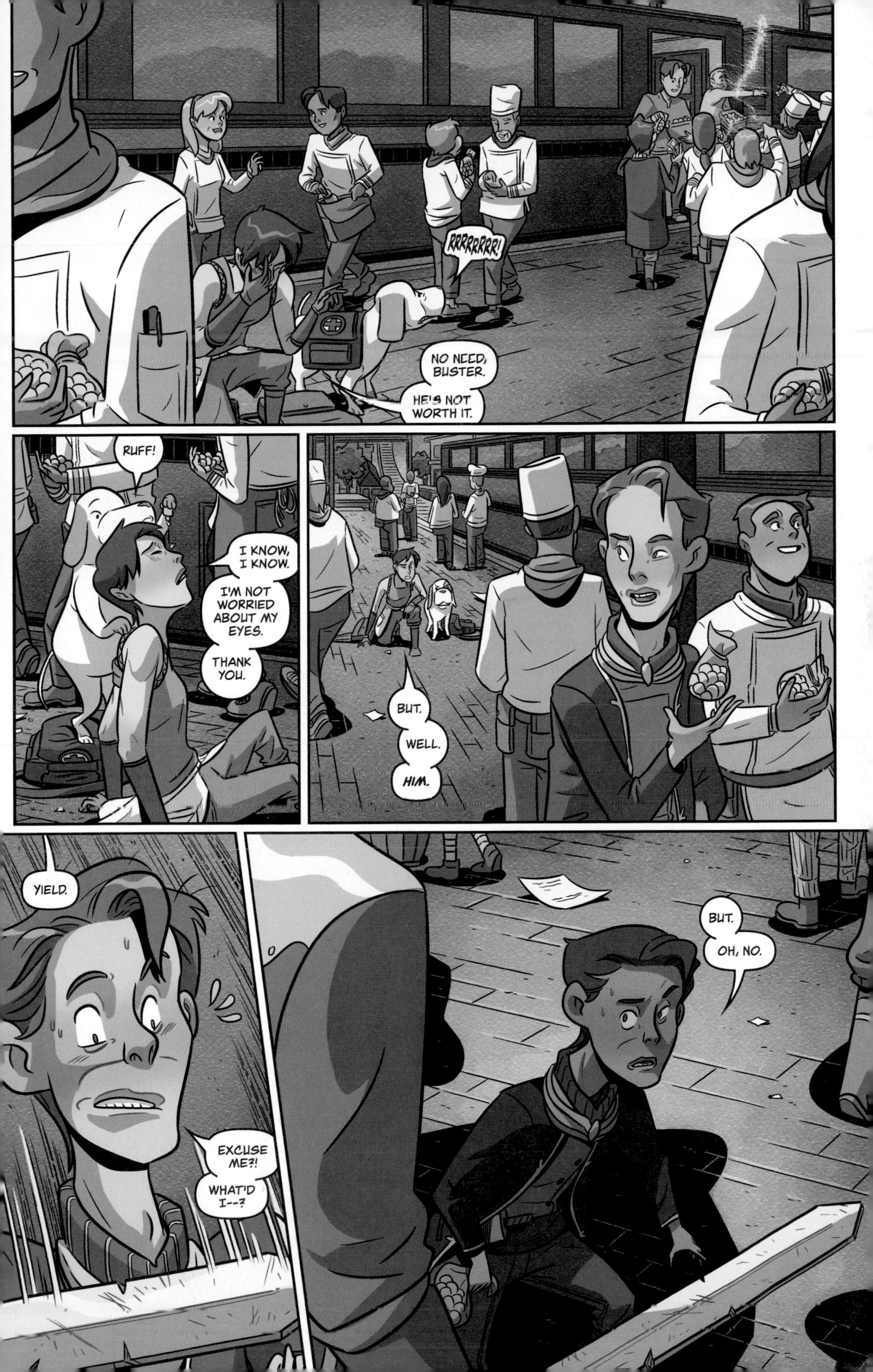
RRRRRRRR!
NO NEED, BUSTER.
HE'S NOT WORTH IT.
RUFF!
I KNOW, I KNOW.
I'M NOT WORRIED ABOUT MY EYES.
THANK YOU.
BUT.
WELL.
HIM.
YIELD.
EXCUSE ME?!
WHAT'D I--?
BUT.
OH, NO.

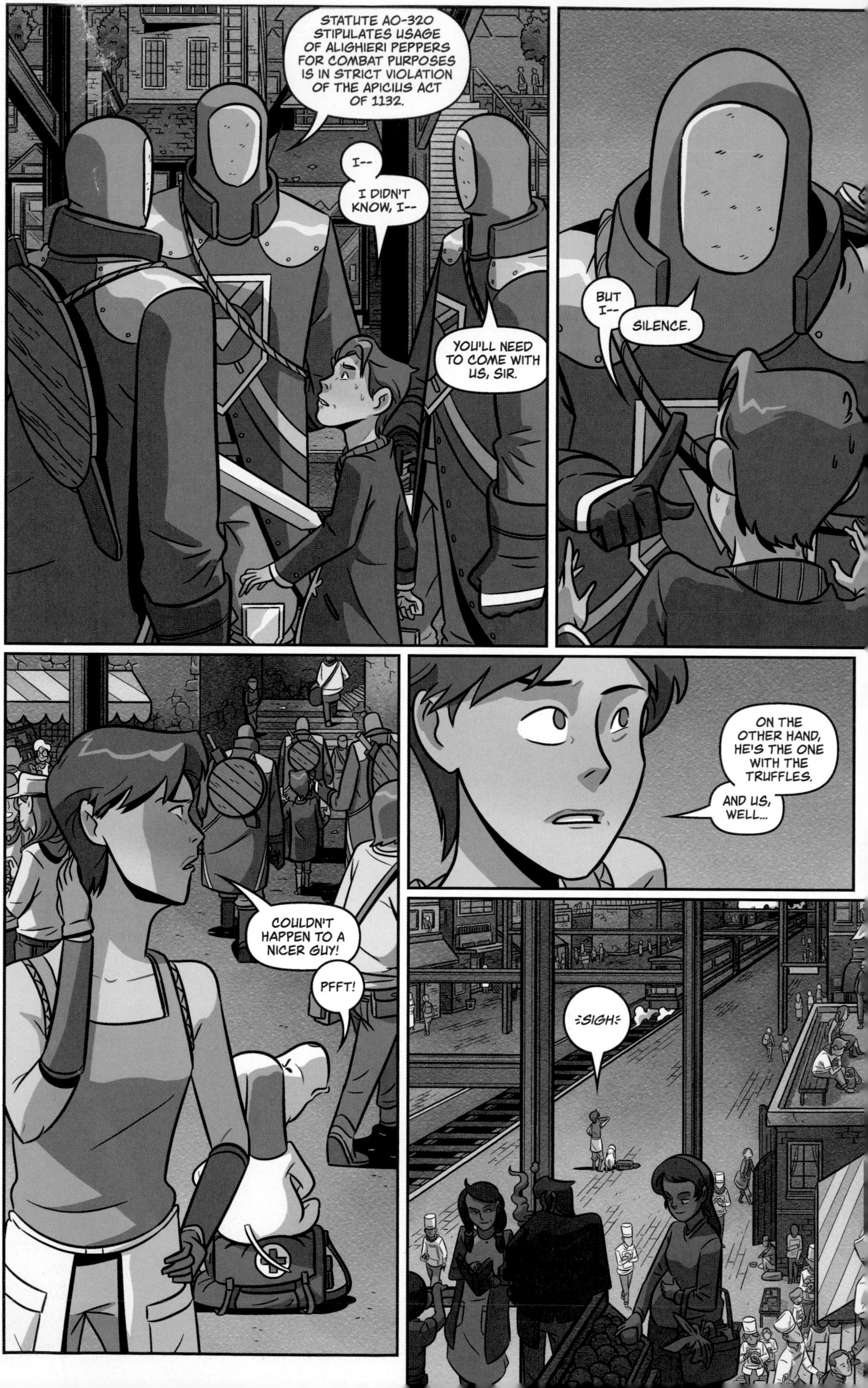
STATUTE AO-320 STIPULATES USAGE OF ALIGHIERI PEPPERS FOR COMBAT PURPOSES IS IN STRICT VIOLATION OF THE APICIUS ACT OF 1132.
I--
I DIDN'T KNOW, I--
YOU'LL NEED TO COME WITH US, SIR.
BUT I--
SILENCE.
COULDN'T HAPPEN TO A NICER GUY!
PFFT!
ON THE OTHER HAND, HE'S THE ONE WITH THE TRUFFLES.
AND US, WELL...
SIGH

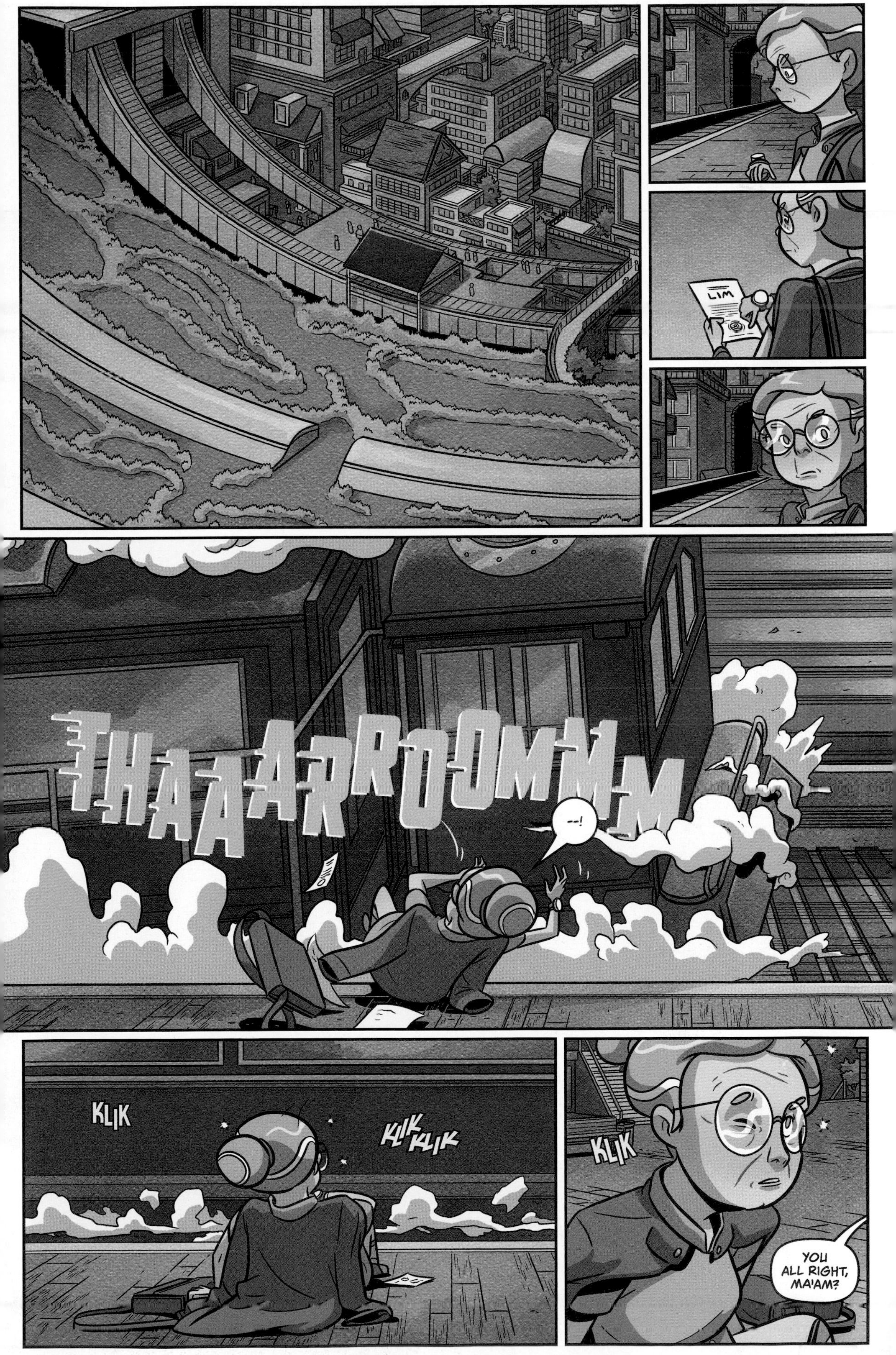
LIM
THAAARROOMMM
--!
KLIK
KLIK KLIK
KLIK
YOU ALL RIGHT, MA'AM?

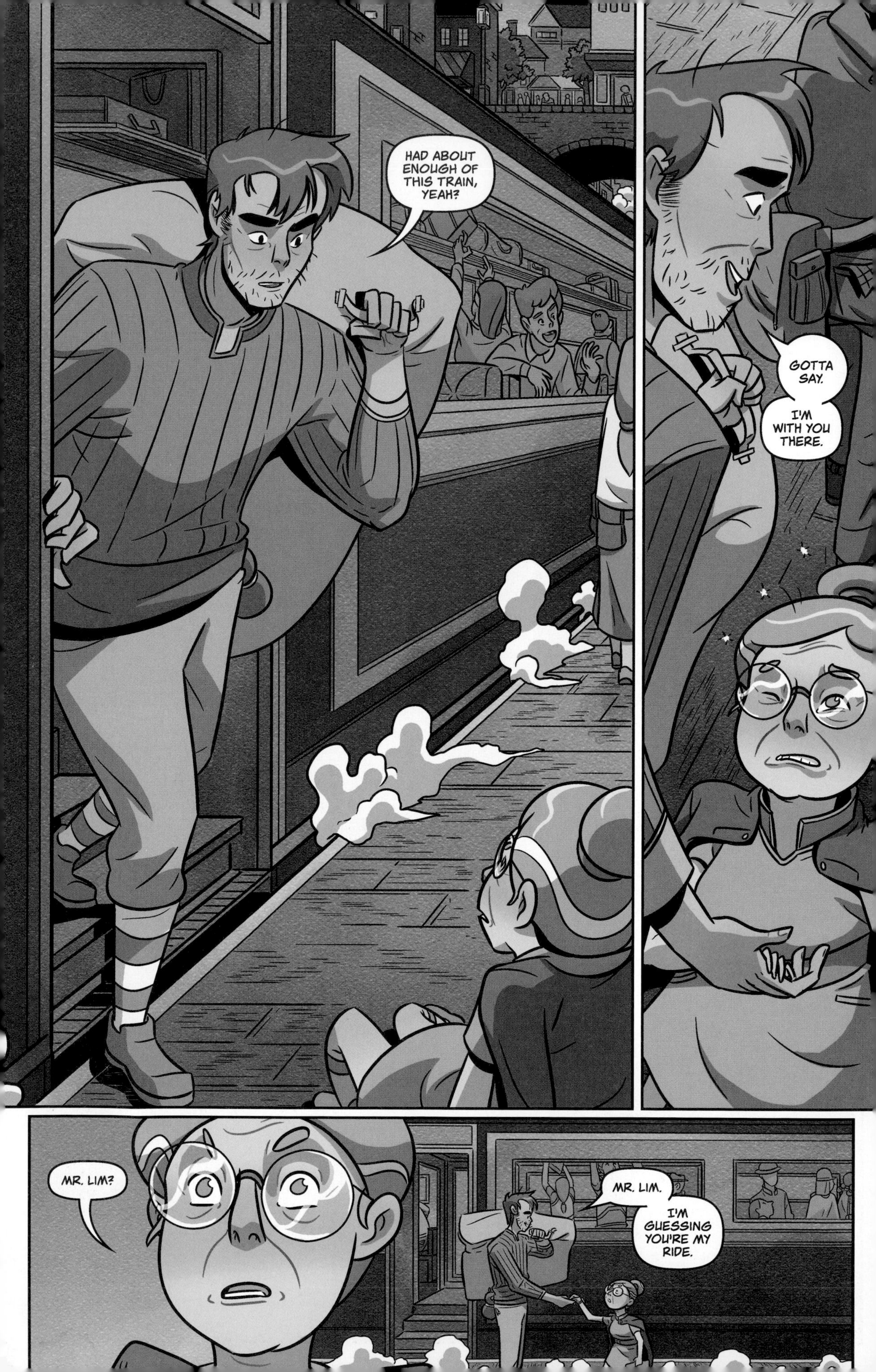

HAD ABOUT ENOUGH OF THIS TRAIN, YEAH?
GOTTA SAY.
I'M WITH YOU THERE.
MR. LIM?
MR. LIM.
I'M GUESSING YOU'RE MY RIDE.

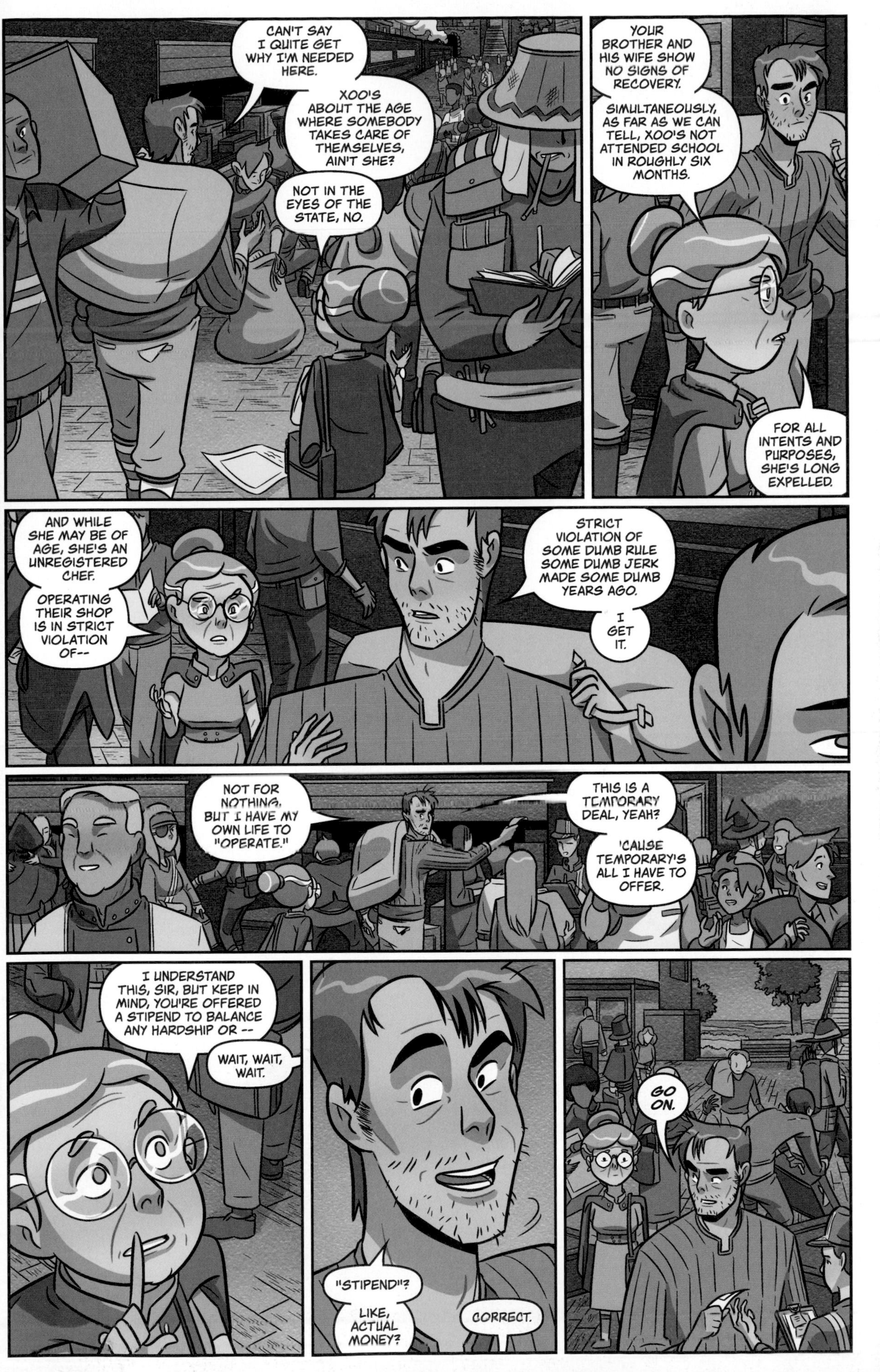
CAN'T SAY I QUITE GET WHY I'M NEEDED HERE.
XOO'S ABOUT THE AGE WHERE SOMEBODY TAKES CARE OF THEMSELVES, AIN'T SHE?
NOT IN THE EYES OF THE STATE, NO.
YOUR BROTHER AND HIS WIFE SHOW NO SIGNS OF RECOVERY.
SIMULTANEOUSLY, AS FAR AS WE CAN TELL, XOO'S NOT ATTENDED SCHOOL IN ROUGHLY SIX MONTHS.
FOR ALL INTENTS AND PURPOSES, SHE'S LONG EXPELLED.
AND WHILE SHE MAY BE OF AGE, SHE'S AN UNREGISTERED CHEF.
OPERATING THEIR SHOP IS IN STRICT VIOLATION OF--
STRICT VIOLATION OF SOME DUMB RULE SOME DUMB JERK MADE SOME DUMB YEARS AGO.
I GET IT.
NOT FOR NOTHING, BUT I HAVE MY OWN LIFE TO "OPERATE."
THIS IS A TEMPORARY DEAL, YEAH?
'CAUSE TEMPORARY'S ALL I HAVE TO OFFER.
I UNDERSTAND THIS, SIR, BUT KEEP IN MIND, YOU'RE OFFERED A STIPEND TO BALANCE ANY HARDSHIP OR --
WAIT, WAIT, WAIT.
"STIPEND"?
LIKE, ACTUAL MONEY?
CORRECT.
GO ON.

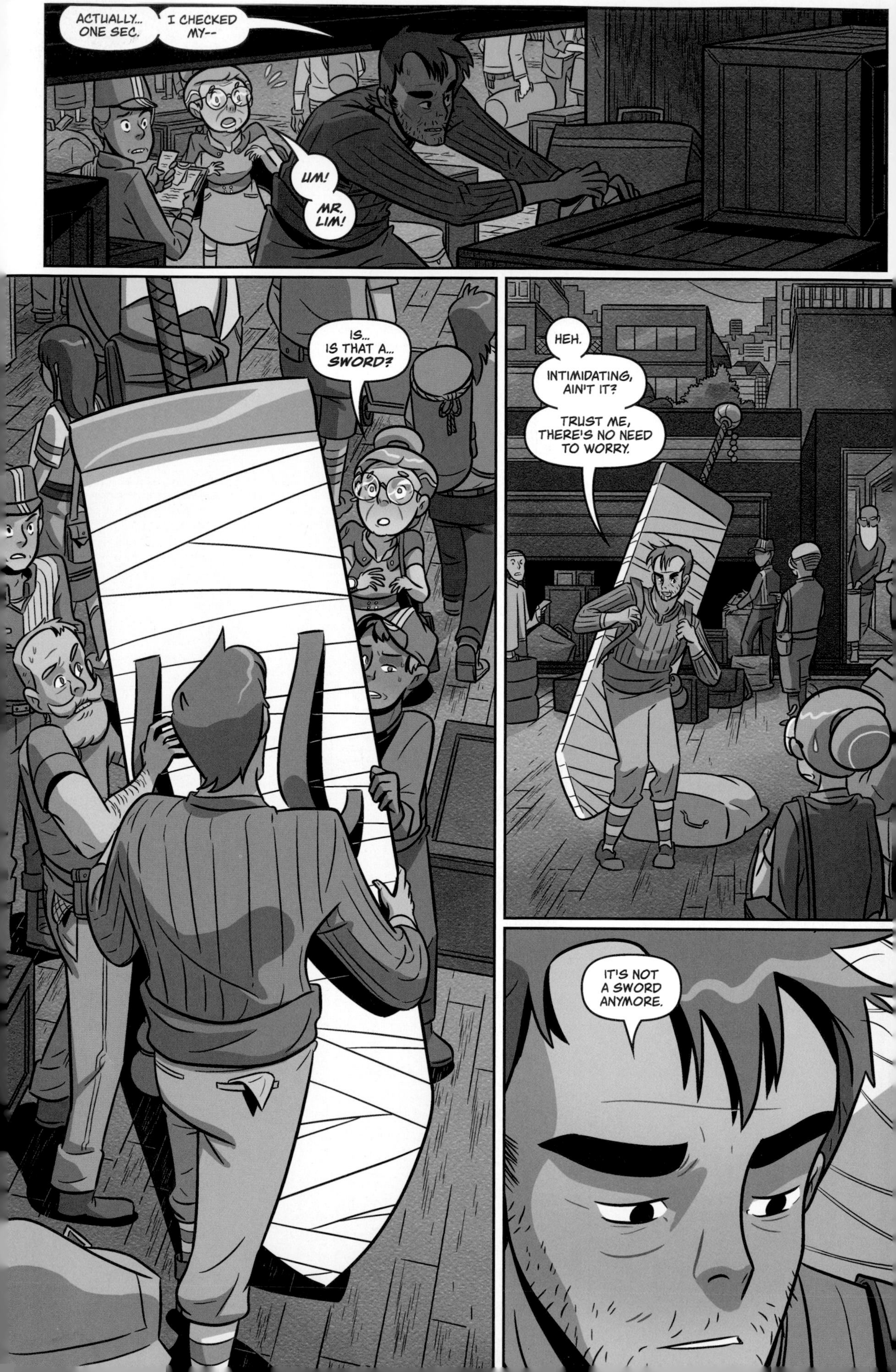
ACTUALLY... ONE SEC.
I CHECKED MY--
UM!
MR. LIM!
IS... IS THAT A... SWORD?
HEH.
INTIMIDATING, AIN'T IT?
TRUST ME, THERE'S NO NEED TO WORRY.
IT'S NOT A SWORD ANYMORE.

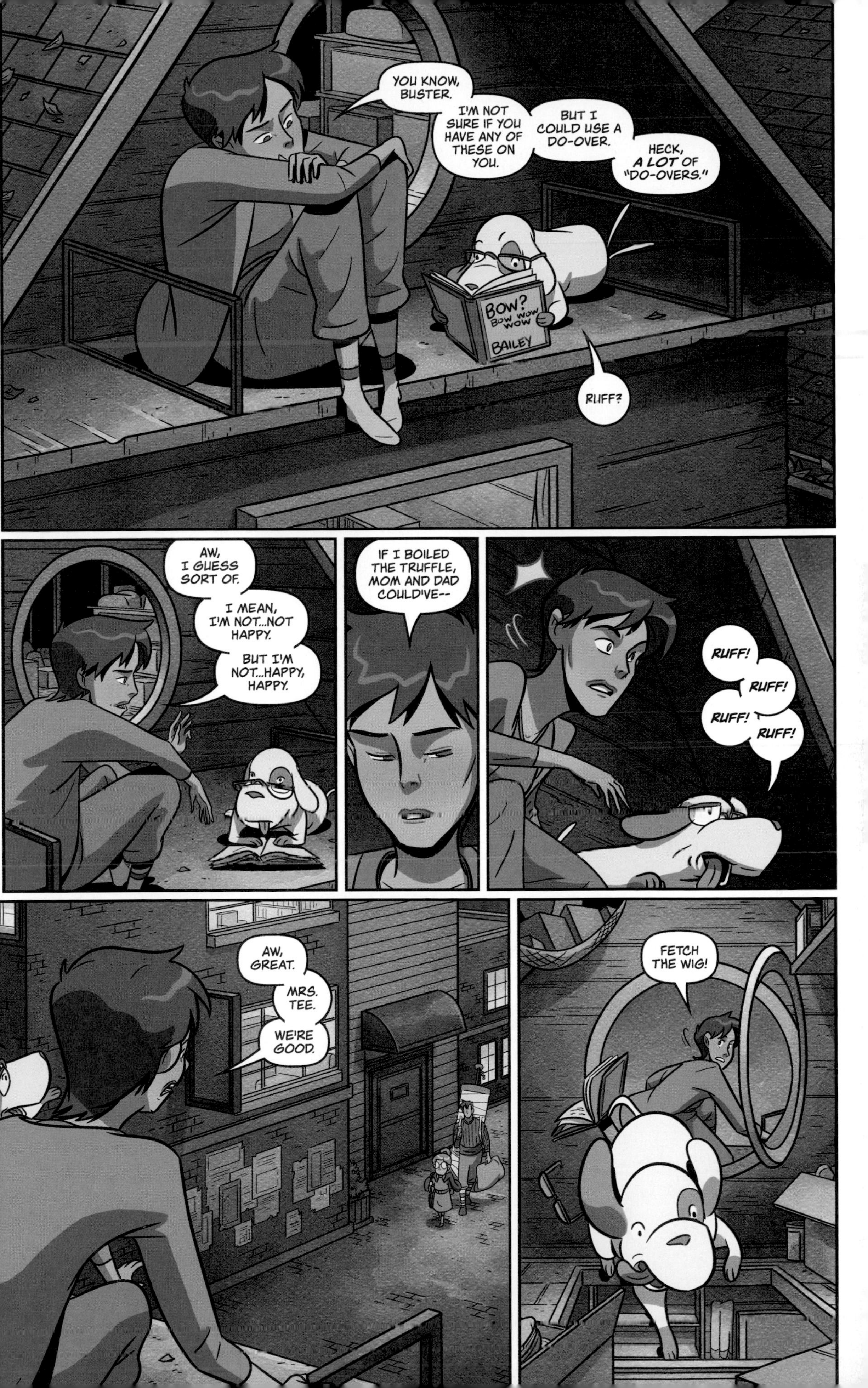
YOU KNOW, BUSTER.
I'M NOT SURE IF YOU HAVE ANY OF THESE ON YOU.
BUT I COULD USE A DO-OVER.
HECK, A LOT OF "DO-OVERS."
BOW? BOW WOW WOW
BAILEY
RUFF?
AW, I GUESS SORT OF.
I MEAN, I'M NOT...NOT HAPPY.
BUT I'M NOT...HAPPY, HAPPY.
IF I BOILED THE TRUFFLE, MOM AND DAD COULD'VE--
RUFF!
RUFF!
RUFF!
RUFF!
AW, GREAT.
MRS. TEE.
WE'RE GOOD.
FETCH THE WIG!

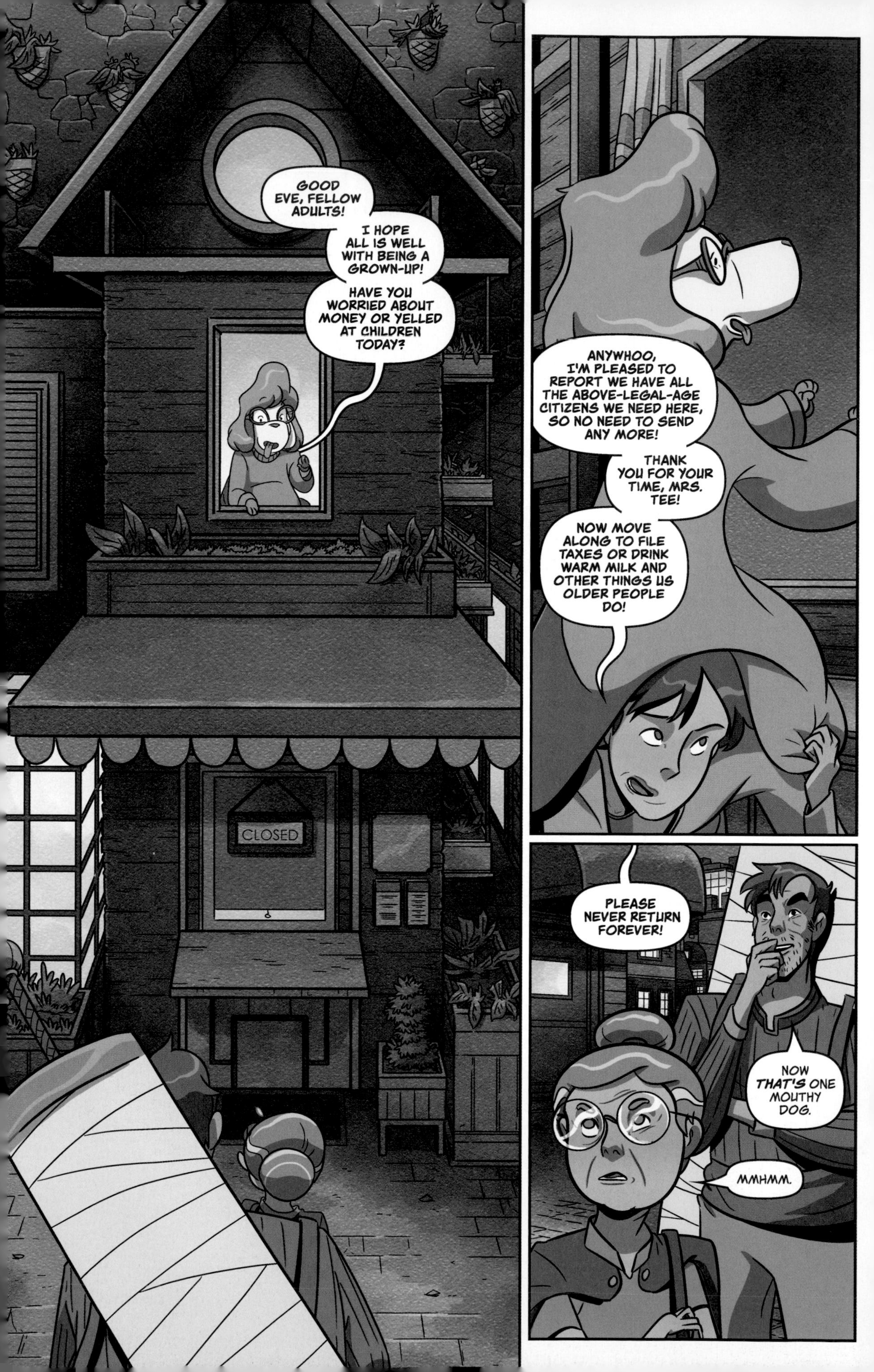
GOOD EVE, FELLOW ADULTS!
I HOPE ALL IS WELL WITH BEING A GROWN-UP!
HAVE YOU WORRIED ABOUT MONEY OR YELLED AT CHILDREN TODAY?
CLOSED
ANYWHOO, I'M PLEASED TO REPORT WE HAVE ALL THE ABOVE-LEGAL-AGE CITIZENS WE NEED HERE, SO NO NEED TO SEND ANY MORE!
THANK YOU FOR YOUR TIME, MRS. TEE!
NOW MOVE ALONG TO FILE TAXES OR DRINK WARM MILK AND OTHER THINGS US OLDER PEOPLE DO!
PLEASE NEVER RETURN FOREVER!
NOW THAT'S ONE MOUTHY DOG.
MMHMM.

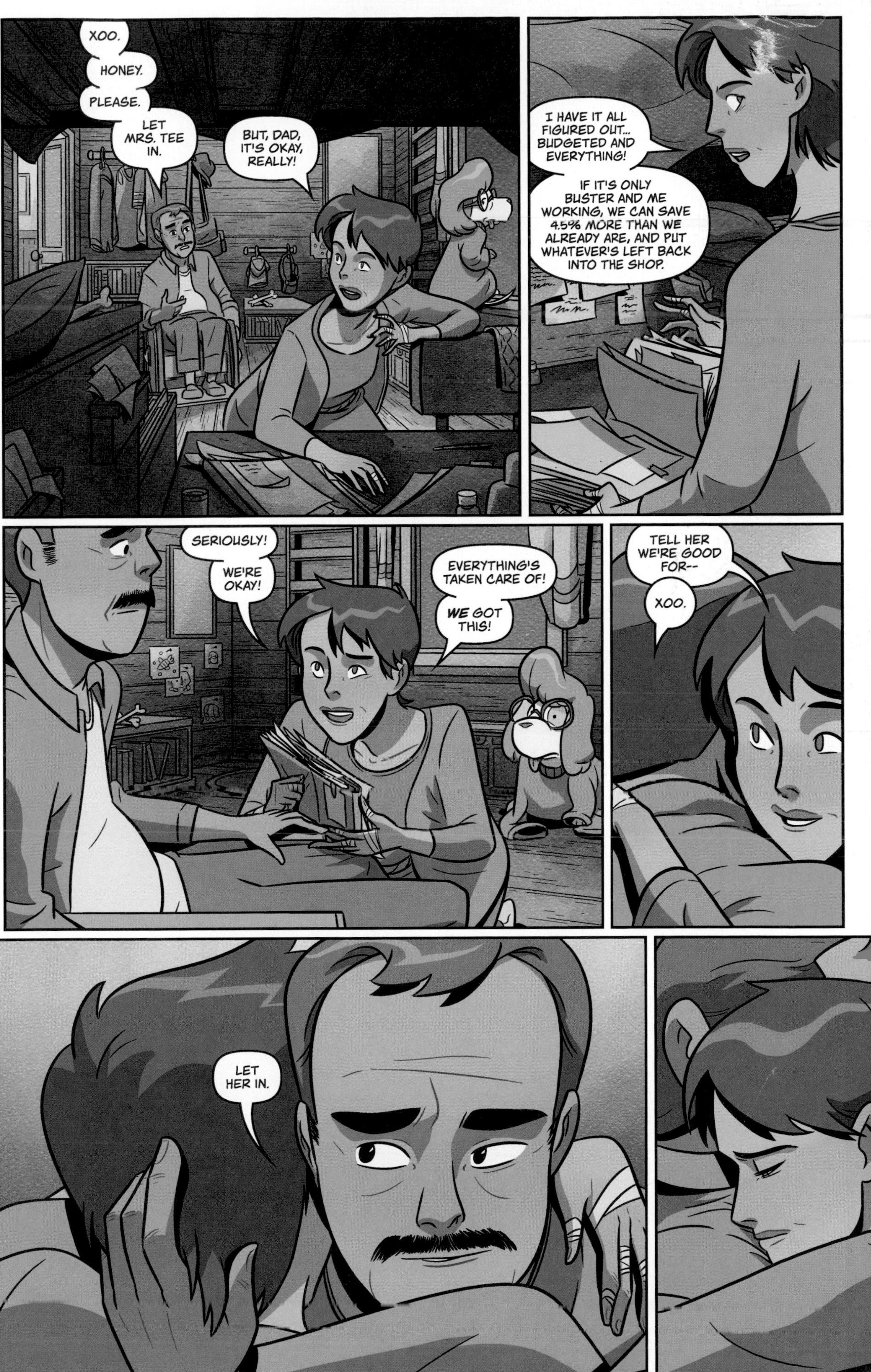
XOO.
HONEY.
PLEASE.
LET MRS. TEE IN.
BUT, DAD, IT'S OKAY, REALLY!
I HAVE IT ALL FIGURED OUT... BUDGETED AND EVERYTHING!
IF IT'S ONLY BUSTER AND ME WORKING, WE CAN SAVE 4.5% MORE THAN WE ALREADY ARE, AND PUT WHATEVER'S LEFT BACK INTO THE SHOP.
SERIOUSLY!
WE'RE OKAY!
EVERYTHING'S TAKEN CARE OF!
WE GOT THIS!
TELL HER WE'RE GOOD FOR--
XOO.
LET HER IN.

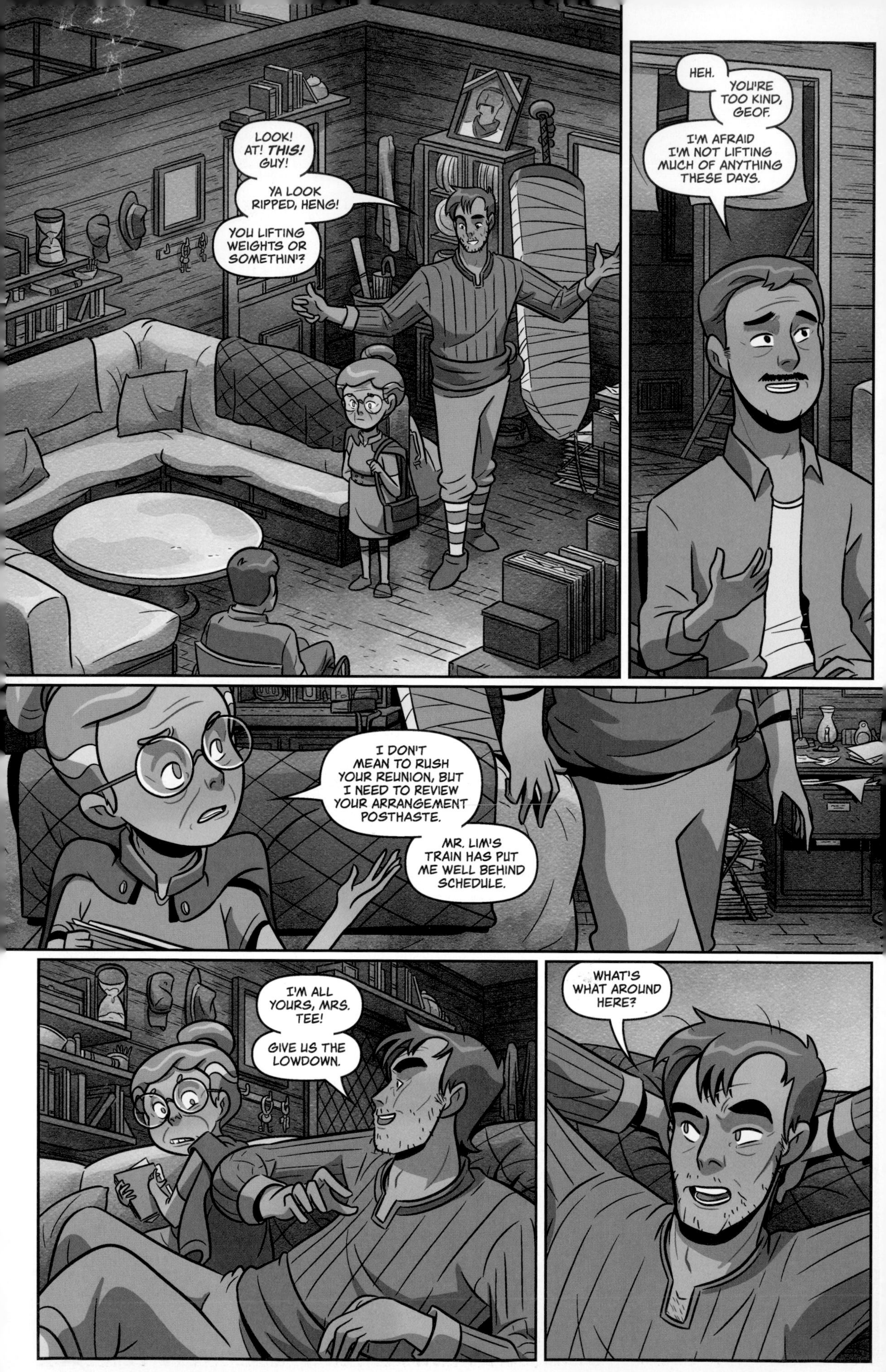
LOOK! AT! THIS! GUY!
YA LOOK RIPPED, HENG!
YOU LIFTING WEIGHTS OR SOMETHIN'?
HEH.
YOU'RE TOO KIND, GEOF.
I'M AFRAID I'M NOT LIFTING MUCH OF ANYTHING THESE DAYS.
I DON'T MEAN TO RUSH YOUR REUNION, BUT I NEED TO REVIEW YOUR ARRANGEMENT POSTHASTE.
MR. LIM'S TRAIN HAS PUT ME WELL BEHIND SCHEDULE.
I'M ALL YOURS, MRS. TEE!
GIVE US THE LOWDOWN.
WHAT'S WHAT AROUND HERE?

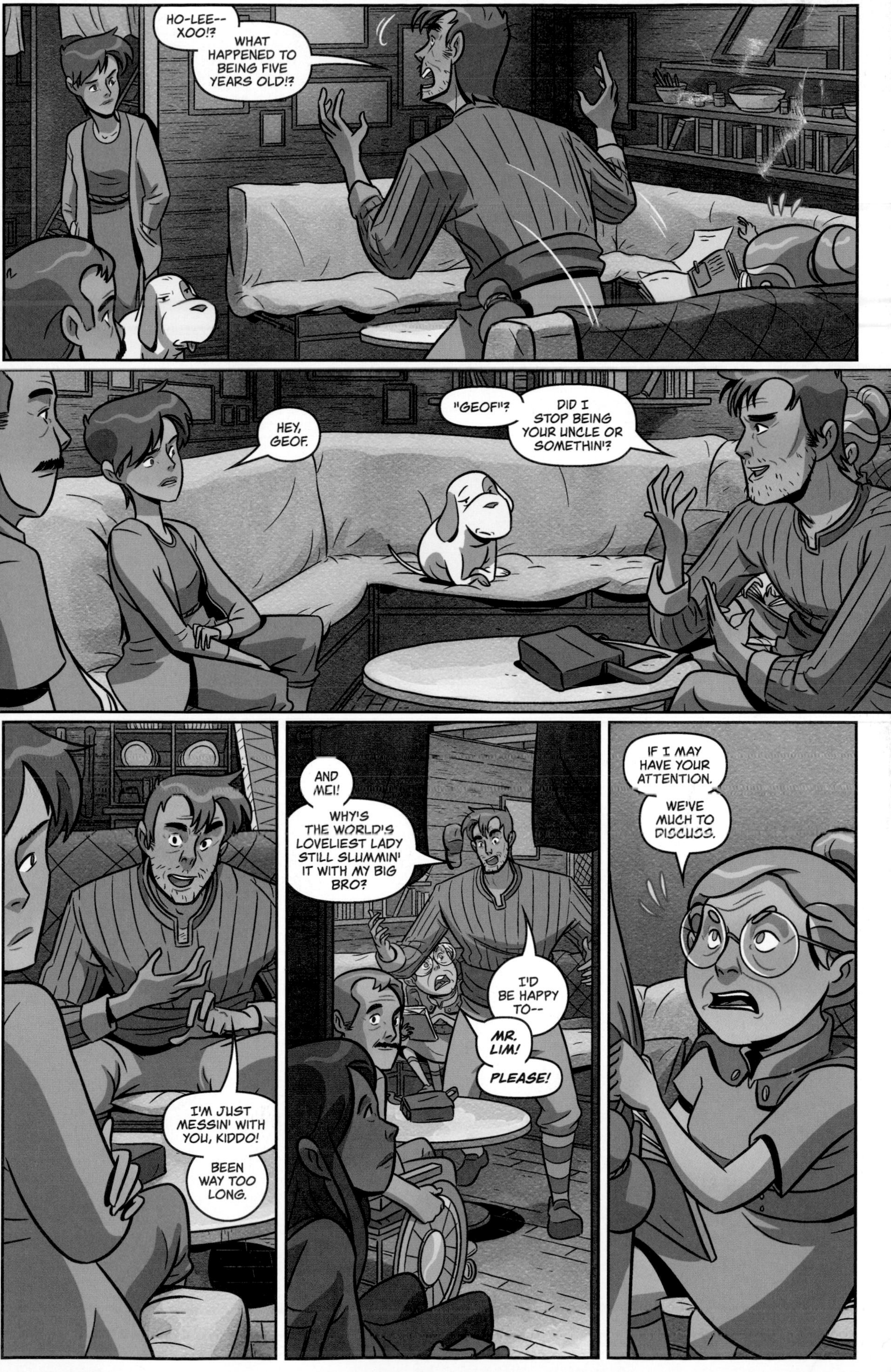
HO-LEE--
XOO!?
WHAT HAPPENED TO BEING FIVE YEARS OLD!?
HEY, GEOF.
"GEOF"?
DID I STOP BEING YOUR UNCLE OR SOMETHIN'?
I'M JUST MESSIN' WITH YOU, KIDDO!
BEEN WAY TOO LONG.
AND MEI!
WHY'S THE WORLD'S LOVELIEST LADY STILL SLUMMIN' IT WITH MY BIG BRO?
I'D BE HAPPY TO--
MR. LIM!
PLEASE!
IF I MAY HAVE YOUR ATTENTION.
WE'VE MUCH TO DISCUSS.

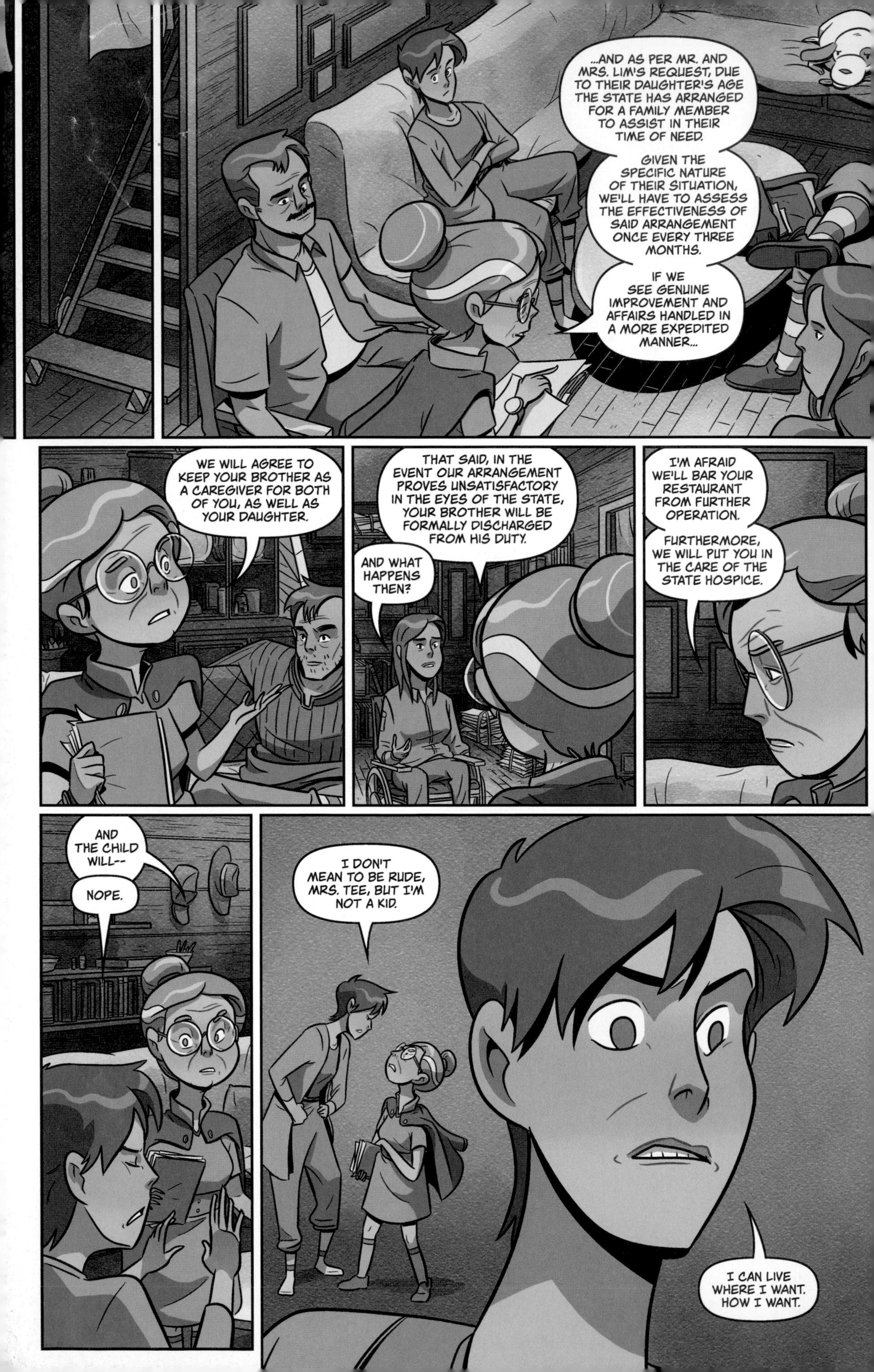
...AND AS PER MR. AND MRS. LIM'S REQUEST, DUE TO THEIR DAUGHTER'S AGE THE STATE HAS ARRANGED FOR A FAMILY MEMBER TO ASSIST IN THEIR TIME OF NEED.
GIVEN THE SPECIFIC NATURE OF THEIR SITUATION, WE'LL HAVE TO ASSESS THE EFFECTIVENESS OF SAID ARRANGEMENT ONCE EVERY THREE MONTHS.
IF WE SEE GENUINE IMPROVEMENT AND AFFAIRS HANDLED IN A MORE EXPEDITED MANNER...
WE WILL AGREE TO KEEP YOUR BROTHER AS A CAREGIVER FOR BOTH OF YOU, AS WELL AS YOUR DAUGHTER.
THAT SAID, IN THE EVENT OUR ARRANGEMENT PROVES UNSATISFACTORY IN THE EYES OF THE STATE, YOUR BROTHER WILL BE FORMALLY DISCHARGED FROM HIS DUTY.
AND WHAT HAPPENS THEN?
I'M AFRAID WE'LL BAR YOUR RESTAURANT FROM FURTHER OPERATION.
FURTHERMORE, WE WILL PUT YOU IN THE CARE OF THE STATE HOSPICE.
AND THE CHILD WILL--
NOPE.
I DON'T MEAN TO BE RUDE, MRS. TEE, BUT I'M NOT A KID.
I CAN LIVE WHERE I WANT. HOW I WANT.

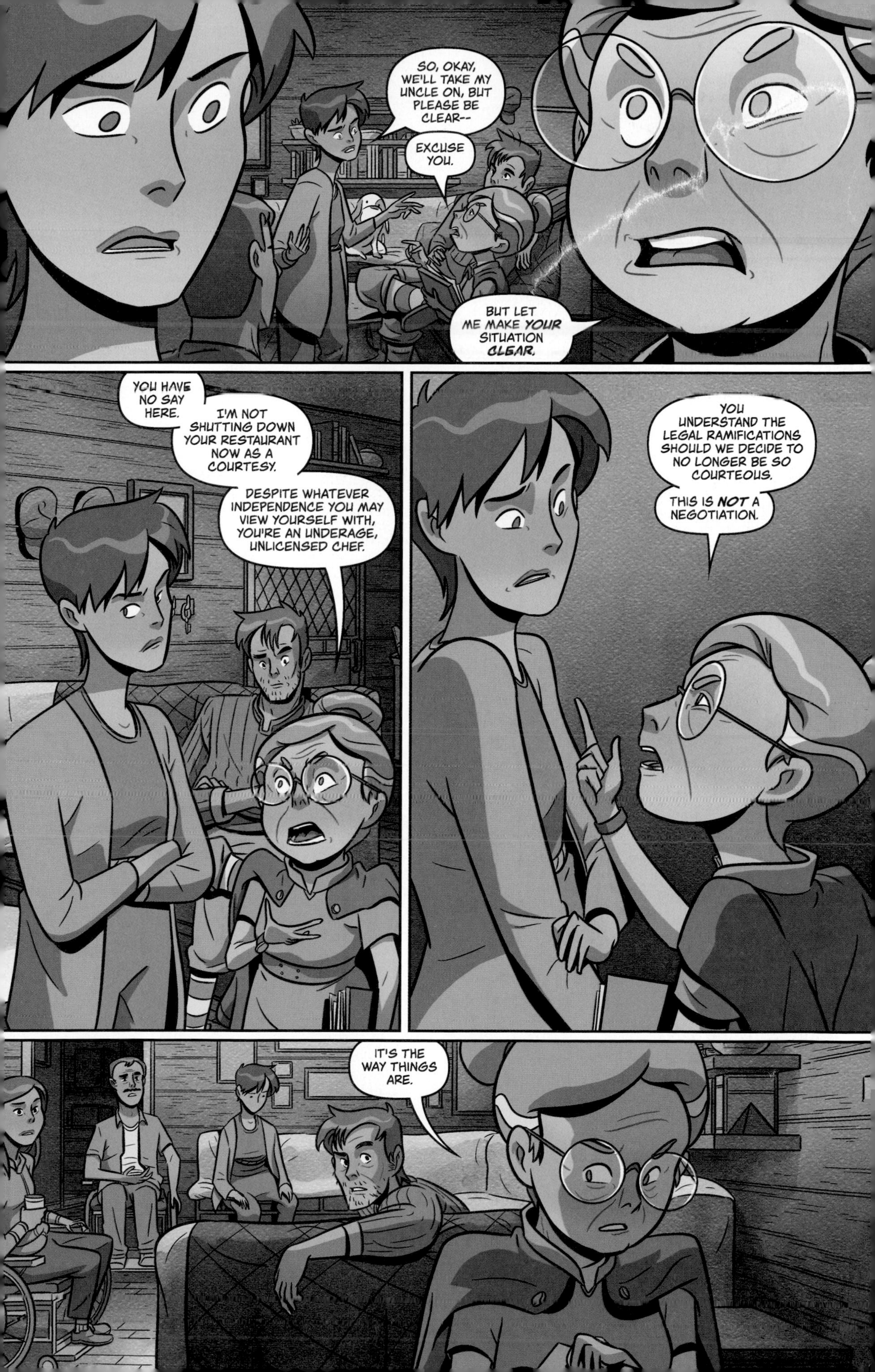
SO, OKAY, WE'LL TAKE MY UNCLE ON, BUT PLEASE BE CLEAR--
EXCUSE YOU.
BUT LET ME MAKE YOUR SITUATION CLEAR.
YOU HAVE NO SAY HERE.
I'M NOT SHUTTING DOWN YOUR RESTAURANT NOW AS A COURTESY.
DESPITE WHATEVER INDEPENDENCE YOU MAY VIEW YOURSELF WITH, YOU'RE AN UNDERAGE, UNLICENSED CHEF.
YOU UNDERSTAND THE LEGAL RAMIFICATIONS SHOULD WE DECIDE TO NO LONGER BE SO COURTEOUS.
THIS IS NOT A NEGOTIATION.
IT'S THE WAY THINGS ARE.

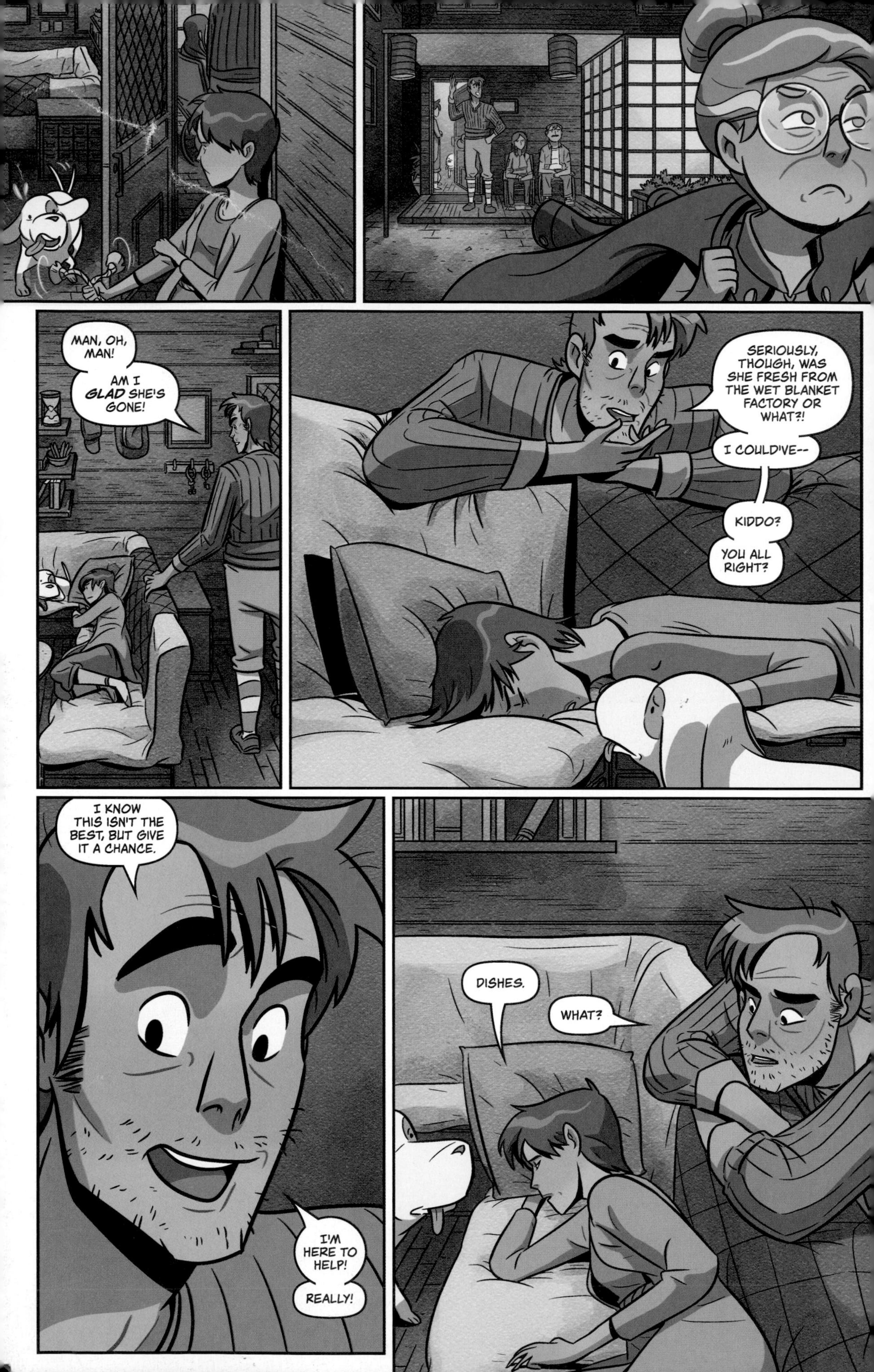
MAN, OH, MAN!
AM I GLAD SHE'S GONE!
SERIOUSLY, THOUGH, WAS SHE FRESH FROM THE WET BLANKET FACTORY OR WHAT?!
I COULD'VE--
KIDDO?
YOU ALL RIGHT?
I KNOW THIS ISN'T THE BEST, BUT GIVE IT A CHANCE.
I'M HERE TO HELP!
REALLY!
DISHES.
WHAT?

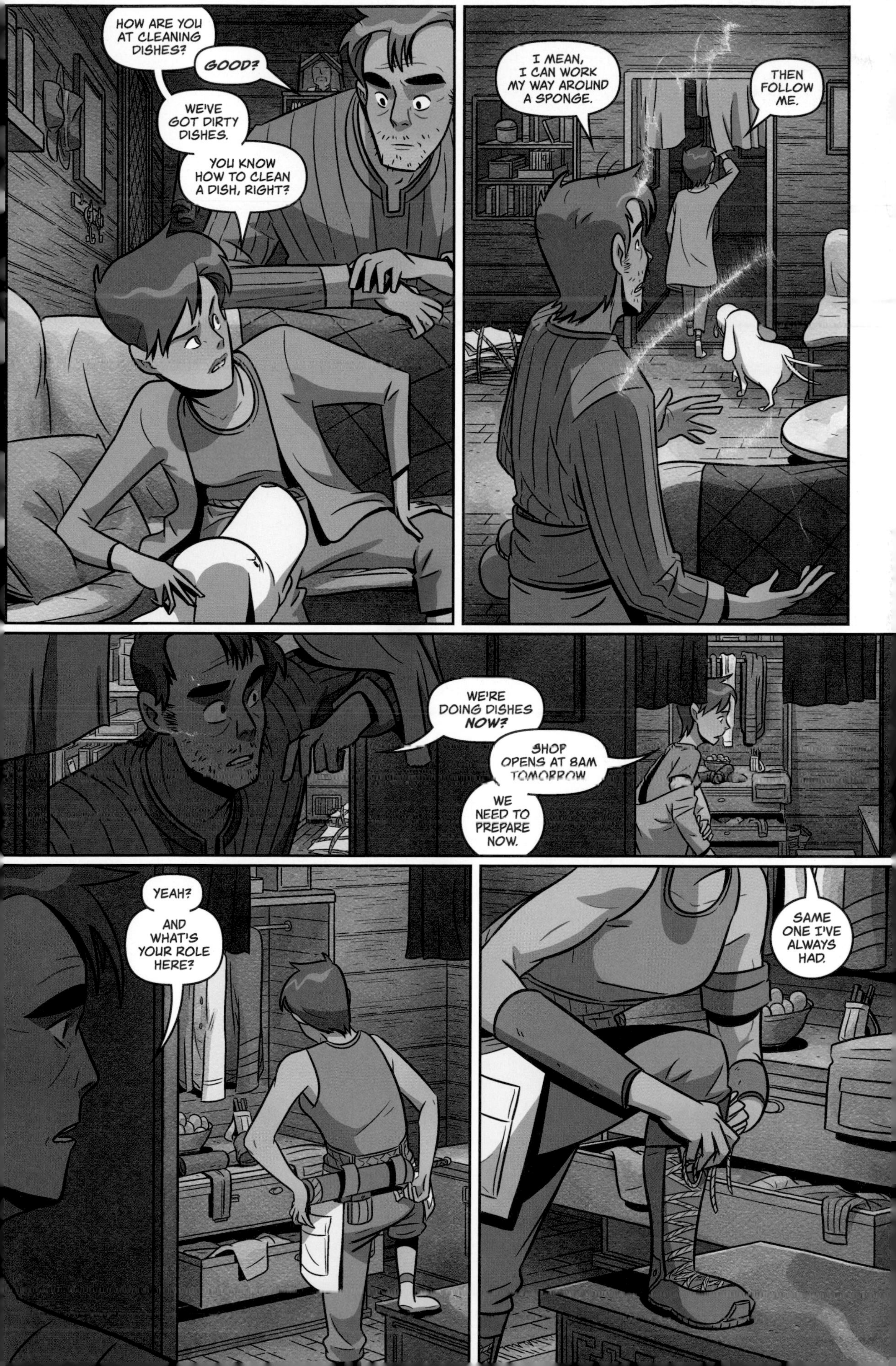
HOW ARE YOU AT CLEANING DISHES?
GOOD?
WE'VE GOT DIRTY DISHES.
YOU KNOW HOW TO CLEAN A DISH, RIGHT?
I MEAN, I CAN WORK MY WAY AROUND A SPONGE.
THEN FOLLOW ME.
WE'RE DOING DISHES NOW?
SHOP OPENS AT 8AM TOMORROW
WE NEED TO PREPARE NOW.
YEAH?
AND WHAT'S YOUR ROLE HERE?
SAME ONE I'VE ALWAYS HAD.

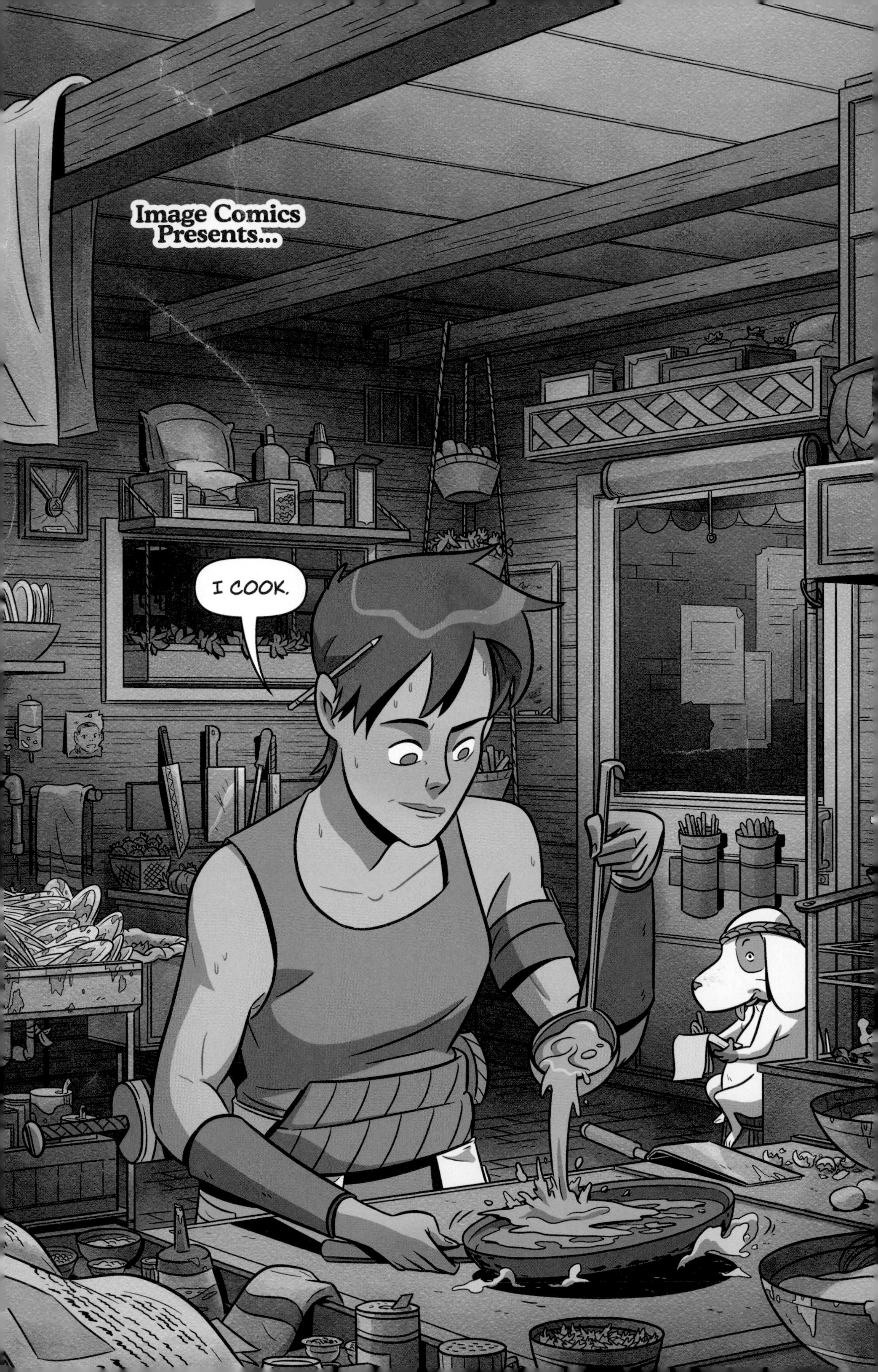
Image Comics
Presents...
I COOK.

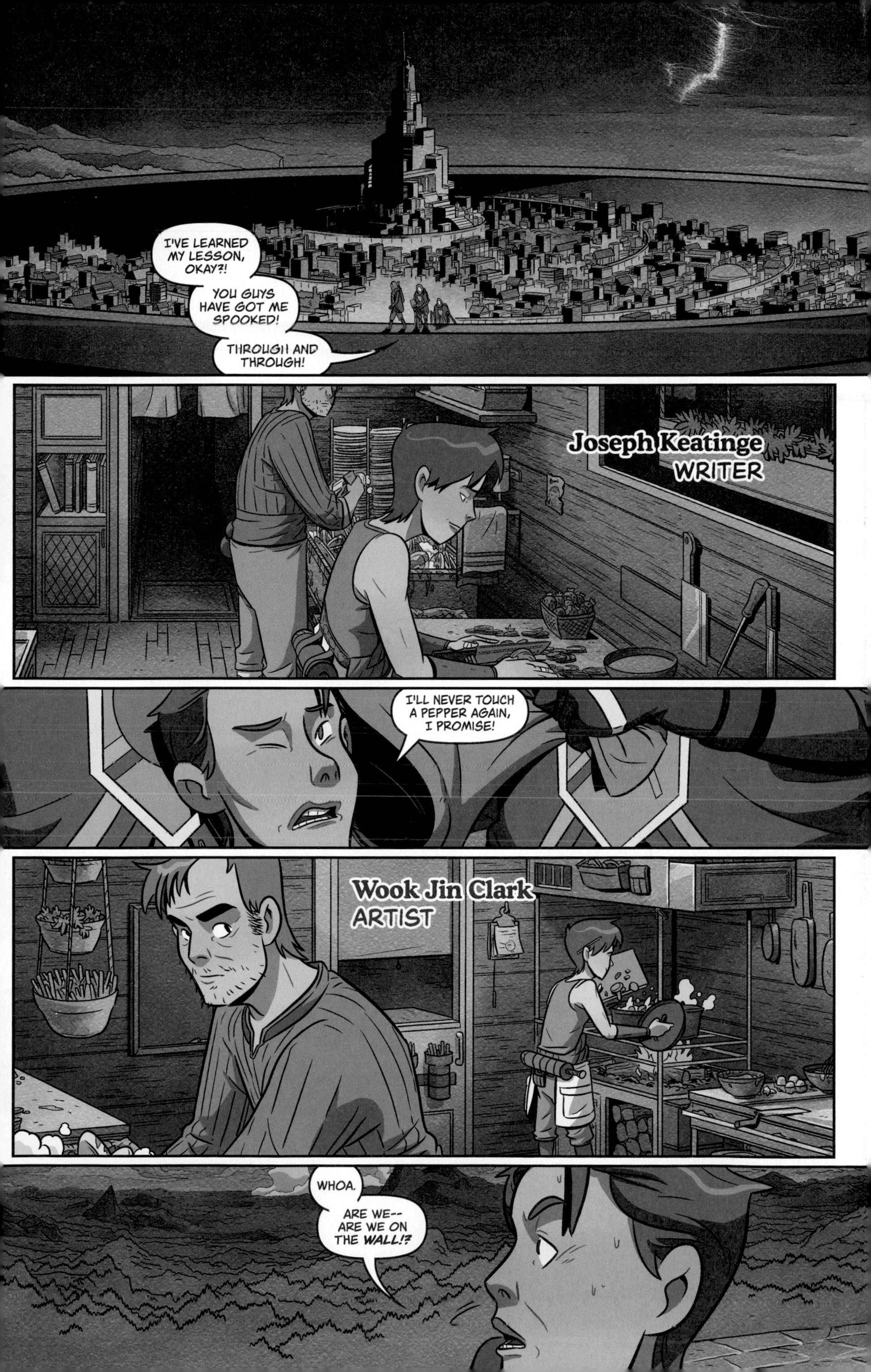

I'VE LEARNED MY LESSON, OKAY?!
YOU GUYS HAVE GOT ME SPOOKED!
THROUGH AND THROUGH!
Joseph Keatinge
WRITER
I'LL NEVER TOUCH A PEPPER AGAIN, I PROMISE!
Wook Jin Clark
ARTIST
WHOA.
ARE WE-- ARE WE ON THE WALL!?

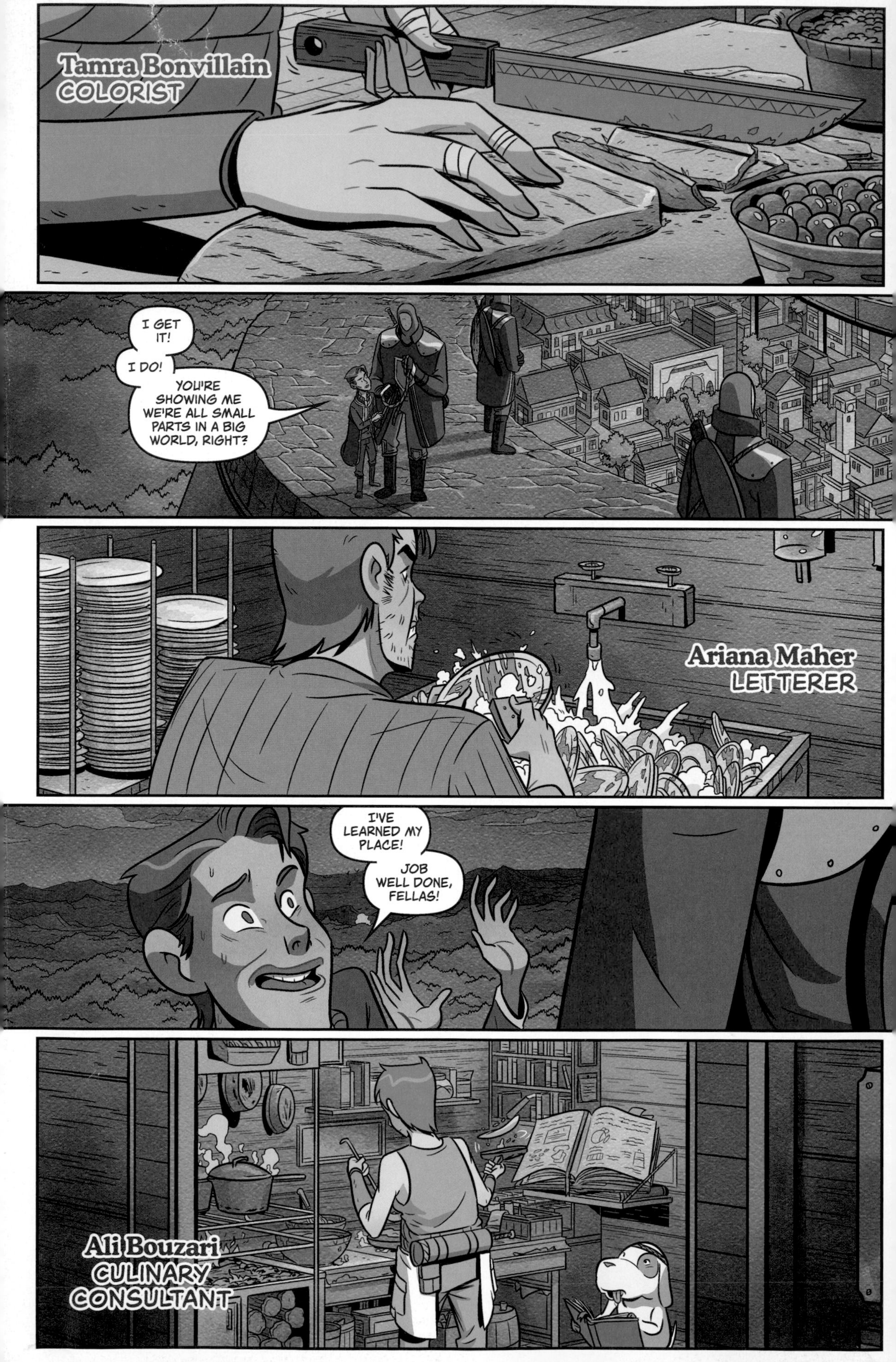

Tamra Bonvillain
COLORIST
I GET IT!
I DO!
YOU'RE SHOWING ME WE'RE ALL SMALL PARTS IN A BIG WORLD, RIGHT?
Ariana Maher
LETTERER
I'VE LEARNED MY PLACE!
JOB WELL DONE, FELLAS!
Ali Bouzari
CULINARY CONSULTANT

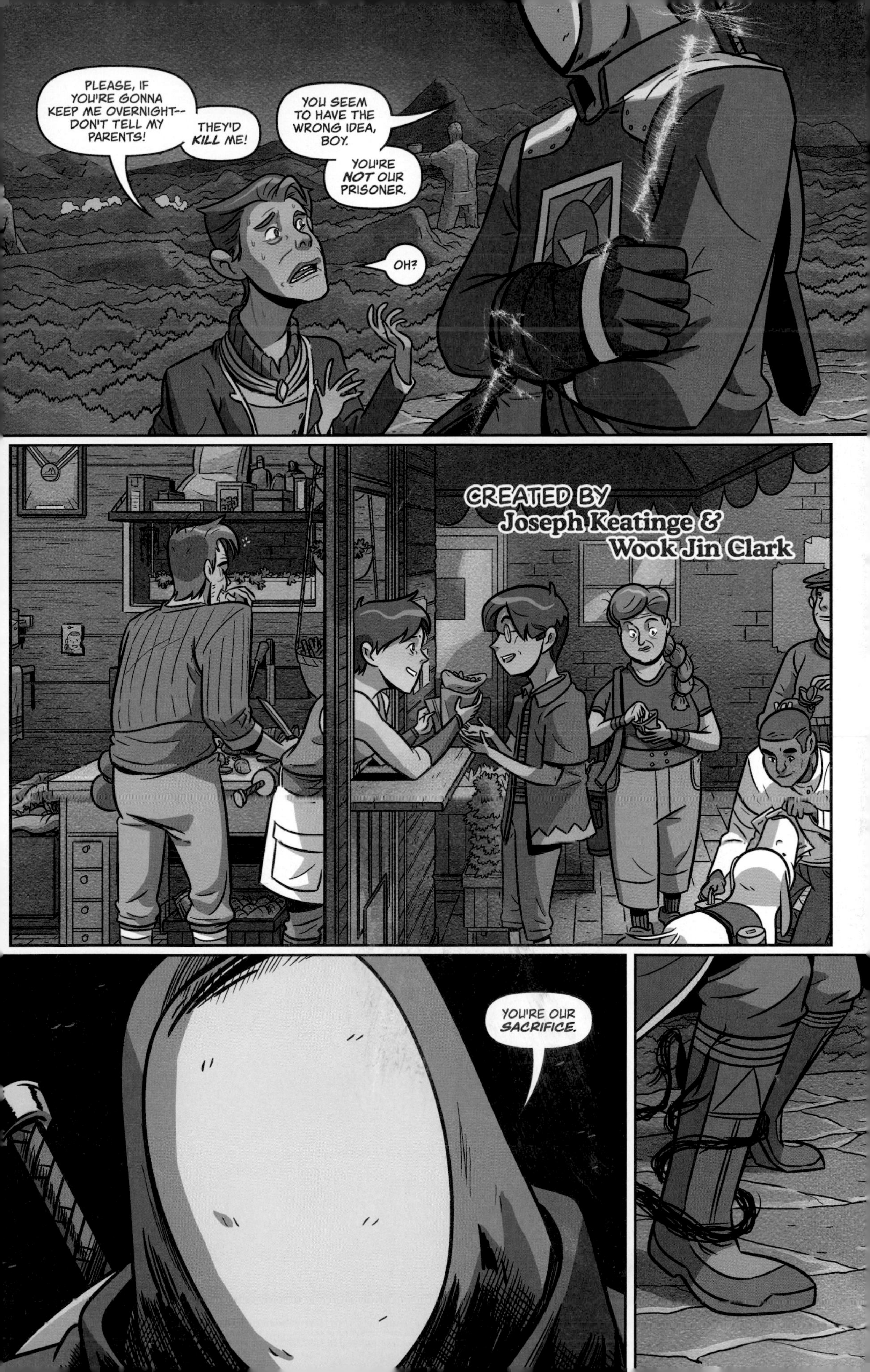
PLEASE, IF YOU'RE GONNA KEEP ME OVERNIGHT-- DON'T TELL MY PARENTS!
THEY'D KILL ME!
YOU SEEM TO HAVE THE WRONG IDEA, BOY.
YOU'RE NOT OUR PRISONER.
OH?
CREATED BY
Joseph Keatinge & Wook Jin Clark
YOU'RE OUR SACRIFICE.

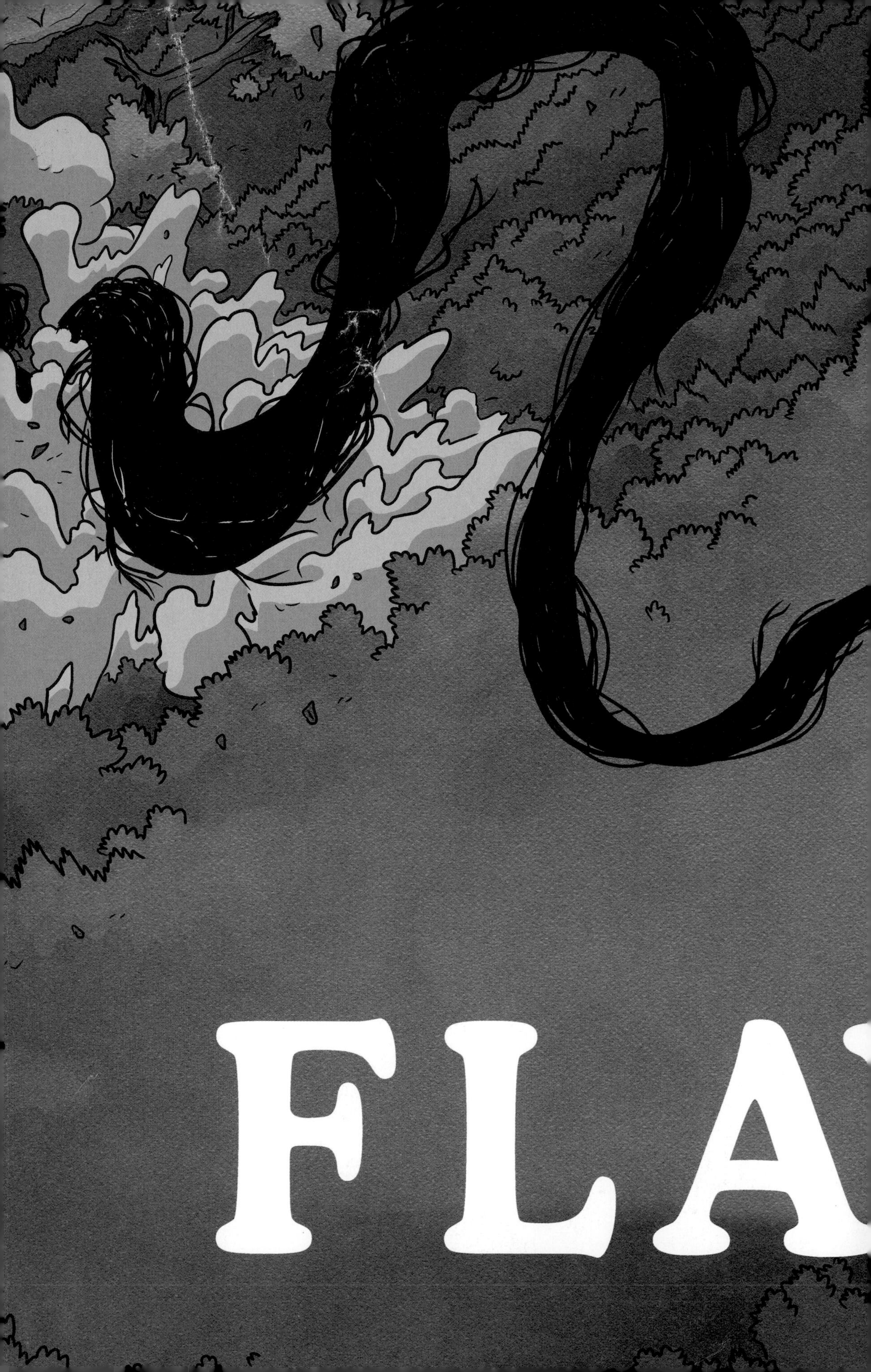
FLA

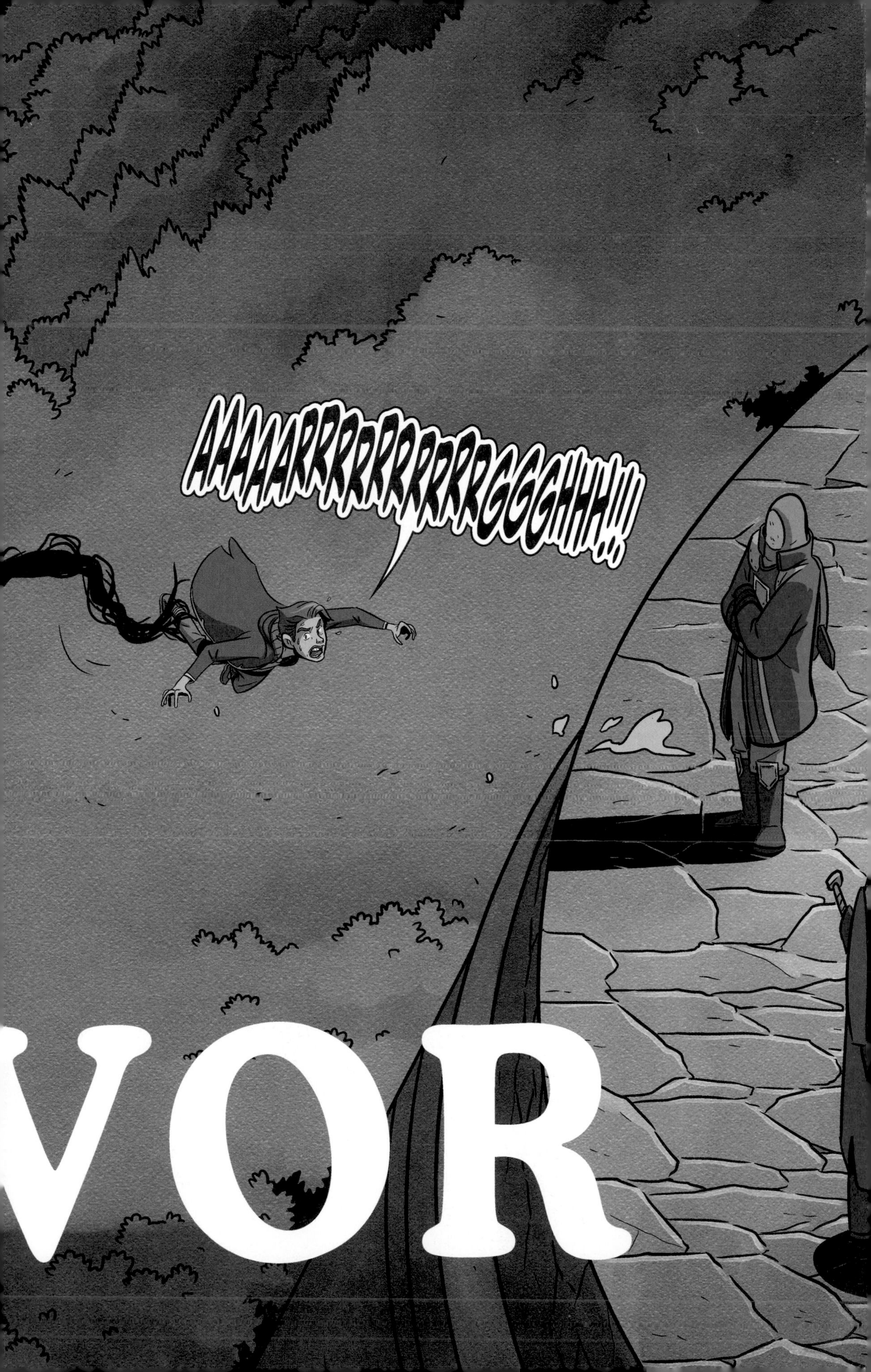
AAAAARRRRRRRRRGGGHHH!!!
VOR

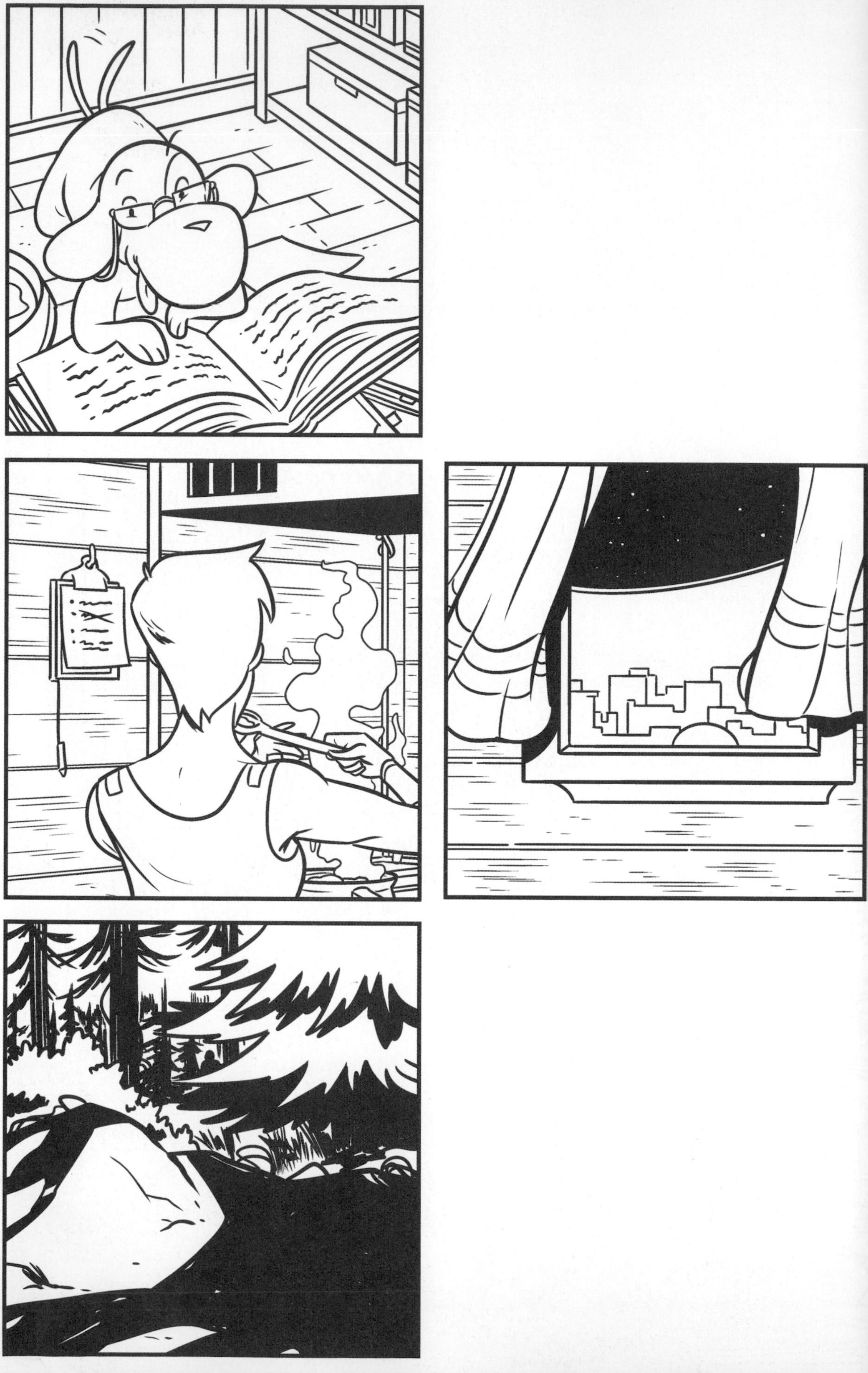

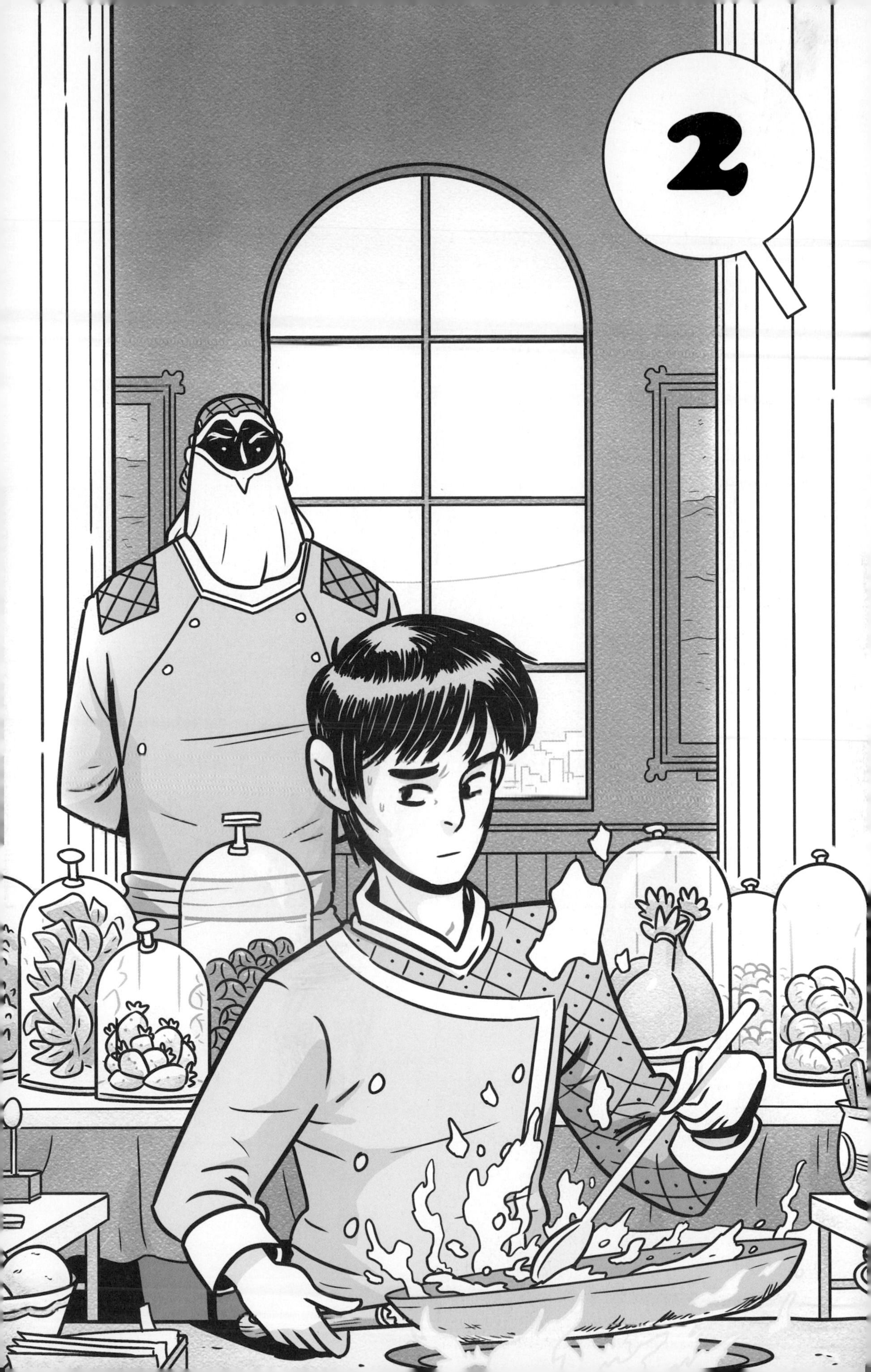
2

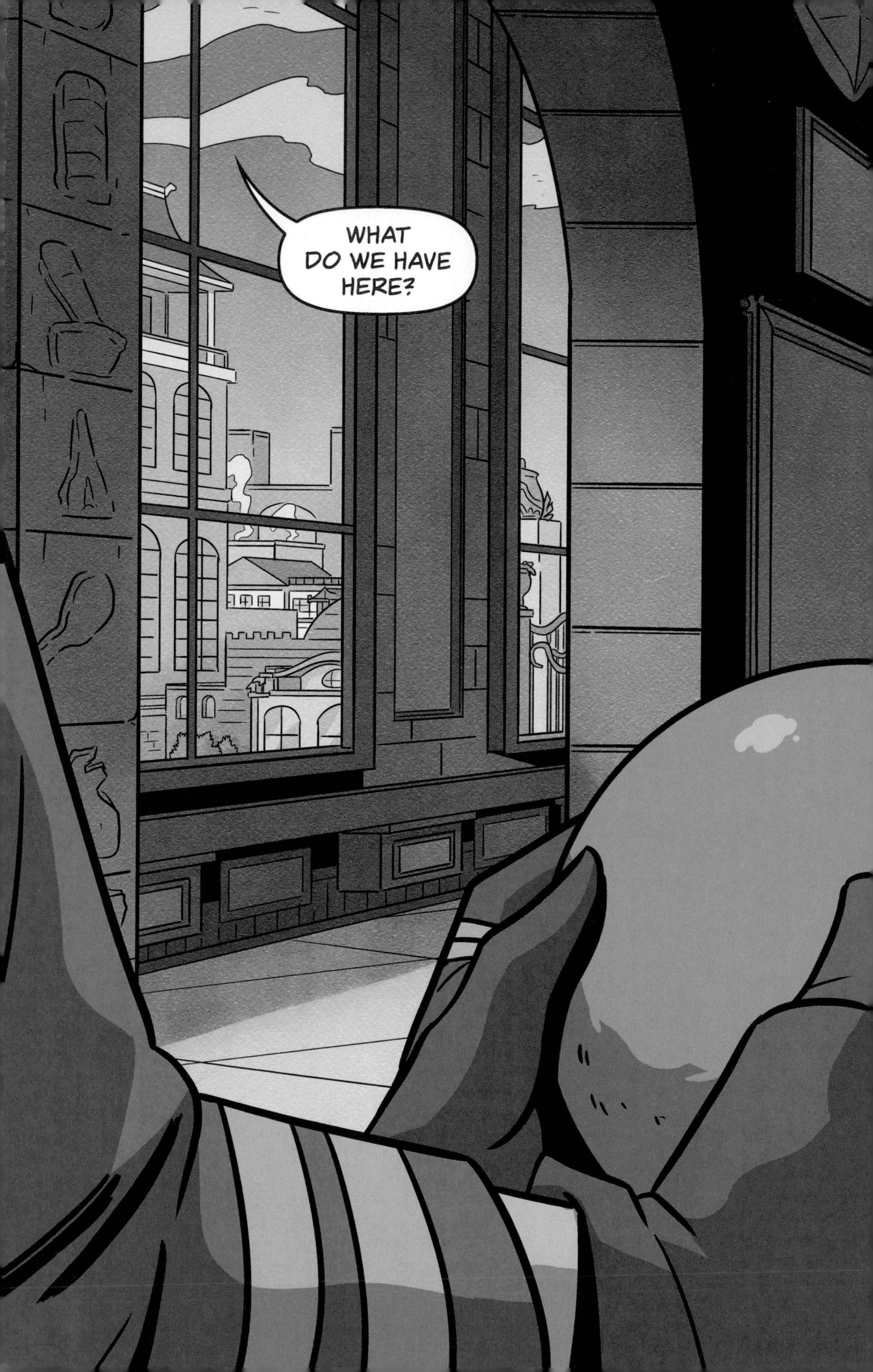
WHAT DO WE HAVE HERE?

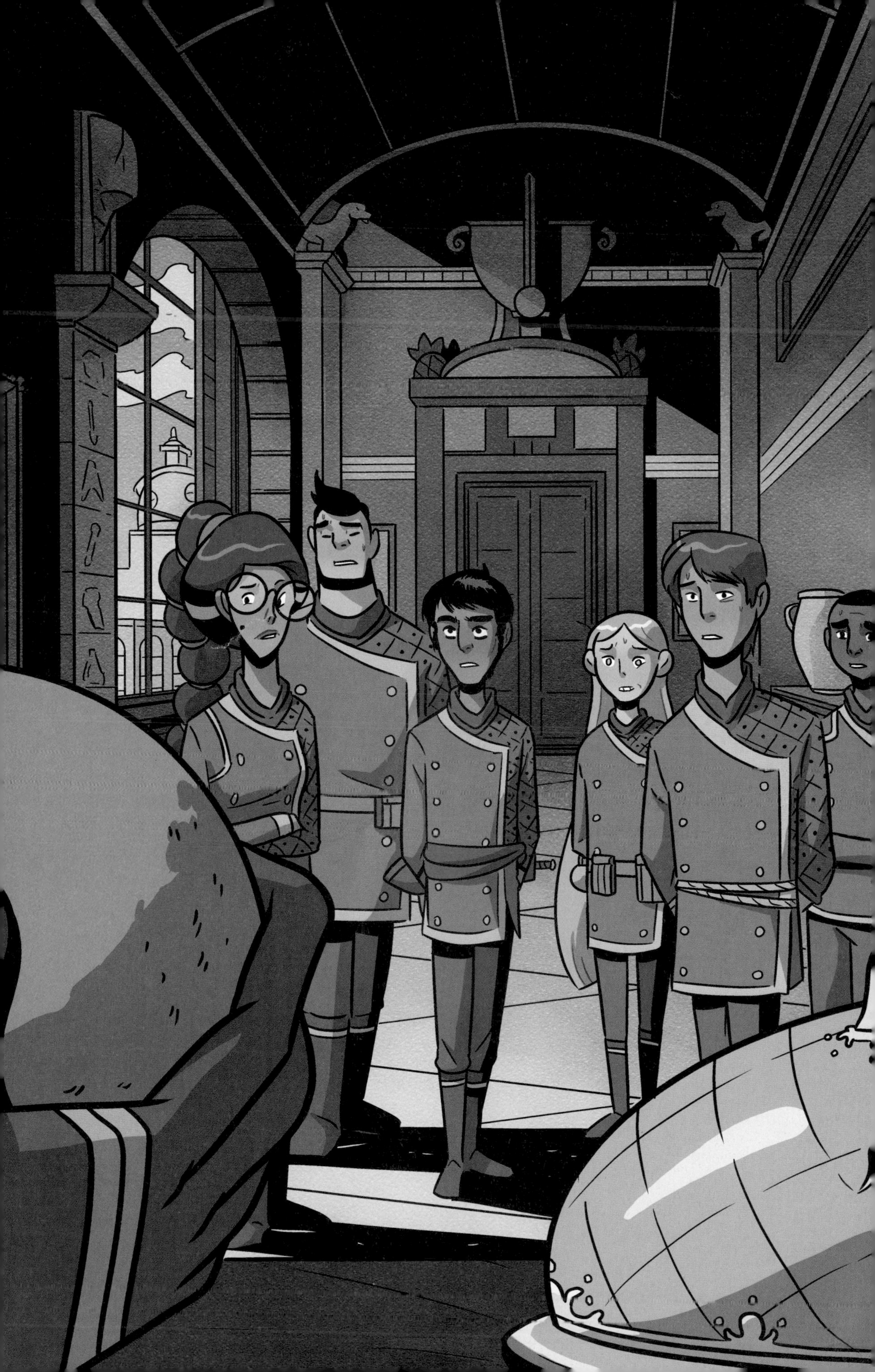

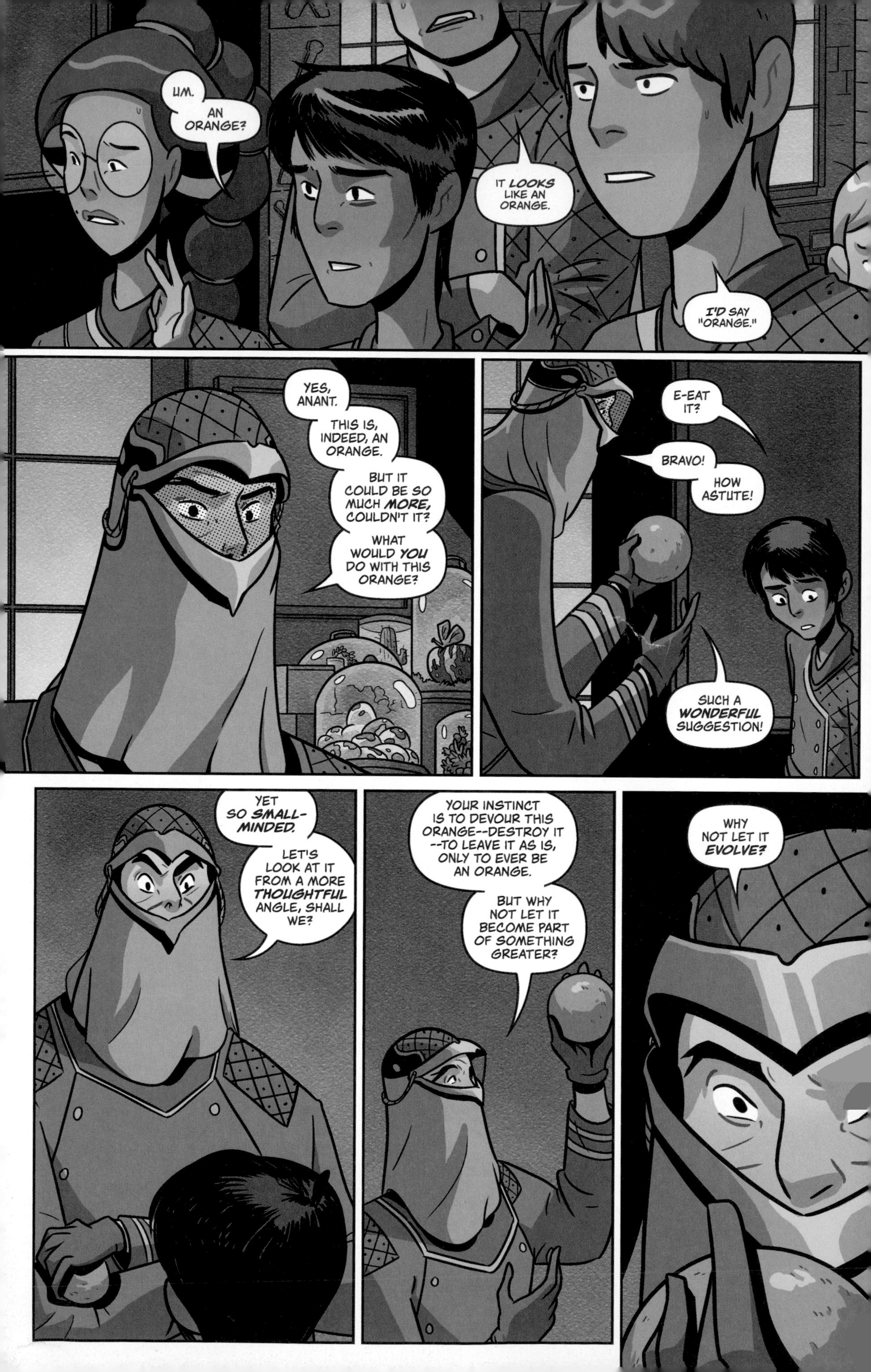
UM.
AN ORANGE?
IT LOOKS LIKE AN ORANGE.
I'D SAY "ORANGE."
YES, ANANT.
THIS IS, INDEED, AN ORANGE.
BUT IT COULD BE SO MUCH MORE, COULDN'T IT?
WHAT WOULD YOU DO WITH THIS ORANGE?
E-EAT IT?
BRAVO!
HOW ASTUTE!
SUCH A WONDERFUL SUGGESTION!
YET SO SMALL-MINDED.
LET'S LOOK AT IT FROM A MORE THOUGHTFUL ANGLE, SHALL WE?
YOUR INSTINCT IS TO DEVOUR THIS ORANGE--DESTROY IT --TO LEAVE IT AS IS, ONLY TO EVER BE AN ORANGE.
BUT WHY NOT LET IT BECOME PART OF SOMETHING GREATER?
WHY NOT LET IT EVOLVE?

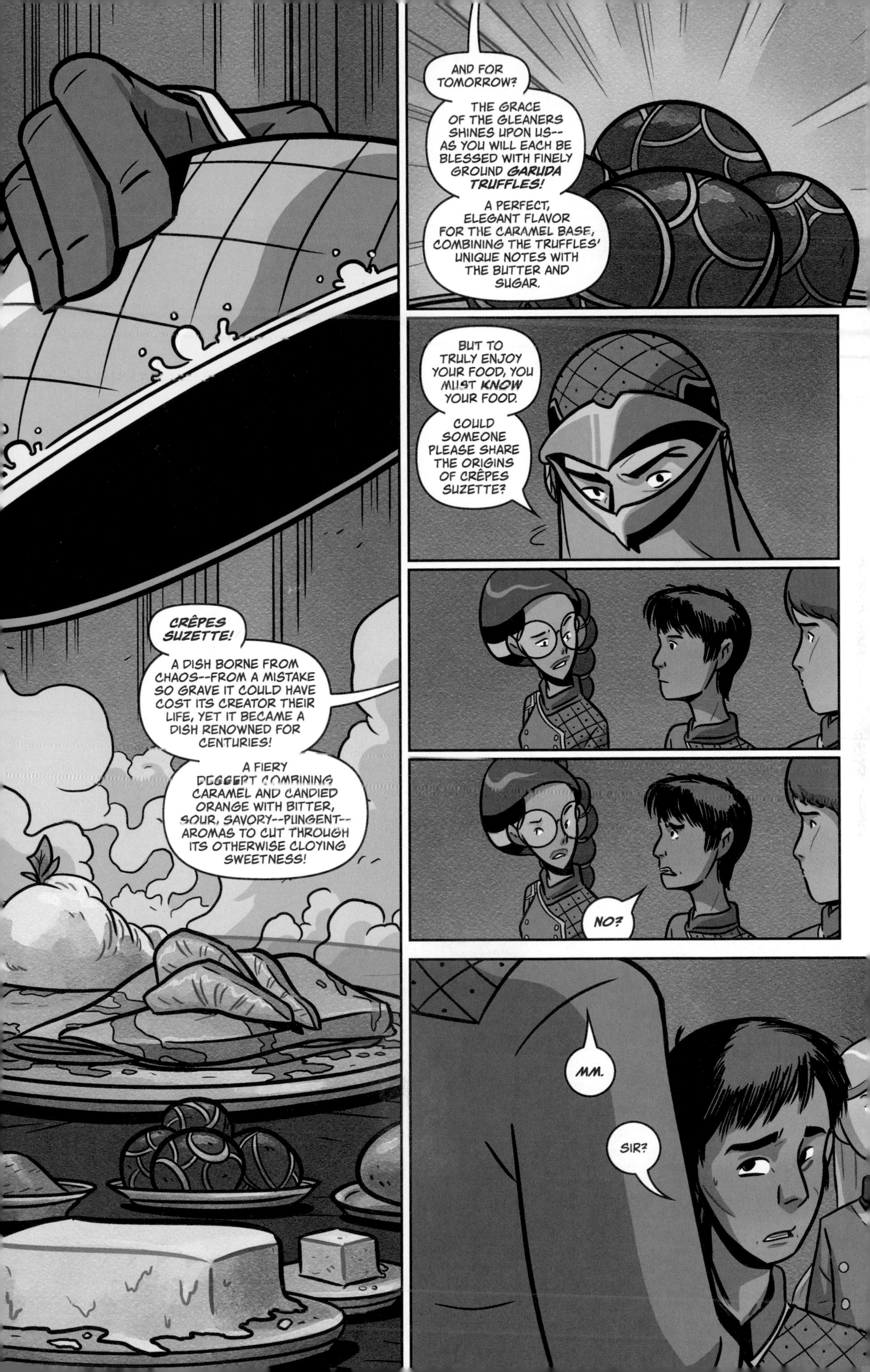

CRÊPES SUZETTE!
A DISH BORNE FROM CHAOS--FROM A MISTAKE SO GRAVE IT COULD HAVE COST ITS CREATOR THEIR LIFE, YET IT BECAME A DISH RENOWNED FOR CENTURIES!
A FIERY DESSERT COMBINING CARAMEL AND CANDIED ORANGE WITH BITTER, SOUR, SAVORY--PUNGENT--AROMAS TO CUT THROUGH ITS OTHERWISE CLOYING SWEETNESS!
AND FOR TOMORROW?
THE GRACE OF THE GLEANERS SHINES UPON US--AS YOU WILL EACH BE BLESSED WITH FINELY GROUND GARUDA TRUFFLES!
A PERFECT, ELEGANT FLAVOR FOR THE CARAMEL BASE, COMBINING THE TRUFFLES' UNIQUE NOTES WITH THE BUTTER AND SUGAR.
BUT TO TRULY ENJOY YOUR FOOD, YOU MUST KNOW YOUR FOOD.
COULD SOMEONE PLEASE SHARE THE ORIGINS OF CRÊPES SUZETTE?
NO?
MM.
SIR?

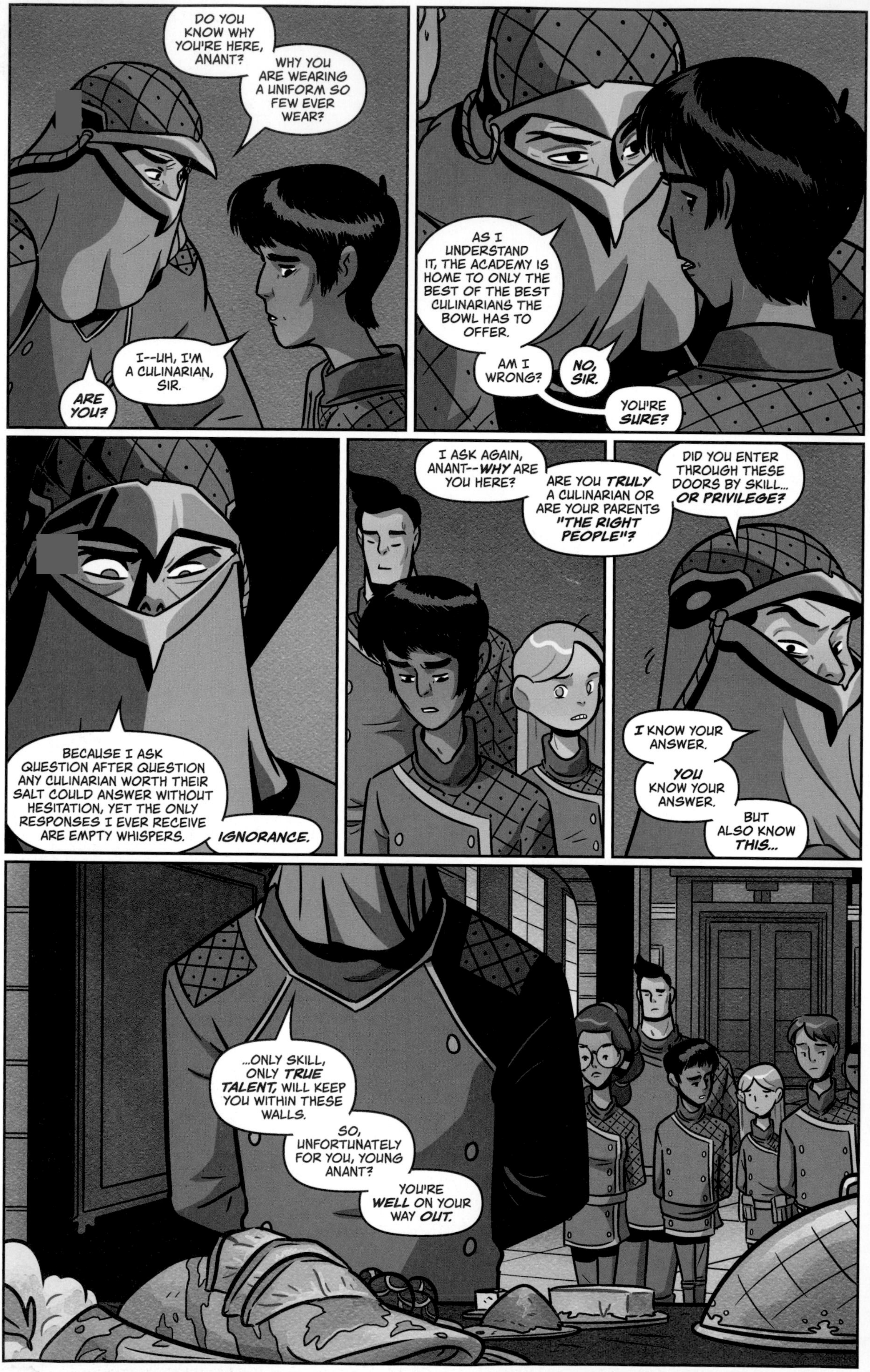
DO YOU KNOW WHY YOU'RE HERE, ANANT?
WHY YOU ARE WEARING A UNIFORM SO FEW EVER WEAR?
I--UH, I'M A CULINARIAN, SIR.
ARE YOU?
AS I UNDERSTAND IT, THE ACADEMY IS HOME TO ONLY THE BEST OF THE BEST CULINARIANS THE BOWL HAS TO OFFER.
AM I WRONG?
NO, SIR.
YOU'RE SURE?
BECAUSE I ASK QUESTION AFTER QUESTION ANY CULINARIAN WORTH THEIR SALT COULD ANSWER WITHOUT HESITATION, YET THE ONLY RESPONSES I EVER RECEIVE ARE EMPTY WHISPERS.
IGNORANCE.
I ASK AGAIN, ANANT--WHY ARE YOU HERE?
ARE YOU TRULY A CULINARIAN OR ARE YOUR PARENTS "THE RIGHT PEOPLE"?
DID YOU ENTER THROUGH THESE DOORS BY SKILL... OR PRIVILEGE?
I KNOW YOUR ANSWER.
YOU KNOW YOUR ANSWER.
BUT ALSO KNOW THIS...
...ONLY SKILL, ONLY TRUE TALENT, WILL KEEP YOU WITHIN THESE WALLS.
SO, UNFORTUNATELY FOR YOU, YOUNG ANANT?
YOU'RE WELL ON YOUR WAY OUT.

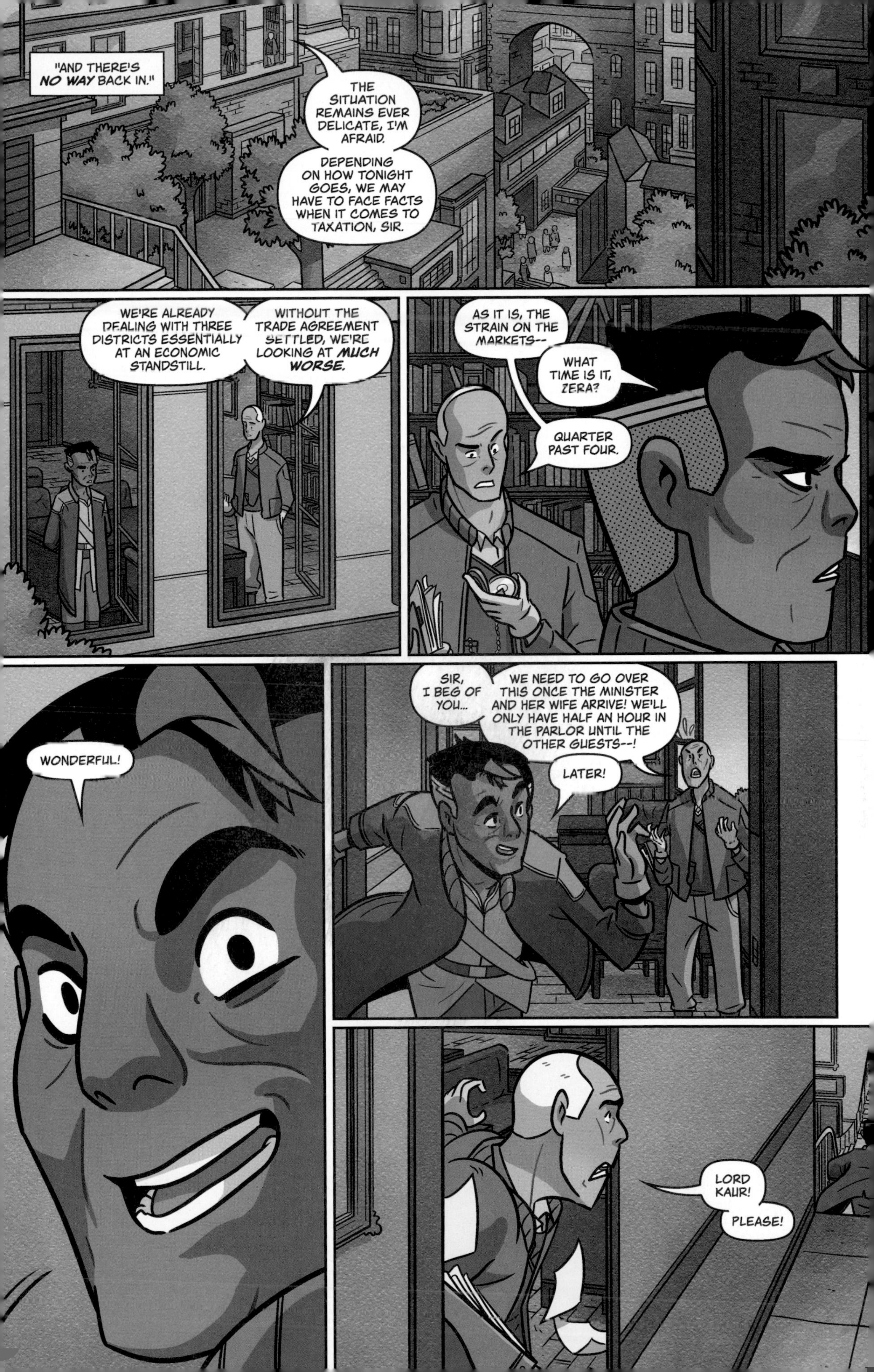
"AND THERE'S NO WAY BACK IN."
THE SITUATION REMAINS EVER DELICATE, I'M AFRAID.
DEPENDING ON HOW TONIGHT GOES, WE MAY HAVE TO FACE FACTS WHEN IT COMES TO TAXATION, SIR.
WE'RE ALREADY DEALING WITH THREE DISTRICTS ESSENTIALLY AT AN ECONOMIC STANDSTILL.
WITHOUT THE TRADE AGREEMENT SETTLED, WE'RE LOOKING AT MUCH WORSE.
AS IT IS, THE STRAIN ON THE MARKETS--
WHAT TIME IS IT, ZERA?
QUARTER PAST FOUR.
WONDERFUL!
SIR, I BEG OF YOU...
WE NEED TO GO OVER THIS ONCE THE MINISTER AND HER WIFE ARRIVE! WE'LL ONLY HAVE HALF AN HOUR IN THE PARLOR UNTIL THE OTHER GUESTS--!
LATER!
LORD KAUR!
PLEASE!

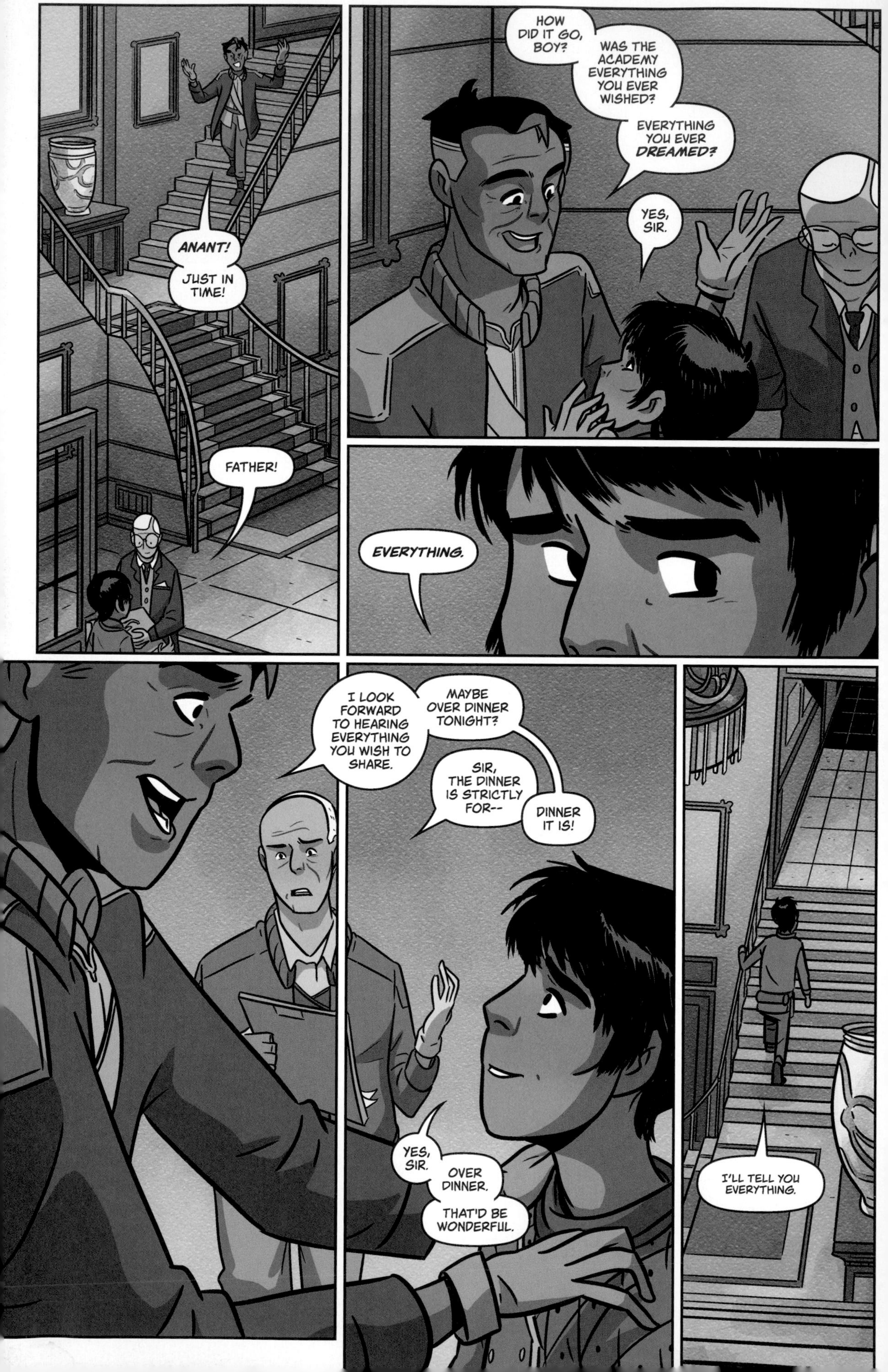
ANANT!
JUST IN TIME!
FATHER!
HOW DID IT GO, BOY?
WAS THE ACADEMY EVERYTHING YOU EVER WISHED?
EVERYTHING YOU EVER DREAMED?
YES, SIR.
EVERYTHING.
I LOOK FORWARD TO HEARING EVERYTHING YOU WISH TO SHARE.
MAYBE OVER DINNER TONIGHT?
SIR, THE DINNER IS STRICTLY FOR--
DINNER IT IS!
YES, SIR.
OVER DINNER.
THAT'D BE WONDERFUL.
I'LL TELL YOU EVERYTHING.

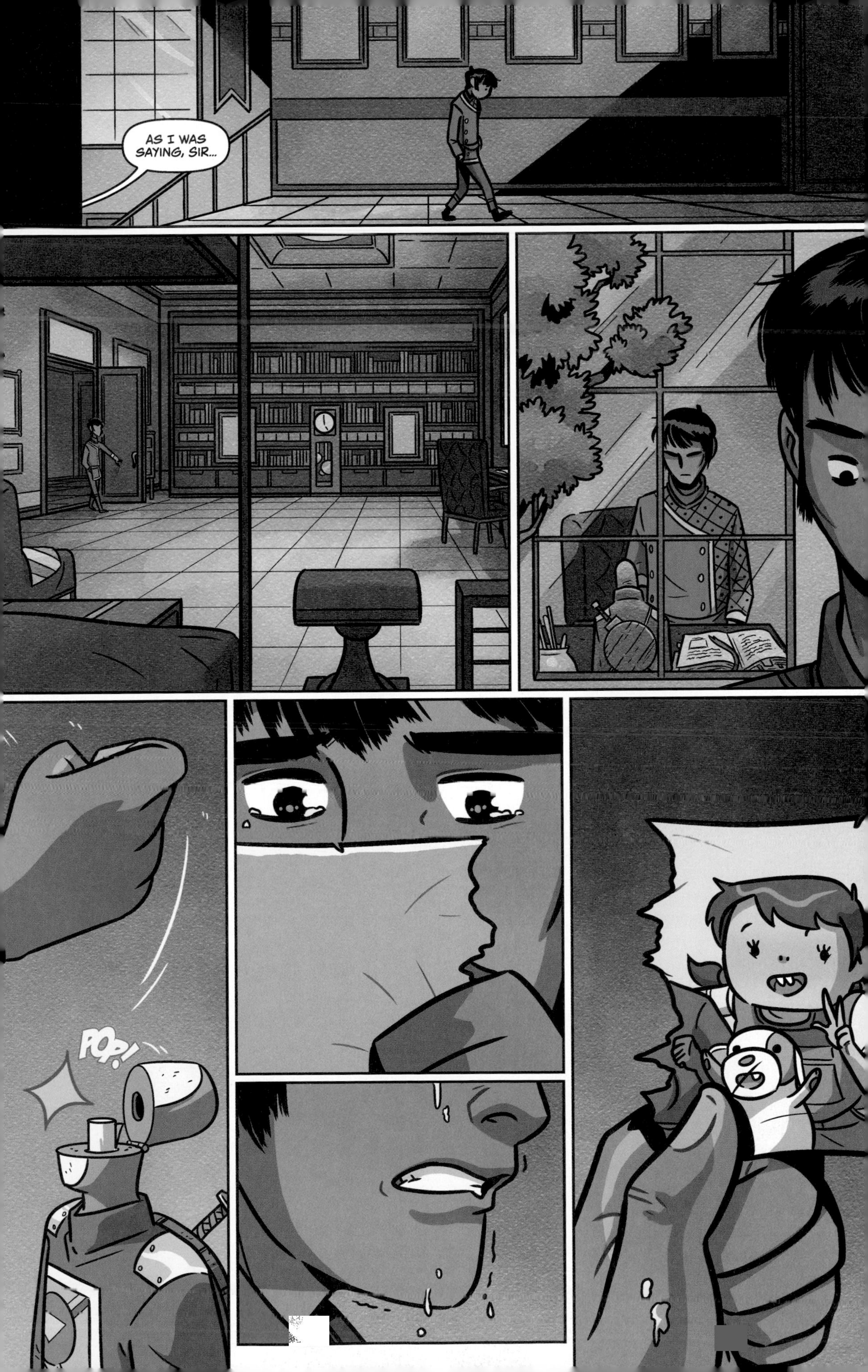
AS I WAS SAYING, SIR...
POP!

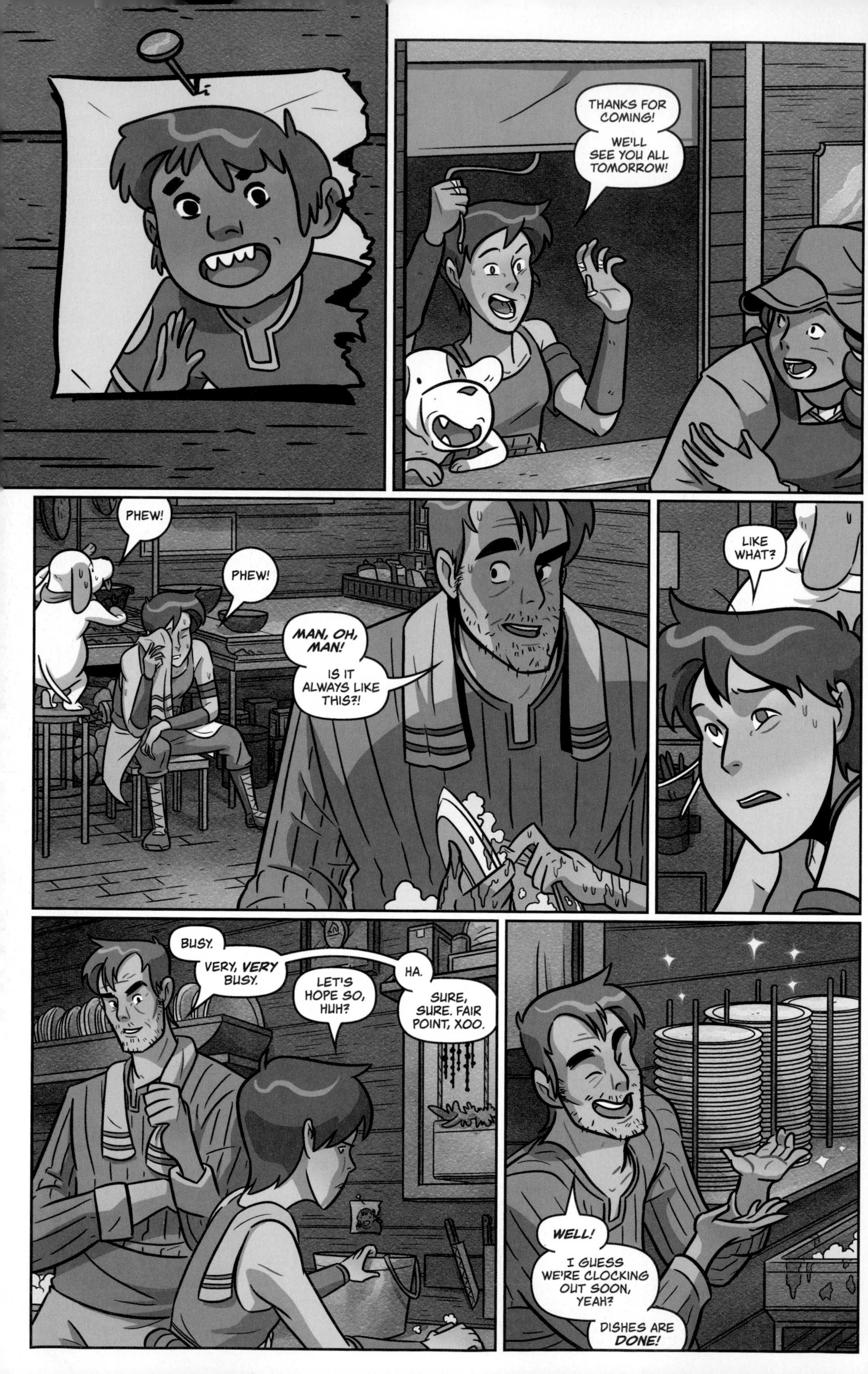
THANKS FOR COMING!
WE'LL SEE YOU ALL TOMORROW!
PHEW!
PHEW!
MAN, OH, MAN!
IS IT ALWAYS LIKE THIS?!
LIKE WHAT?
BUSY.
VERY, VERY BUSY.
LET'S HOPE SO, HUH?
HA.
SURE, SURE. FAIR POINT, XOO.
WELL!
I GUESS WE'RE CLOCKING OUT SOON, YEAH?
DISHES ARE DONE!

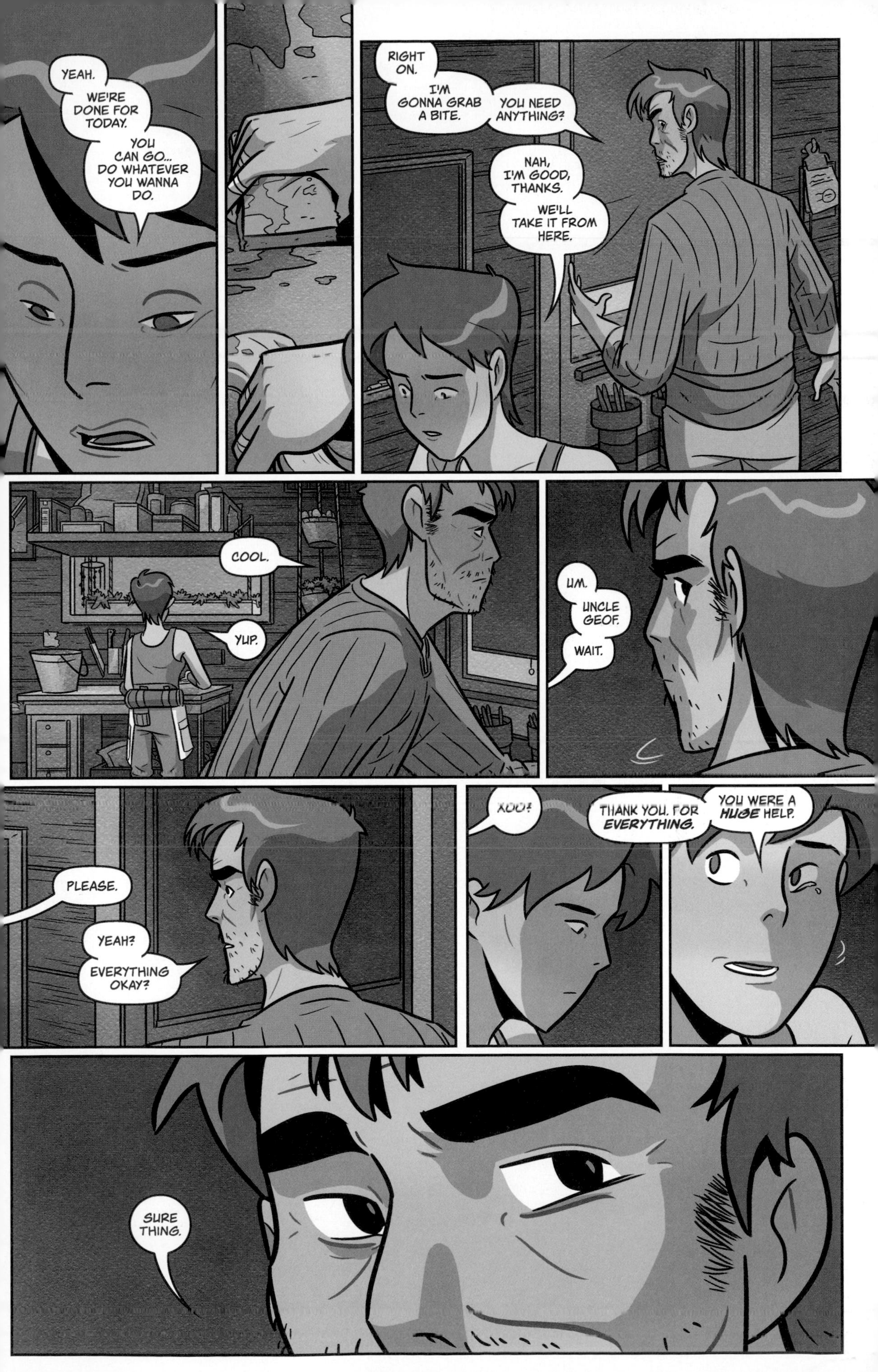
YEAH.
WE'RE DONE FOR TODAY.
YOU CAN GO... DO WHATEVER YOU WANNA DO.
RIGHT ON.
I'M GONNA GRAB A BITE.
YOU NEED ANYTHING?
NAH, I'M GOOD, THANKS.
WE'LL TAKE IT FROM HERE.
COOL.
YUP.
UM.
UNCLE GEOF.
WAIT.
PLEASE.
YEAH?
EVERYTHING OKAY?
YOU?
THANK YOU. FOR EVERYTHING.
YOU WERE A HUGE HELP.
SURE THING.

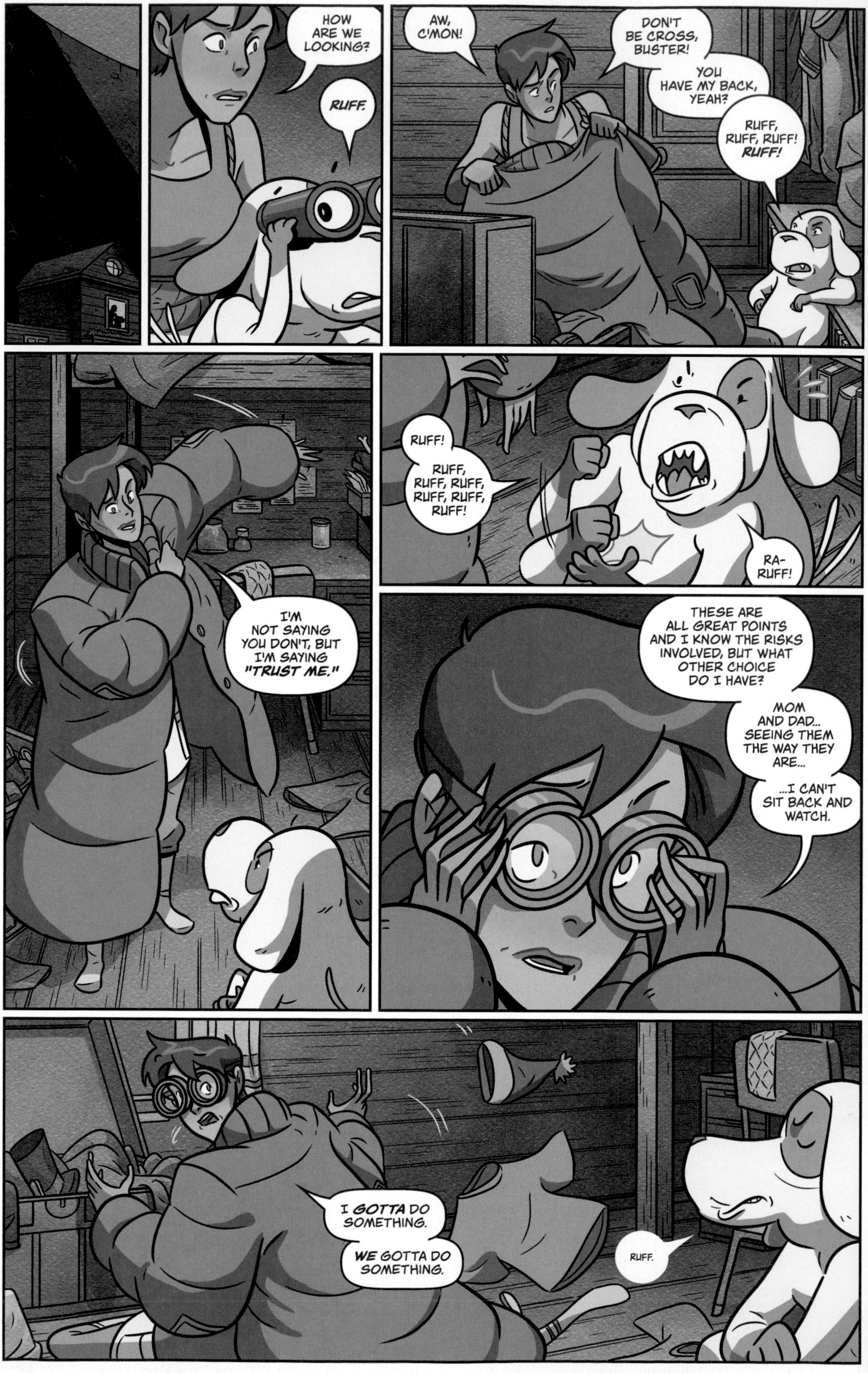

HOW ARE WE LOOKING?
RUFF.
AW, C'MON!
DON'T BE CROSS, BUSTER!
YOU HAVE MY BACK, YEAH?
RUFF, RUFF, RUFF! RUFF!
I'M NOT SAYING YOU DON'T, BUT I'M SAYING "TRUST ME."
RUFF!
RUFF, RUFF, RUFF, RUFF, RUFF, RUFF!
RA-RUFF!
THESE ARE ALL GREAT POINTS AND I KNOW THE RISKS INVOLVED, BUT WHAT OTHER CHOICE DO I HAVE?
MOM AND DAD... SEEING THEM THE WAY THEY ARE...
...I CAN'T SIT BACK AND WATCH.
I GOTTA DO SOMETHING.
WE GOTTA DO SOMETHING.
RUFF.

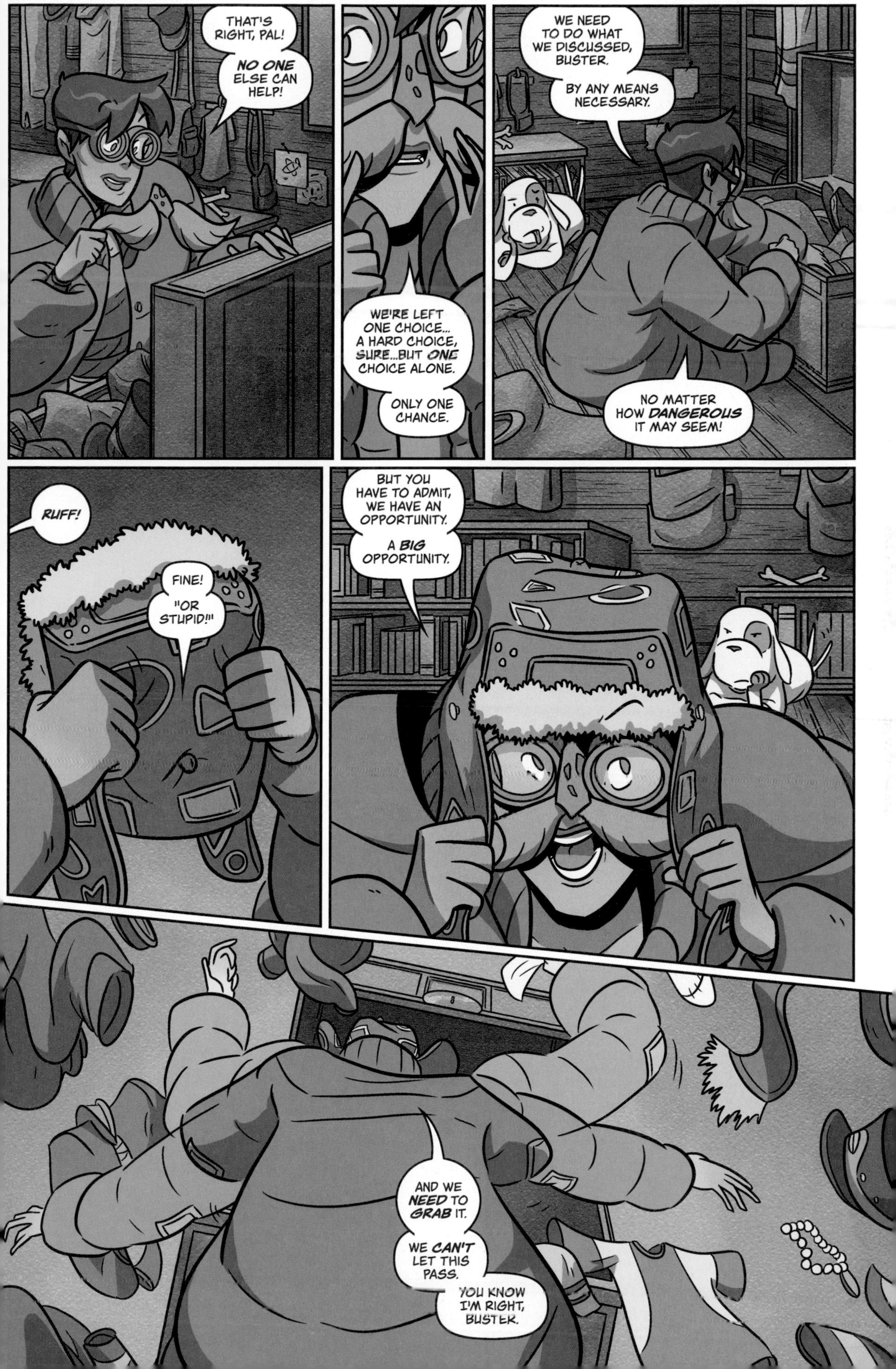
THAT'S RIGHT, PAL!
NO ONE ELSE CAN HELP!
WE'RE LEFT ONE CHOICE... A HARD CHOICE, SURE...BUT ONE CHOICE ALONE.
ONLY ONE CHANCE.
WE NEED TO DO WHAT WE DISCUSSED, BUSTER.
BY ANY MEANS NECESSARY.
NO MATTER HOW DANGEROUS IT MAY SEEM!
RUFF!
FINE!
"OR STUPID!"
BUT YOU HAVE TO ADMIT, WE HAVE AN OPPORTUNITY.
A BIG OPPORTUNITY.
AND WE NEED TO GRAB IT.
WE CAN'T LET THIS PASS.
YOU KNOW I'M RIGHT, BUSTER.

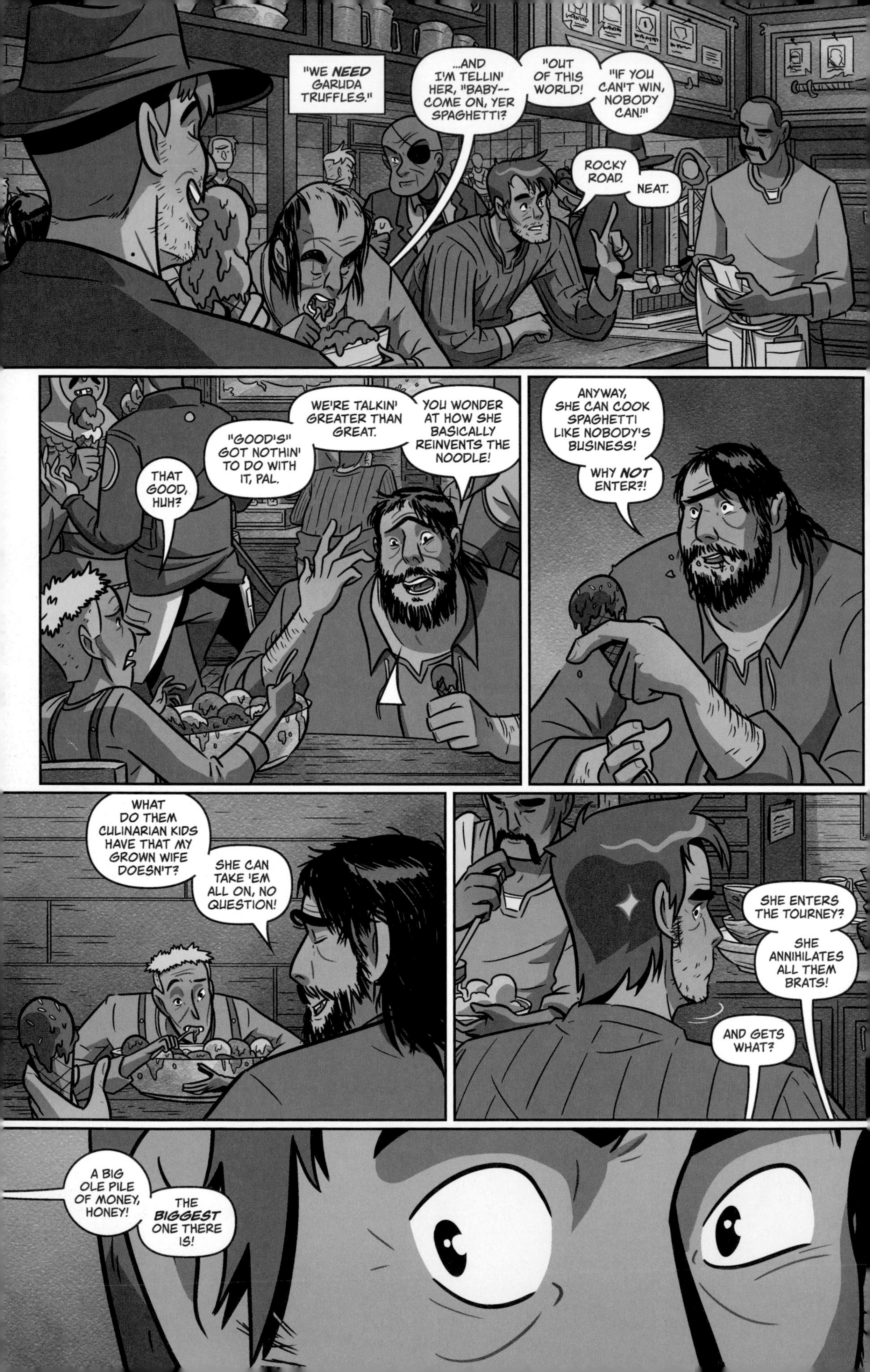
"WE NEED GARUDA TRUFFLES."
...AND I'M TELLIN' HER, "BABY-- COME ON, YER SPAGHETTI?
"OUT OF THIS WORLD!
"IF YOU CAN'T WIN, NOBODY CAN!"
ROCKY ROAD.
NEAT.
THAT GOOD, HUH?
"GOOD'S" GOT NOTHIN' TO DO WITH IT, PAL.
WE'RE TALKIN' GREATER THAN GREAT.
YOU WONDER AT HOW SHE BASICALLY REINVENTS THE NOODLE!
ANYWAY, SHE CAN COOK SPAGHETTI LIKE NOBODY'S BUSINESS!
WHY NOT ENTER?!
WHAT DO THEM CULINARIAN KIDS HAVE THAT MY GROWN WIFE DOESN'T?
SHE CAN TAKE 'EM ALL ON, NO QUESTION!
SHE ENTERS THE TOURNEY?
SHE ANNIHILATES ALL THEM BRATS!
AND GETS WHAT?
A BIG OLE PILE OF MONEY, HONEY!
THE BIGGEST ONE THERE IS!

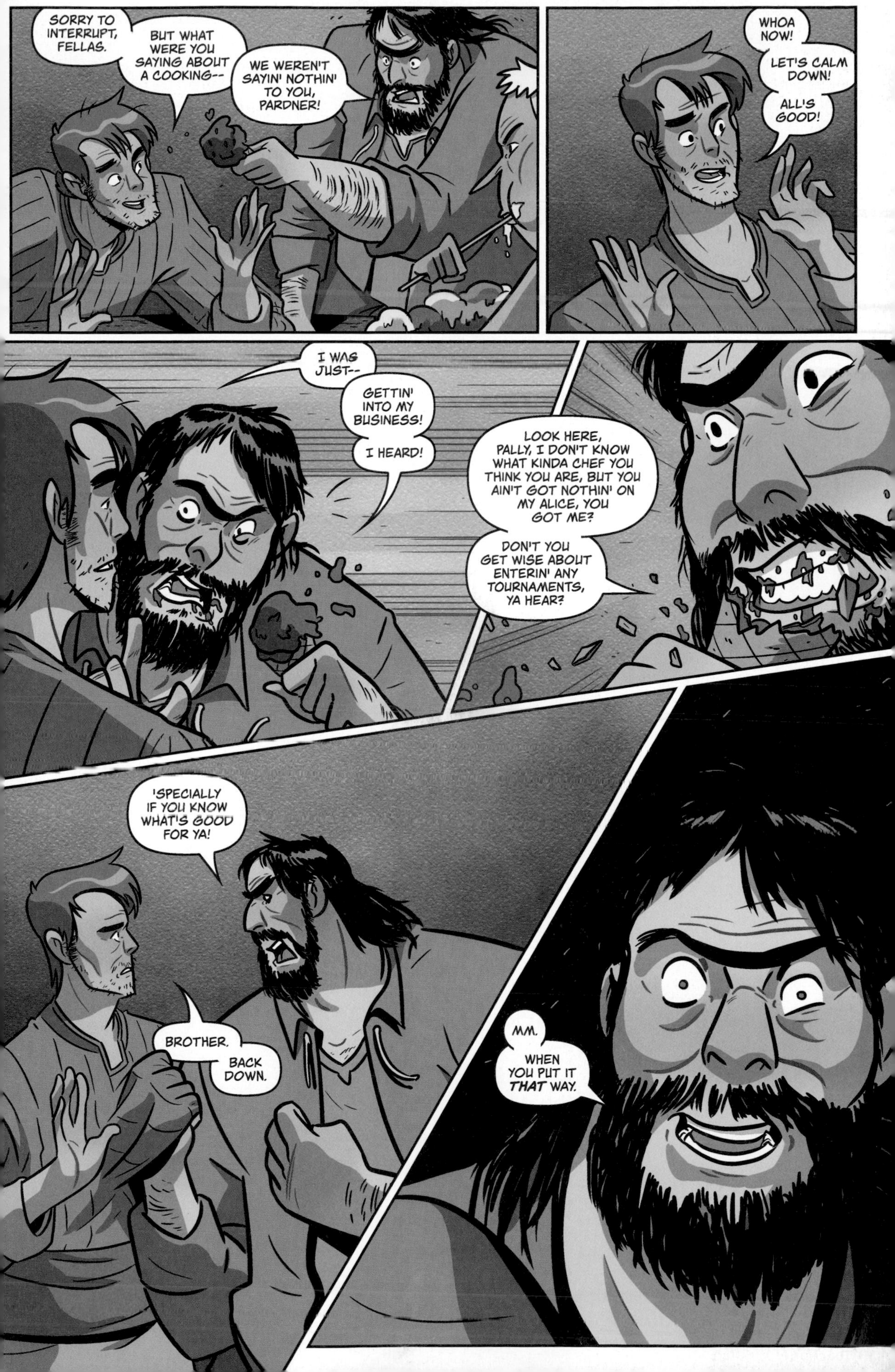
SORRY TO INTERRUPT, FELLAS.
BUT WHAT WERE YOU SAYING ABOUT A COOKING--
WE WEREN'T SAYIN' NOTHIN' TO YOU, PARDNER!
WHOA NOW!
LET'S CALM DOWN!
ALL'S GOOD!
I WAS JUST--
GETTIN' INTO MY BUSINESS!
I HEARD!
LOOK HERE, PALLY, I DON'T KNOW WHAT KINDA CHEF YOU THINK YOU ARE, BUT YOU AIN'T GOT NOTHIN' ON MY ALICE, YOU GOT ME?
DON'T YOU GET WISE ABOUT ENTERIN' ANY TOURNAMENTS, YA HEAR?
'SPECIALLY IF YOU KNOW WHAT'S GOOD FOR YA!
BROTHER.
BACK DOWN.
MM.
WHEN YOU PUT IT *THAT* WAY.

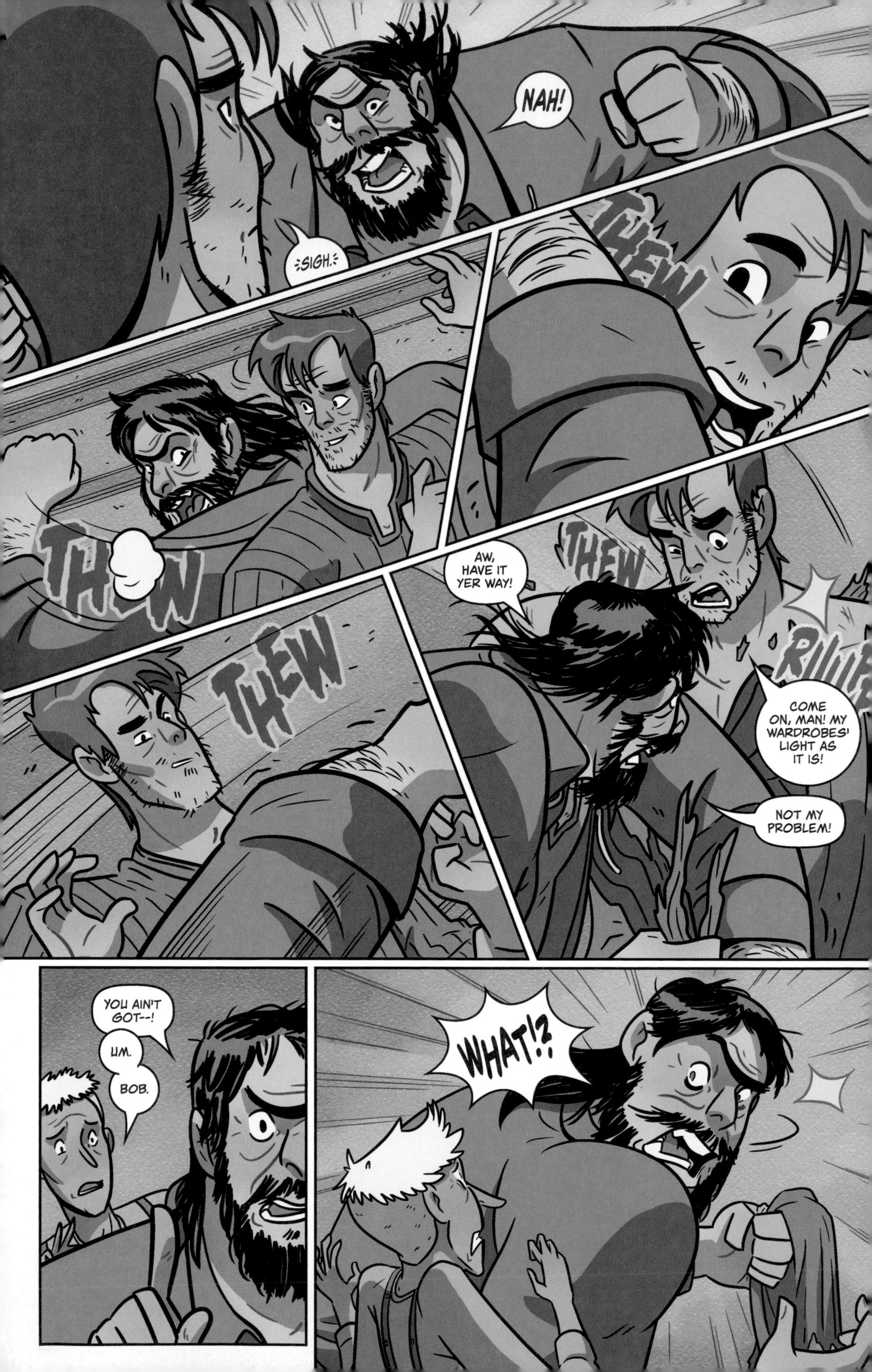
NAH!
SIGH.
THEW
THEW
THEW
AW, HAVE IT YER WAY!
THEW
RIIIIP
COME ON, MAN! MY WARDROBES' LIGHT AS IT IS!
NOT MY PROBLEM!
YOU AIN'T GOT--!
UM.
BOB.
WHAT!?

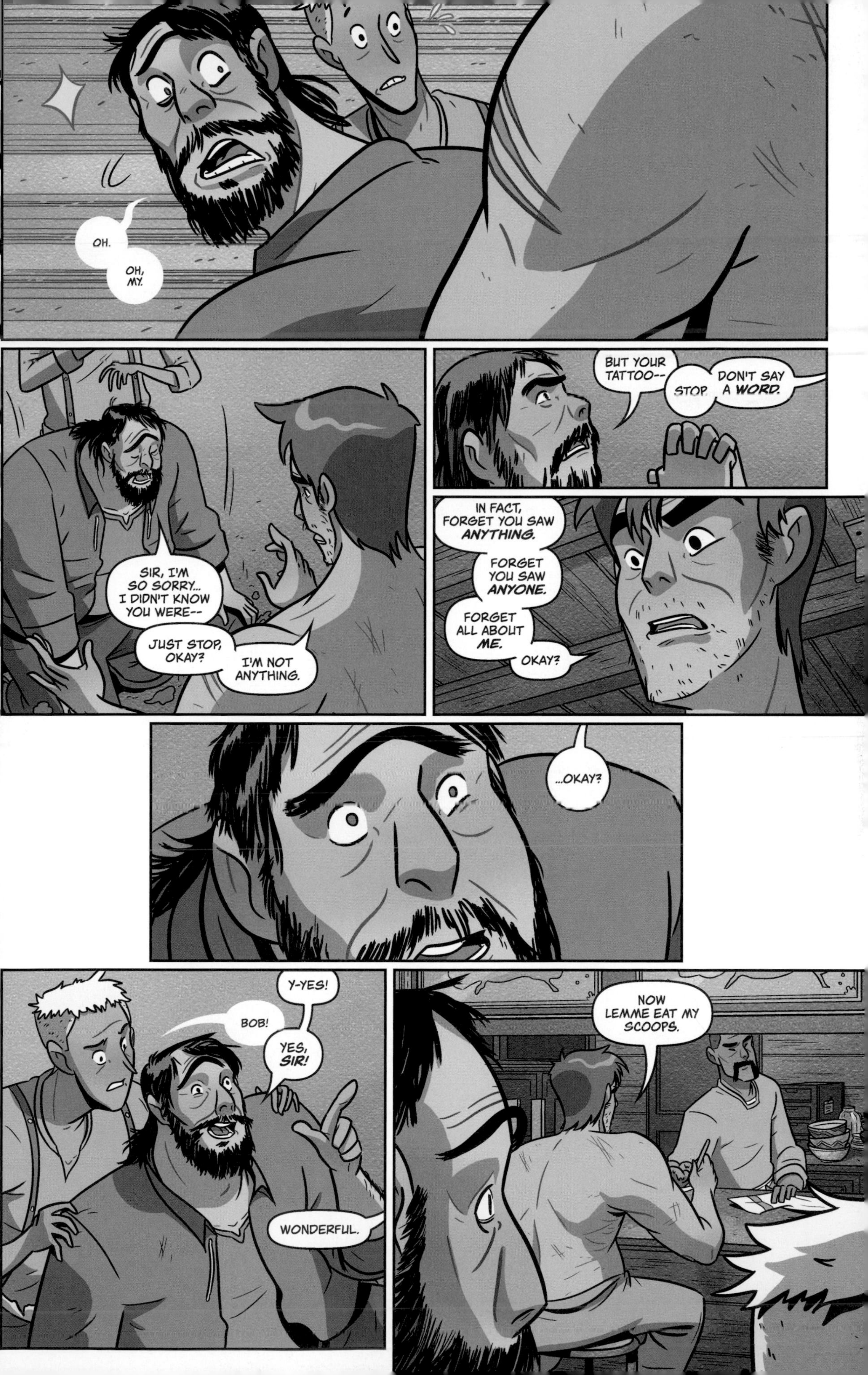
OH.
OH, MY.
SIR, I'M SO SORRY... I DIDN'T KNOW YOU WERE--
JUST STOP, OKAY?
I'M NOT ANYTHING.
BUT YOUR TATTOO--
STOP.
DON'T SAY A WORD.
IN FACT, FORGET YOU SAW ANYTHING.
FORGET YOU SAW ANYONE.
FORGET ALL ABOUT ME.
OKAY?
...OKAY?
Y-YES!
BOB!
YES, SIR!
WONDERFUL.
NOW LEMME EAT MY SCOOPS.

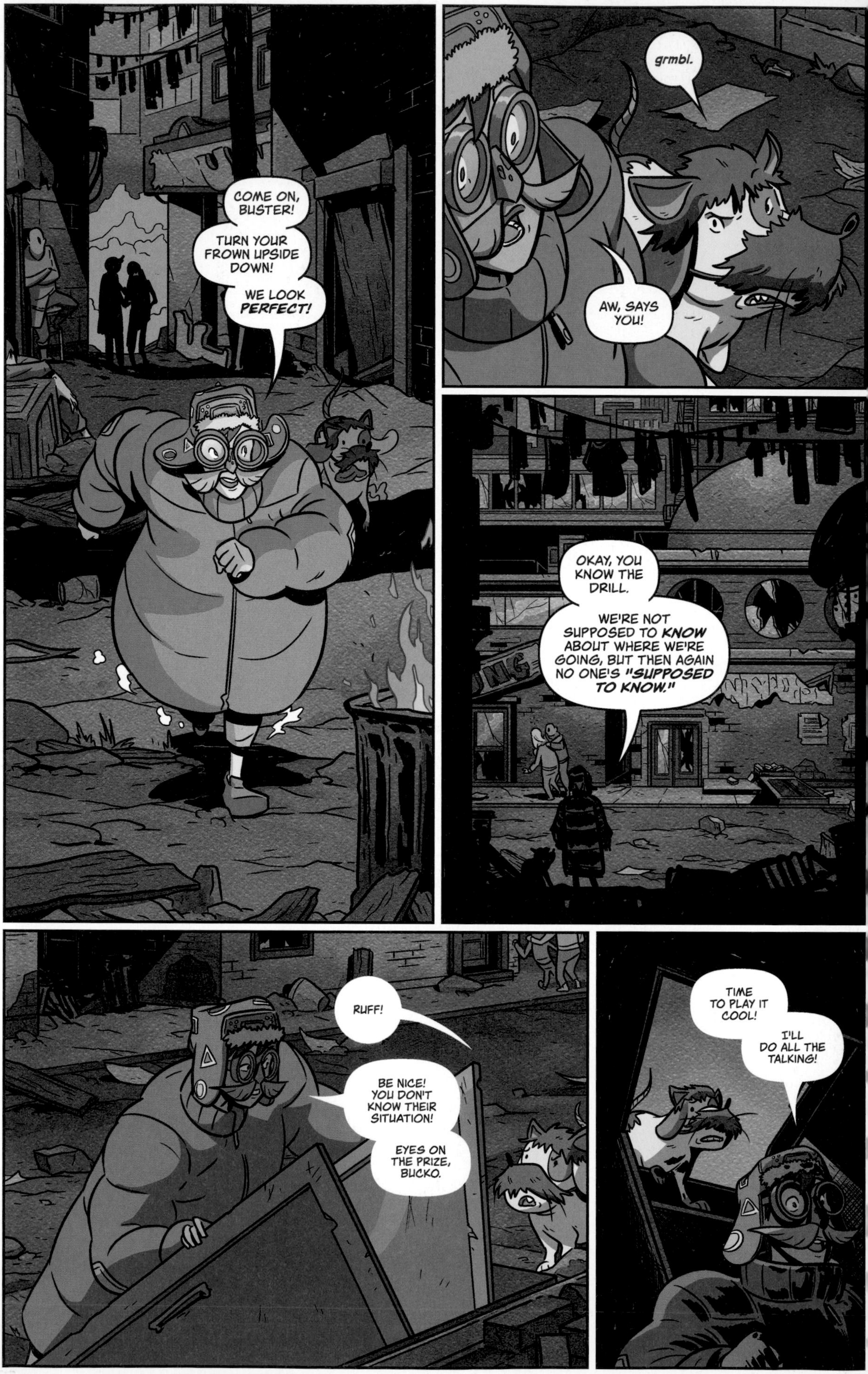
COME ON, BUSTER!
TURN YOUR FROWN UPSIDE DOWN!
WE LOOK *PERFECT!*
grmbl.
AW, SAYS YOU!
OKAY, YOU KNOW THE DRILL.
WE'RE NOT SUPPOSED TO *KNOW* ABOUT WHERE WE'RE GOING, BUT THEN AGAIN NO ONE'S *"SUPPOSED TO KNOW."*
RUFF!
BE NICE! YOU DON'T KNOW THEIR SITUATION!
EYES ON THE PRIZE, BUCKO.
TIME TO PLAY IT COOL!
I'LL DO ALL THE TALKING!

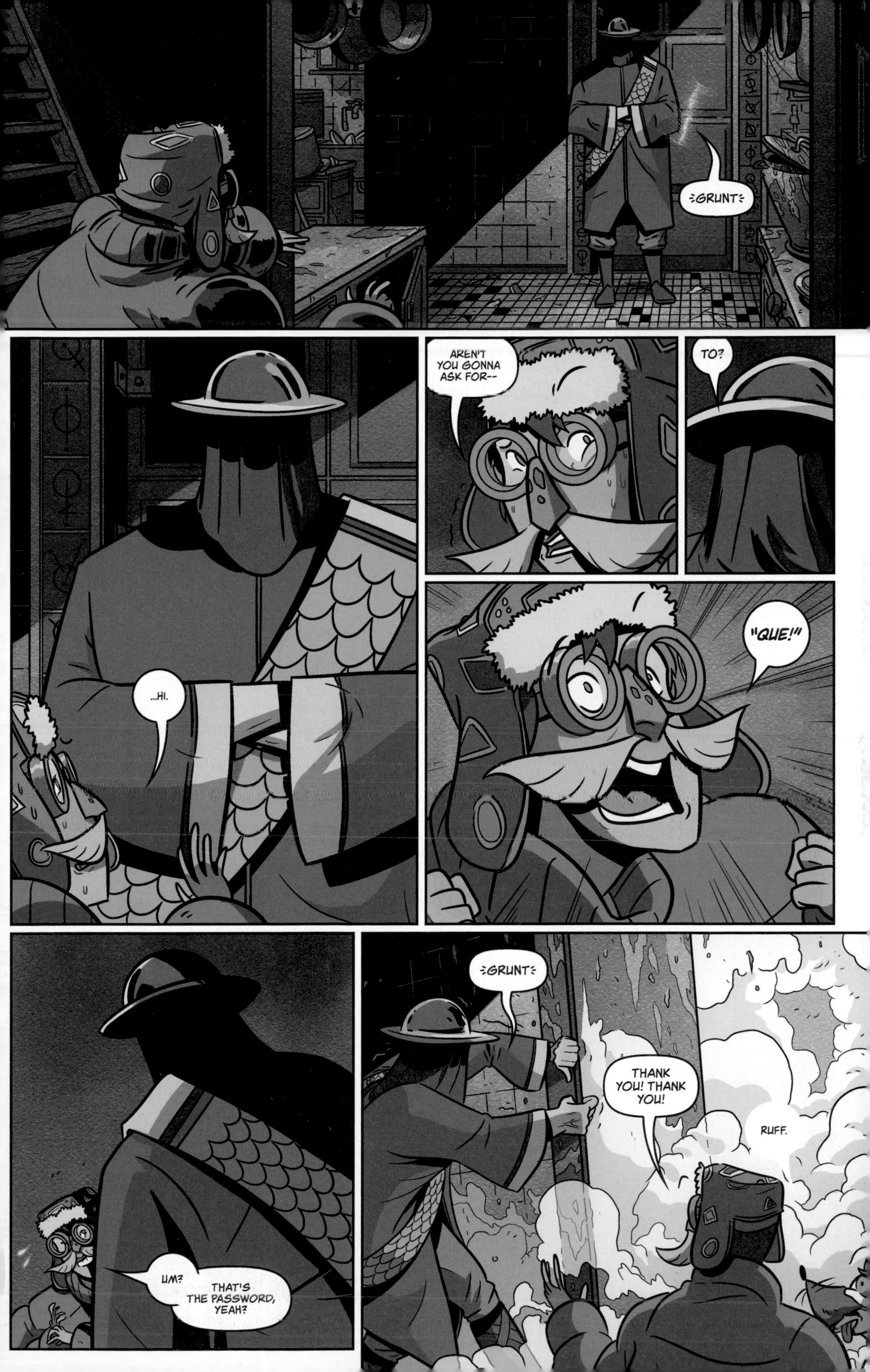
GRUNT
...HI.
AREN'T YOU GONNA ASK FOR--
TO?
"QUE!"
UM?
THAT'S THE PASSWORD, YEAH?
GRUNT
THANK YOU! THANK YOU!
RUFF.

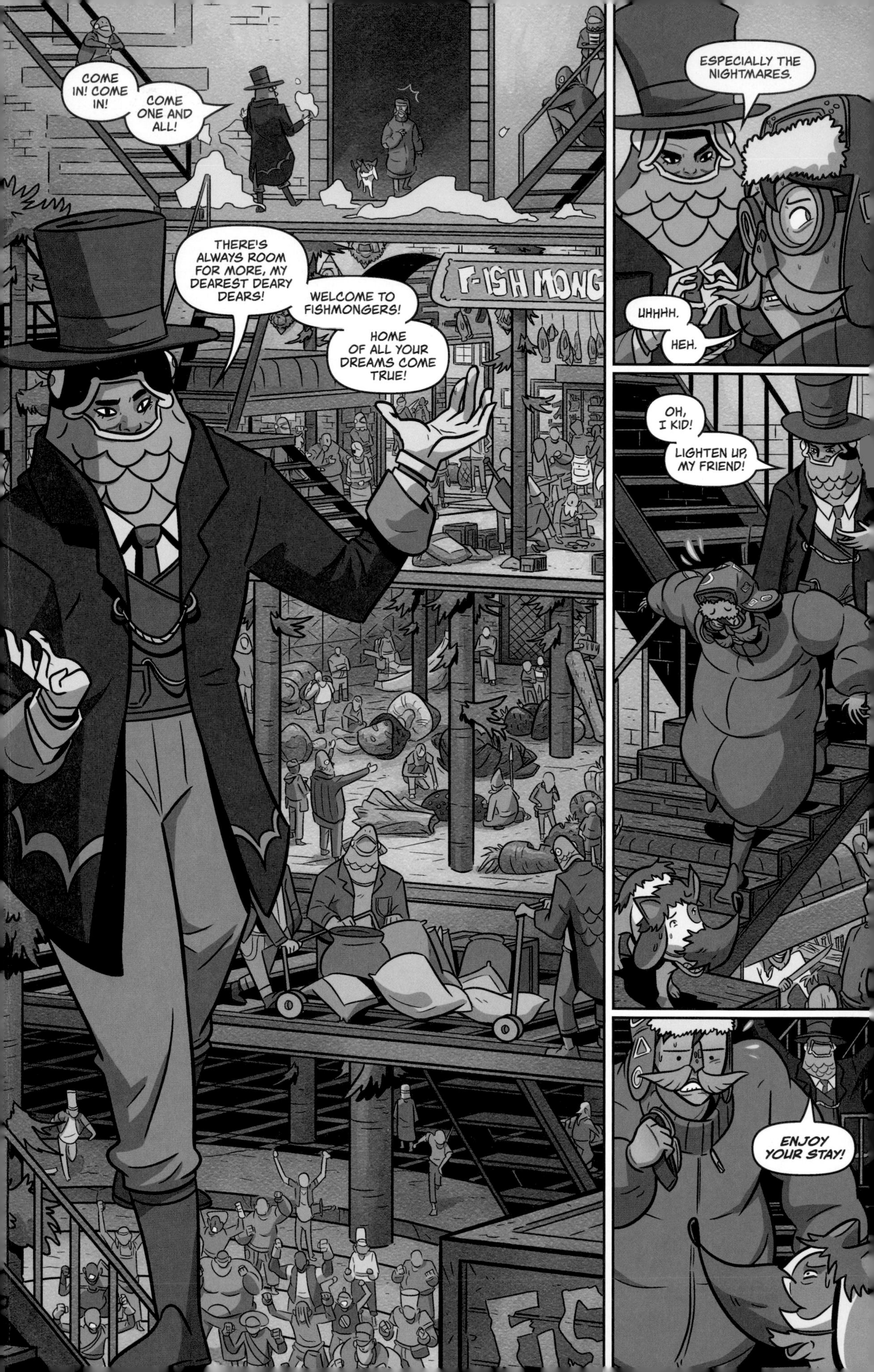
COME IN! COME IN!
COME ONE AND ALL!
THERE'S ALWAYS ROOM FOR MORE, MY DEAREST DEARY DEARS!
F-ISH MONG
WELCOME TO FISHMONGERS!
HOME OF ALL YOUR DREAMS COME TRUE!
ESPECIALLY THE NIGHTMARES.
UHHHH.
HEH.
OH, I KID!
LIGHTEN UP, MY FRIEND!
ENJOY YOUR STAY!

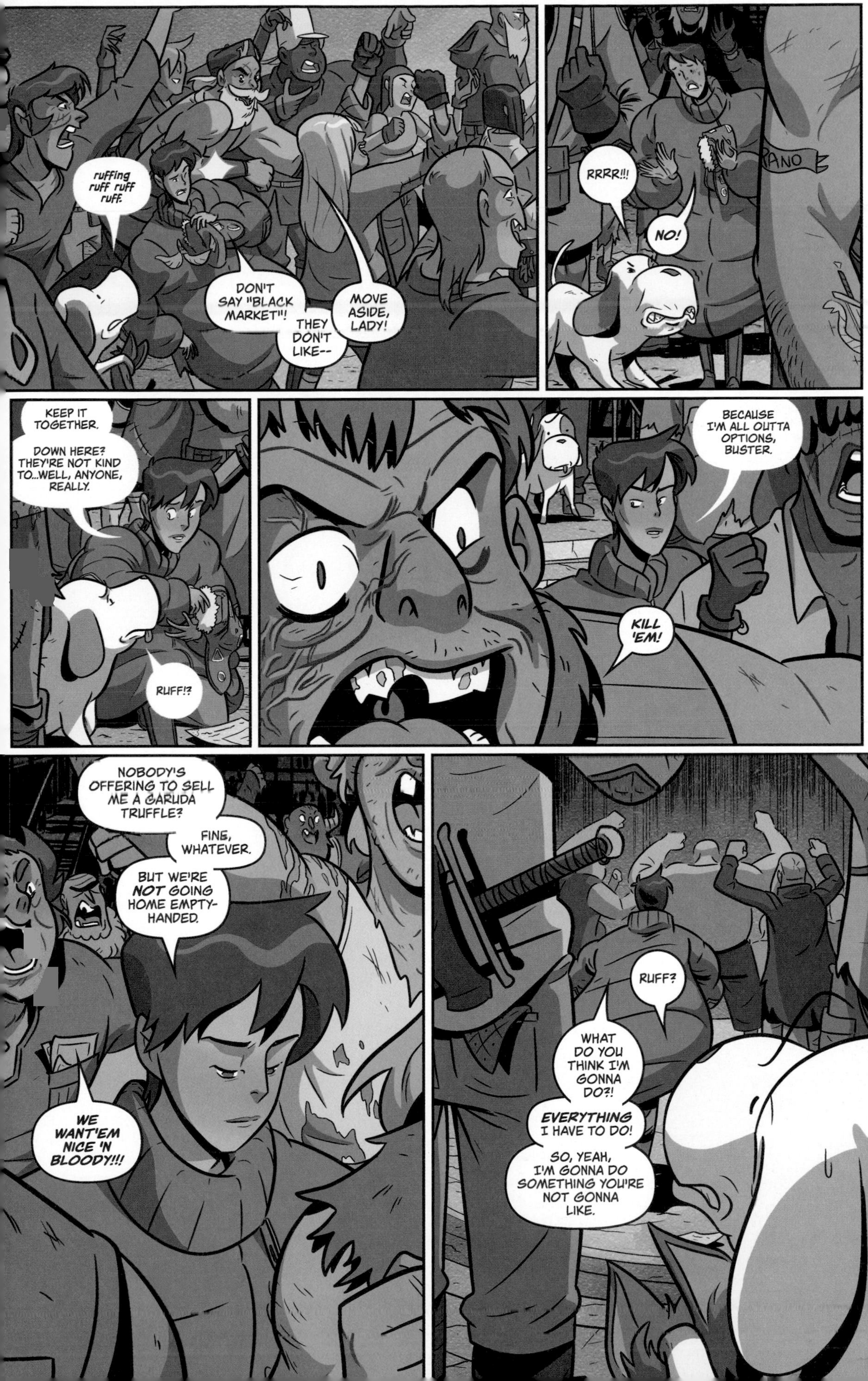
ruffing ruff ruff ruff.
DON'T SAY "BLACK MARKET"!
THEY DON'T LIKE--
MOVE ASIDE, LADY!
RANO
RRRR!!!
NO!
KEEP IT TOGETHER.
DOWN HERE? THEY'RE NOT KIND TO...WELL, ANYONE, REALLY.
RUFF!?
BECAUSE I'M ALL OUTTA OPTIONS, BUSTER.
KILL 'EM!
NOBODY'S OFFERING TO SELL ME A GARUDA TRUFFLE?
FINE, WHATEVER.
BUT WE'RE NOT GOING HOME EMPTY-HANDED.
WE WANT'EM NICE 'N BLOODY!!!
RUFF?
WHAT DO YOU THINK I'M GONNA DO?!
EVERYTHING I HAVE TO DO!
SO, YEAH, I'M GONNA DO SOMETHING YOU'RE NOT GONNA LIKE.

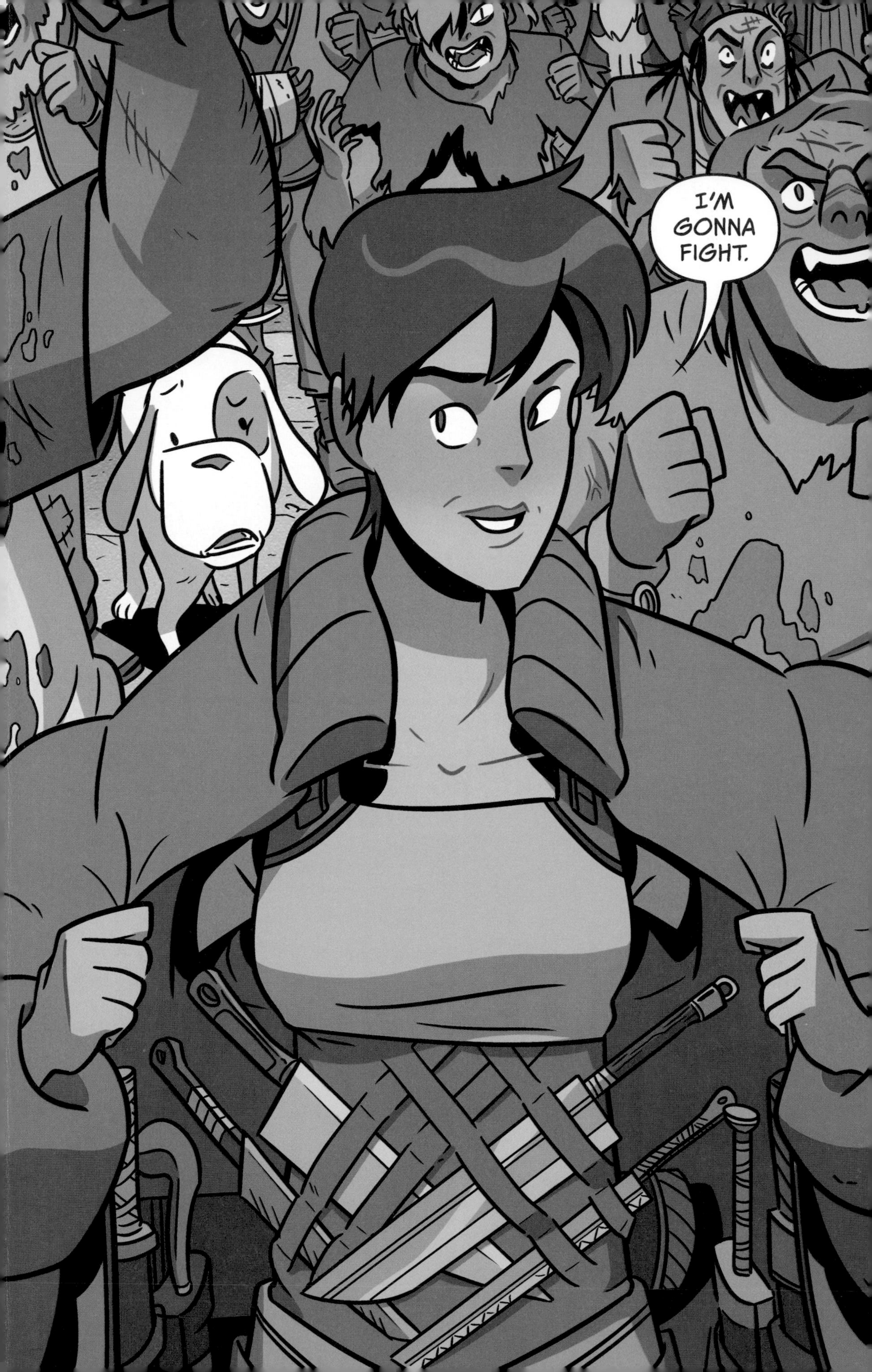
I'M GONNA FIGHT.

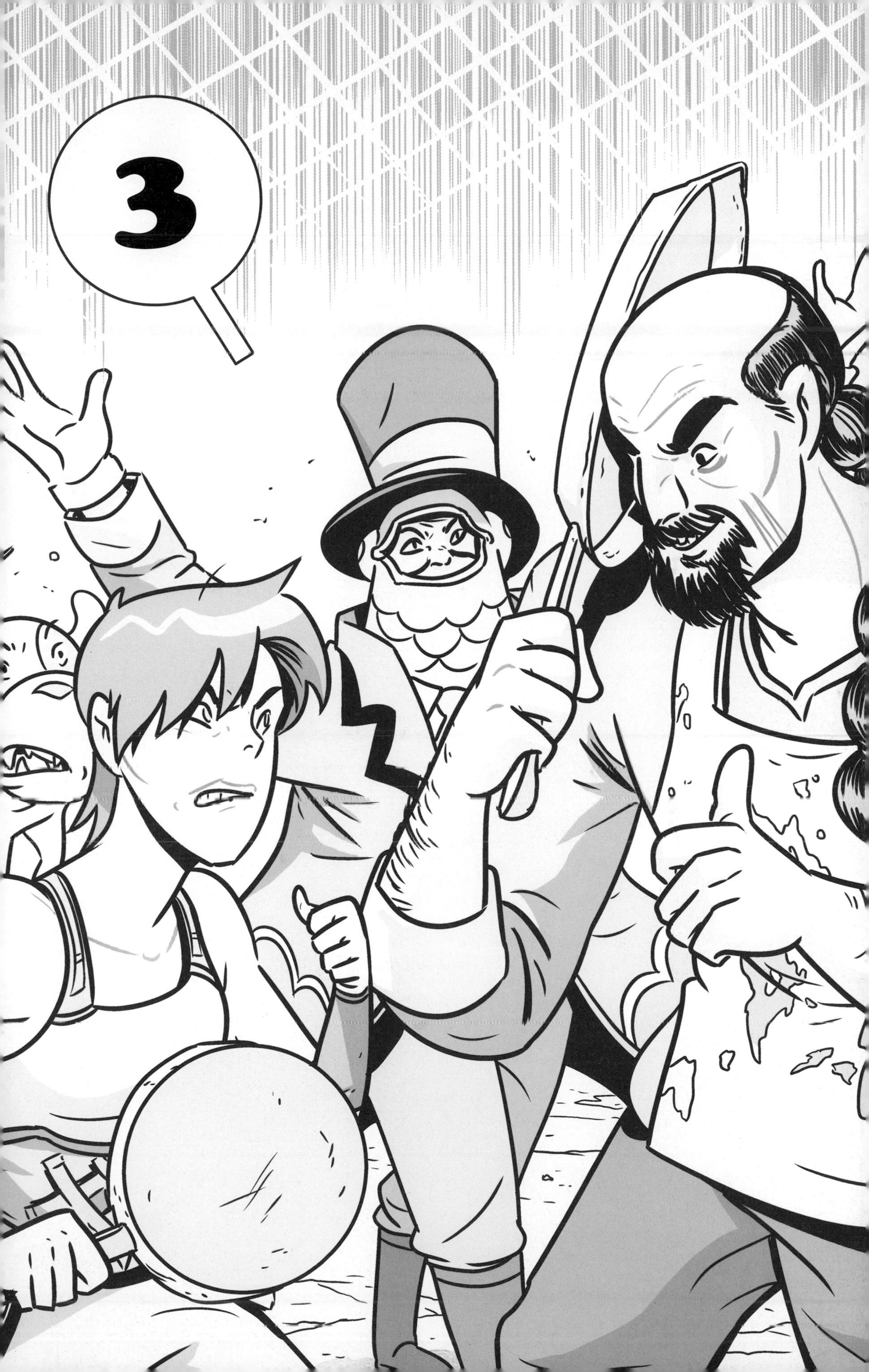
3

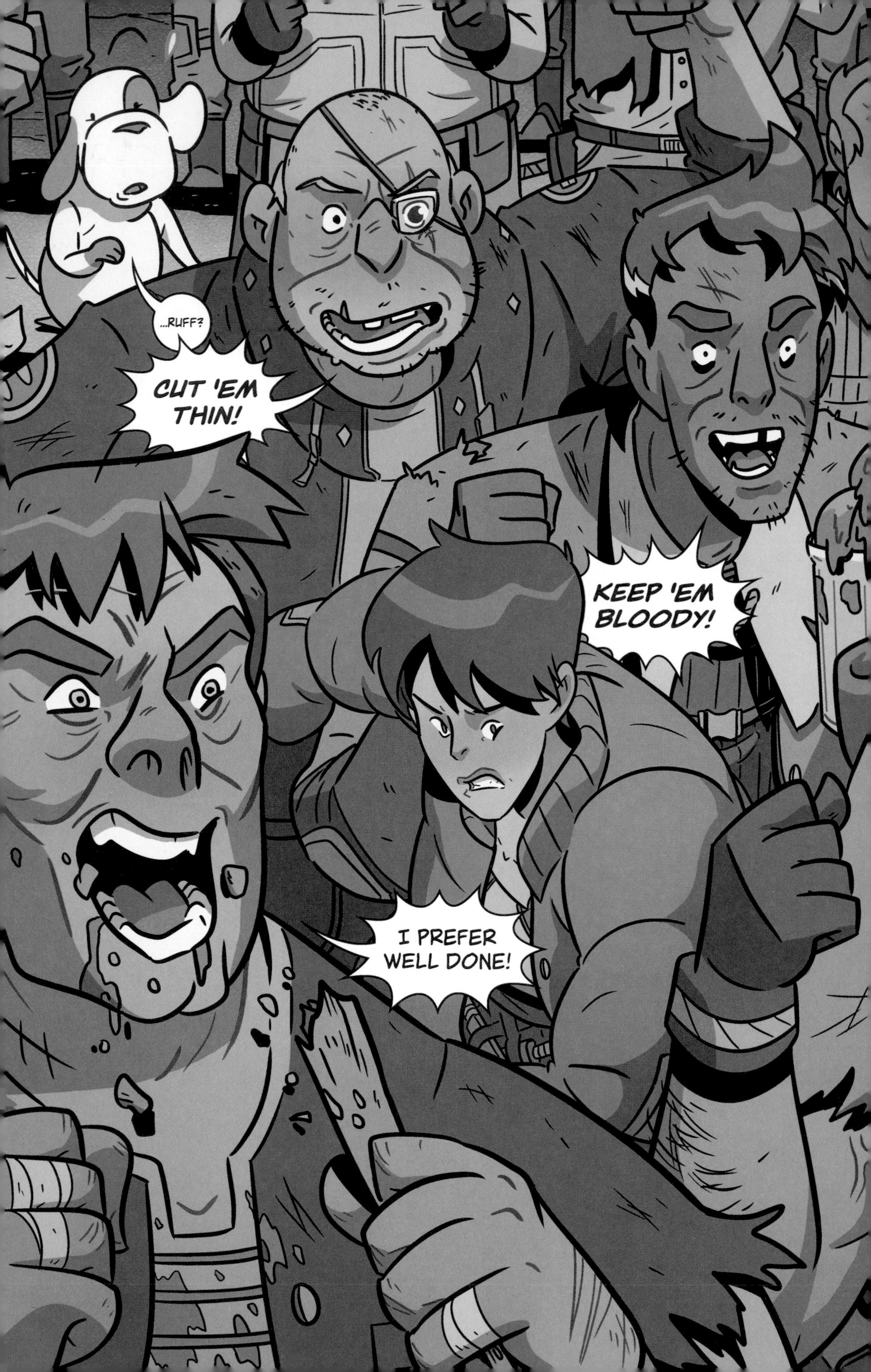
...RUFF?
CUT 'EM THIN!
KEEP 'EM BLOODY!
I PREFER WELL DONE!

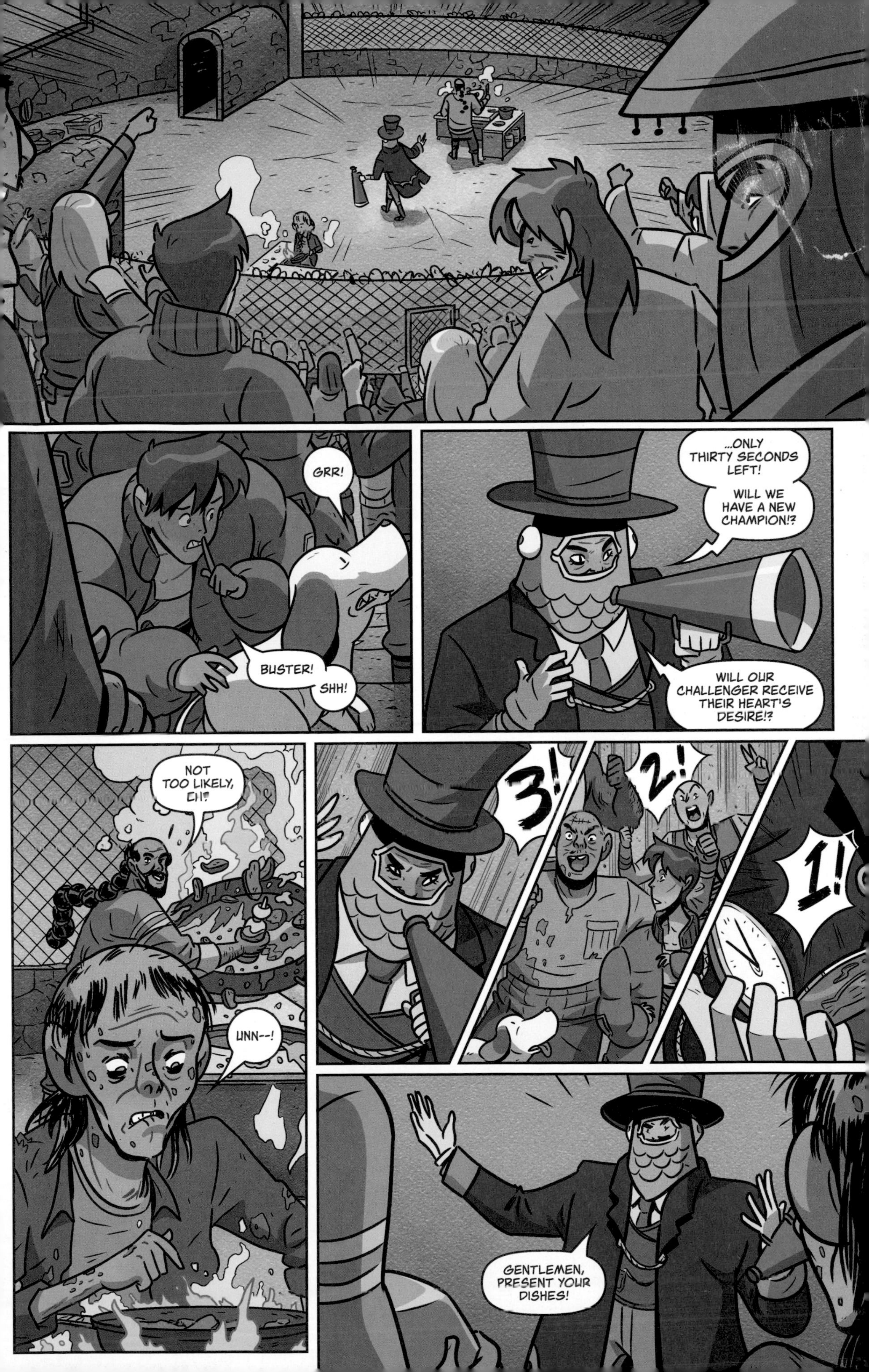
GRR!
BUSTER!
SHH!
...ONLY THIRTY SECONDS LEFT!
WILL WE HAVE A NEW CHAMPION!?
WILL OUR CHALLENGER RECEIVE THEIR HEART'S DESIRE!?
NOT TOO LIKELY, EH!?
UNN--!
3!
2!
1!
GENTLEMEN, PRESENT YOUR DISHES!

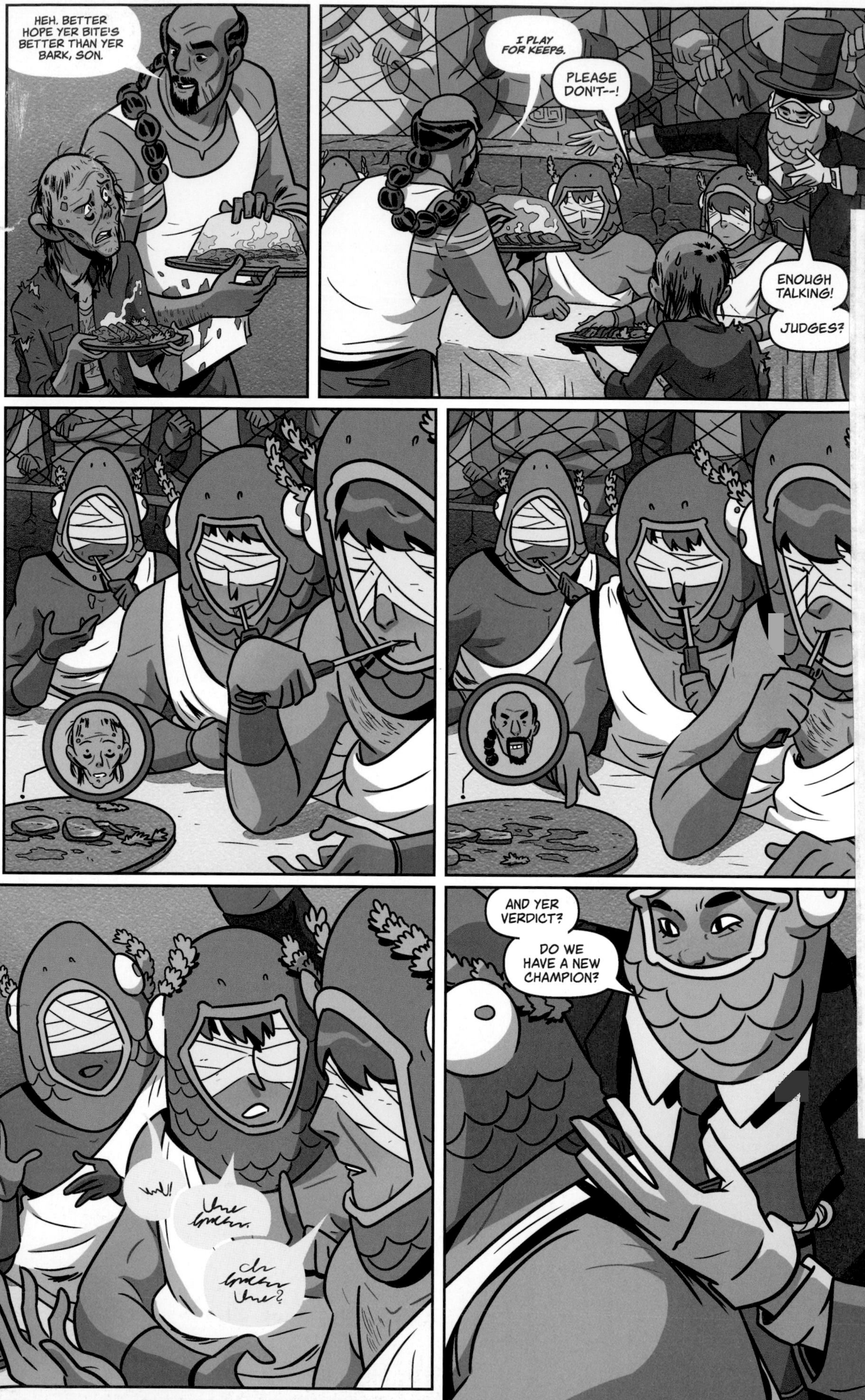
HEH. BETTER HOPE YER BITE'S BETTER THAN YER BARK, SON.
I PLAY FOR KEEPS.
PLEASE DON'T--!
ENOUGH TALKING!
JUDGES?
AND YER VERDICT?
DO WE HAVE A NEW CHAMPION?

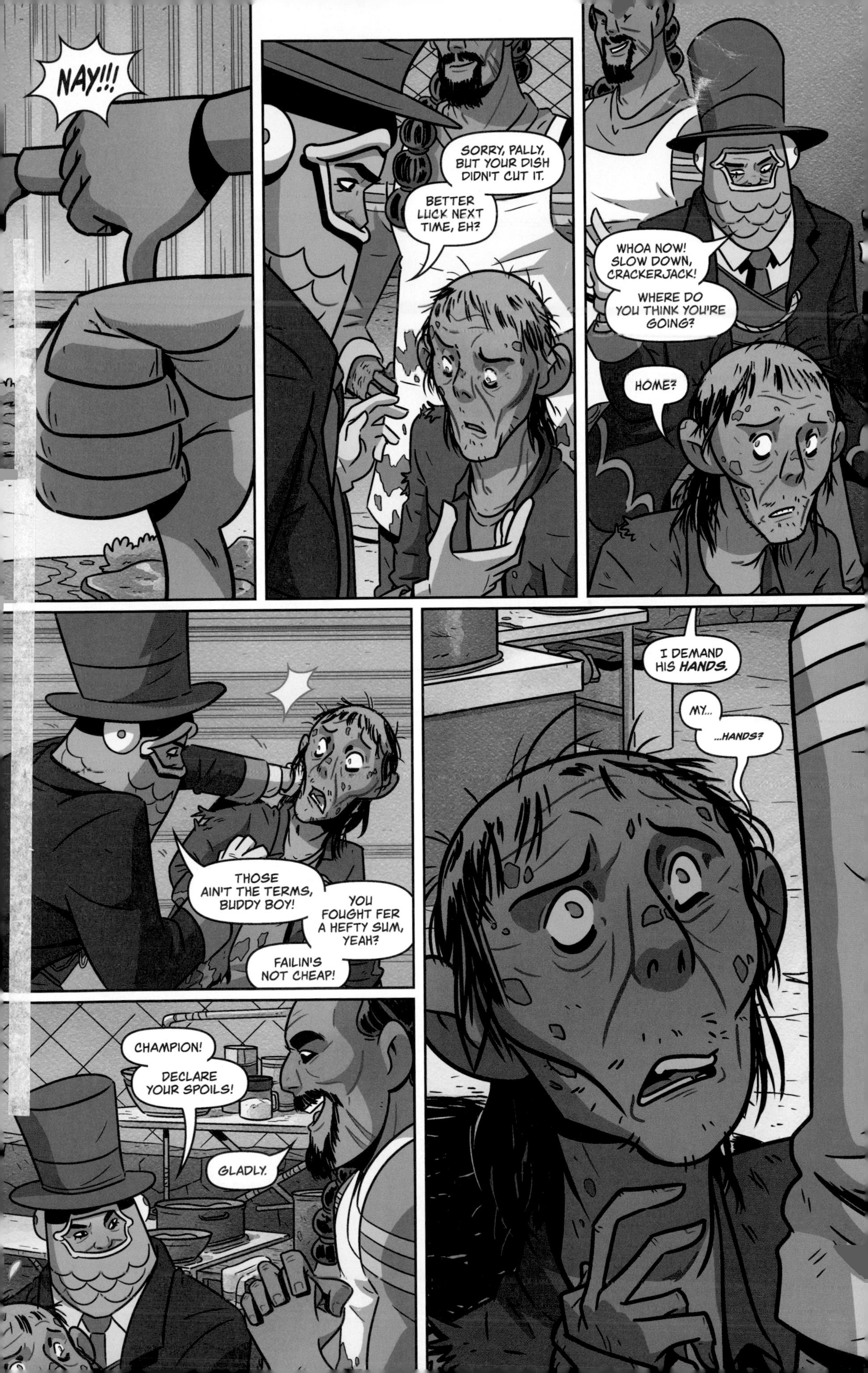
NAY!!!
SORRY, PALLY, BUT YOUR DISH DIDN'T CUT IT.
BETTER LUCK NEXT TIME, EH?
WHOA NOW! SLOW DOWN, CRACKERJACK!
WHERE DO YOU THINK YOU'RE GOING?
HOME?
THOSE AIN'T THE TERMS, BUDDY BOY!
YOU FOUGHT FER A HEFTY SUM, YEAH?
FAILIN'S NOT CHEAP!
I DEMAND HIS HANDS.
MY...
...HANDS?
CHAMPION!
DECLARE YOUR SPOILS!
GLADLY.

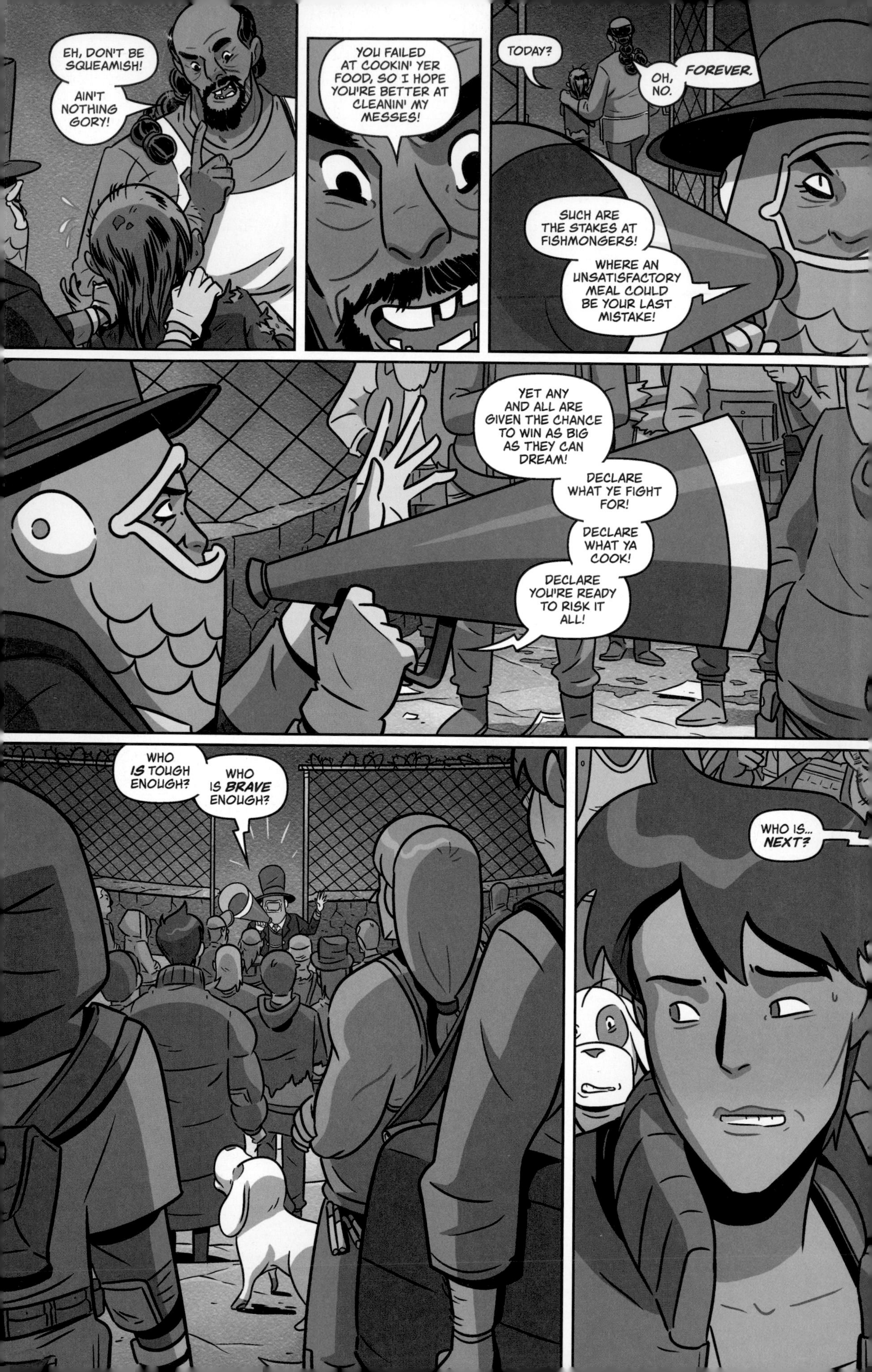
EH, DON'T BE SQUEAMISH!
AIN'T NOTHING GORY!
YOU FAILED AT COOKIN' YER FOOD, SO I HOPE YOU'RE BETTER AT CLEANIN' MY MESSES!
TODAY?
OH, NO.
FOREVER.
SUCH ARE THE STAKES AT FISHMONGERS!
WHERE AN UNSATISFACTORY MEAL COULD BE YOUR LAST MISTAKE!
YET ANY AND ALL ARE GIVEN THE CHANCE TO WIN AS BIG AS THEY CAN DREAM!
DECLARE WHAT YE FIGHT FOR!
DECLARE WHAT YA COOK!
DECLARE YOU'RE READY TO RISK IT ALL!
WHO IS TOUGH ENOUGH?
WHO IS BRAVE ENOUGH?
WHO IS... NEXT?

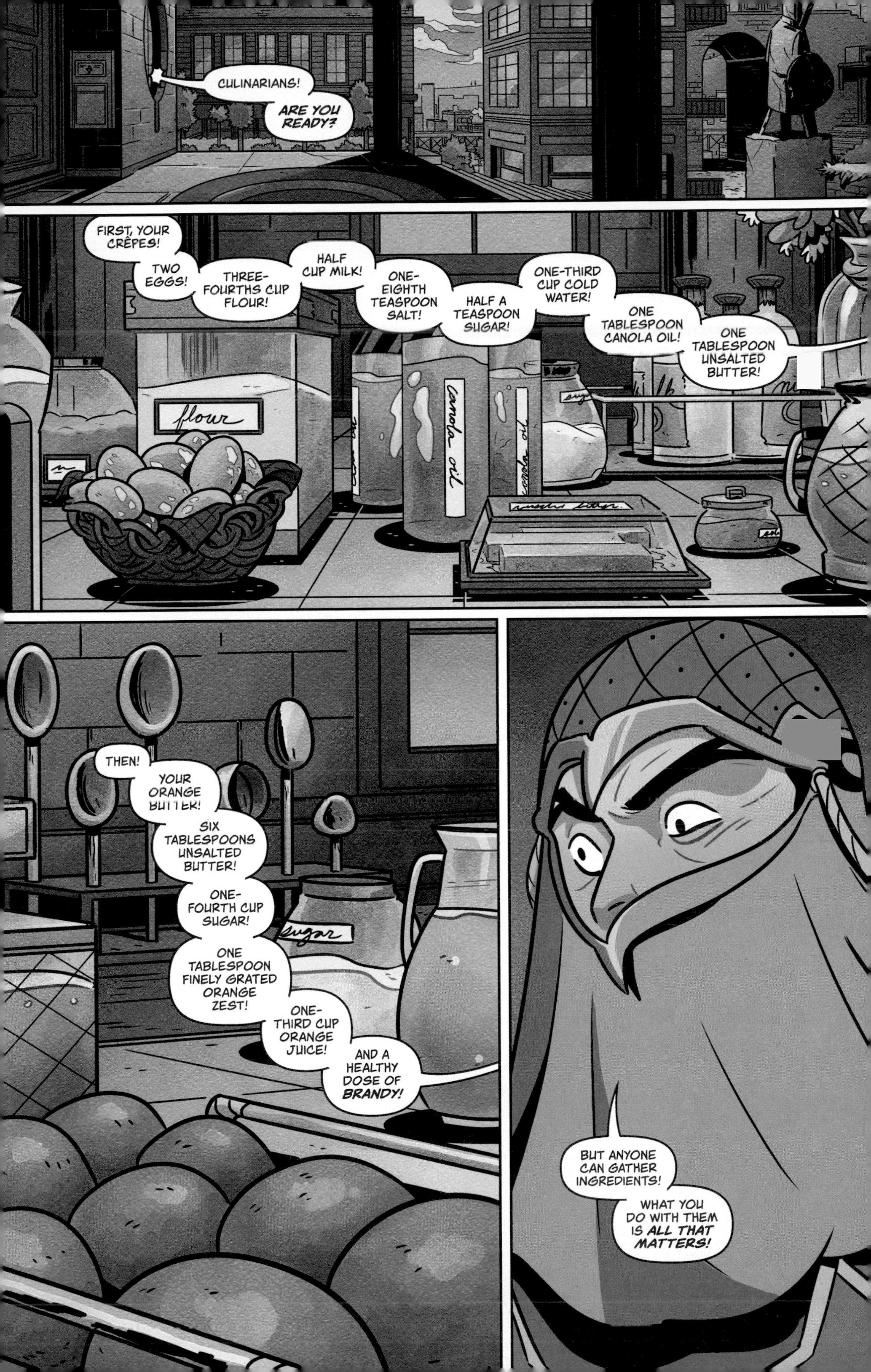
CULINARIANS!
ARE YOU READY?
FIRST, YOUR CRÊPES!
TWO EGGS!
THREE-FOURTHS CUP FLOUR!
HALF CUP MILK!
ONE-EIGHTH TEASPOON SALT!
HALF A TEASPOON SUGAR!
ONE-THIRD CUP COLD WATER!
ONE TABLESPOON CANOLA OIL!
ONE TABLESPOON UNSALTED BUTTER!
flour
canola oil
THEN!
YOUR ORANGE BUTTER!
SIX TABLESPOONS UNSALTED BUTTER!
ONE-FOURTH CUP SUGAR!
ONE TABLESPOON FINELY GRATED ORANGE ZEST!
ONE-THIRD CUP ORANGE JUICE!
AND A HEALTHY DOSE OF BRANDY!
sugar
BUT ANYONE CAN GATHER INGREDIENTS!
WHAT YOU DO WITH THEM IS ALL THAT MATTERS!

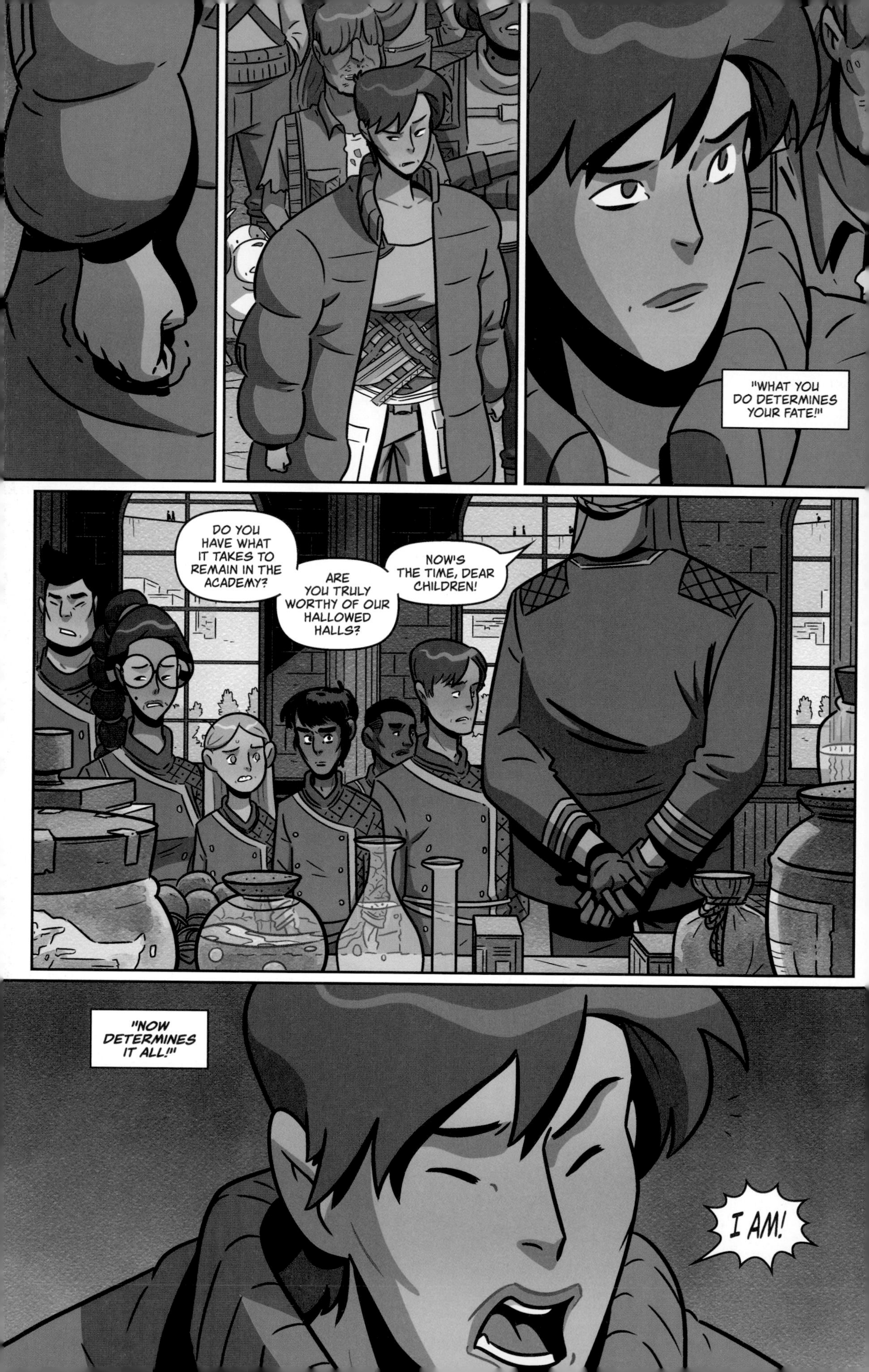
"WHAT YOU DO DETERMINES YOUR FATE!"
DO YOU HAVE WHAT IT TAKES TO REMAIN IN THE ACADEMY?
ARE YOU TRULY WORTHY OF OUR HALLOWED HALLS?
NOW'S THE TIME, DEAR CHILDREN!
"NOW DETERMINES IT ALL!"
I AM!

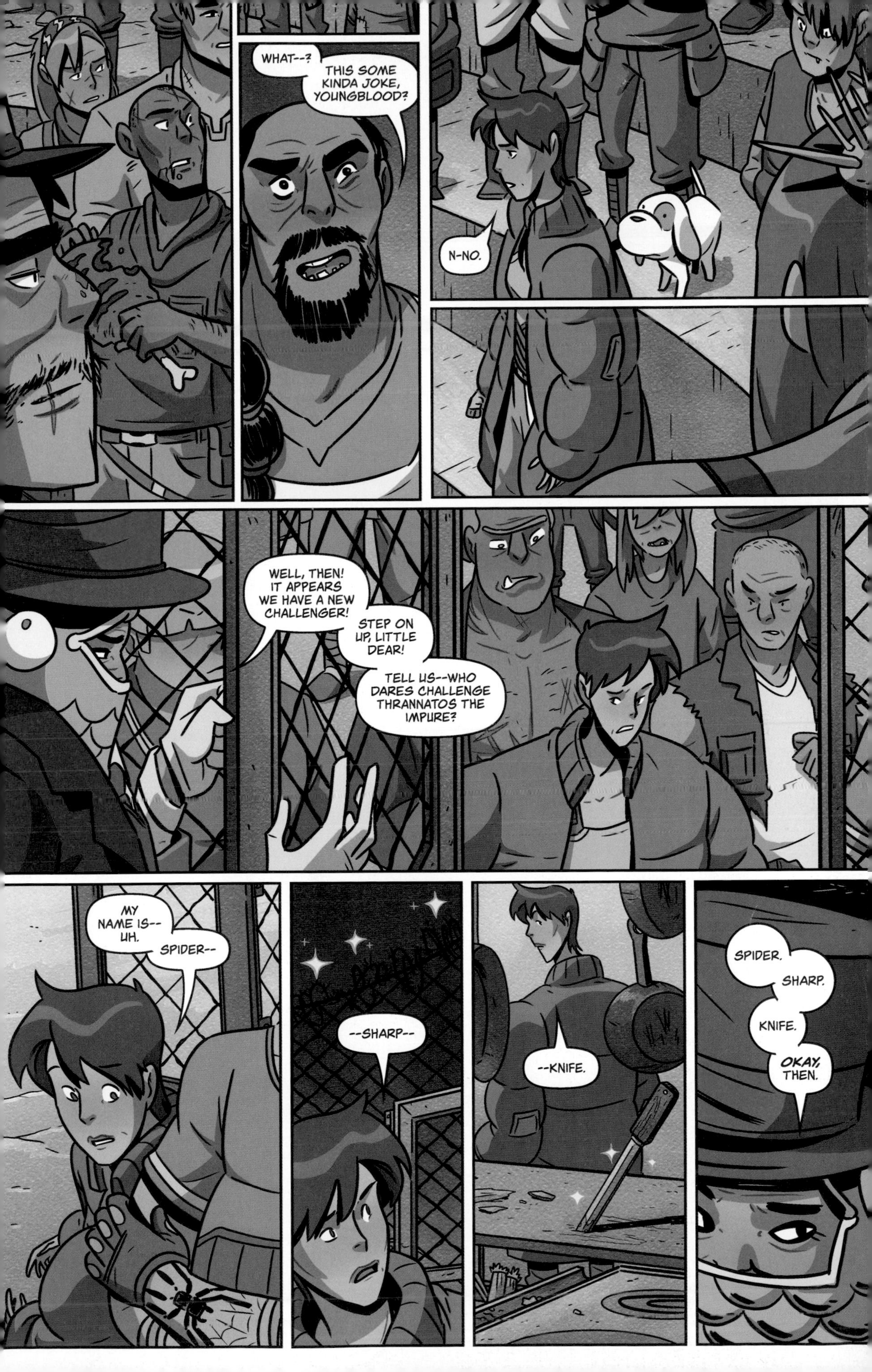
WHAT--?
THIS SOME KINDA JOKE, YOUNGBLOOD?
N-NO.
WELL, THEN! IT APPEARS WE HAVE A NEW CHALLENGER!
STEP ON UP, LITTLE DEAR!
TELL US--WHO DARES CHALLENGE THRANNATOS THE IMPURE?
MY NAME IS-- UH.
SPIDER--
--SHARP--
--KNIFE.
SPIDER.
SHARP.
KNIFE.
OKAY, THEN.

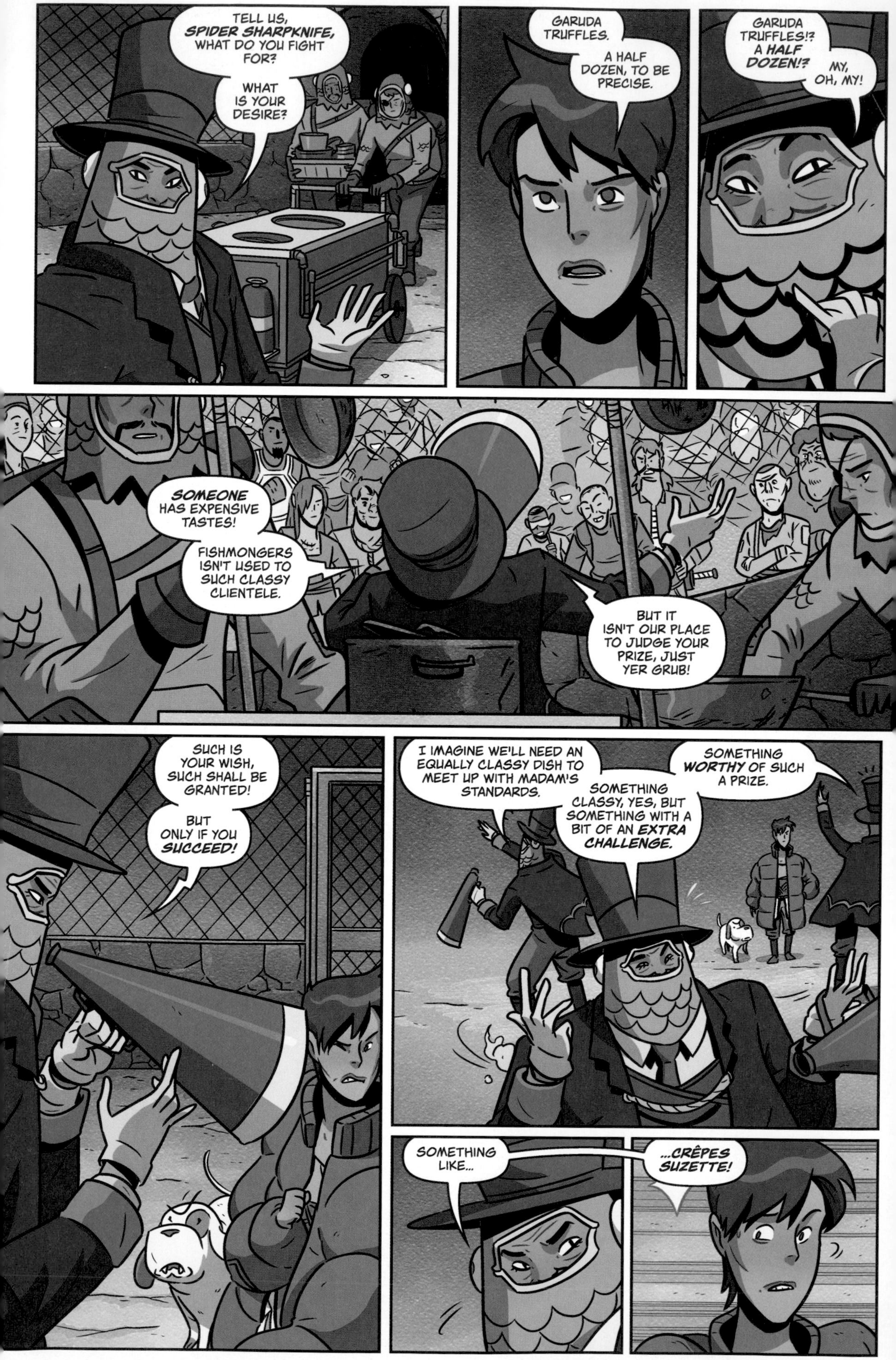
TELL US, SPIDER SHARPKNIFE, WHAT DO YOU FIGHT FOR?
WHAT IS YOUR DESIRE?
GARUDA TRUFFLES.
A HALF DOZEN, TO BE PRECISE.
GARUDA TRUFFLES!? A HALF DOZEN!?
MY, OH, MY!
SOMEONE HAS EXPENSIVE TASTES!
FISHMONGERS ISN'T USED TO SUCH CLASSY CLIENTELE.
BUT IT ISN'T OUR PLACE TO JUDGE YOUR PRIZE, JUST YER GRUB!
SUCH IS YOUR WISH, SUCH SHALL BE GRANTED!
BUT ONLY IF YOU SUCCEED!
I IMAGINE WE'LL NEED AN EQUALLY CLASSY DISH TO MEET UP WITH MADAM'S STANDARDS.
SOMETHING WORTHY OF SUCH A PRIZE.
SOMETHING CLASSY, YES, BUT SOMETHING WITH A BIT OF AN EXTRA CHALLENGE.
SOMETHING LIKE...
...CRÊPES SUZETTE!

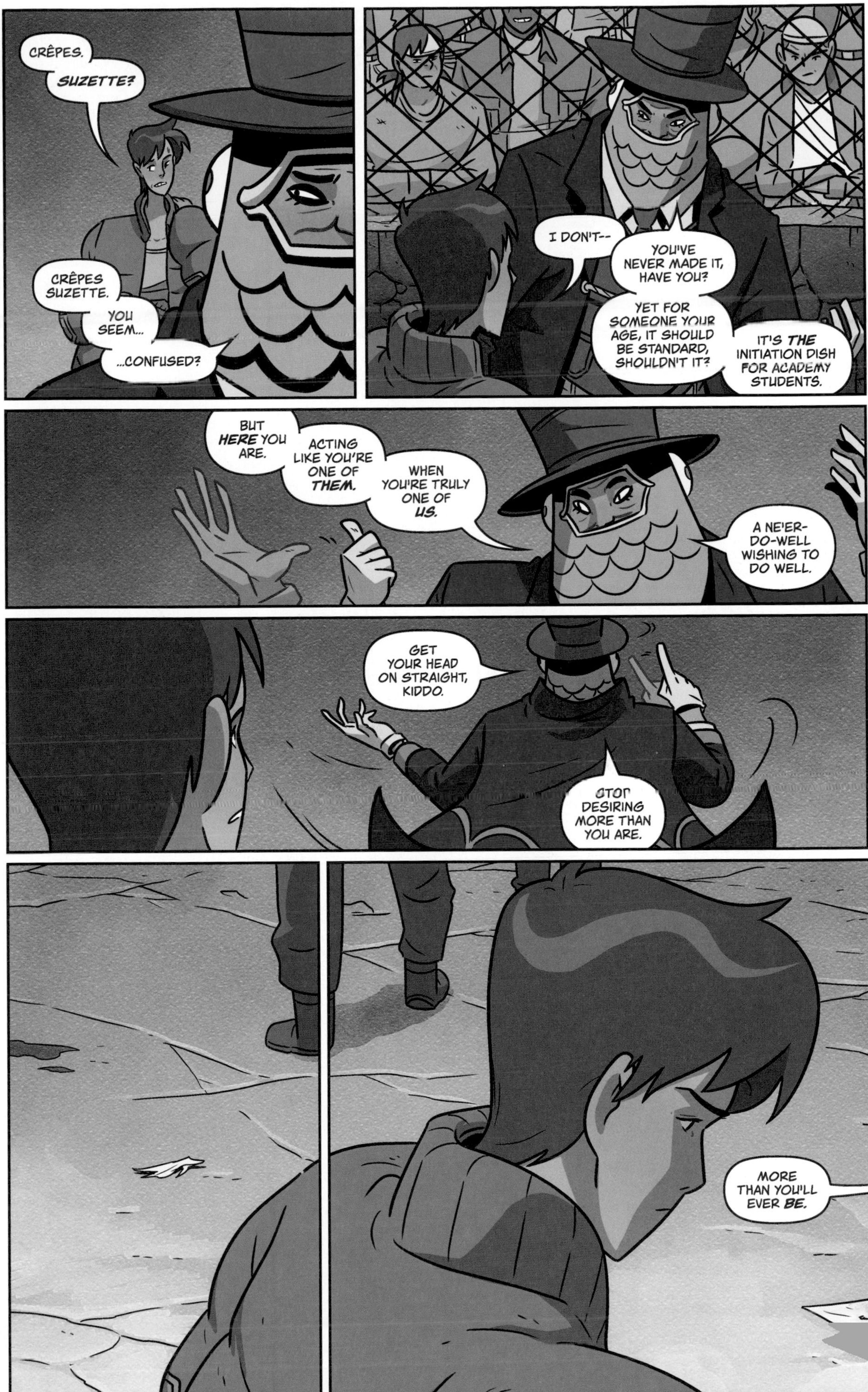
CRÊPES.
SUZETTE?
CRÊPES SUZETTE.
YOU SEEM...
...CONFUSED?
I DON'T--
YOU'VE NEVER MADE IT, HAVE YOU?
YET FOR SOMEONE YOUR AGE, IT SHOULD BE STANDARD, SHOULDN'T IT?
IT'S THE INITIATION DISH FOR ACADEMY STUDENTS.
BUT HERE YOU ARE.
ACTING LIKE YOU'RE ONE OF THEM.
WHEN YOU'RE TRULY ONE OF US.
A NE'ER-DO-WELL WISHING TO DO WELL.
GET YOUR HEAD ON STRAIGHT, KIDDO.
STOP DESIRING MORE THAN YOU ARE.
MORE THAN YOU'LL EVER BE.

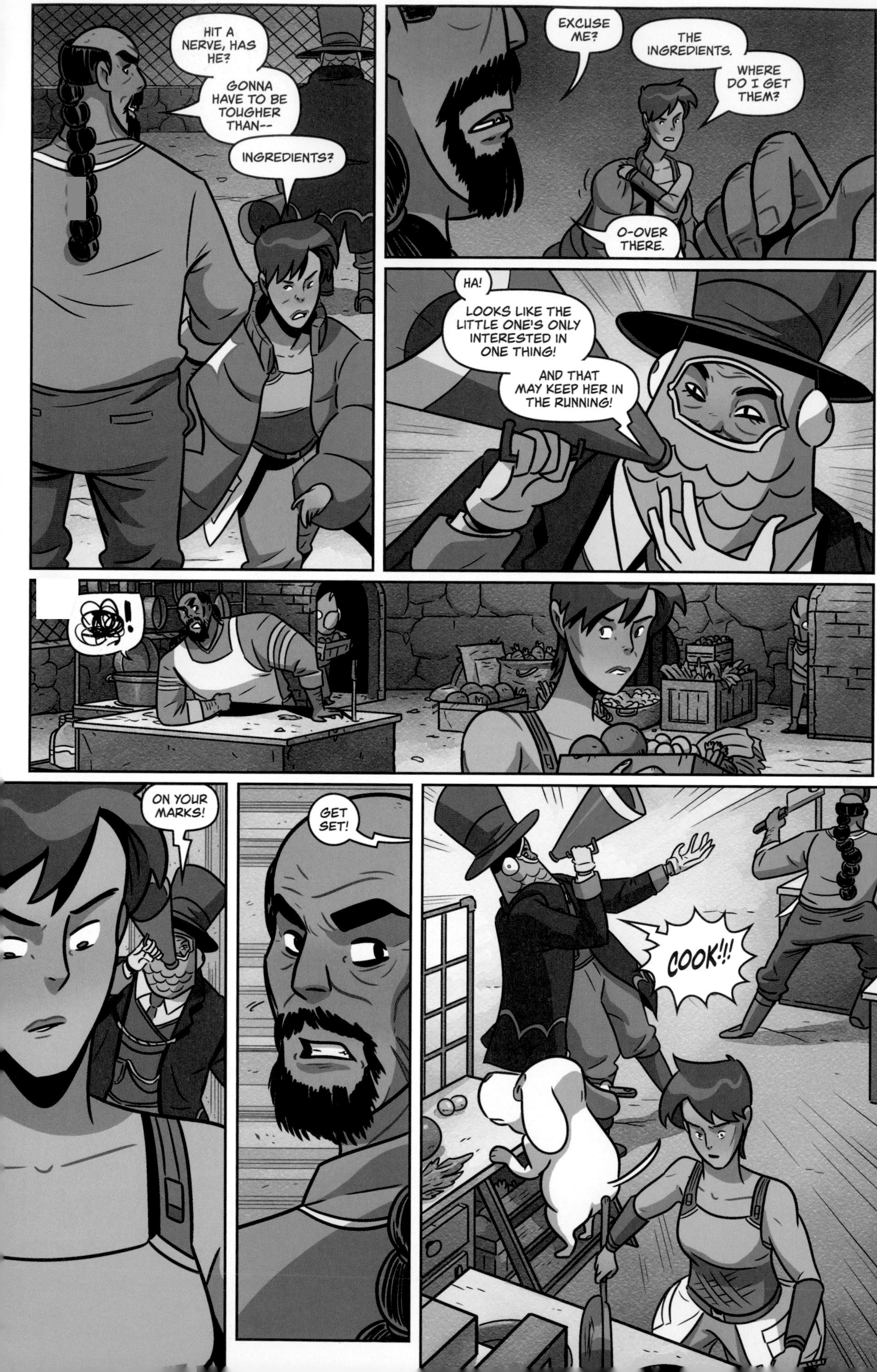
HIT A NERVE, HAS HE?
GONNA HAVE TO BE TOUGHER THAN--
INGREDIENTS?
EXCUSE ME?
THE INGREDIENTS.
WHERE DO I GET THEM?
O-OVER THERE.
HA!
LOOKS LIKE THE LITTLE ONE'S ONLY INTERESTED IN ONE THING!
AND THAT MAY KEEP HER IN THE RUNNING!
!
ON YOUR MARKS!
GET SET!
COOK!!!

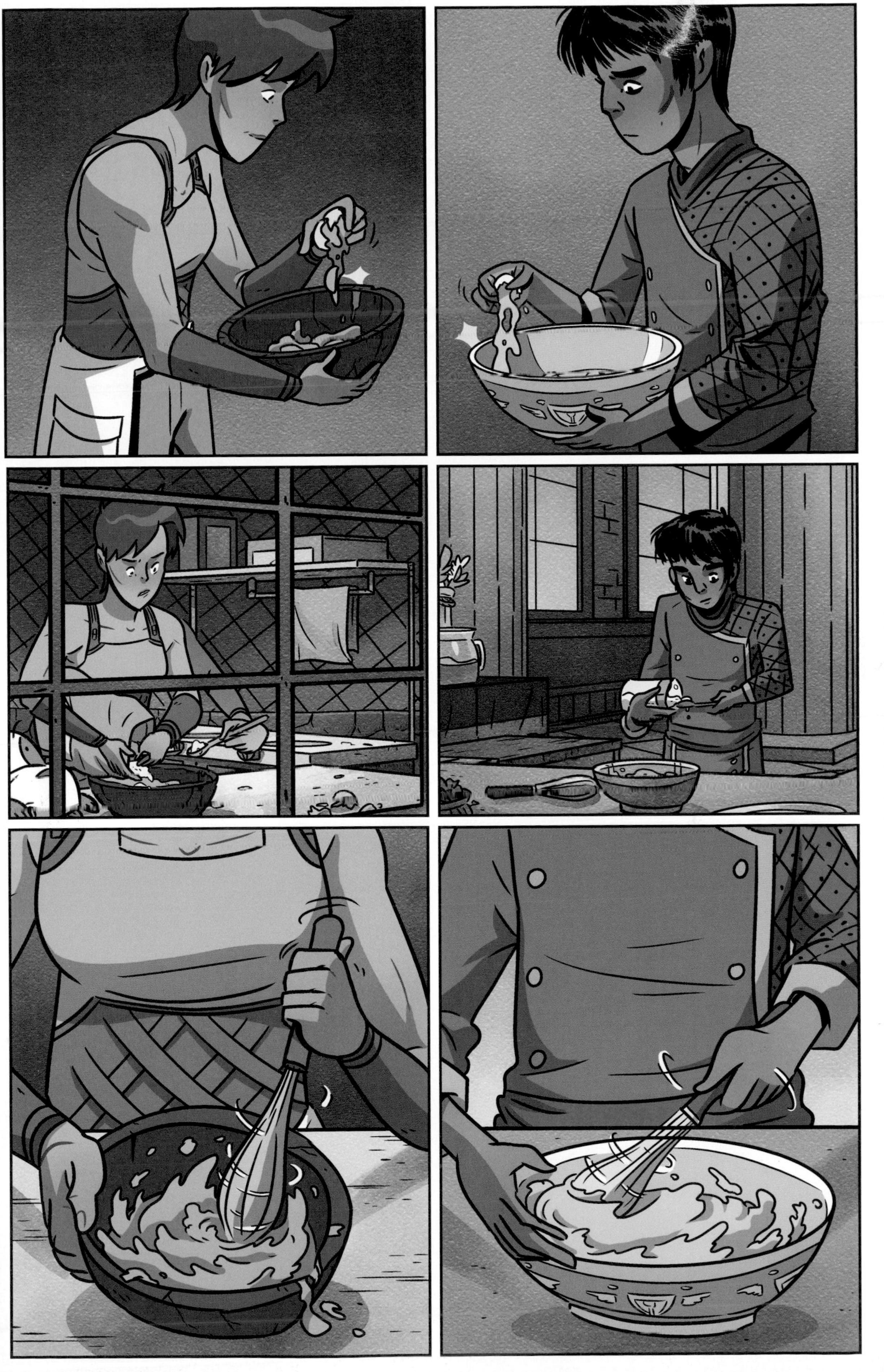

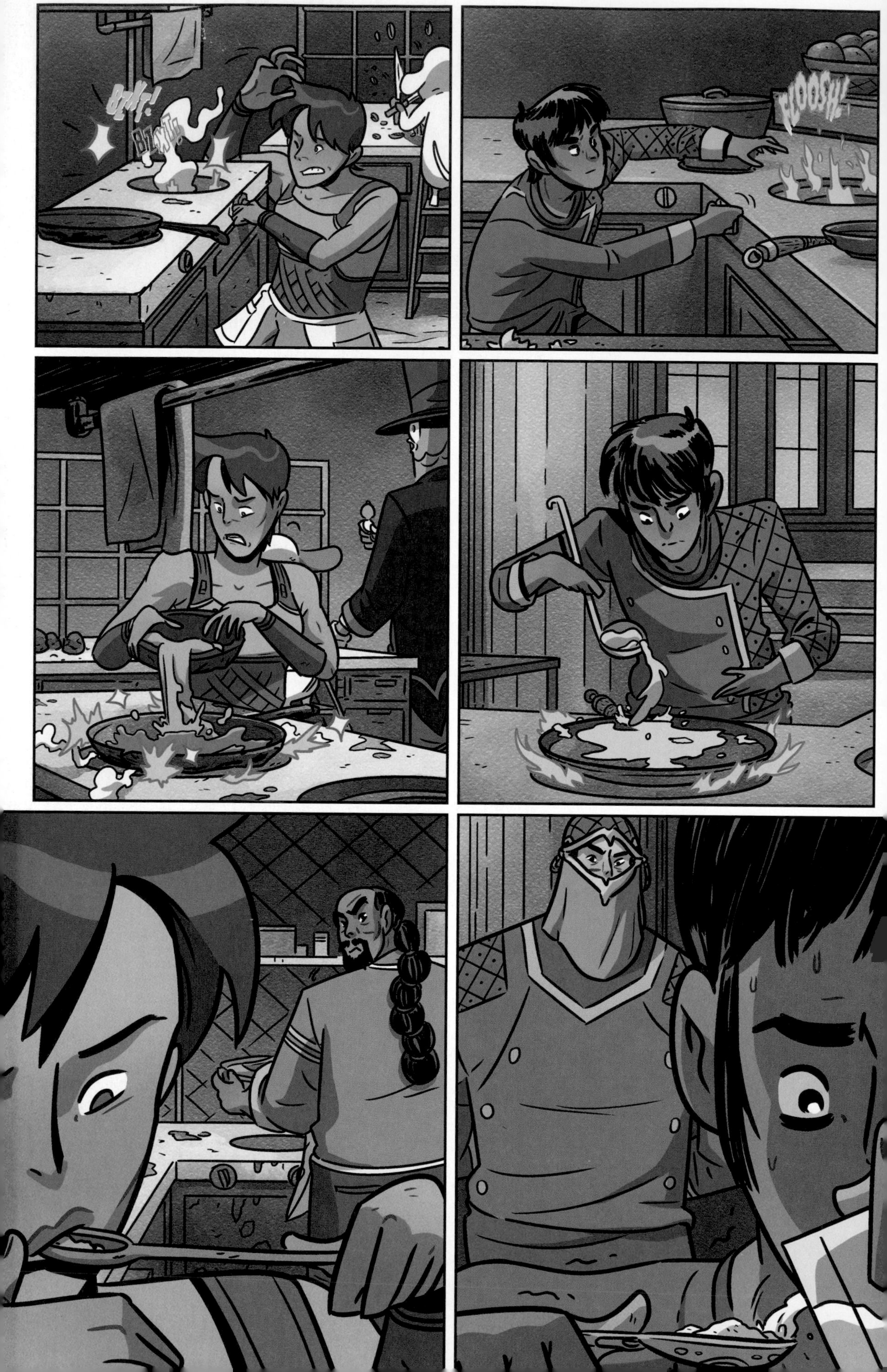
BZZT!
FLOOSH!

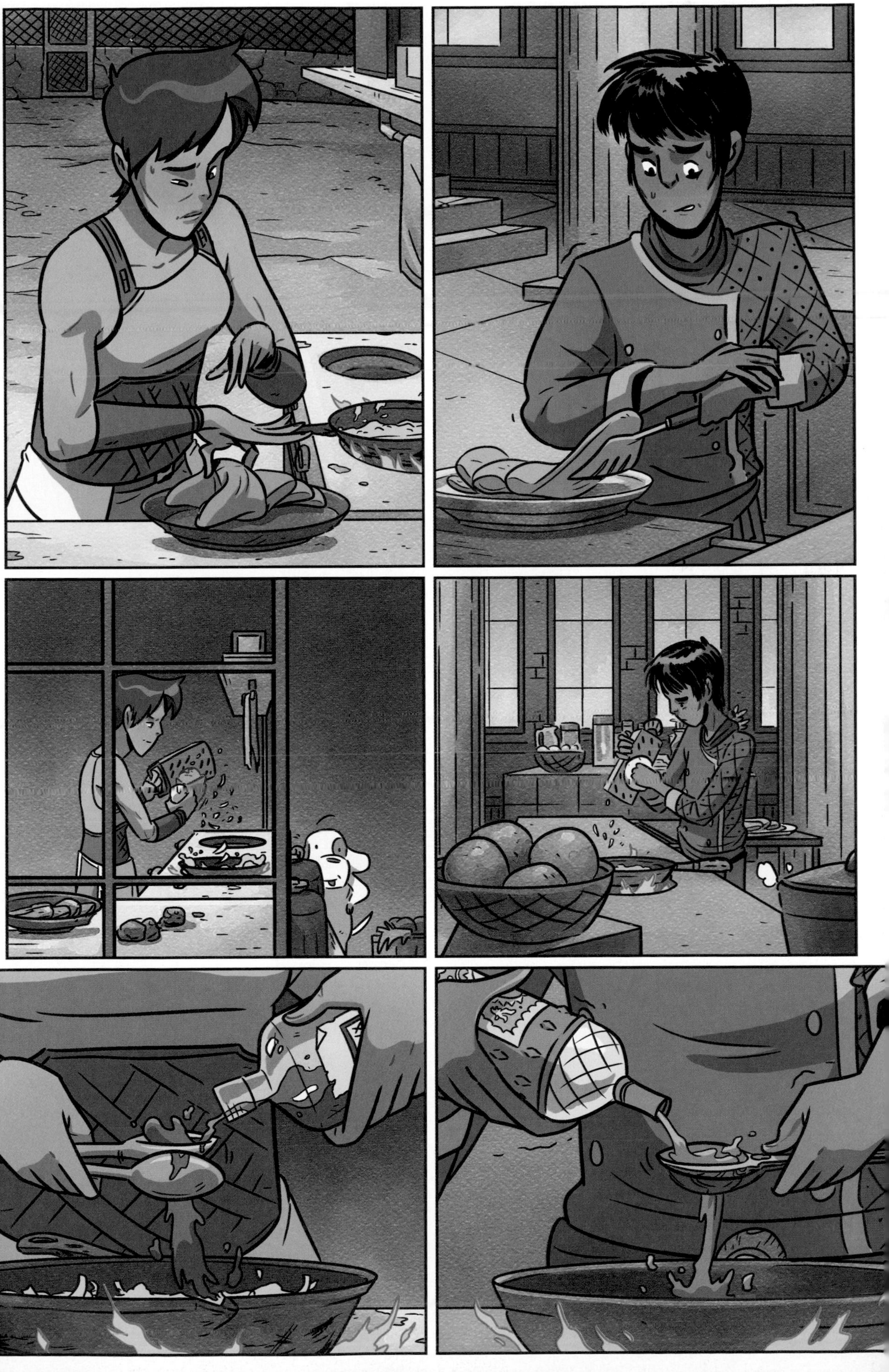

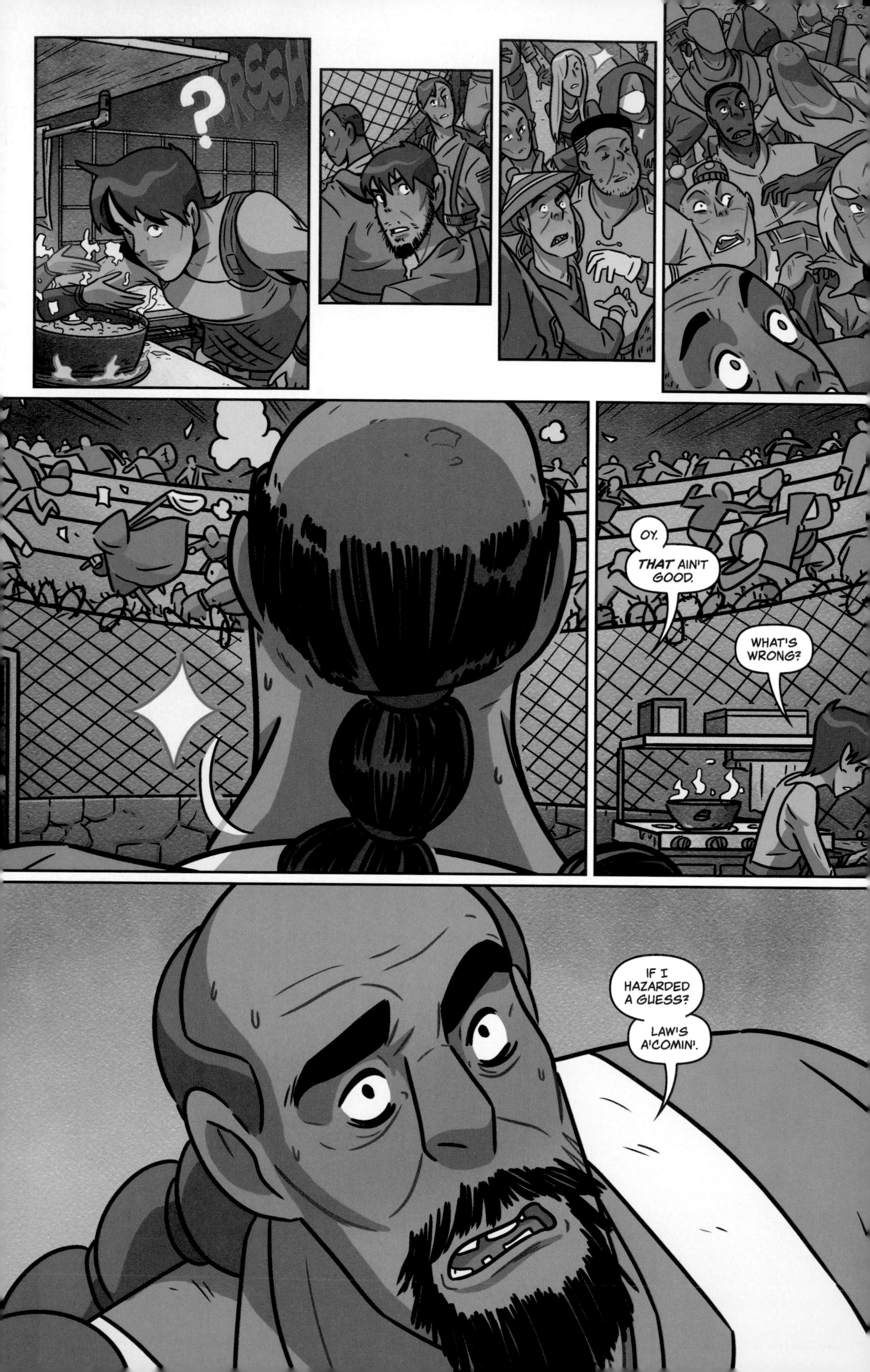
?
KRSSH
OY.
THAT AIN'T GOOD.
WHAT'S WRONG?
IF I HAZARDED A GUESS?
LAW'S A'COMIN'.

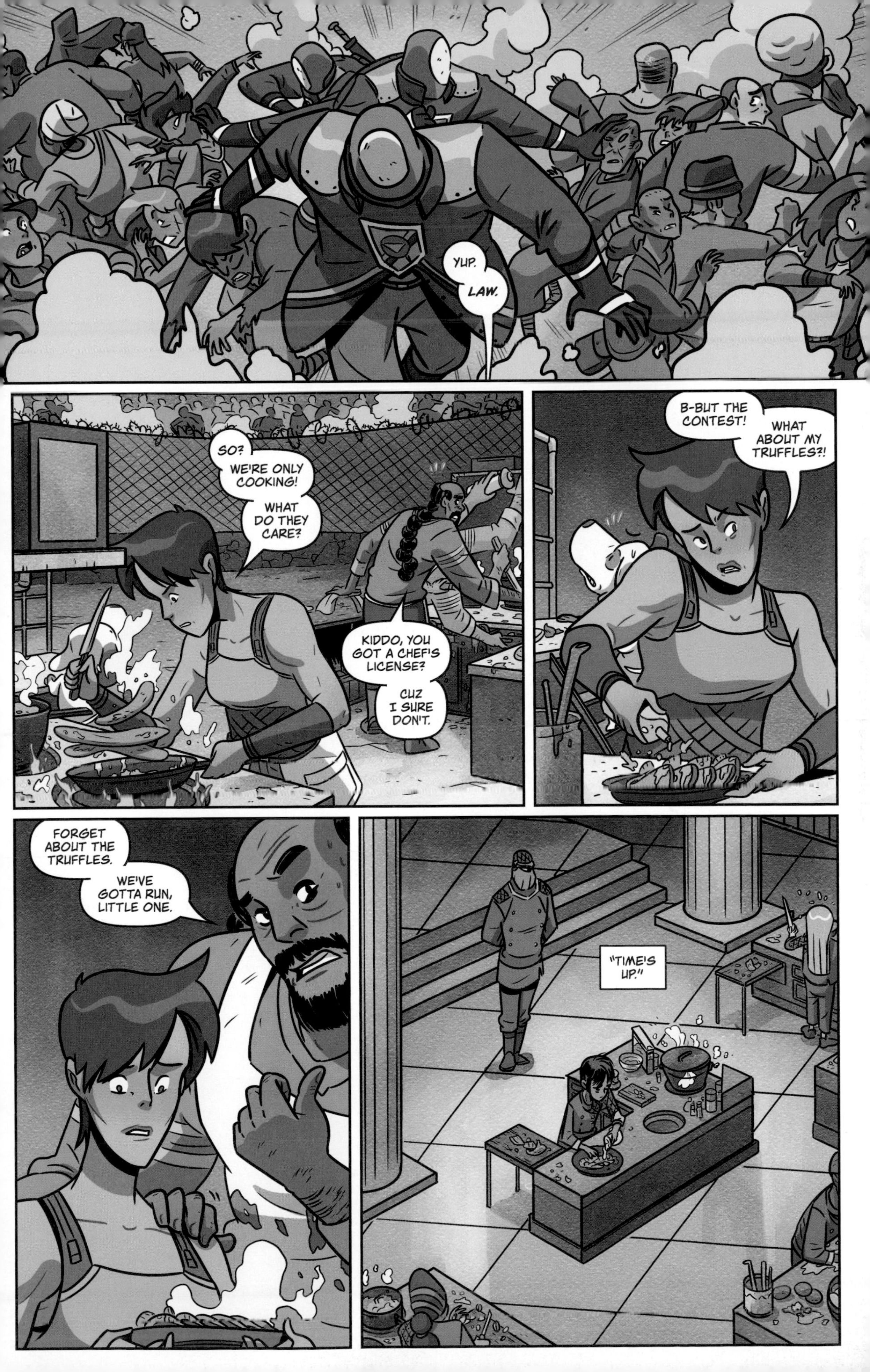
YUP.
LAW.
SO?
WE'RE ONLY COOKING!
WHAT DO THEY CARE?
KIDDO, YOU GOT A CHEF'S LICENSE?
CUZ I SURE DON'T.
B-BUT THE CONTEST!
WHAT ABOUT MY TRUFFLES?!
FORGET ABOUT THE TRUFFLES.
WE'VE GOTTA RUN, LITTLE ONE.
"TIME'S UP."

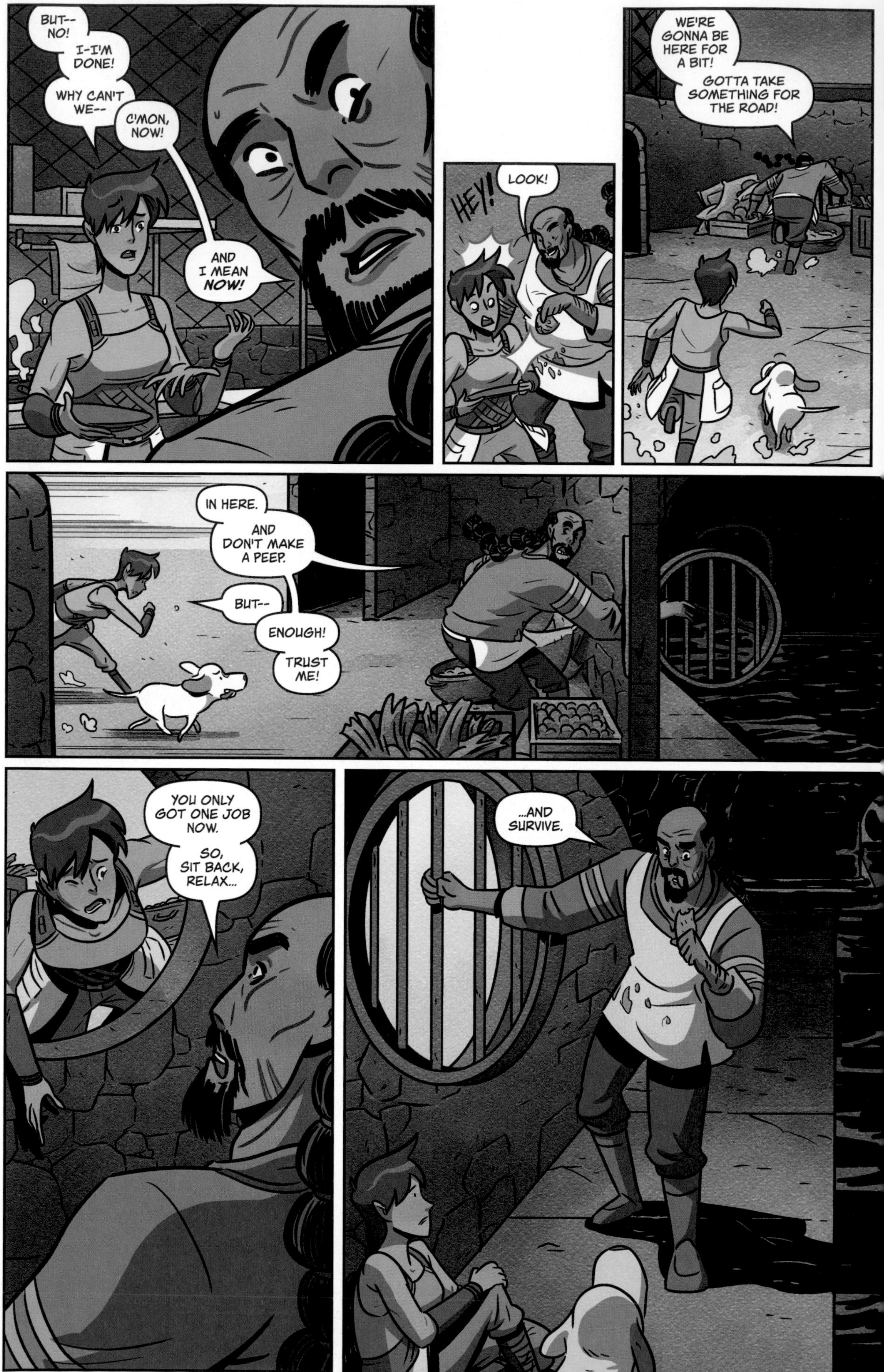
BUT--
NO!
I-I'M DONE!
WHY CAN'T WE--
C'MON, NOW!
AND I MEAN NOW!
HEY!
LOOK!
WE'RE GONNA BE HERE FOR A BIT!
GOTTA TAKE SOMETHING FOR THE ROAD!
IN HERE.
AND DON'T MAKE A PEEP.
BUT--
ENOUGH!
TRUST ME!
YOU ONLY GOT ONE JOB NOW.
SO, SIT BACK, RELAX...
...AND SURVIVE.

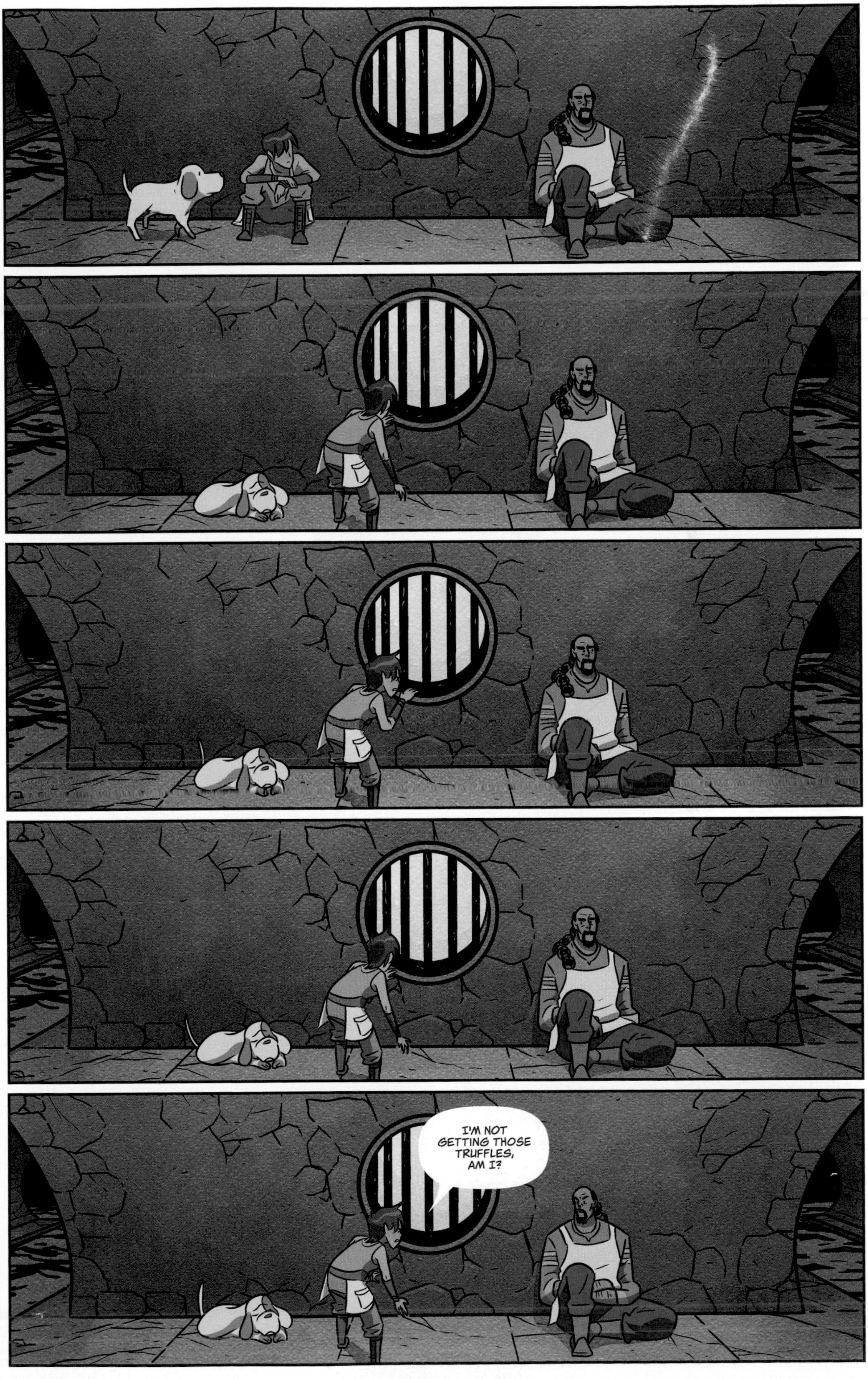
I'M NOT GETTING THOSE TRUFFLES, AM I?

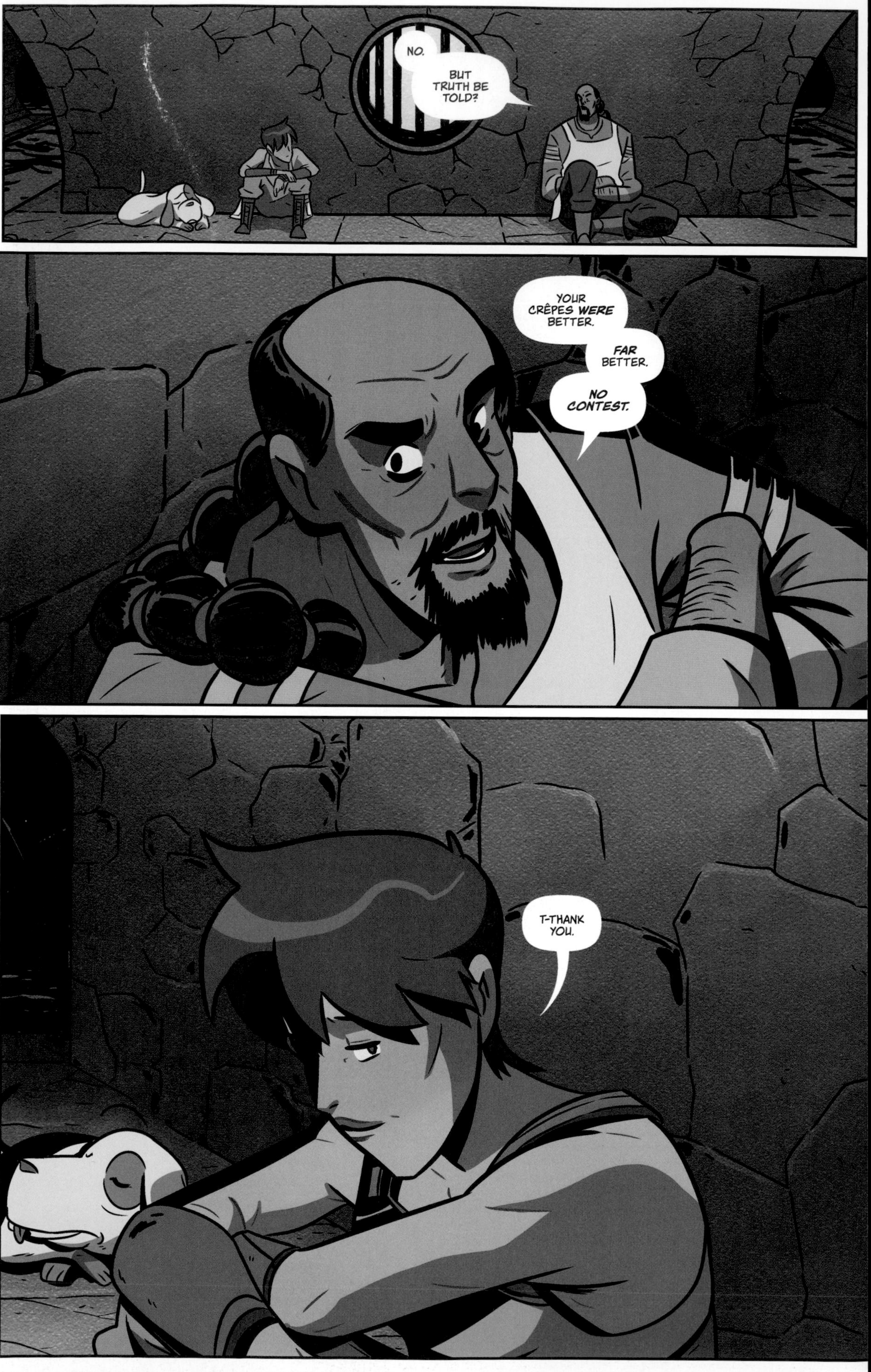
NO.
BUT TRUTH BE TOLD?
YOUR CRÊPES **WERE** BETTER.
FAR BETTER.
NO CONTEST.
T-THANK YOU.

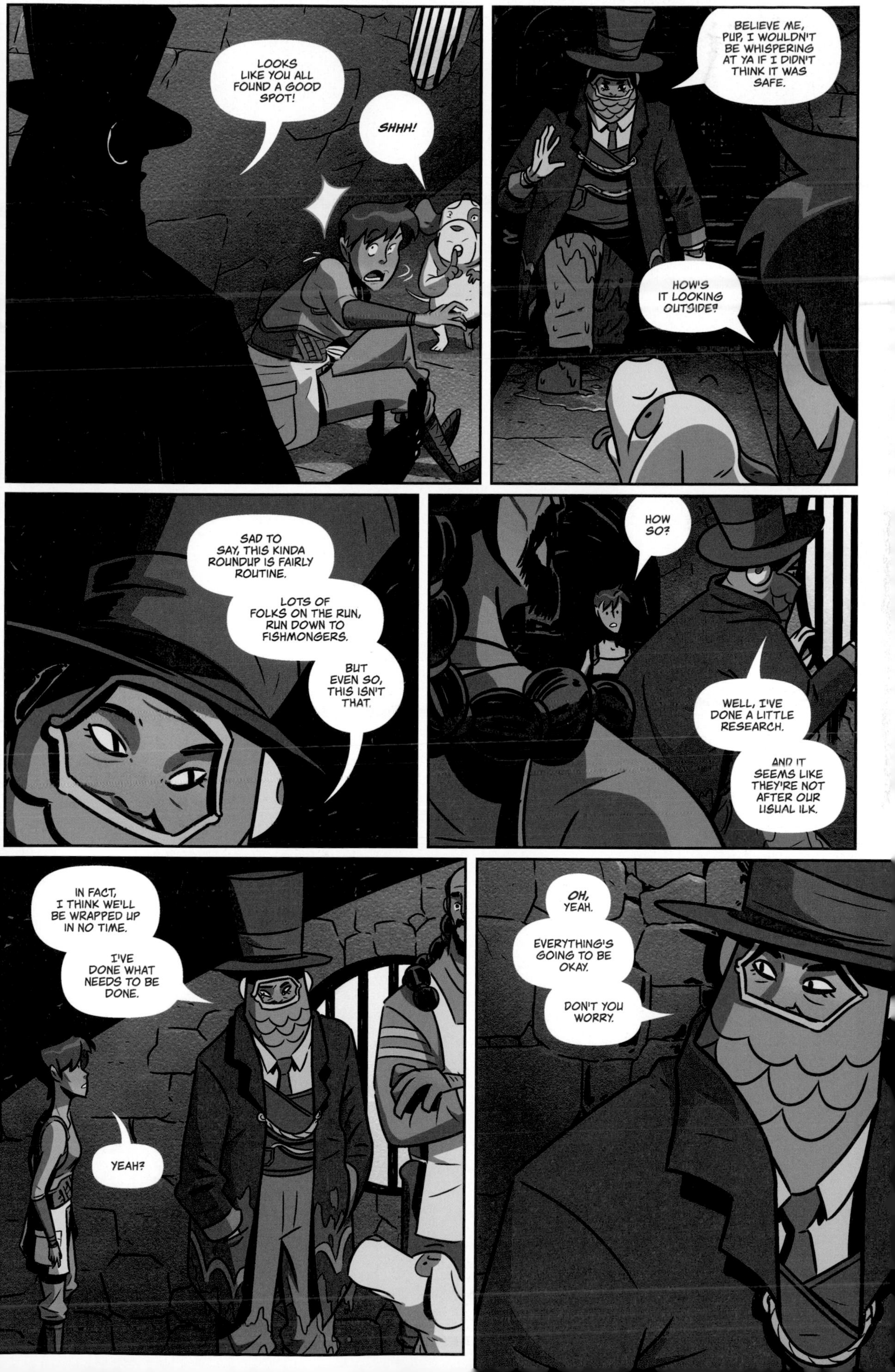
LOOKS LIKE YOU ALL FOUND A GOOD SPOT!
SHHH!
BELIEVE ME, PUP, I WOULDN'T BE WHISPERING AT YA IF I DIDN'T THINK IT WAS SAFE.
HOW'S IT LOOKING OUTSIDE?
SAD TO SAY, THIS KINDA ROUNDUP IS FAIRLY ROUTINE.
LOTS OF FOLKS ON THE RUN, RUN DOWN TO FISHMONGERS.
BUT EVEN SO, THIS ISN'T THAT.
HOW SO?
WELL, I'VE DONE A LITTLE RESEARCH.
AND IT SEEMS LIKE THEY'RE NOT AFTER OUR USUAL ILK.
IN FACT, I THINK WE'LL BE WRAPPED UP IN NO TIME.
I'VE DONE WHAT NEEDS TO BE DONE.
YEAH?
OH, YEAH.
EVERYTHING'S GOING TO BE OKAY.
DON'T YOU WORRY.

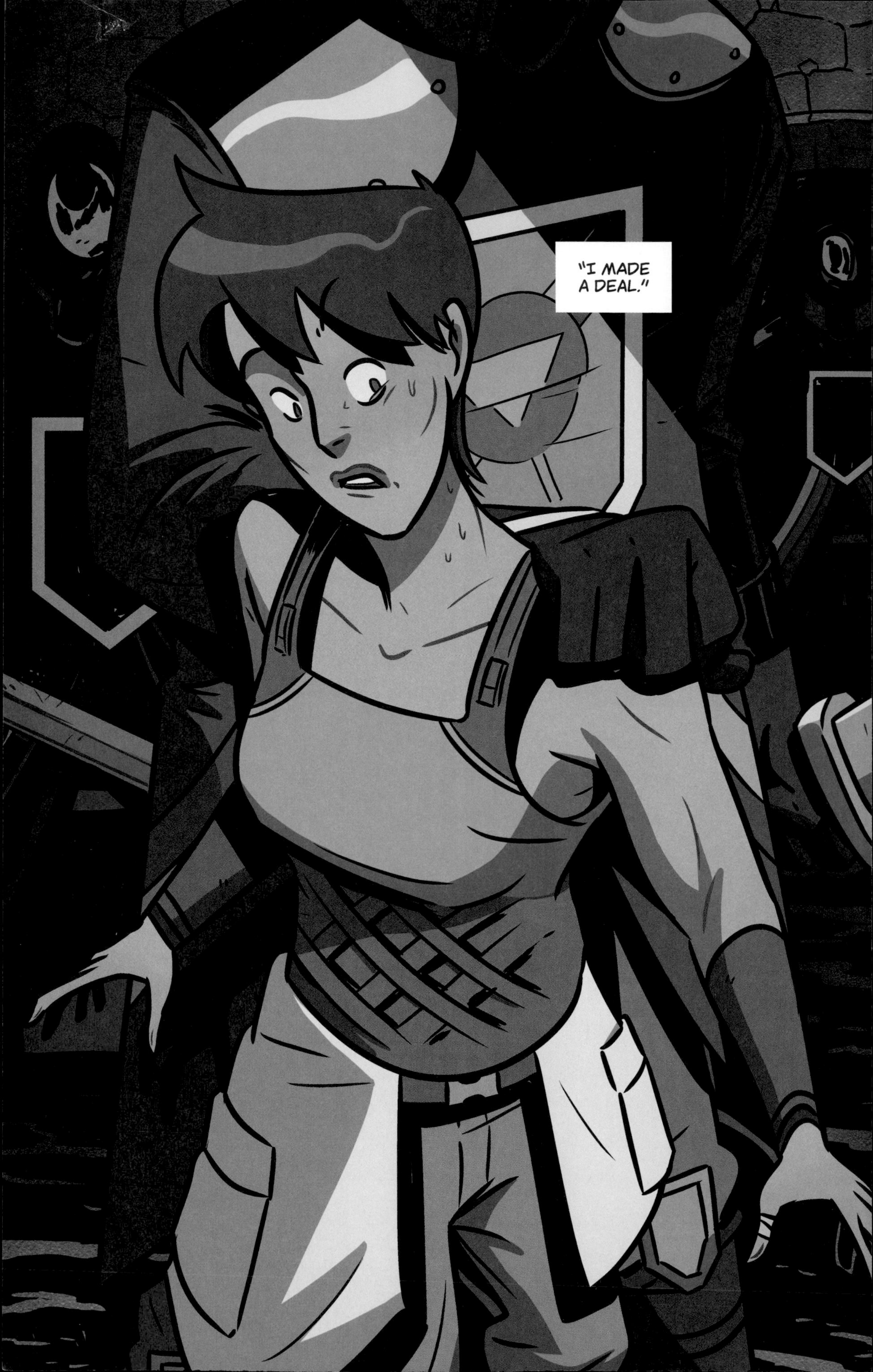
"I MADE A DEAL."

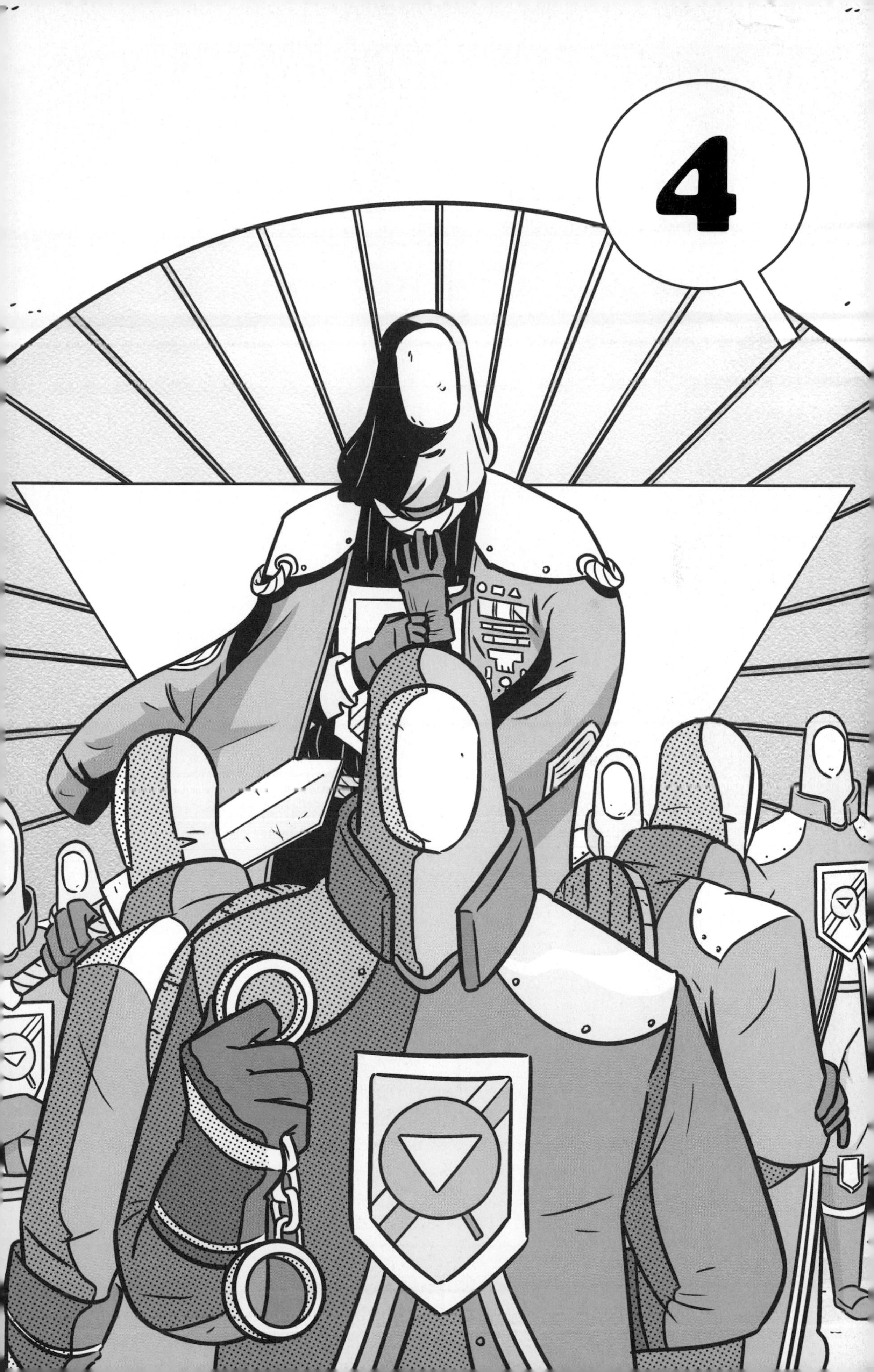
4

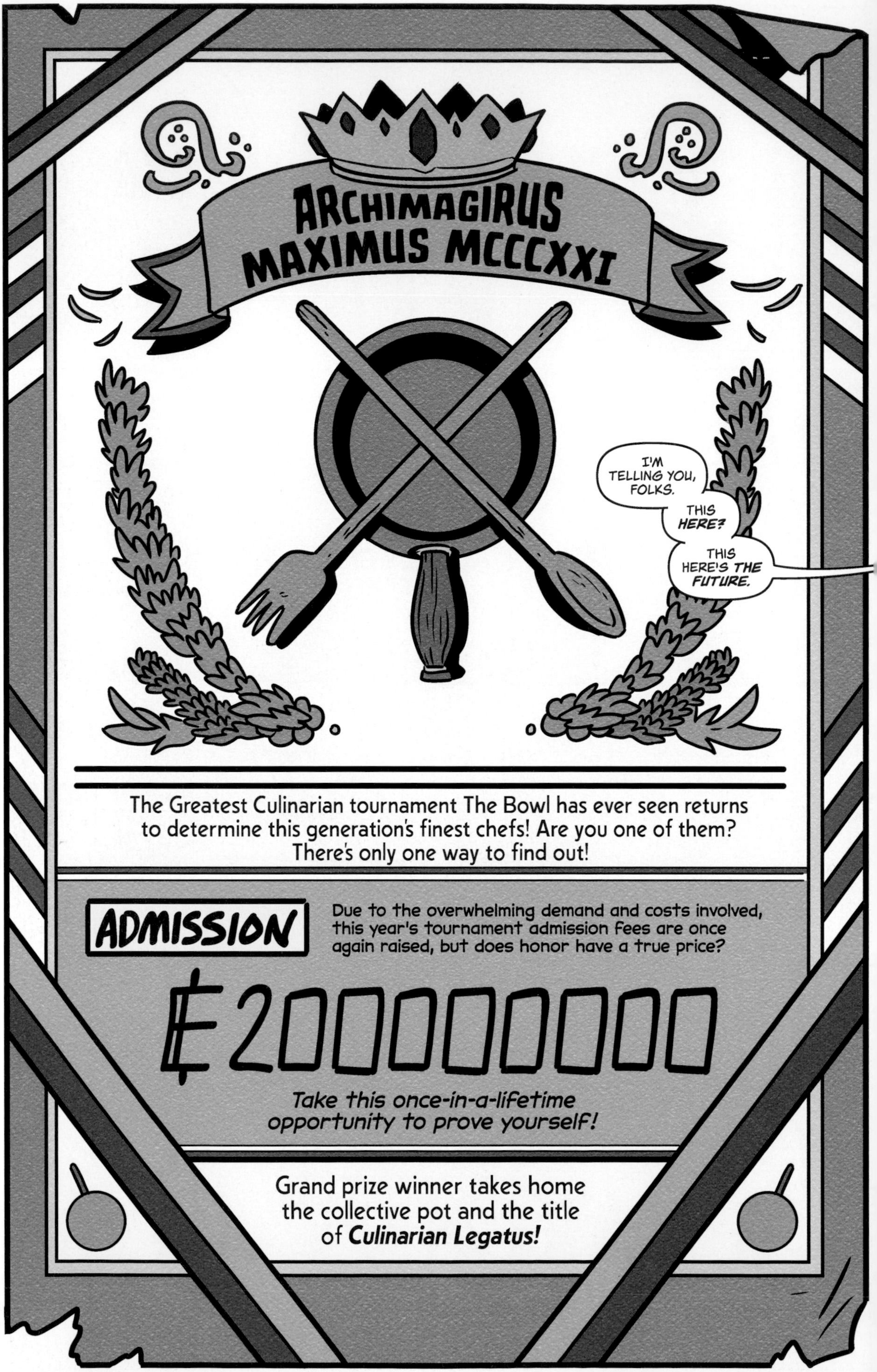
ARCHIMAGIRUS MAXIMUS MCCCXXI
I'M TELLING YOU, FOLKS.
THIS *HERE?*
THIS HERE'S ***THE FUTURE.***
The Greatest Culinarian tournament The Bowl has ever seen returns to determine this generation's finest chefs! Are you one of them? There's only one way to find out!
ADMISSION
Due to the overwhelming demand and costs involved, this year's tournament admission fees are once again raised, but does honor have a true price?
₤200000000
Take this once-in-a-lifetime opportunity to prove yourself!
Grand prize winner takes home the collective pot and the title of ***Culinarian Legatus!***

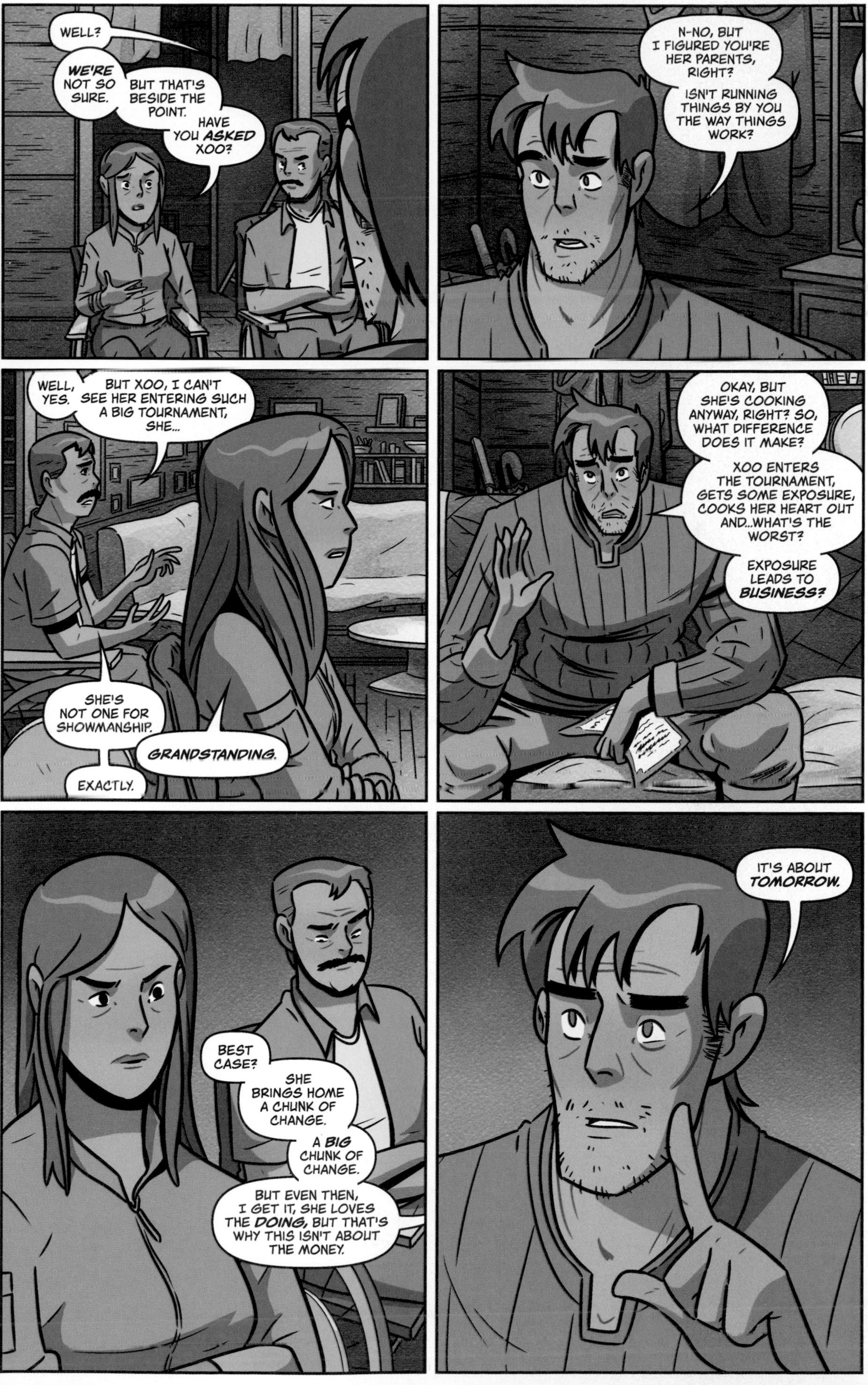
WELL?
WE'RE NOT SO SURE.
BUT THAT'S BESIDE THE POINT.
HAVE YOU ASKED XOO?
N-NO, BUT I FIGURED YOU'RE HER PARENTS, RIGHT?
ISN'T RUNNING THINGS BY YOU THE WAY THINGS WORK?
WELL, YES.
BUT XOO, I CAN'T SEE HER ENTERING SUCH A BIG TOURNAMENT, SHE...
SHE'S NOT ONE FOR SHOWMANSHIP.
GRANDSTANDING.
EXACTLY.
OKAY, BUT SHE'S COOKING ANYWAY, RIGHT? SO, WHAT DIFFERENCE DOES IT MAKE?
XOO ENTERS THE TOURNAMENT, GETS SOME EXPOSURE, COOKS HER HEART OUT AND...WHAT'S THE WORST?
EXPOSURE LEADS TO BUSINESS?
BEST CASE?
SHE BRINGS HOME A CHUNK OF CHANGE.
A BIG CHUNK OF CHANGE.
BUT EVEN THEN, I GET IT, SHE LOVES THE DOING, BUT THAT'S WHY THIS ISN'T ABOUT THE MONEY.
IT'S ABOUT TOMORROW.

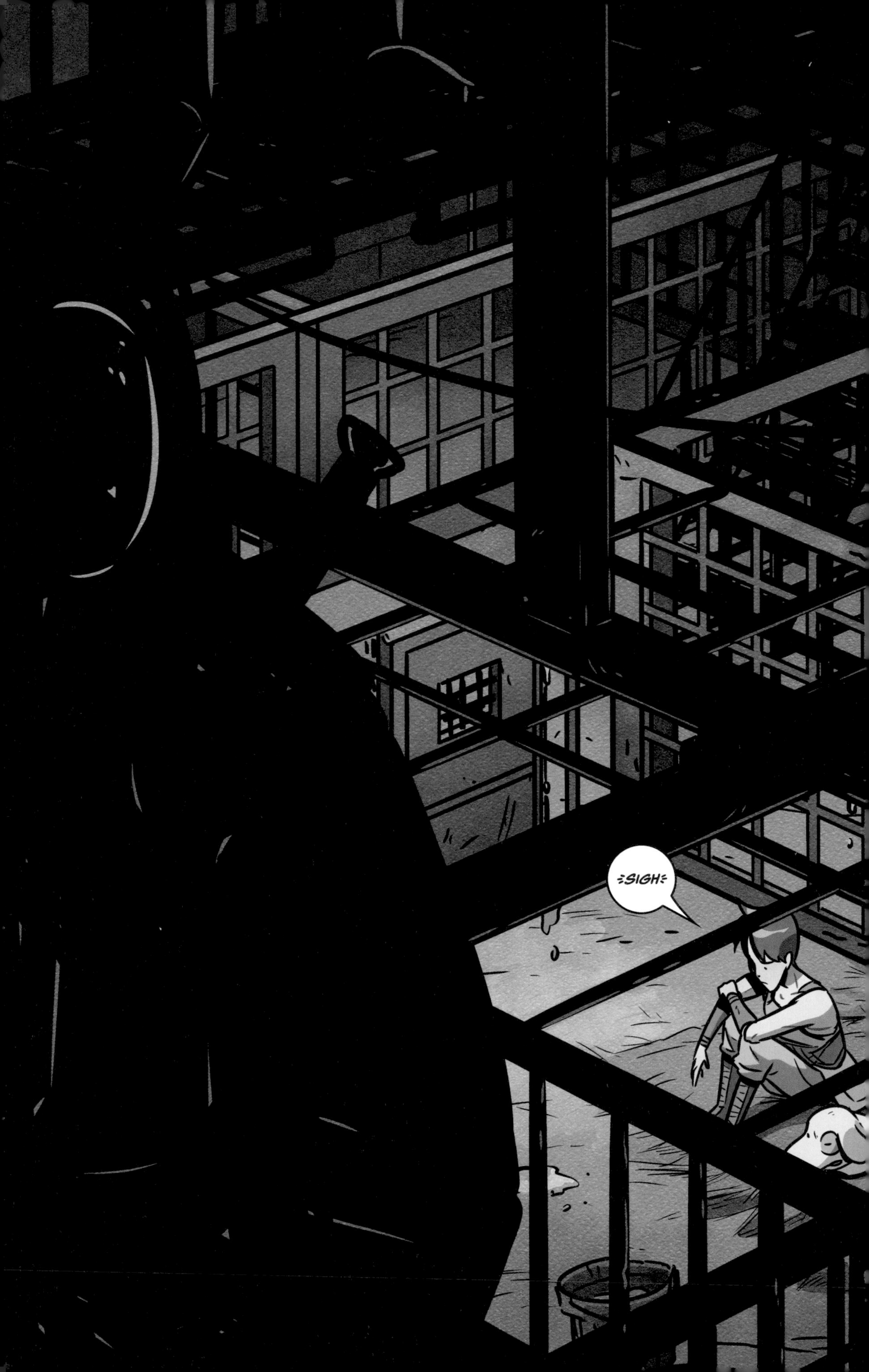
SIGH

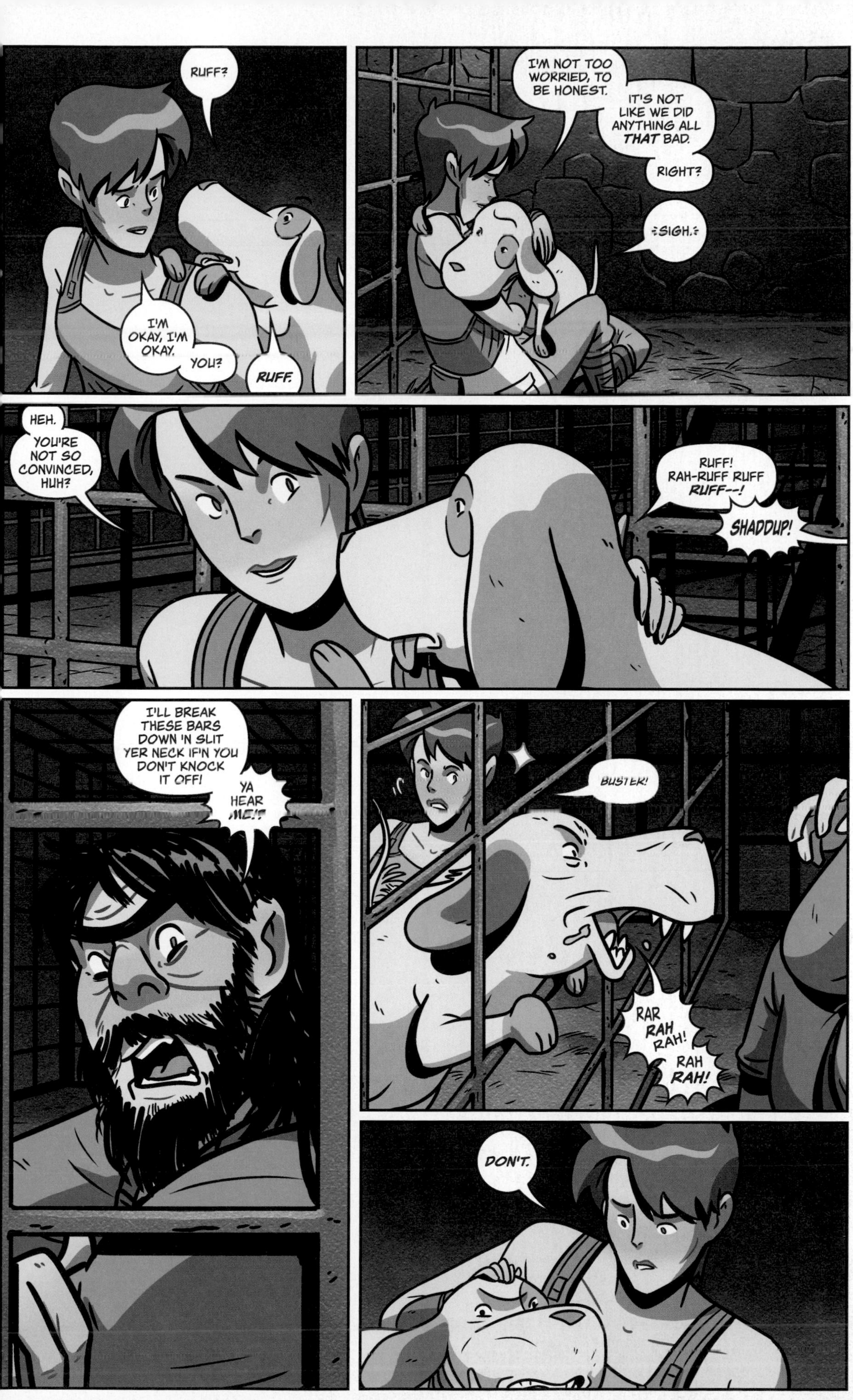
RUFF?
I'M OKAY, I'M OKAY.
YOU?
RUFF.
I'M NOT TOO WORRIED, TO BE HONEST.
IT'S NOT LIKE WE DID ANYTHING ALL THAT BAD.
RIGHT?
SIGH.
HEH.
YOU'RE NOT SO CONVINCED, HUH?
RUFF! RAH-RUFF RUFF RUFF--!
SHADDUP!
I'LL BREAK THESE BARS DOWN 'N SLIT YER NECK IF'N YOU DON'T KNOCK IT OFF!
YA HEAR ME!?
BUSTER!
RAR RAH RAH!
RAH RAH!
DON'T.

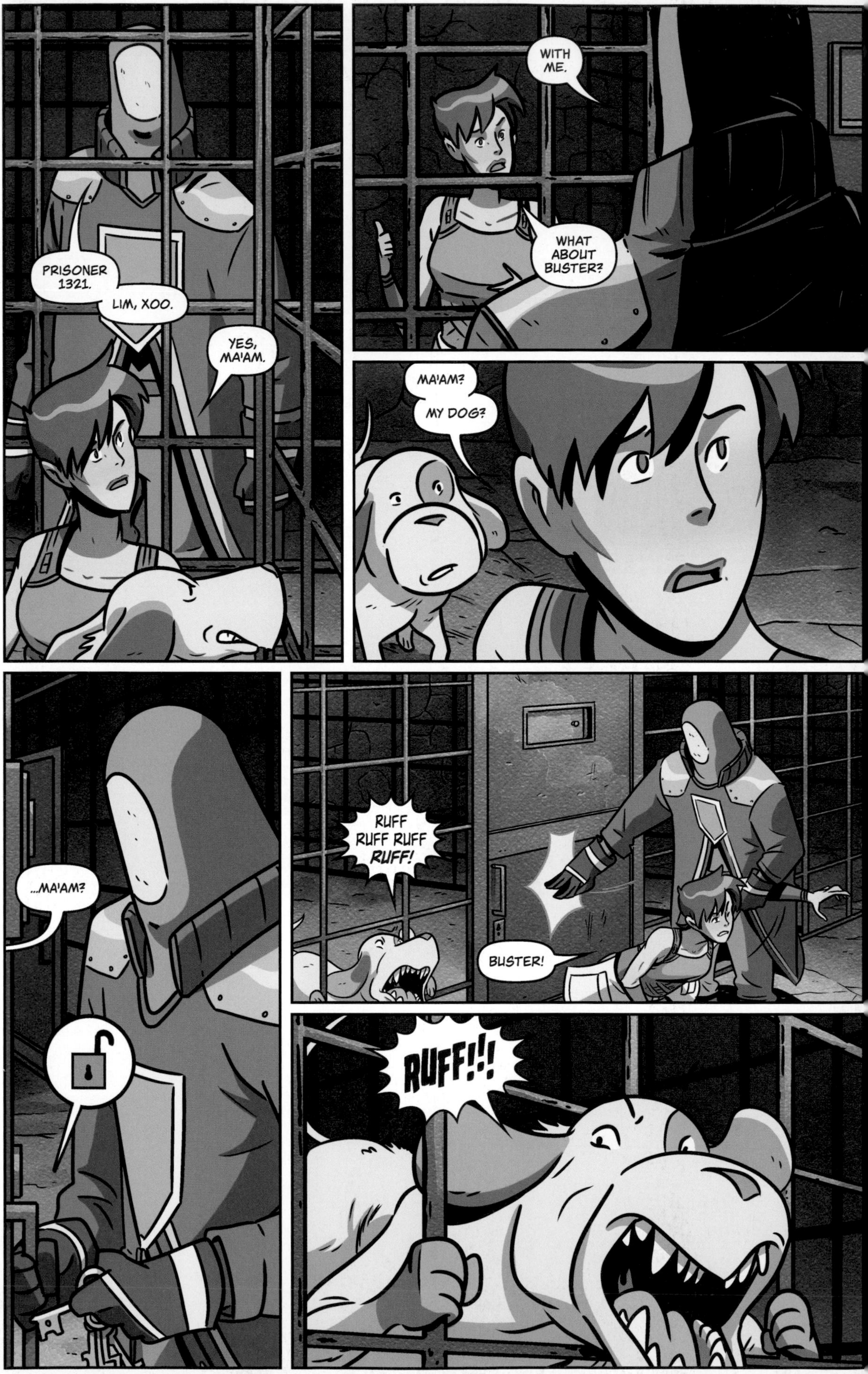
PRISONER 1321.
LIM, XOO.
YES, MA'AM.
WITH ME.
WHAT ABOUT BUSTER?
MA'AM?
MY DOG?
...MA'AM?
RUFF RUFF RUFF RUFF!
BUSTER!
RUFF!!!

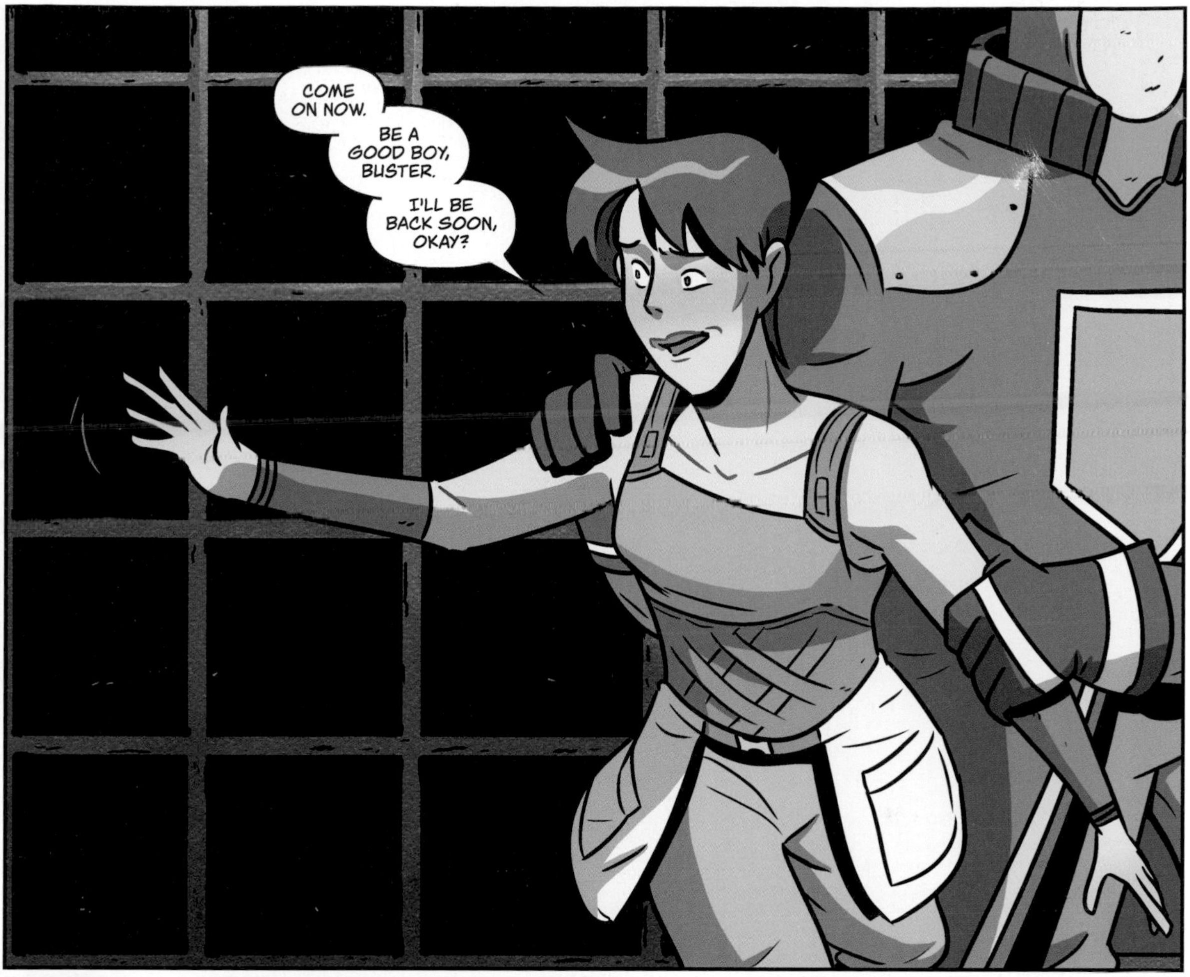
COME ON NOW.
BE A GOOD BOY, BUSTER.
I'LL BE BACK SOON, OKAY?
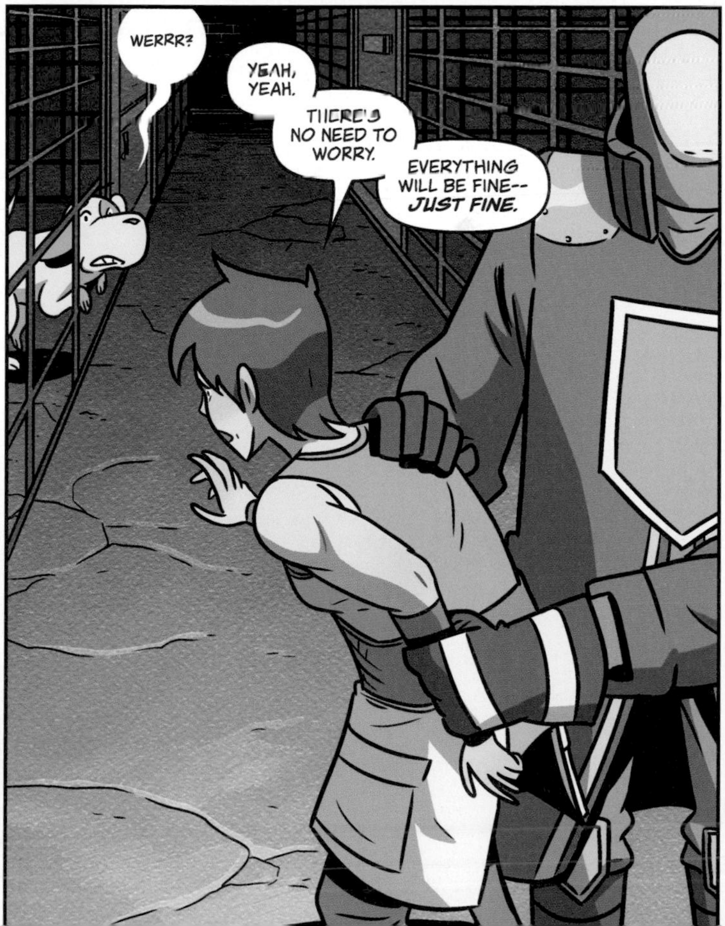
WERRR?
YEAH, YEAH.
THERE'S NO NEED TO WORRY.
EVERYTHING WILL BE FINE-- *JUST FINE.*
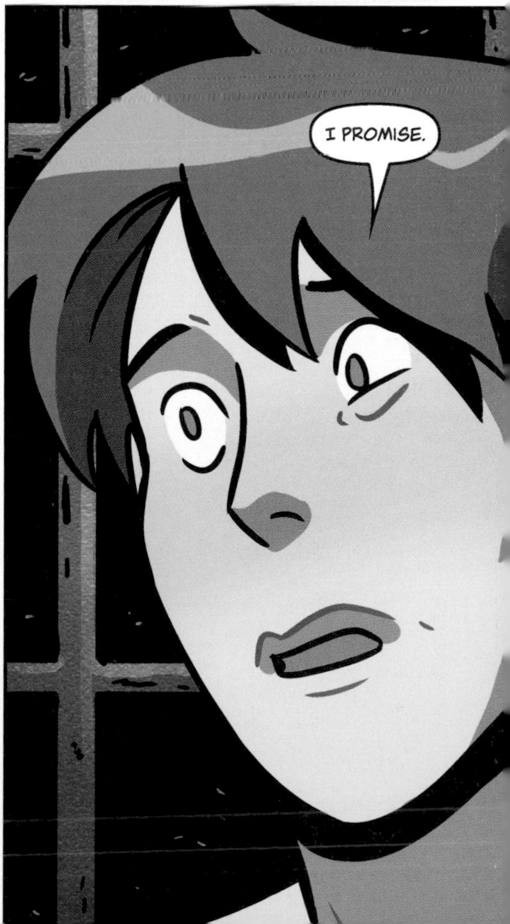
I PROMISE.

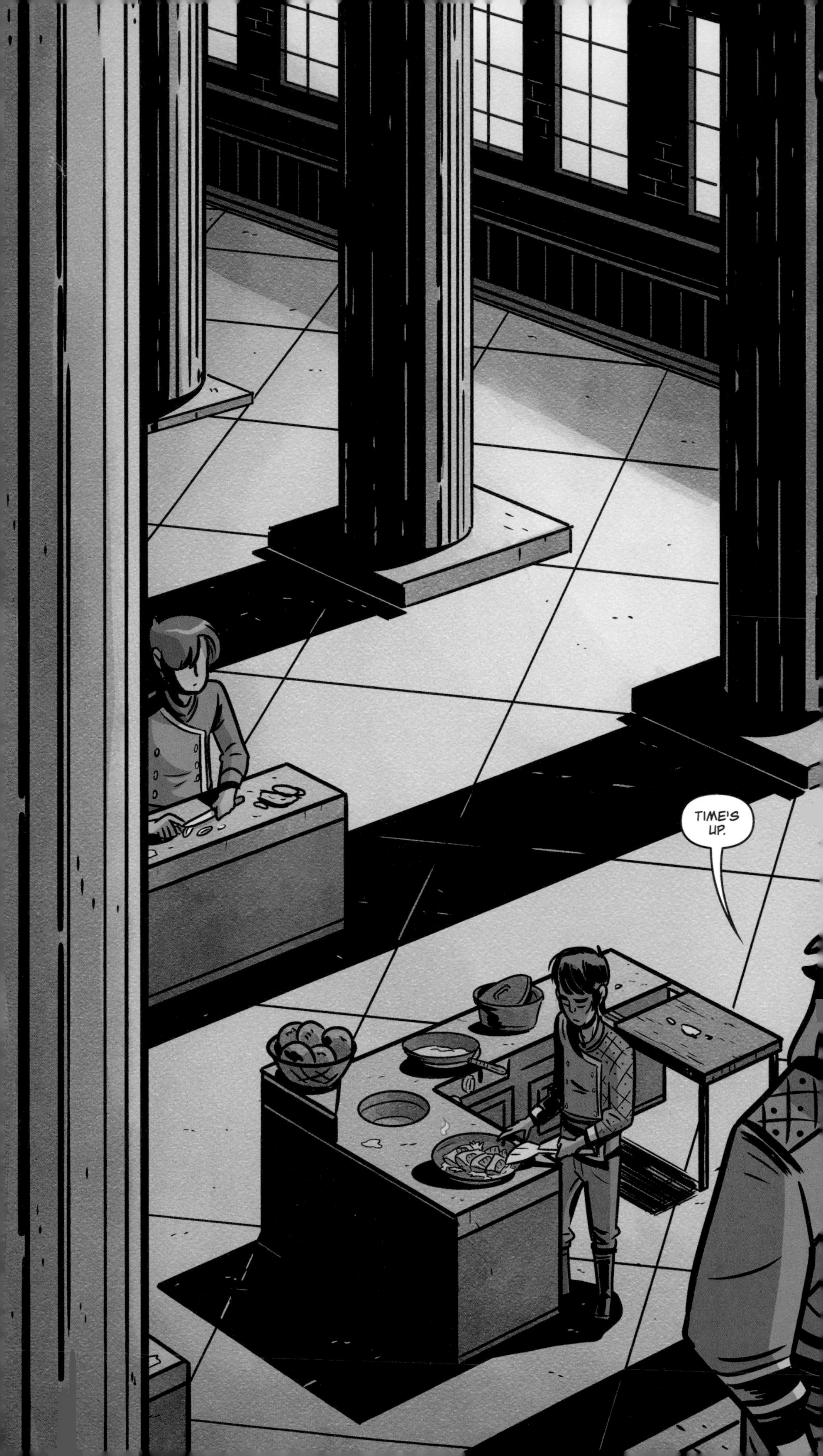
TIME'S UP.

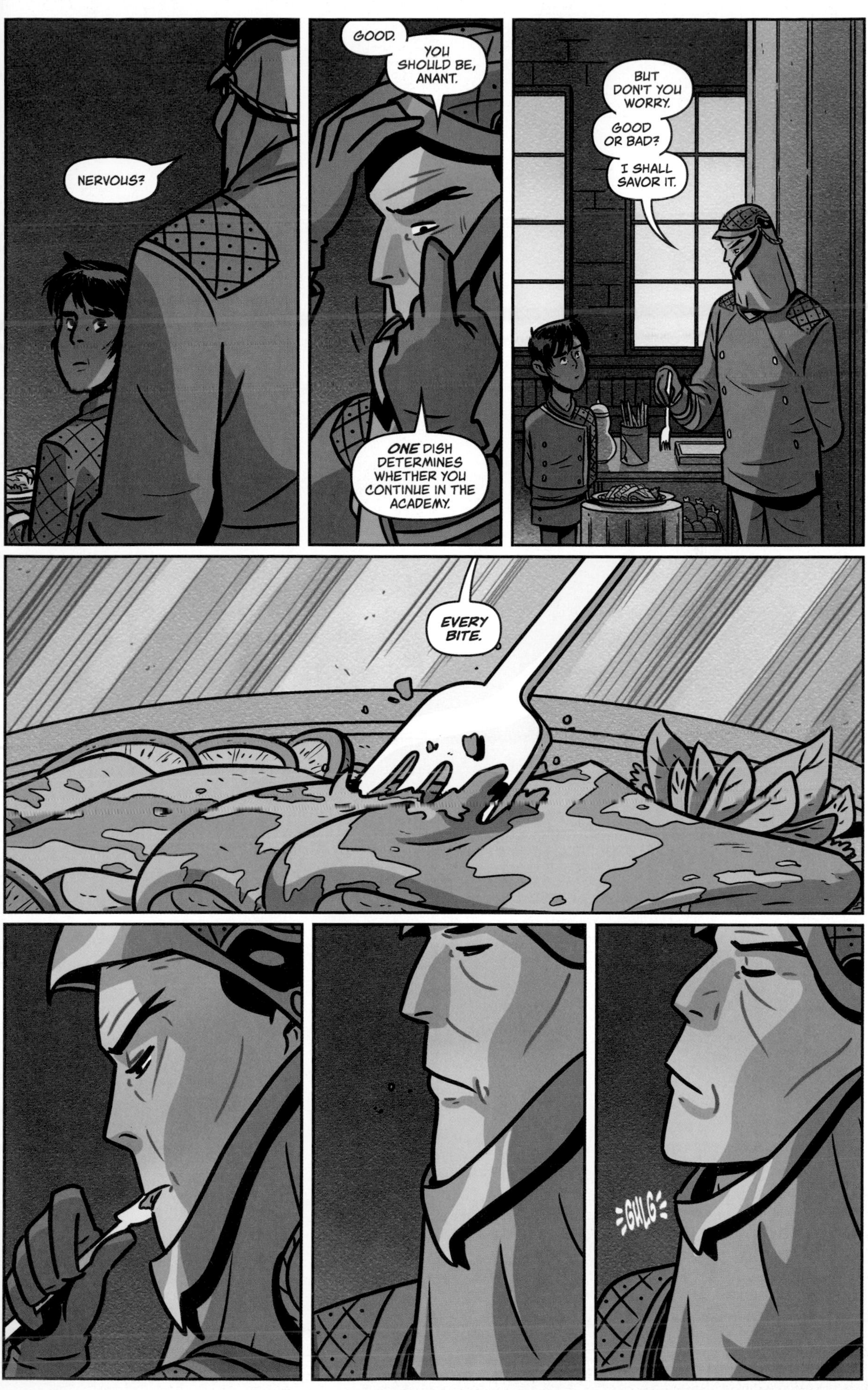
NERVOUS?
GOOD.
YOU SHOULD BE, ANANT.
ONE DISH DETERMINES WHETHER YOU CONTINUE IN THE ACADEMY.
BUT DON'T YOU WORRY.
GOOD OR BAD?
I SHALL SAVOR IT.
EVERY BITE.
GULG

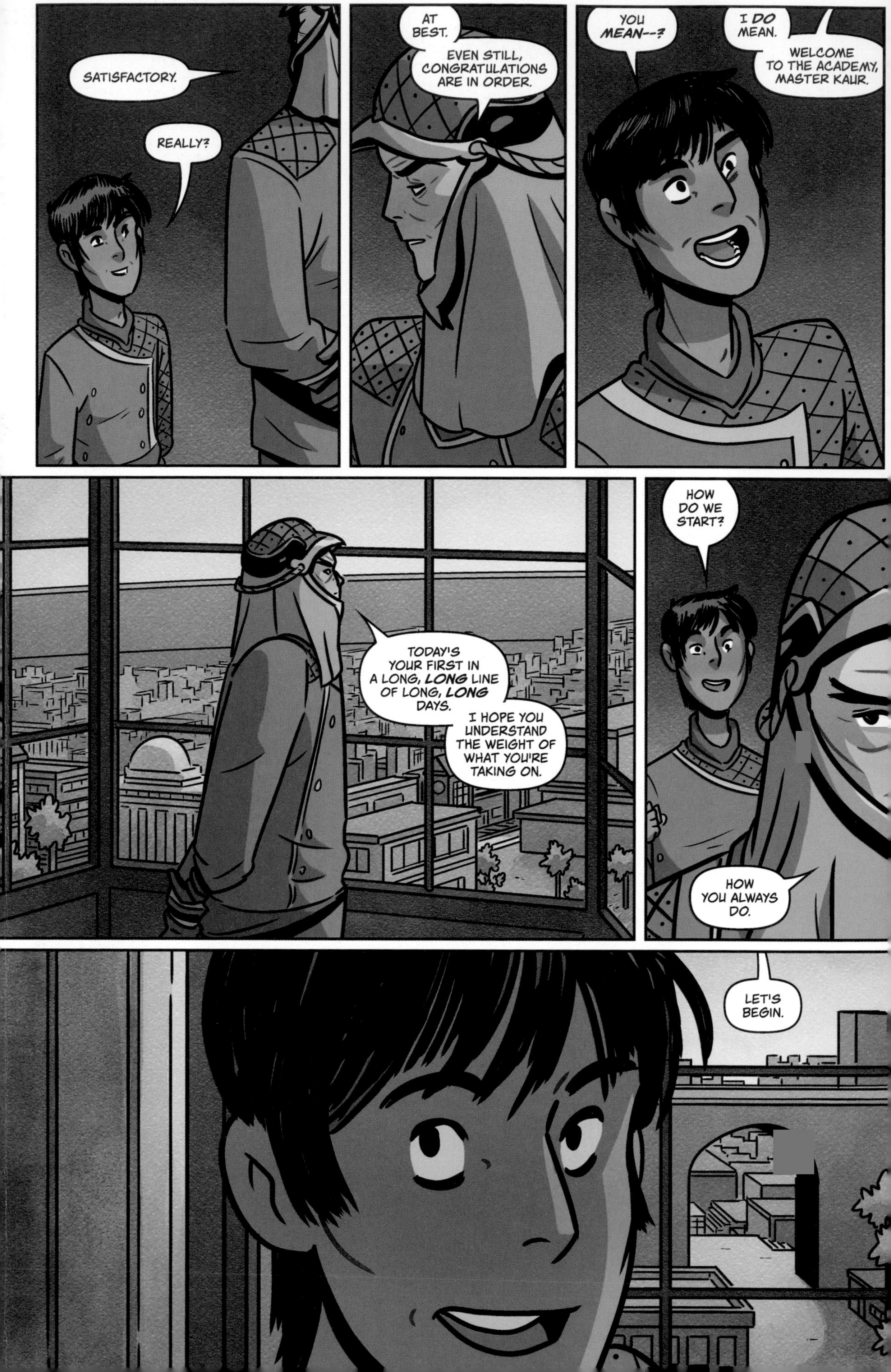
SATISFACTORY.
REALLY?
AT BEST.
EVEN STILL, CONGRATULATIONS ARE IN ORDER.
YOU *MEAN--?*
I *DO* MEAN.
WELCOME TO THE ACADEMY, MASTER KAUR.
TODAY'S YOUR FIRST IN A LONG, *LONG* LINE OF LONG, *LONG* DAYS.
I HOPE YOU UNDERSTAND THE WEIGHT OF WHAT YOU'RE TAKING ON.
HOW DO WE START?
HOW YOU ALWAYS DO.
LET'S BEGIN.

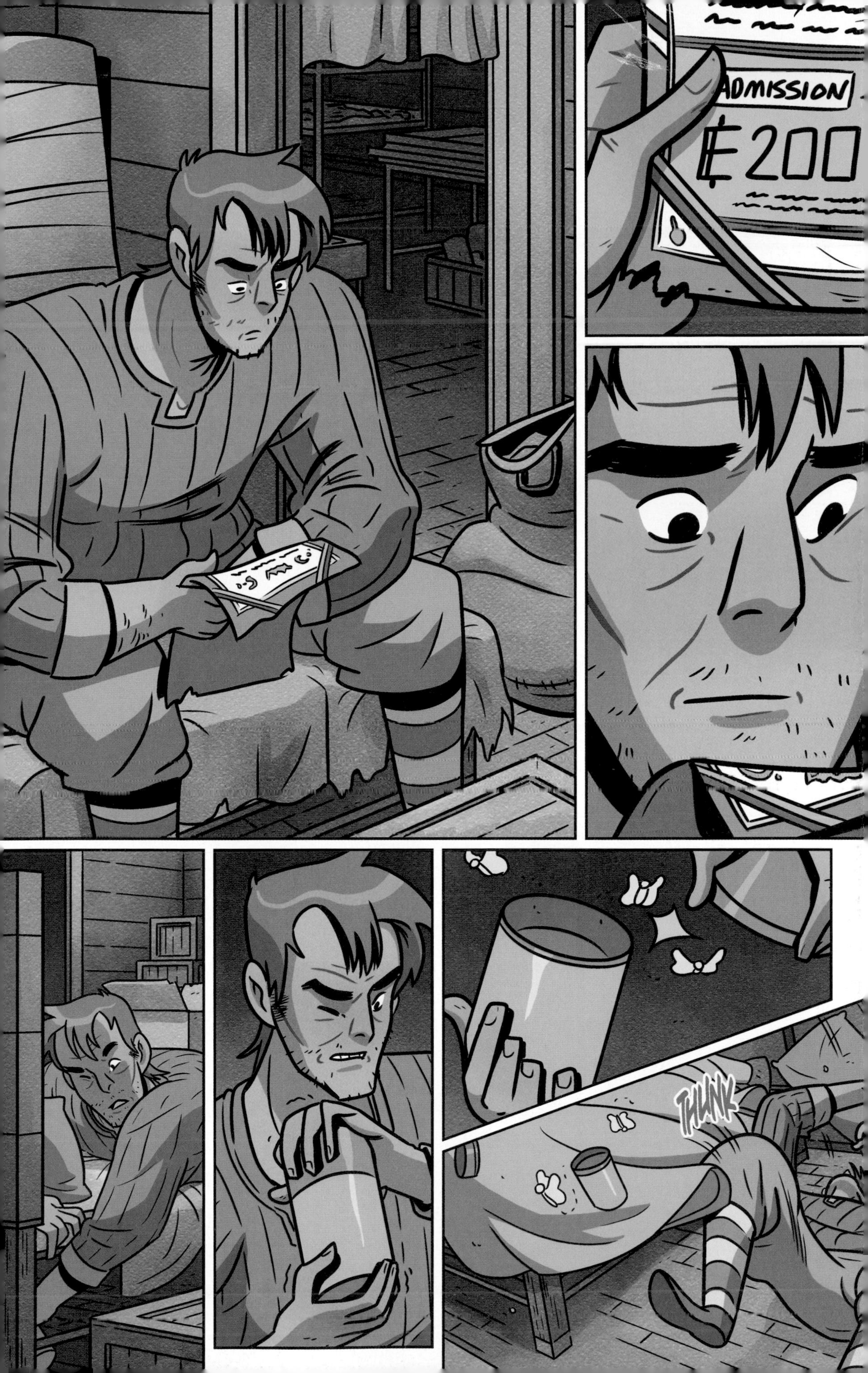

ADMISSION
₤200
THUNK

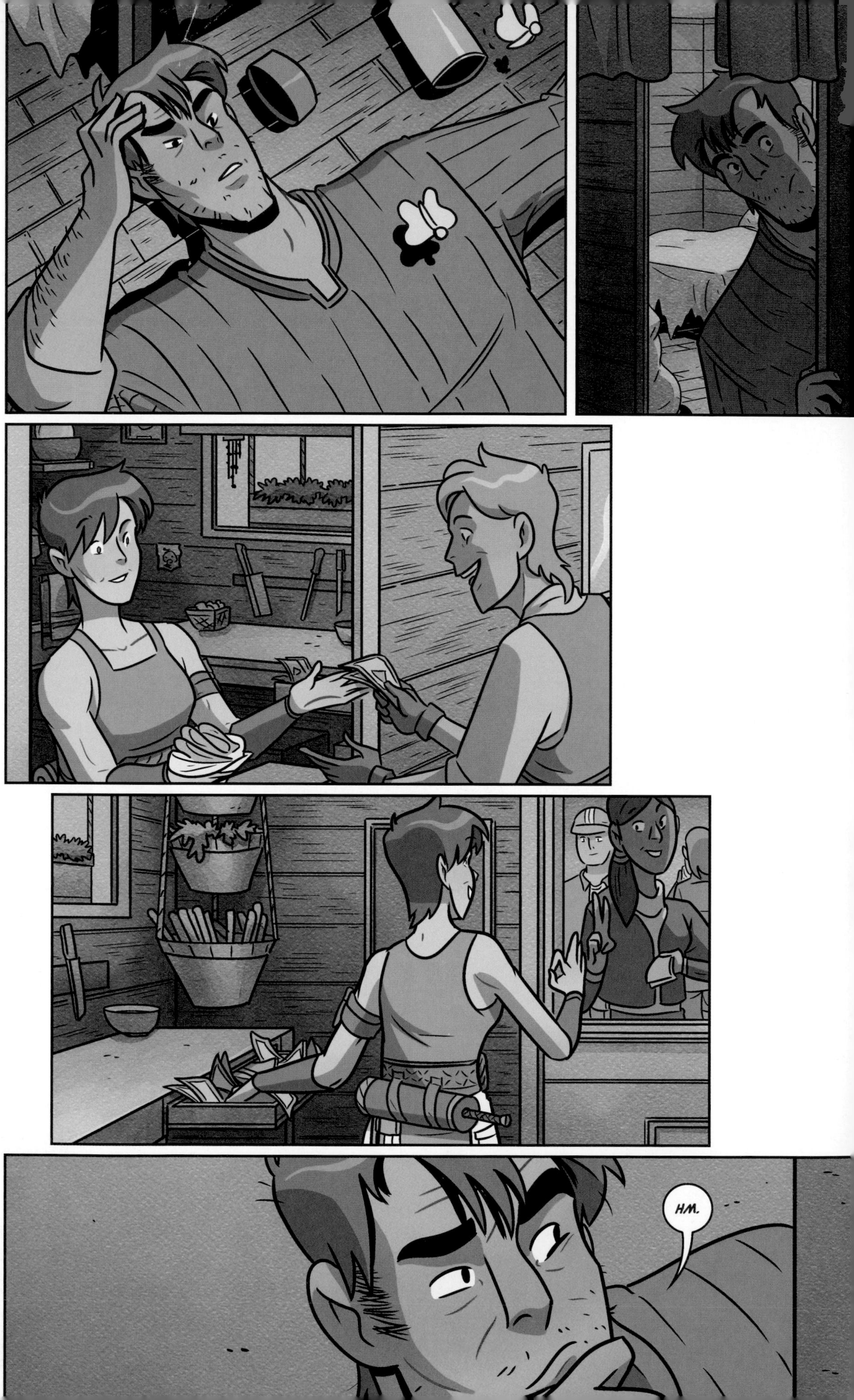
HM.

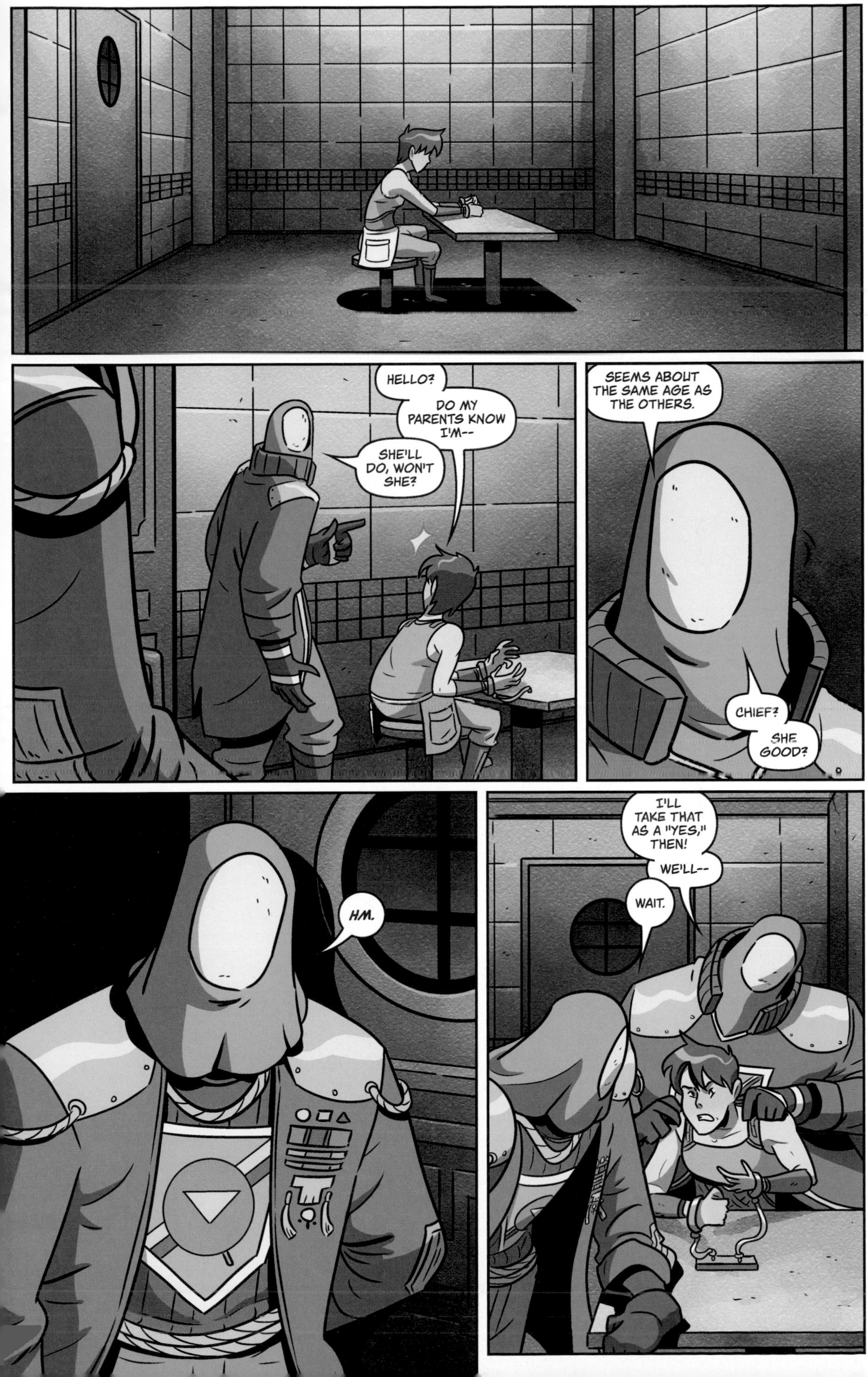
HELLO?
DO MY PARENTS KNOW I'M--
SHE'LL DO, WON'T SHE?
SEEMS ABOUT THE SAME AGE AS THE OTHERS.
CHIEF?
SHE GOOD?
HM.
I'LL TAKE THAT AS A "YES," THEN!
WE'LL--
WAIT.

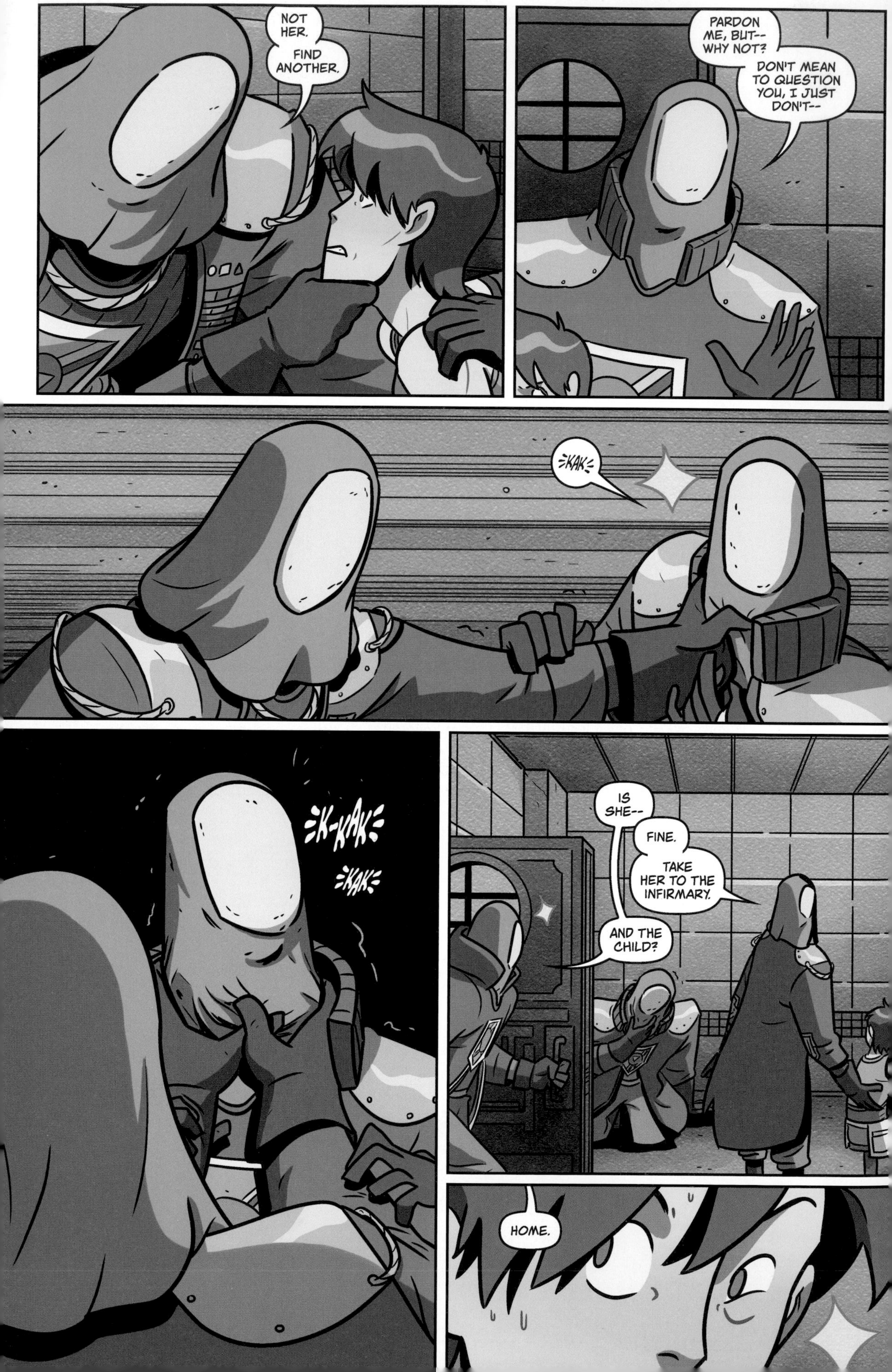
NOT HER.
FIND ANOTHER.
PARDON ME, BUT-- WHY NOT?
DON'T MEAN TO QUESTION YOU, I JUST DON'T--
KAK
K-KAK
KAK
IS SHE--
FINE.
TAKE HER TO THE INFIRMARY.
AND THE CHILD?
HOME.

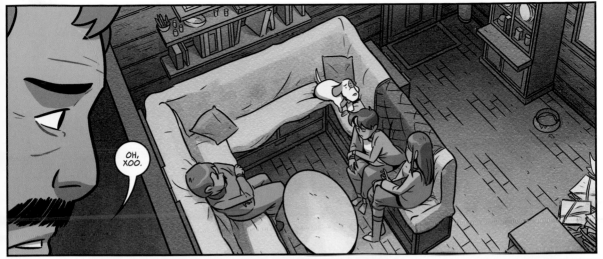

OH, XOO.

YOU WENT-- *WHERE!?*

WHY!?

I-I'M SO SORRY.

I DIDN'T MEAN TO--

HONEY, YOU'RE OKAY NOW.

BUT.

BUT WHILE WE'RE *NOT* HERE TO SCOLD YOU, WE NEED YOU TO BE OPEN WITH US.

WE'RE HERE TO *HELP.*

I KNOW, I KNOW.

ME TOO.

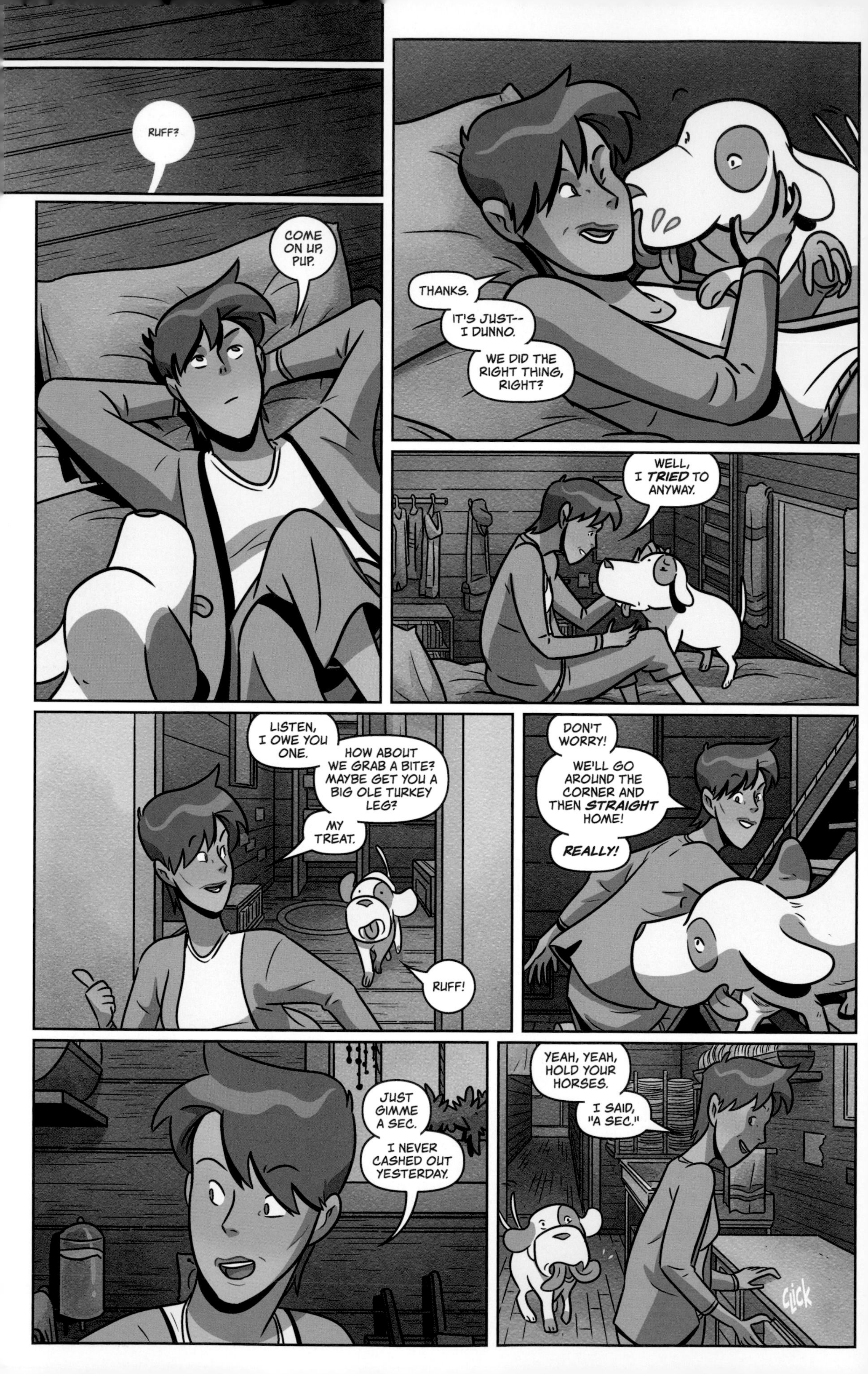
RUFF?
COME ON UP, PUP.
THANKS.
IT'S JUST-- I DUNNO.
WE DID THE RIGHT THING, RIGHT?
WELL, I TRIED TO ANYWAY.
LISTEN, I OWE YOU ONE.
HOW ABOUT WE GRAB A BITE? MAYBE GET YOU A BIG OLE TURKEY LEG?
MY TREAT.
RUFF!
DON'T WORRY!
WE'LL GO AROUND THE CORNER AND THEN STRAIGHT HOME!
REALLY!
JUST GIMME A SEC.
I NEVER CASHED OUT YESTERDAY.
YEAH, YEAH, HOLD YOUR HORSES.
I SAID, "A SEC."
CLICK

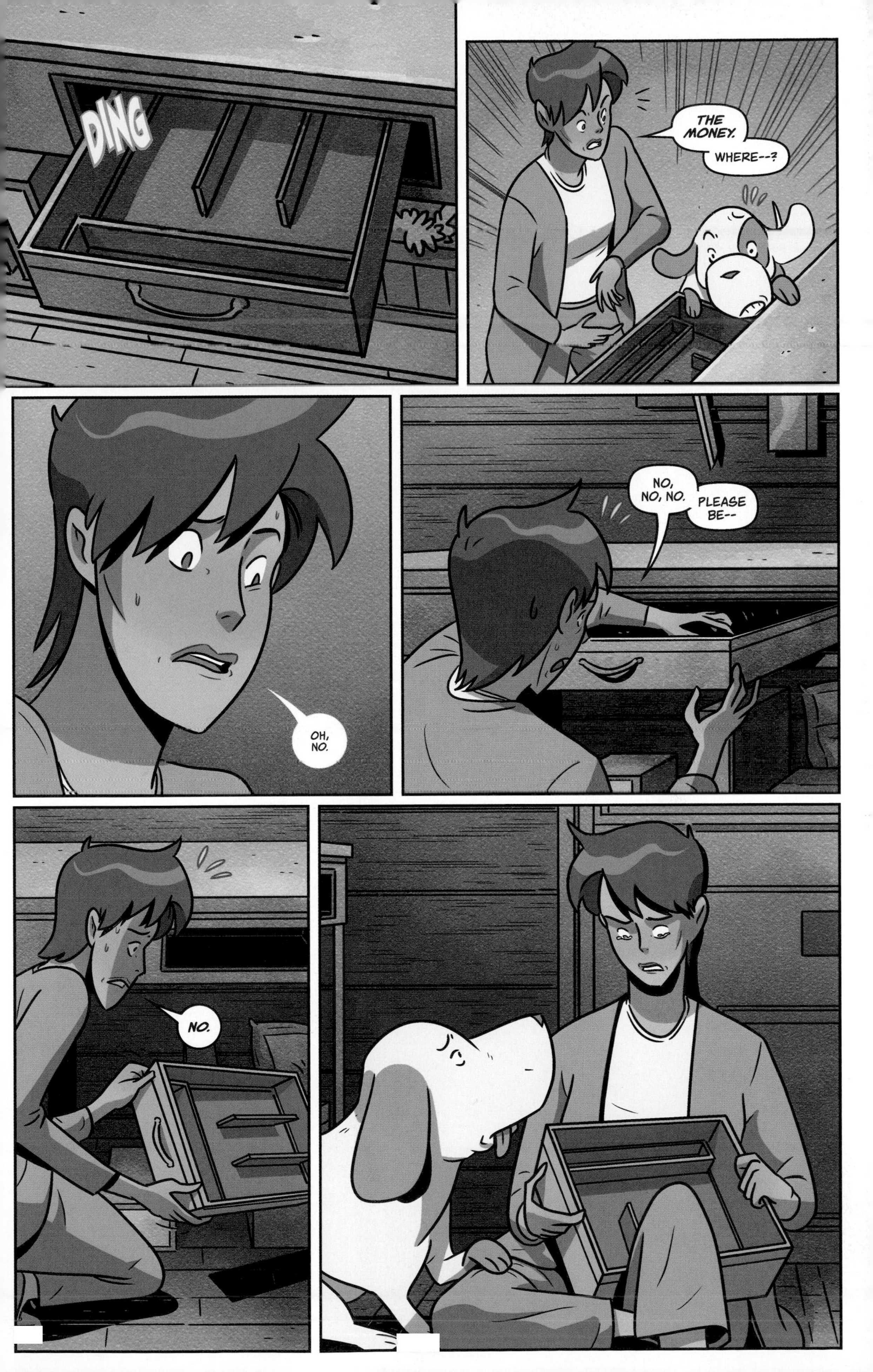
DING
THE MONEY.
WHERE--?
OH, NO.
NO, NO, NO.
PLEASE BE--
NO.

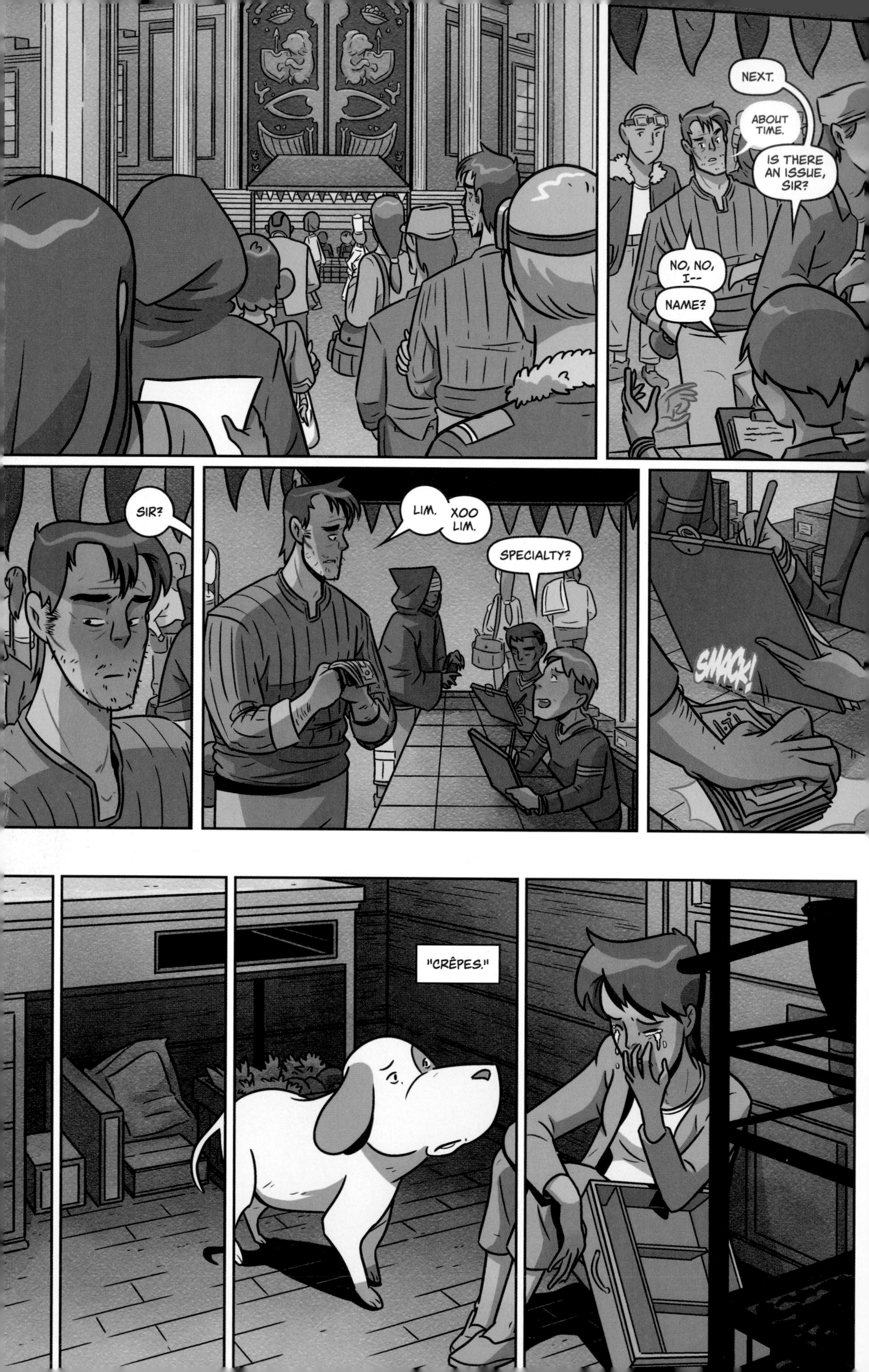
NEXT.
ABOUT TIME.
IS THERE AN ISSUE, SIR?
NO, NO, I--
NAME?
SIR?
LIM.
XOO LIM.
SPECIALTY?
SMACK!
"CRÊPES."

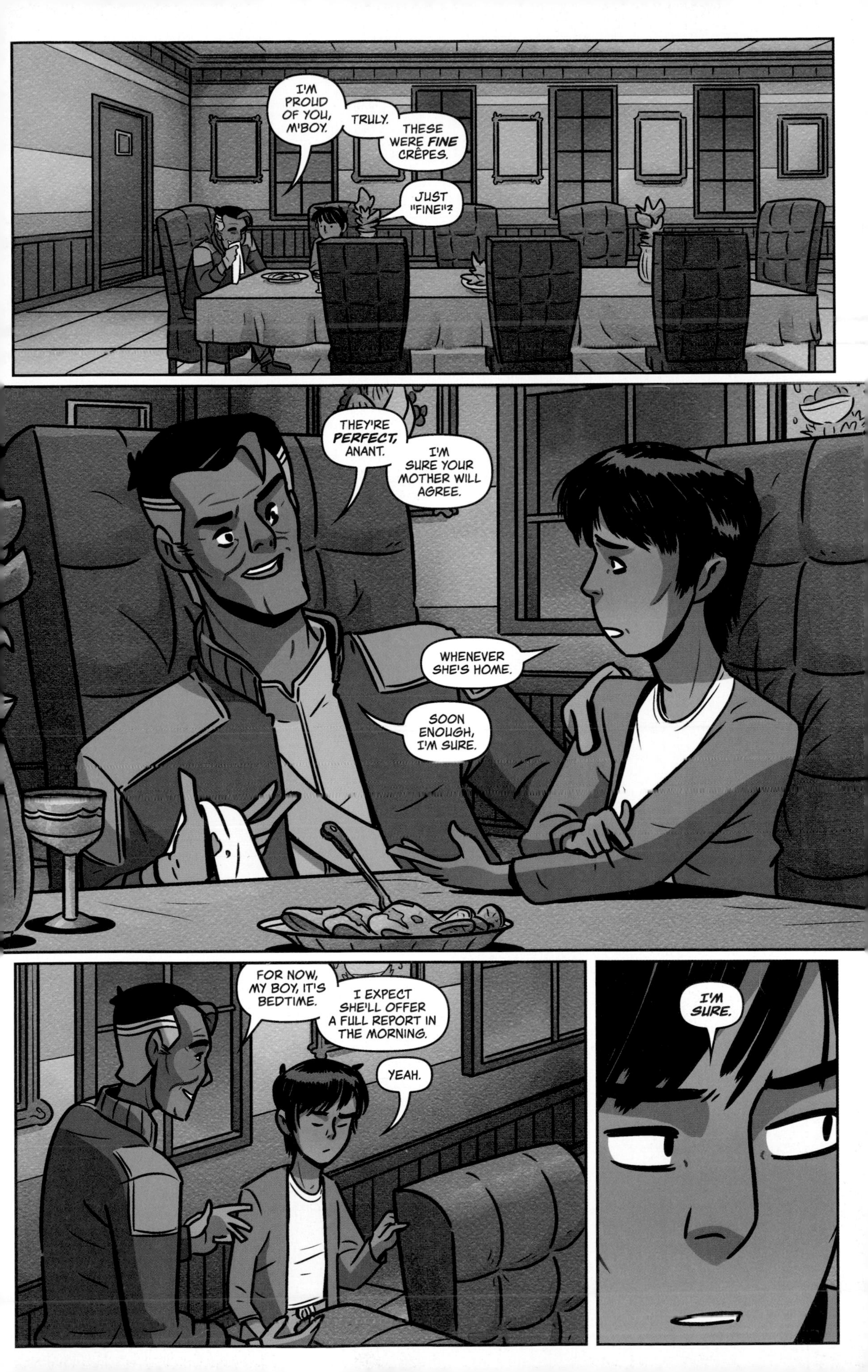
I'M PROUD OF YOU, M'BOY.
TRULY.
THESE WERE *FINE* CRÊPES.
JUST "FINE"?
THEY'RE *PERFECT,* ANANT.
I'M SURE YOUR MOTHER WILL AGREE.
WHENEVER SHE'S HOME.
SOON ENOUGH, I'M SURE.
FOR NOW, MY BOY, IT'S BEDTIME.
I EXPECT SHE'LL OFFER A FULL REPORT IN THE MORNING.
YEAH.
I'M SURE.

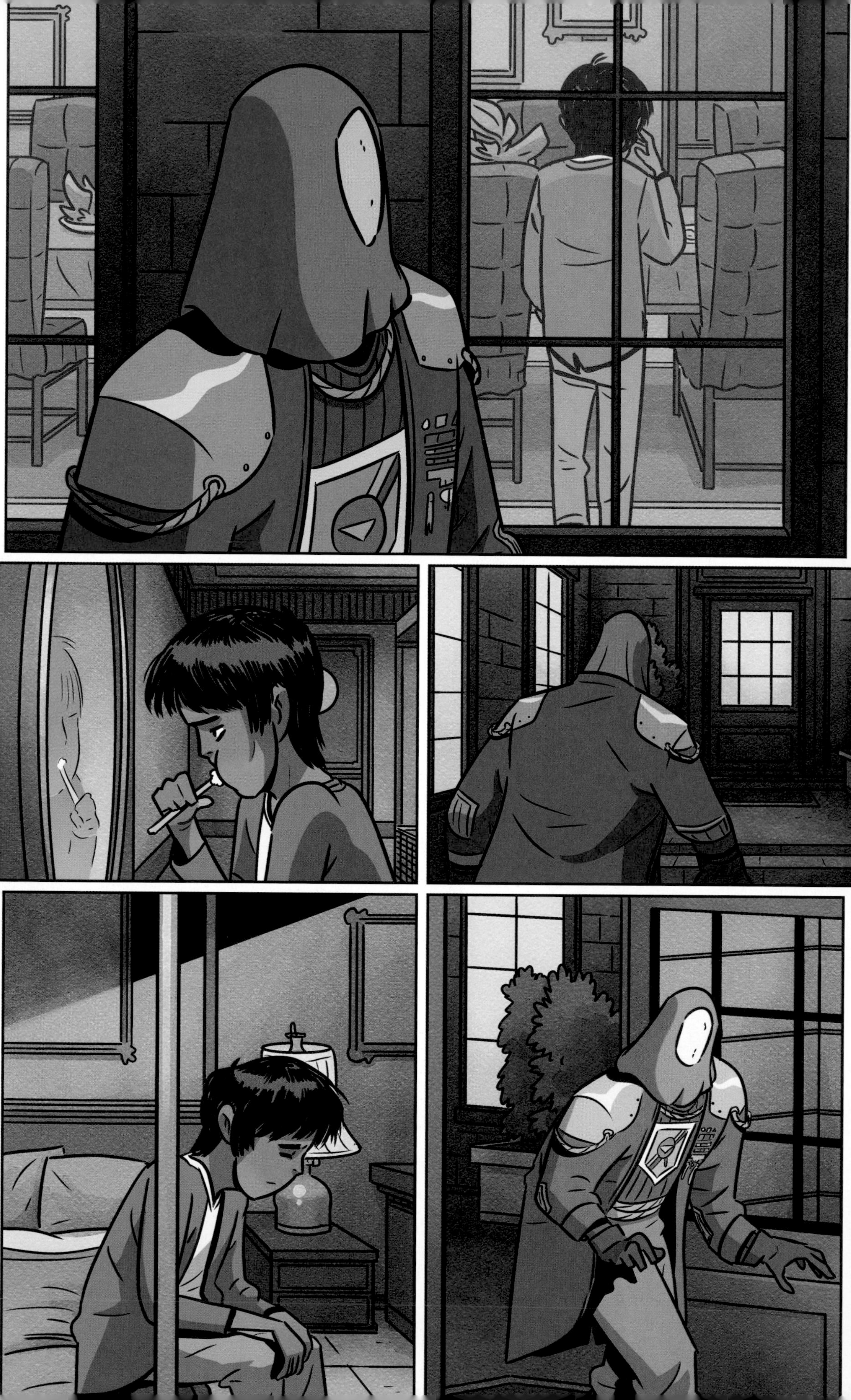

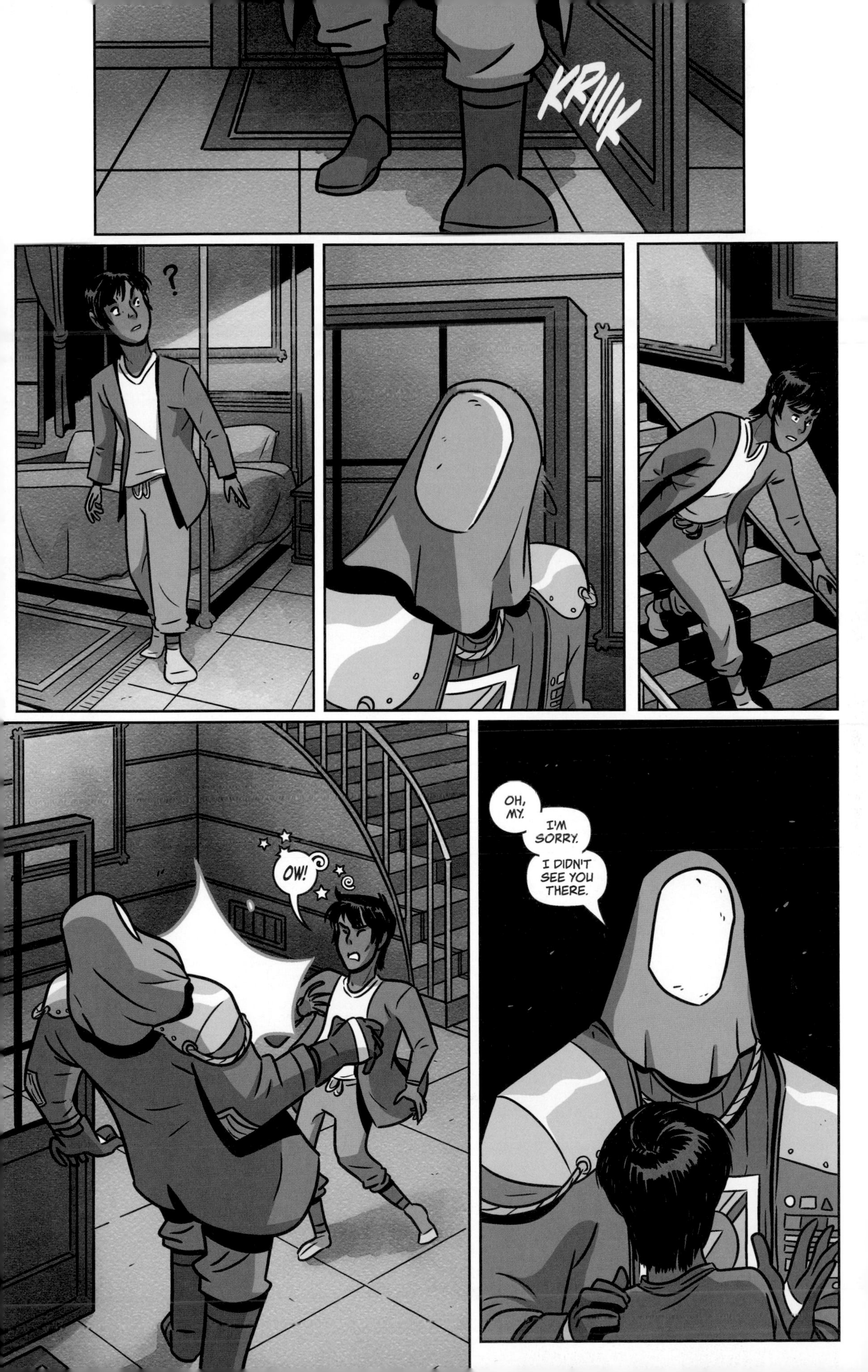
KRIIIK
?
OW!
OH, MY.
I'M SORRY.
I DIDN'T SEE YOU THERE.

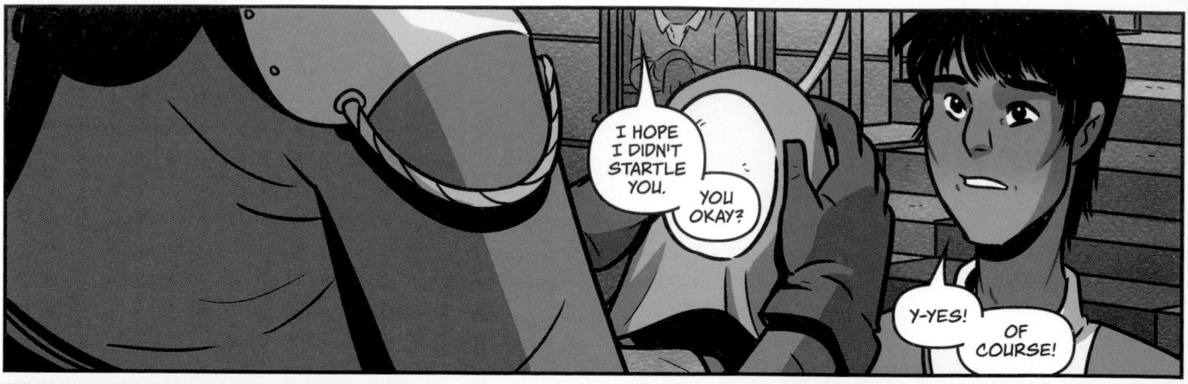
I HOPE I DIDN'T STARTLE YOU.
YOU OKAY?
Y-YES!
OF COURSE!
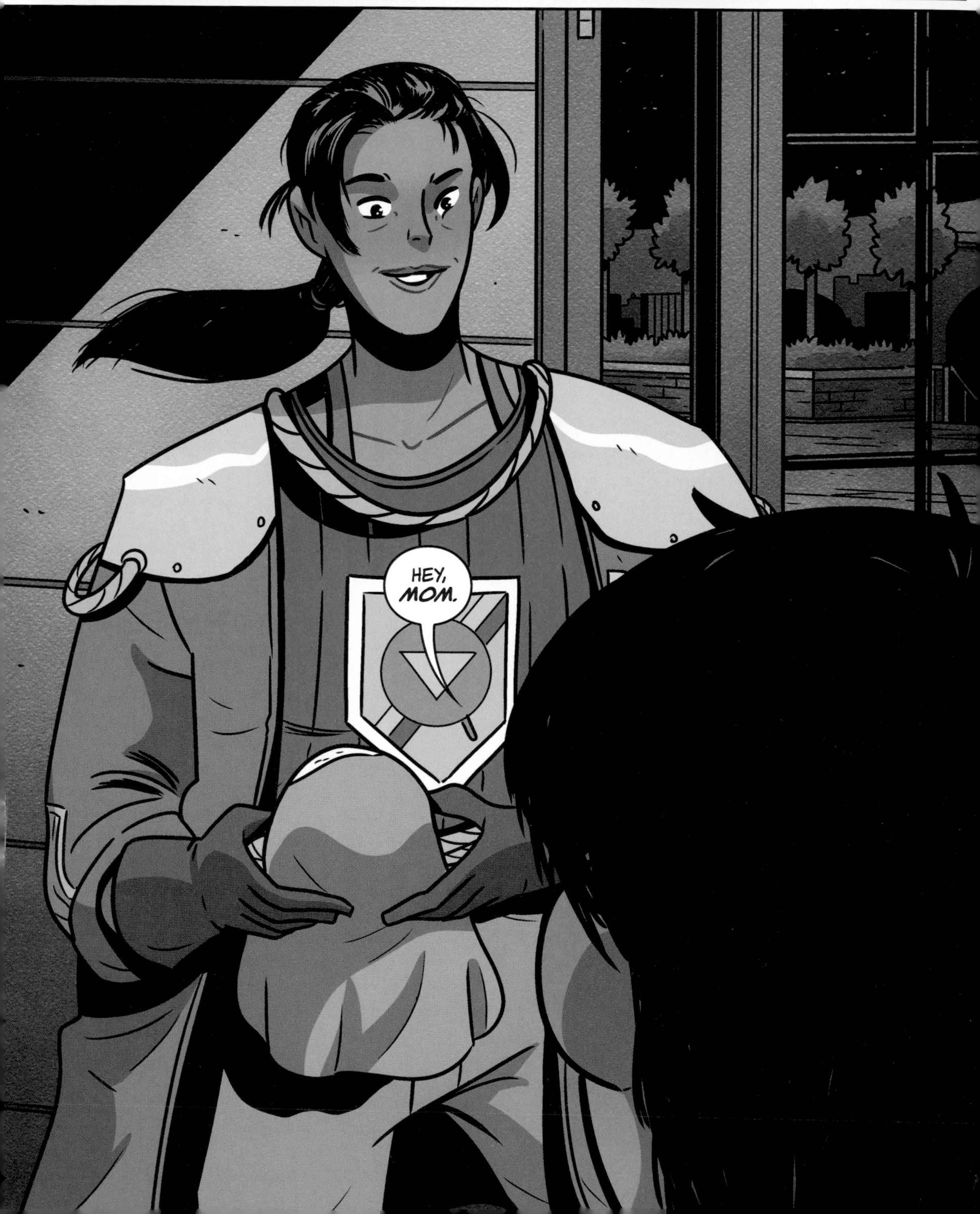
HEY, MOM.

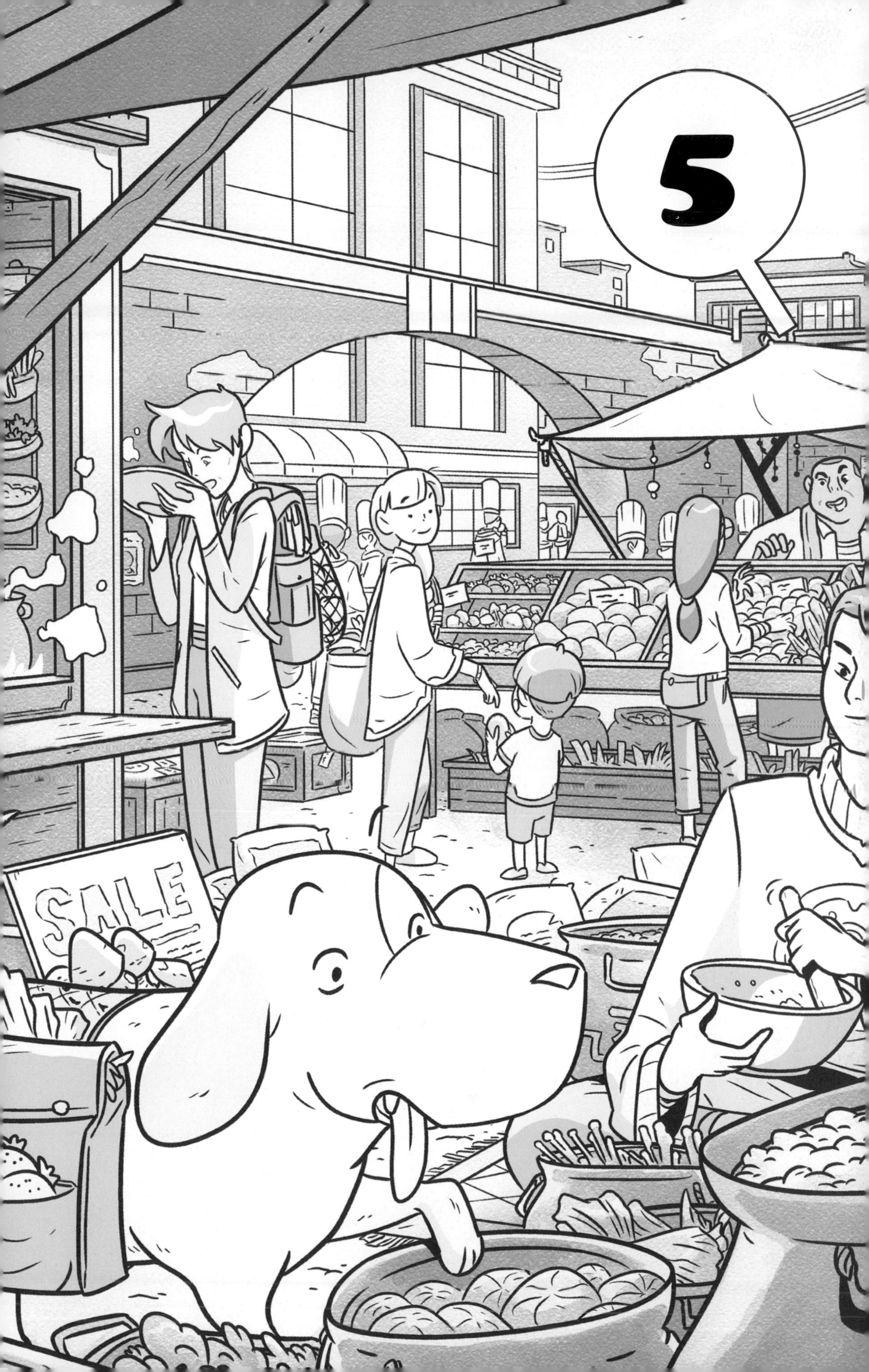
5
SALE

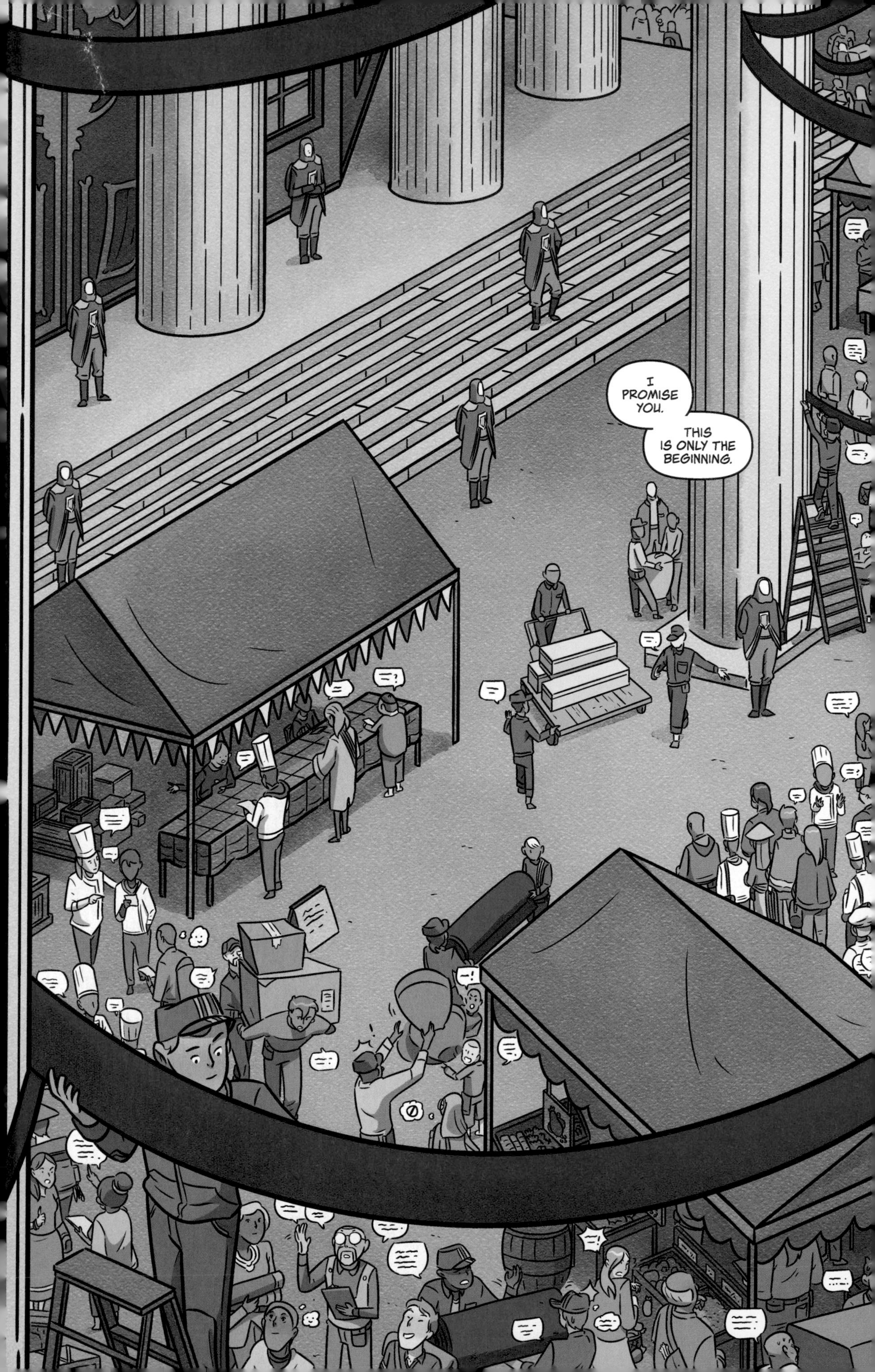
I PROMISE YOU.
THIS IS ONLY THE BEGINNING.

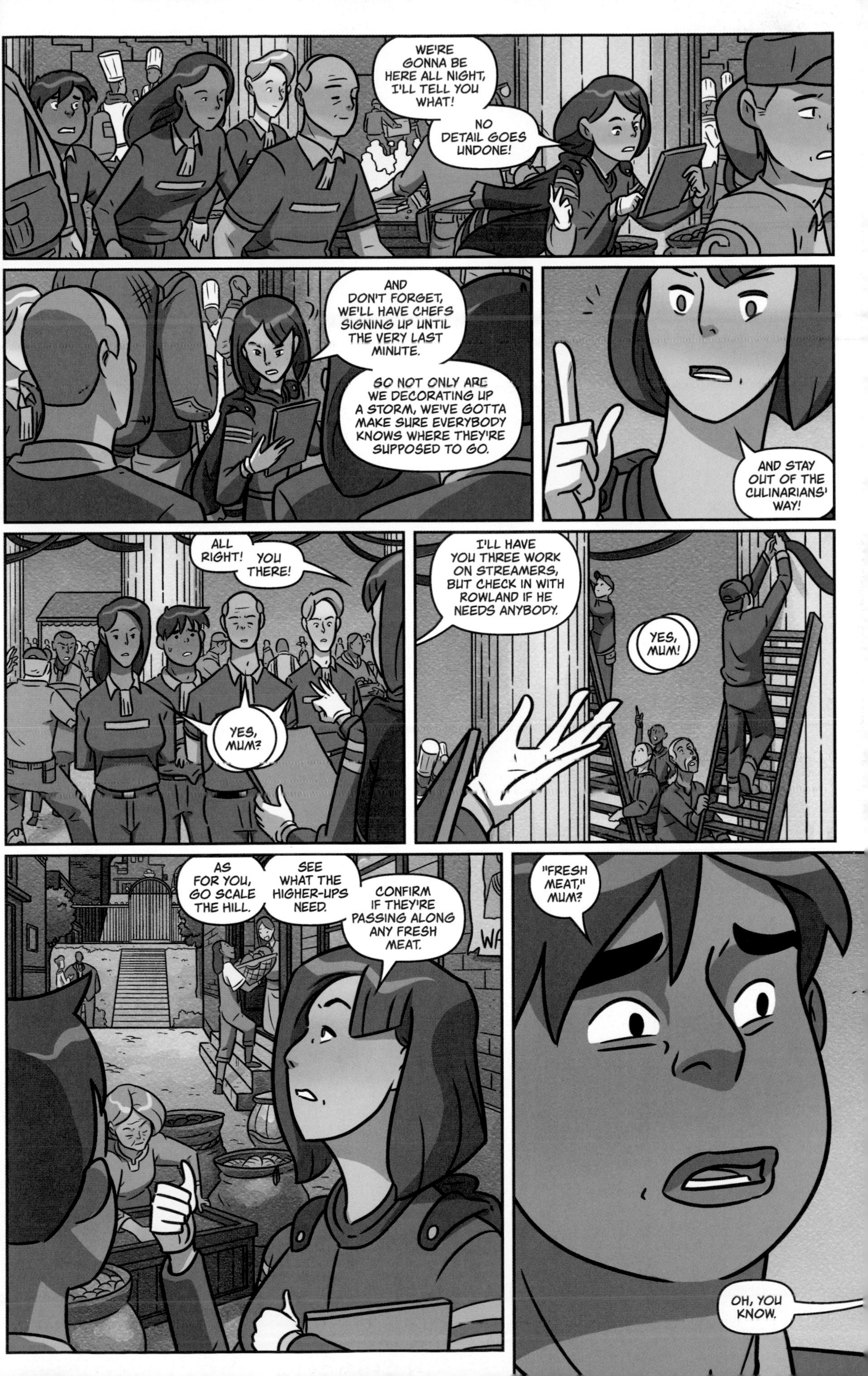

WE'RE GONNA BE HERE ALL NIGHT, I'LL TELL YOU WHAT!
NO DETAIL GOES UNDONE!
AND DON'T FORGET, WE'LL HAVE CHEFS SIGNING UP UNTIL THE VERY LAST MINUTE.
SO NOT ONLY ARE WE DECORATING UP A STORM, WE'VE GOTTA MAKE SURE EVERYBODY KNOWS WHERE THEY'RE SUPPOSED TO GO.
AND STAY OUT OF THE CULINARIANS' WAY!
ALL RIGHT!
YOU THERE!
YES, MUM?
I'LL HAVE YOU THREE WORK ON STREAMERS, BUT CHECK IN WITH ROWLAND IF HE NEEDS ANYBODY.
YES, MUM!
AS FOR YOU, GO SCALE THE HILL.
SEE WHAT THE HIGHER-UPS NEED.
CONFIRM IF THEY'RE PASSING ALONG ANY FRESH MEAT.
"FRESH MEAT," MUM?
OH, YOU KNOW.

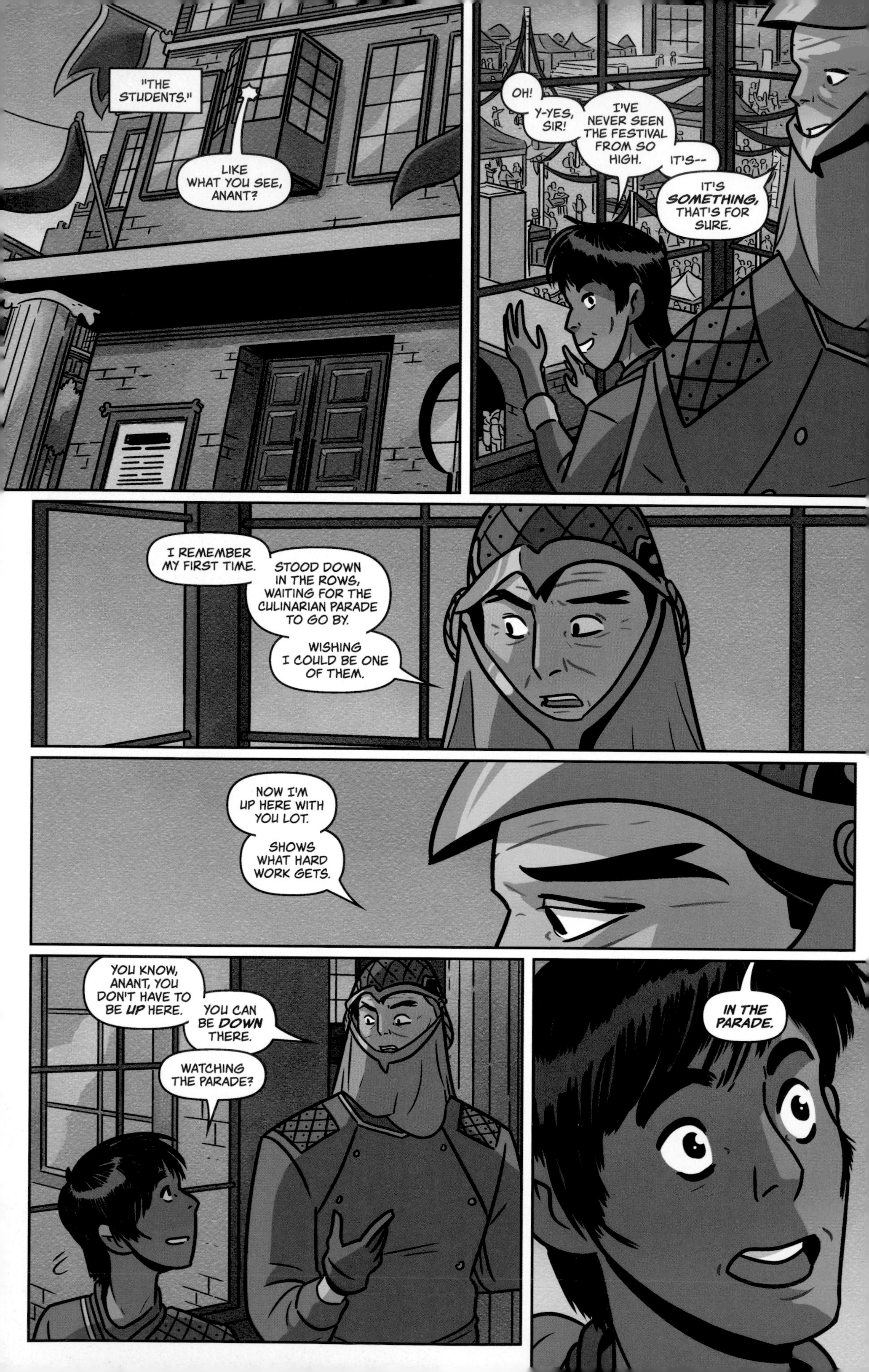
"THE STUDENTS."
LIKE WHAT YOU SEE, ANANT?
OH!
Y-YES, SIR!
I'VE NEVER SEEN THE FESTIVAL FROM SO HIGH.
IT'S--
IT'S *SOMETHING,* THAT'S FOR SURE.
I REMEMBER MY FIRST TIME.
STOOD DOWN IN THE ROWS, WAITING FOR THE CULINARIAN PARADE TO GO BY.
WISHING I COULD BE ONE OF THEM.
NOW I'M UP HERE WITH YOU LOT.
SHOWS WHAT HARD WORK GETS.
YOU KNOW, ANANT, YOU DON'T HAVE TO BE *UP* HERE.
YOU CAN BE *DOWN* THERE.
WATCHING THE PARADE?
IN THE PARADE.

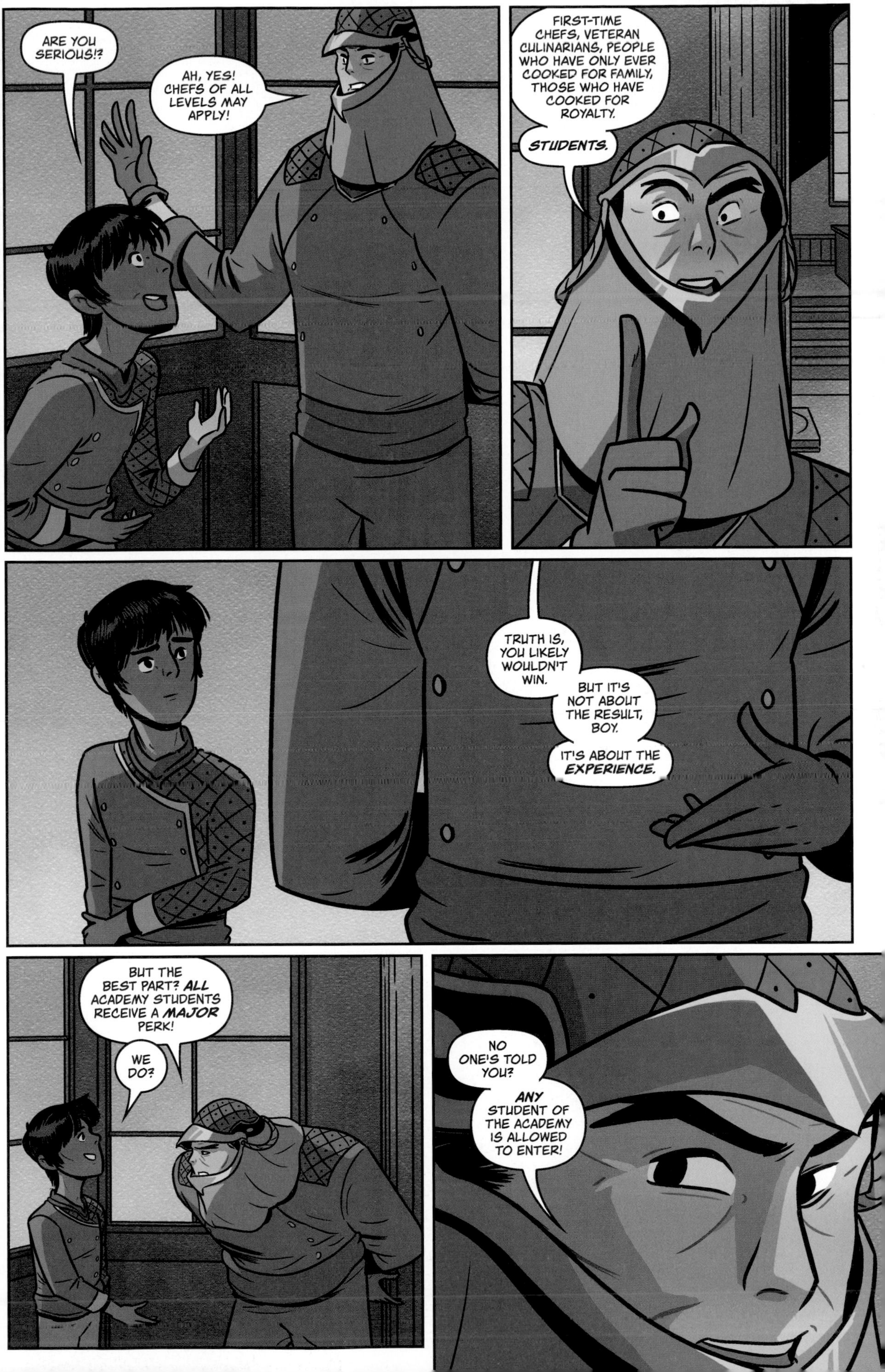
ARE YOU SERIOUS!?
AH, YES! CHEFS OF ALL LEVELS MAY APPLY!
FIRST-TIME CHEFS, VETERAN CULINARIANS, PEOPLE WHO HAVE ONLY EVER COOKED FOR FAMILY, THOSE WHO HAVE COOKED FOR ROYALTY.
STUDENTS.
TRUTH IS, YOU LIKELY WOULDN'T WIN.
BUT IT'S NOT ABOUT THE RESULT, BOY.
IT'S ABOUT THE EXPERIENCE.
BUT THE BEST PART? ALL ACADEMY STUDENTS RECEIVE A MAJOR PERK!
WE DO?
NO ONE'S TOLD YOU?
ANY STUDENT OF THE ACADEMY IS ALLOWED TO ENTER!

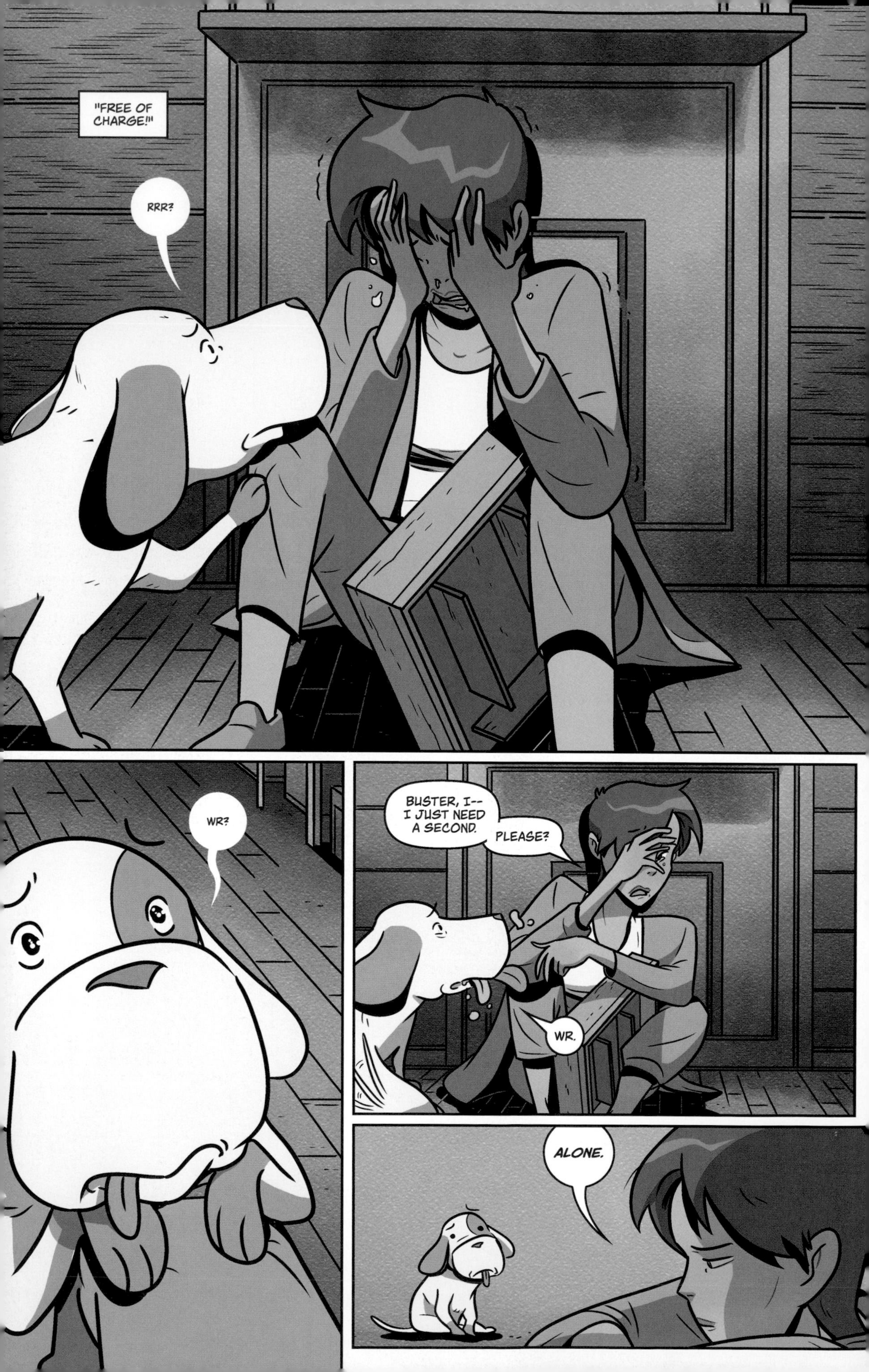
"FREE OF CHARGE!"
RRR?
WR?
BUSTER, I-- I JUST NEED A SECOND.
PLEASE?
WR.
ALONE.

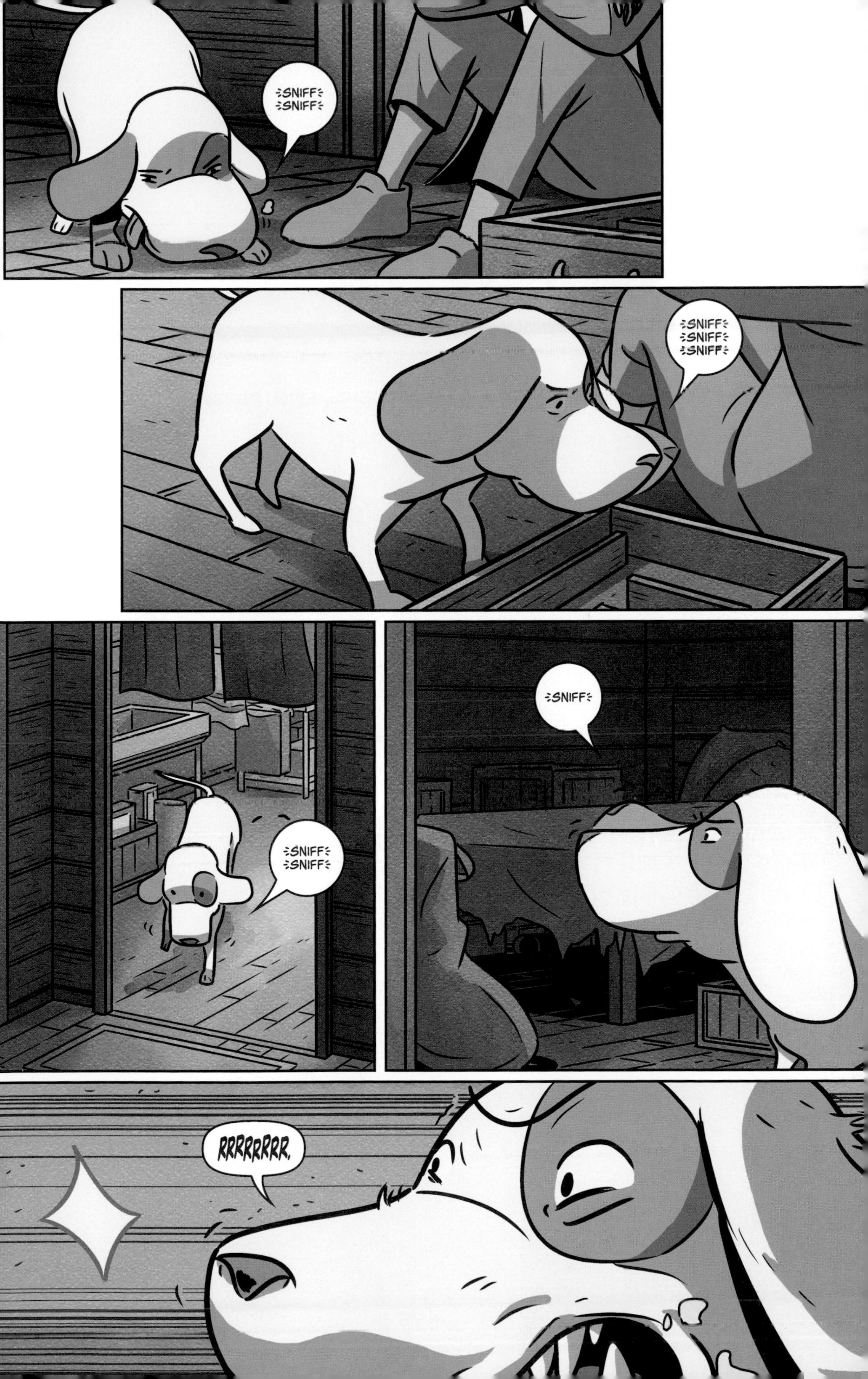
SNIFF
SNIFF
SNIFF
SNIFF
SNIFF
SNIFF
SNIFF
SNIFF
RRRRRRRR.

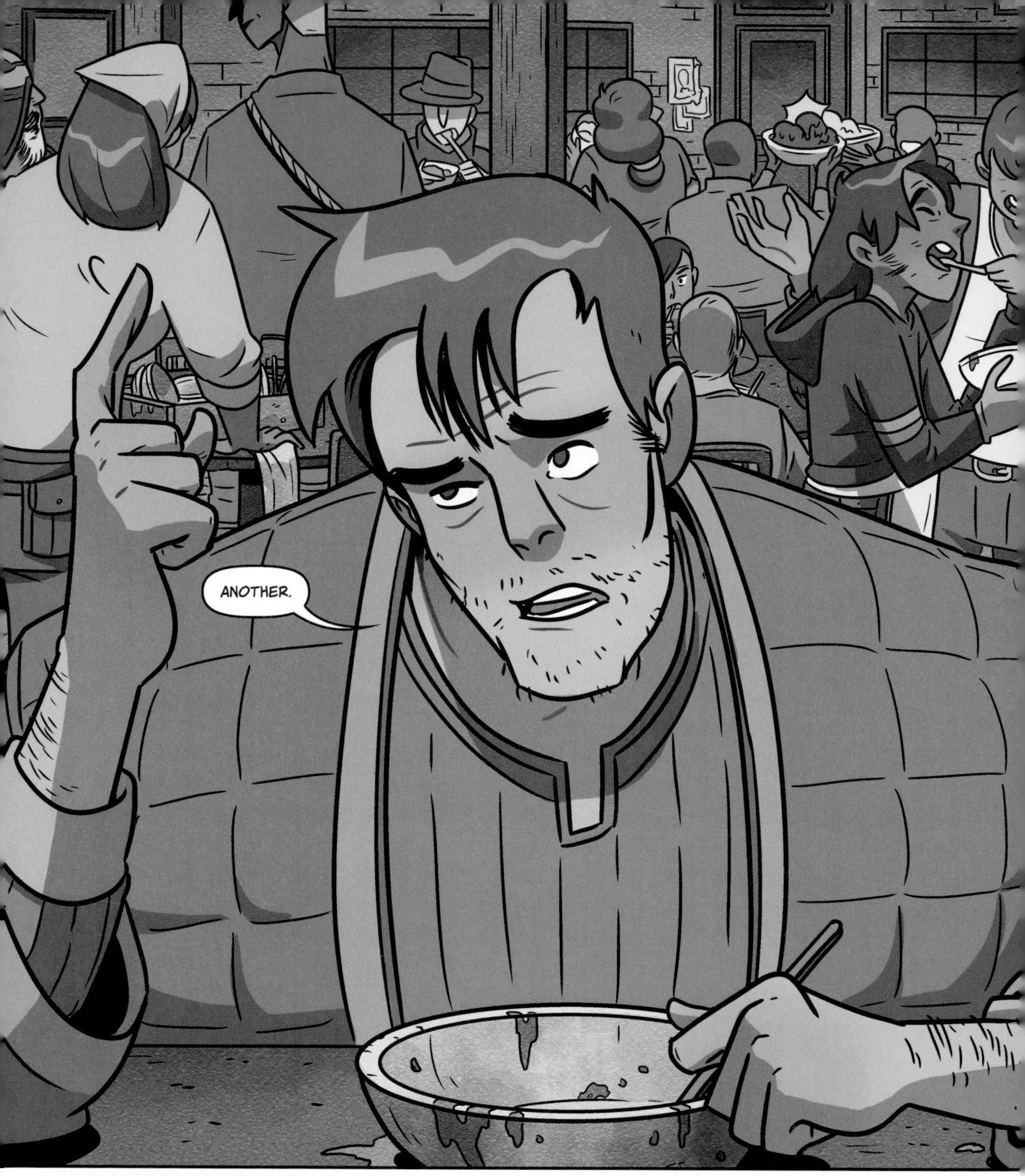
ANOTHER.

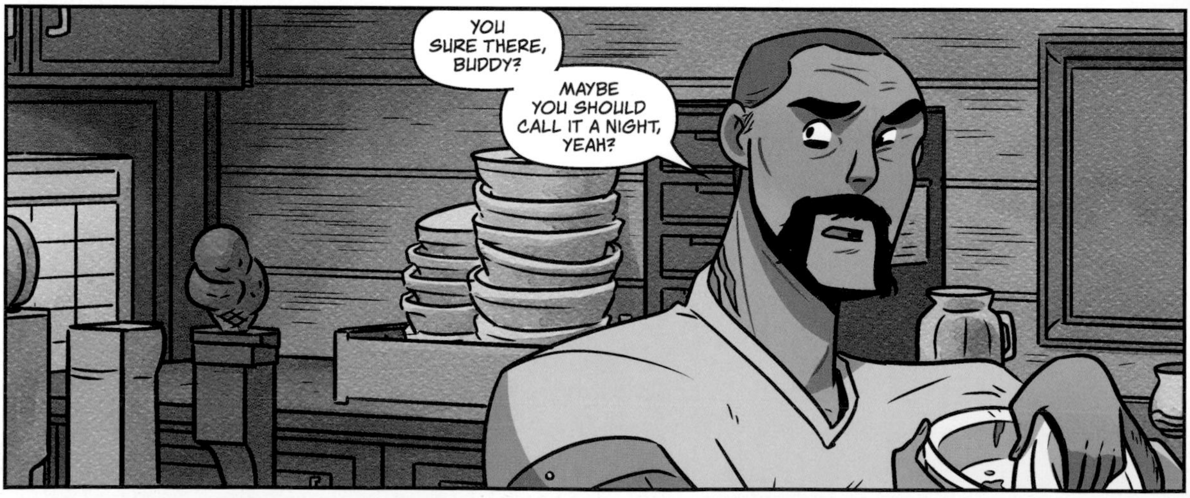
YOU SURE THERE, BUDDY?
MAYBE YOU SHOULD CALL IT A NIGHT, YEAH?

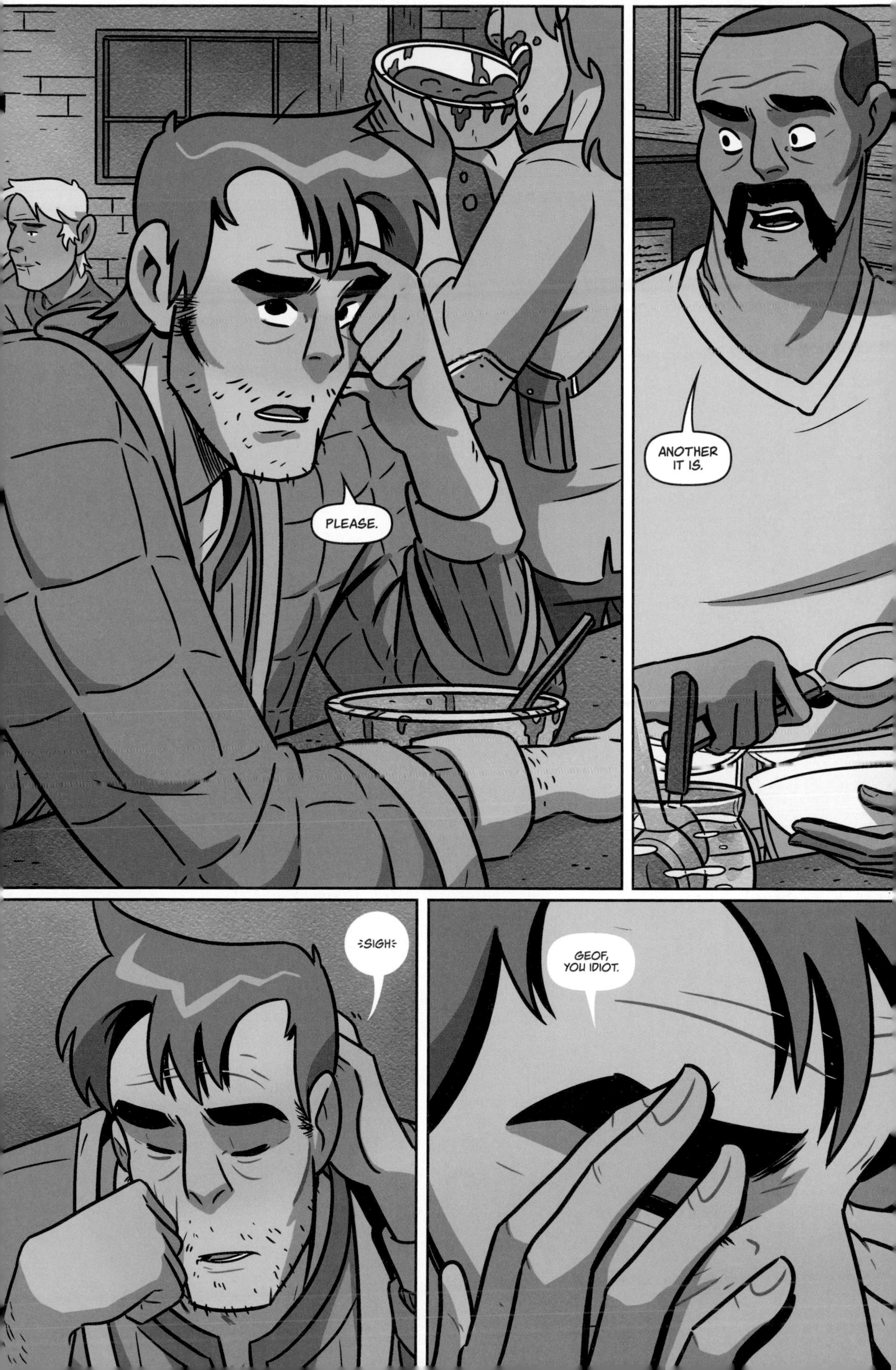
PLEASE.
ANOTHER IT IS.
=SIGH=
GEOF, YOU IDIOT.

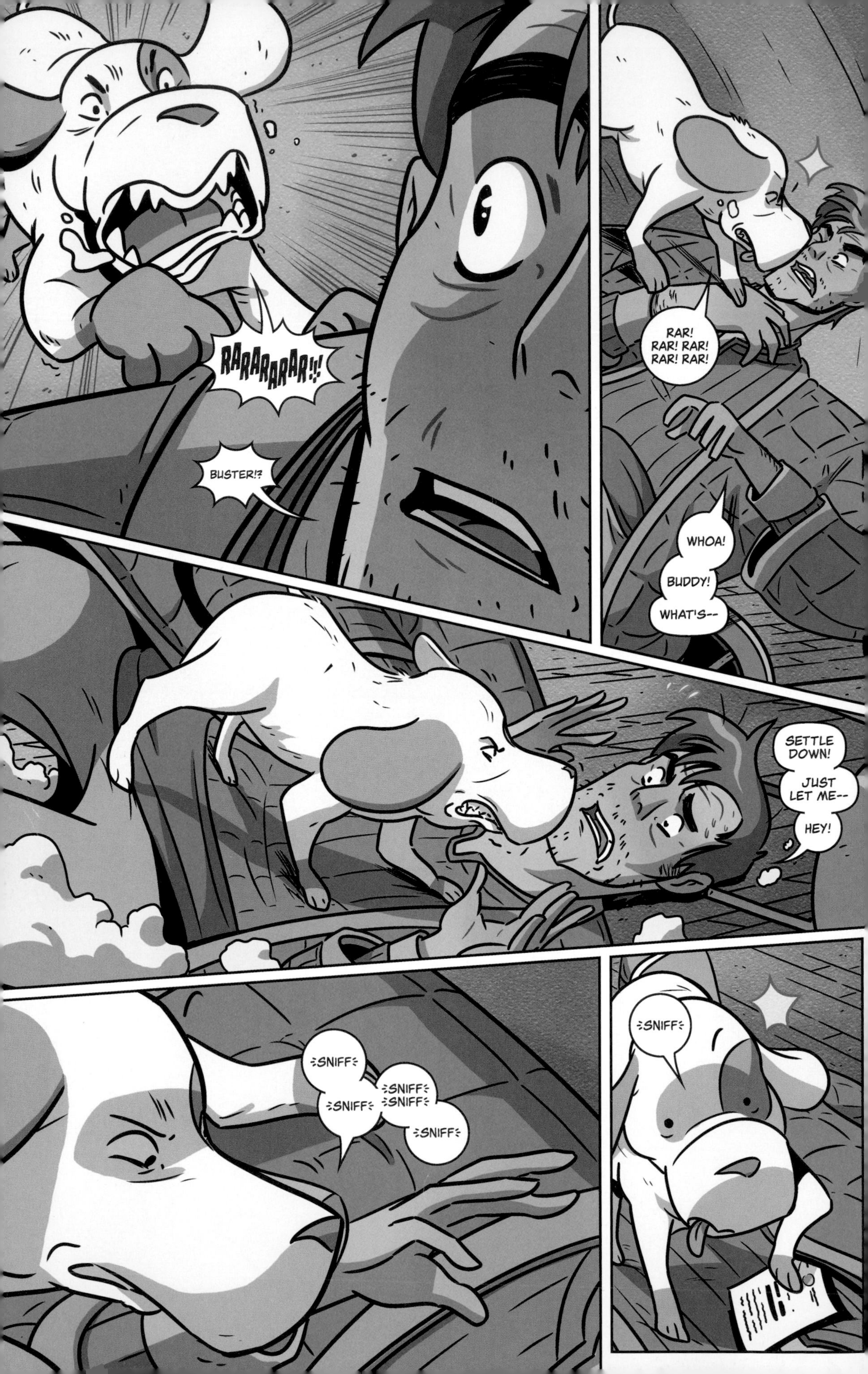
RARARARAR!!!
BUSTER!?
RAR! RAR! RAR! RAR! RAR!
WHOA!
BUDDY!
WHAT'S--
SETTLE DOWN!
JUST LET ME--
HEY!
SNIFF
SNIFF
SNIFF
SNIFF
SNIFF
SNIFF

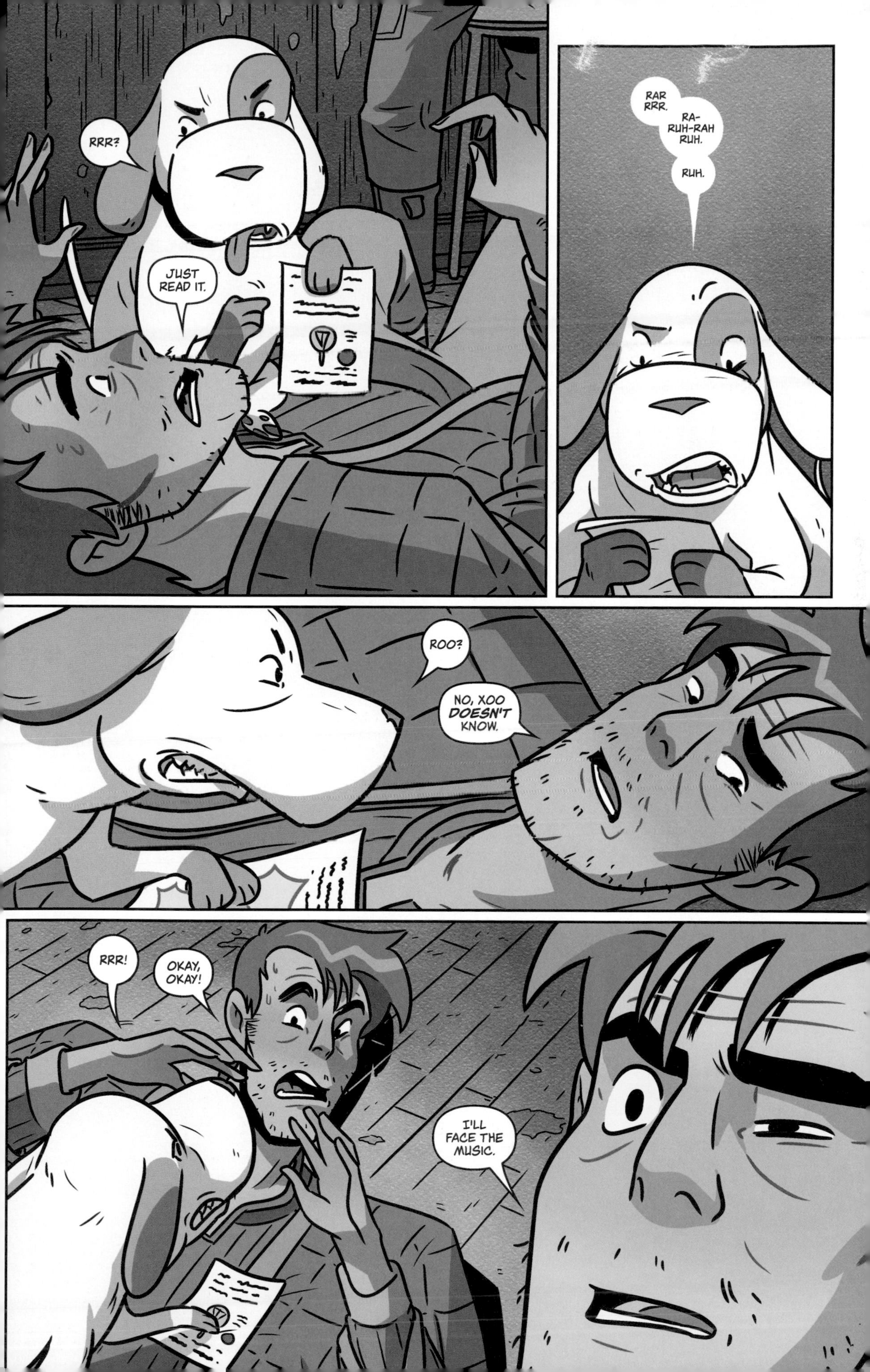
RRR?
JUST READ IT.
RAR RRR.
RA-RUH-RAH RUH.
RUH.
ROO?
NO, XOO DOESN'T KNOW.
RRR!
OKAY, OKAY!
I'LL FACE THE MUSIC.

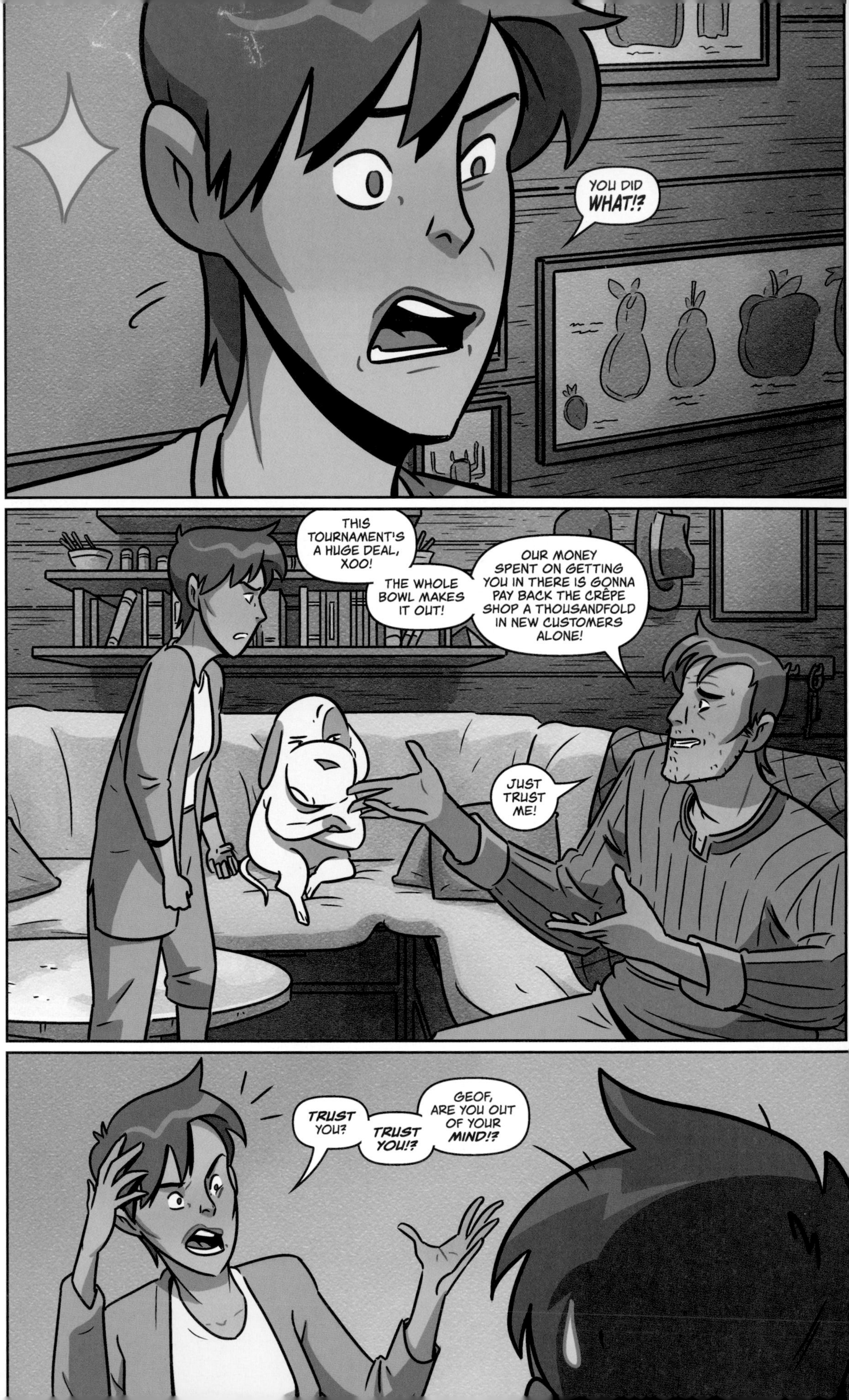
YOU DID WHAT!?
THIS TOURNAMENT'S A HUGE DEAL, XOO!
THE WHOLE BOWL MAKES IT OUT!
OUR MONEY SPENT ON GETTING YOU IN THERE IS GONNA PAY BACK THE CRÊPE SHOP A THOUSANDFOLD IN NEW CUSTOMERS ALONE!
JUST TRUST ME!
TRUST YOU?
TRUST YOU!?
GEOF, ARE YOU OUT OF YOUR MIND!?

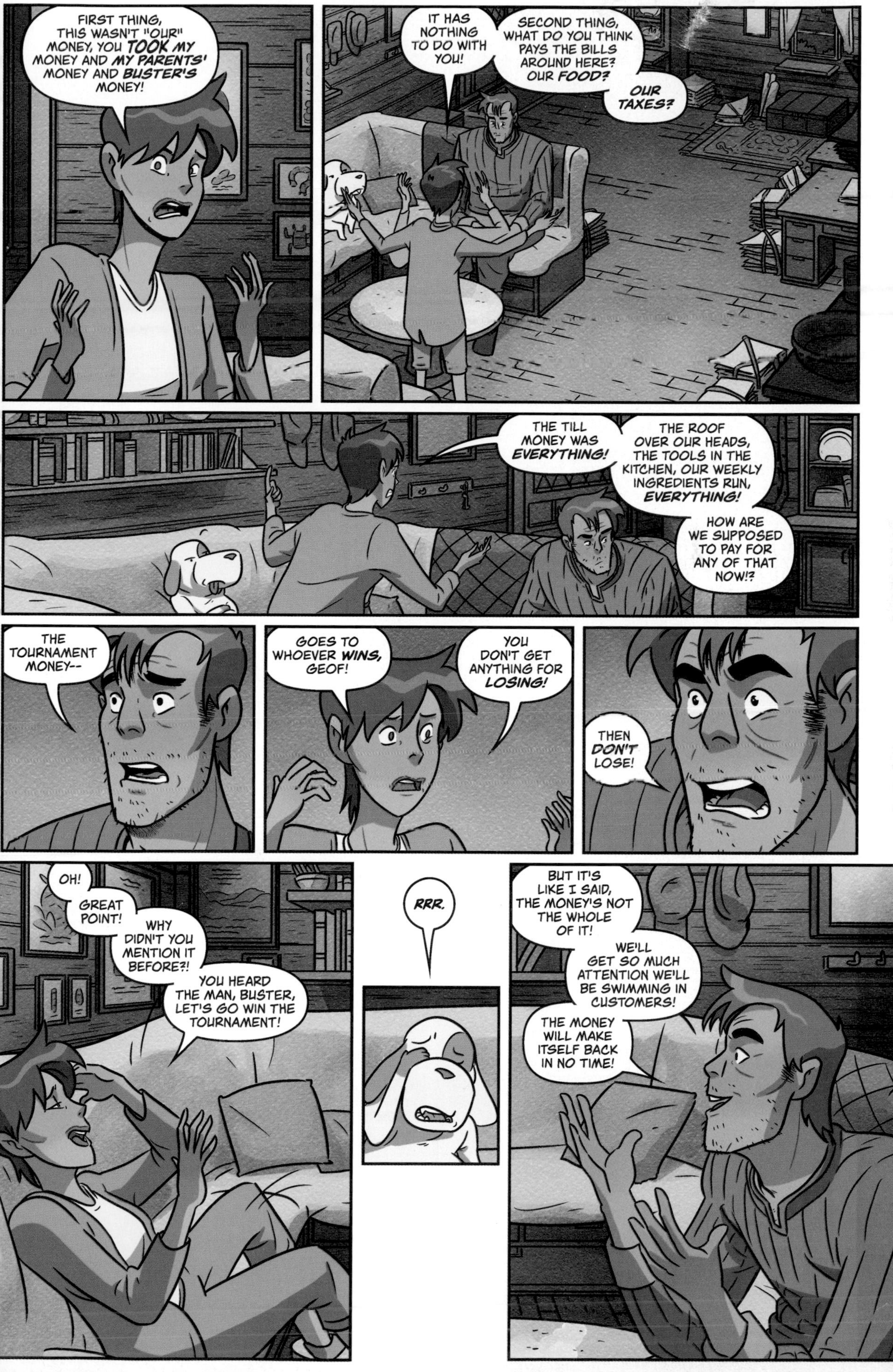
FIRST THING, THIS WASN'T "OUR" MONEY, YOU TOOK MY MONEY AND MY PARENTS' MONEY AND BUSTER'S MONEY!
IT HAS NOTHING TO DO WITH YOU!
SECOND THING, WHAT DO YOU THINK PAYS THE BILLS AROUND HERE? OUR FOOD?
OUR TAXES?
THE TILL MONEY WAS EVERYTHING!
THE ROOF OVER OUR HEADS, THE TOOLS IN THE KITCHEN, OUR WEEKLY INGREDIENTS RUN, EVERYTHING!
HOW ARE WE SUPPOSED TO PAY FOR ANY OF THAT NOW!?
THE TOURNAMENT MONEY--
GOES TO WHOEVER WINS, GEOF!
YOU DON'T GET ANYTHING FOR LOSING!
THEN DON'T LOSE!
OH!
GREAT POINT!
WHY DIDN'T YOU MENTION IT BEFORE?!
YOU HEARD THE MAN, BUSTER, LET'S GO WIN THE TOURNAMENT!
RRR.
BUT IT'S LIKE I SAID, THE MONEY'S NOT THE WHOLE OF IT!
WE'LL GET SO MUCH ATTENTION WE'LL BE SWIMMING IN CUSTOMERS!
THE MONEY WILL MAKE ITSELF BACK IN NO TIME!

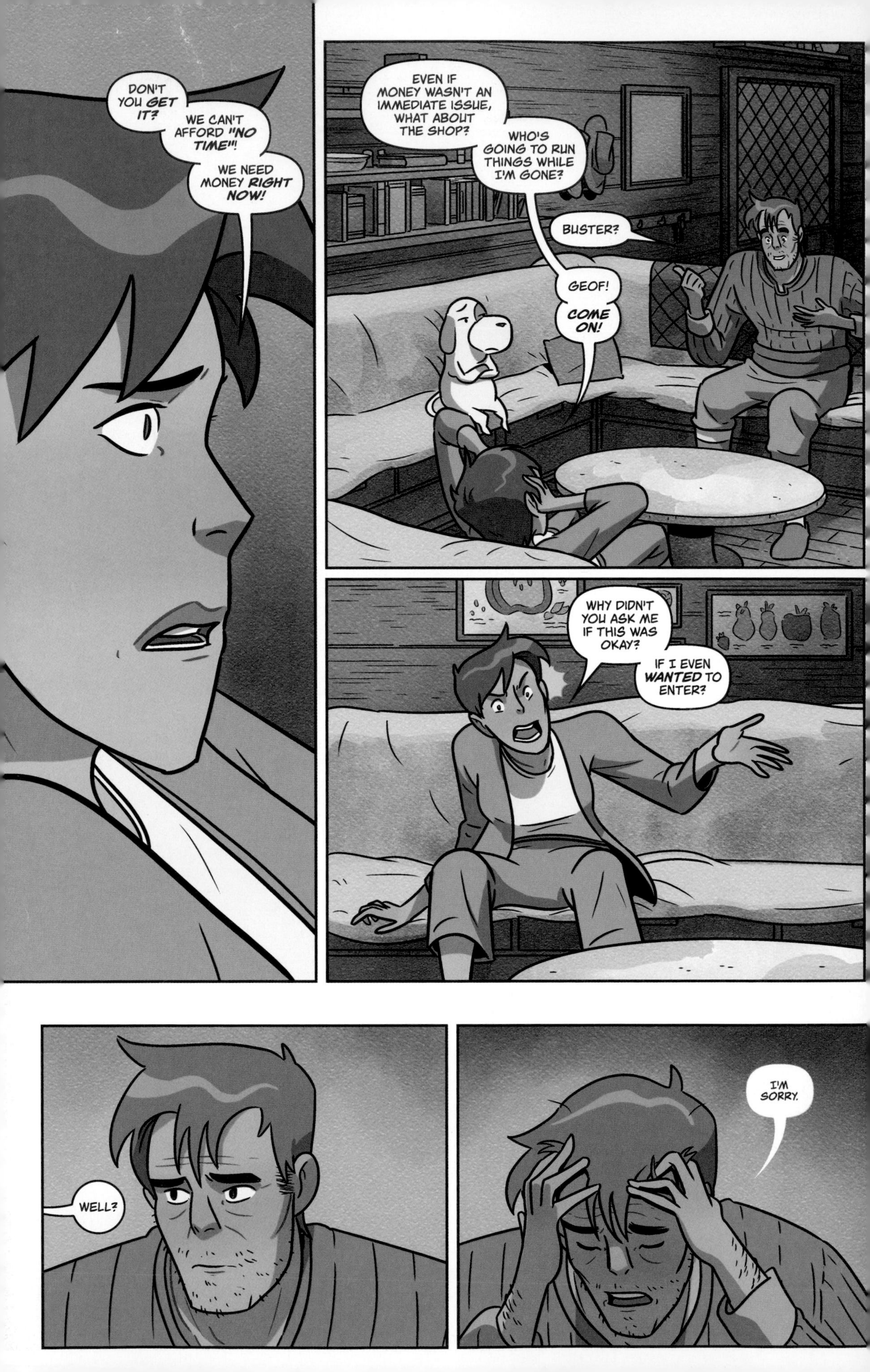
DON'T YOU GET IT?
WE CAN'T AFFORD "NO TIME"!
WE NEED MONEY RIGHT NOW!
EVEN IF MONEY WASN'T AN IMMEDIATE ISSUE, WHAT ABOUT THE SHOP?
WHO'S GOING TO RUN THINGS WHILE I'M GONE?
BUSTER?
GEOF!
COME ON!
WHY DIDN'T YOU ASK ME IF THIS WAS OKAY?
IF I EVEN WANTED TO ENTER?
WELL?
I'M SORRY.

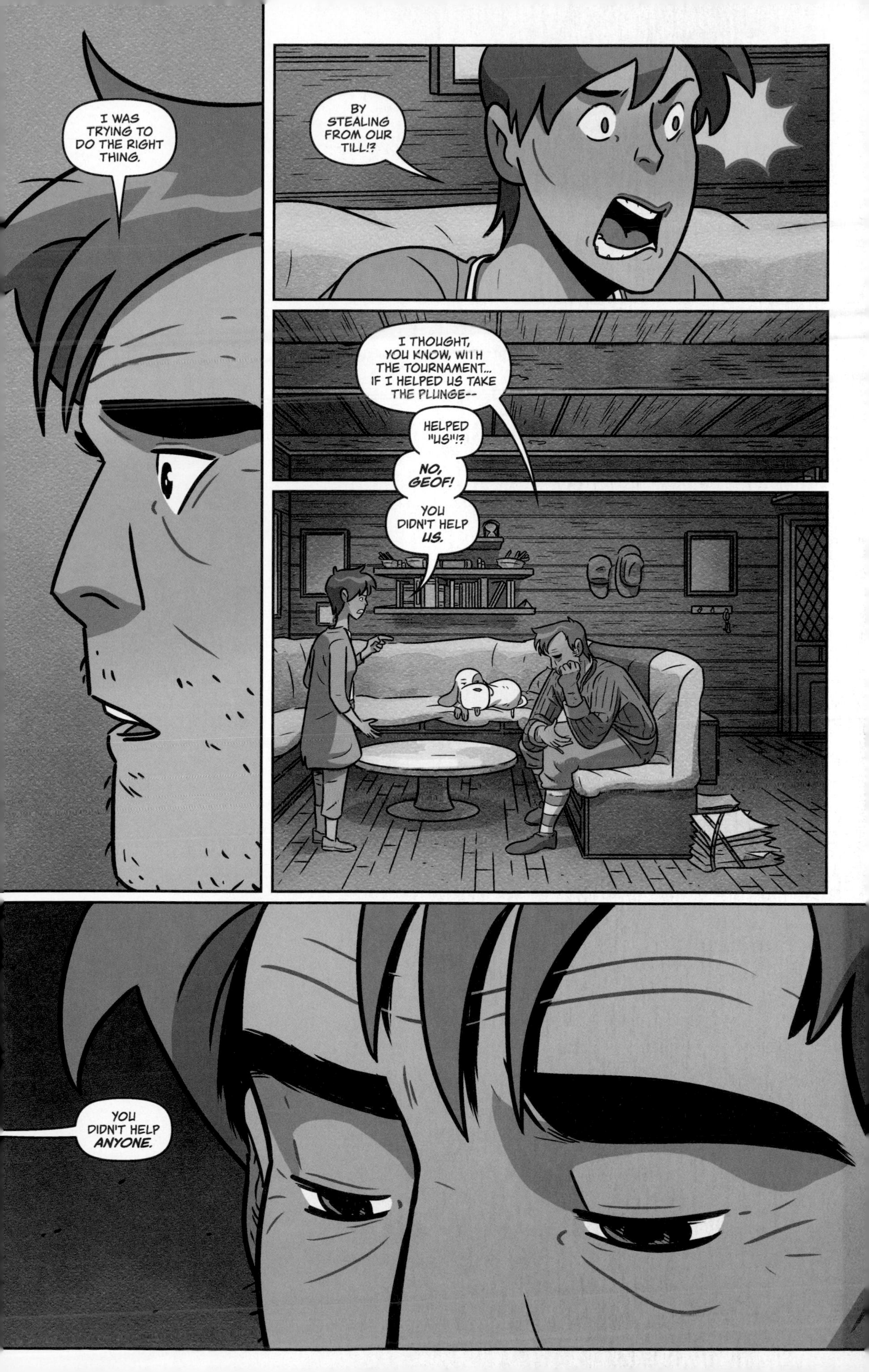
I WAS TRYING TO DO THE RIGHT THING.
BY STEALING FROM OUR TILL!?
I THOUGHT, YOU KNOW, WITH THE TOURNAMENT... IF I HELPED US TAKE THE PLUNGE--
HELPED "US"!?
NO, GEOF!
YOU DIDN'T HELP US.
YOU DIDN'T HELP ANYONE.

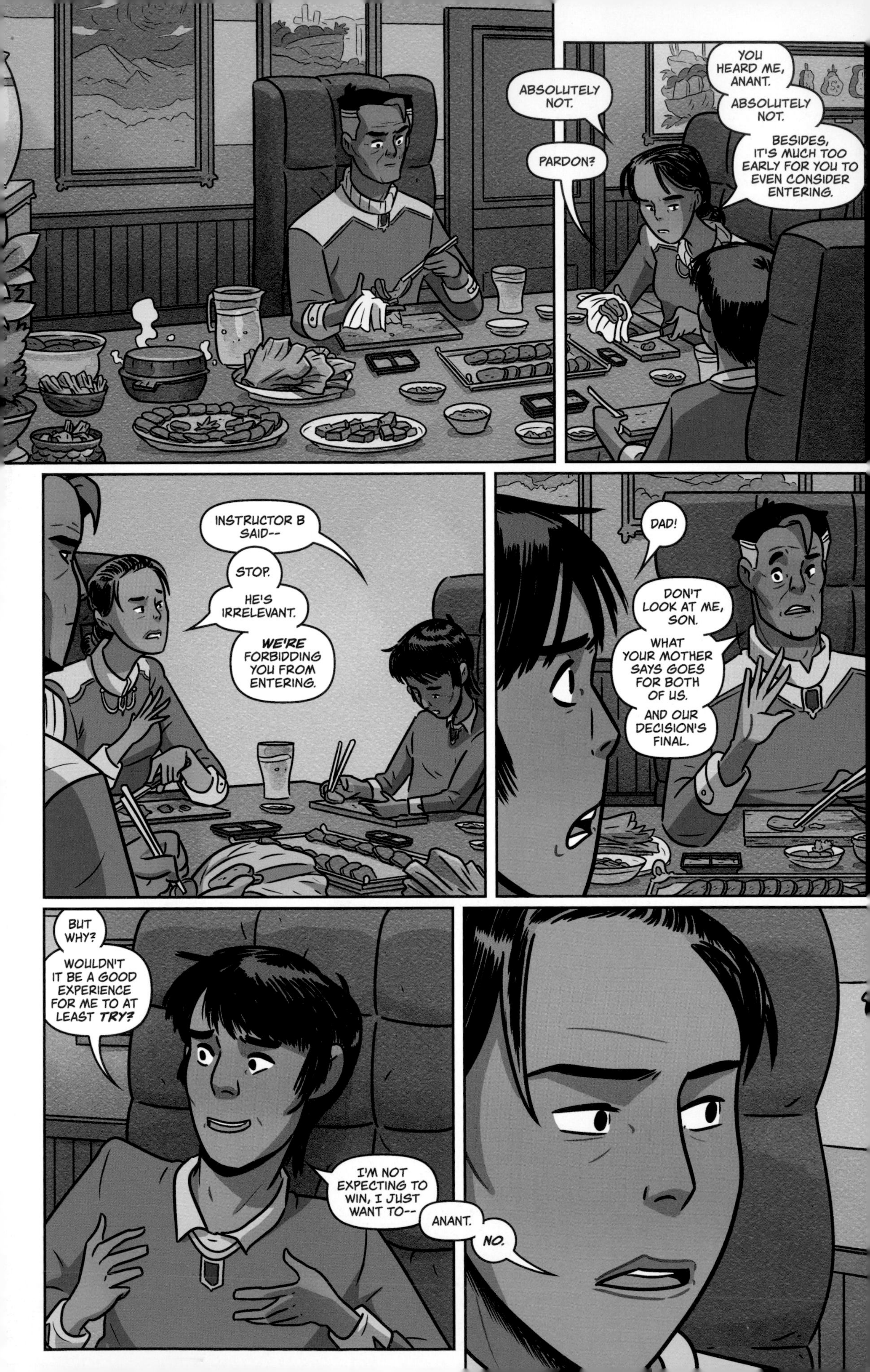
ABSOLUTELY NOT.
PARDON?
YOU HEARD ME, ANANT.
ABSOLUTELY NOT.
BESIDES, IT'S MUCH TOO EARLY FOR YOU TO EVEN CONSIDER ENTERING.
INSTRUCTOR B SAID--
STOP.
HE'S IRRELEVANT.
WE'RE FORBIDDING YOU FROM ENTERING.
DAD!
DON'T LOOK AT ME, SON.
WHAT YOUR MOTHER SAYS GOES FOR BOTH OF US.
AND OUR DECISION'S FINAL.
BUT WHY?
WOULDN'T IT BE A GOOD EXPERIENCE FOR ME TO AT LEAST *TRY?*
I'M NOT EXPECTING TO WIN, I JUST WANT TO--
ANANT.
NO.

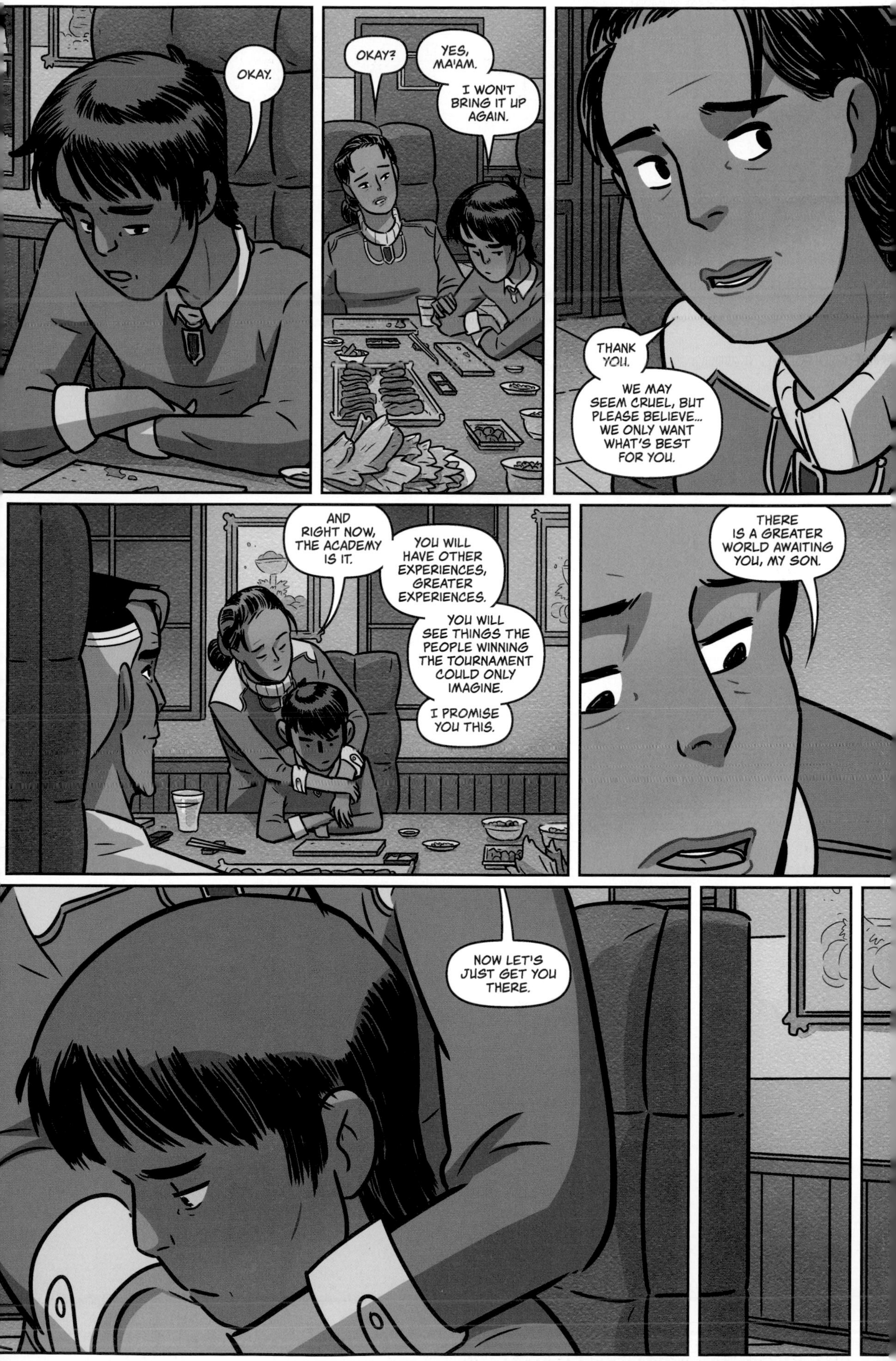
OKAY.
OKAY?
YES, MA'AM.
I WON'T BRING IT UP AGAIN.
THANK YOU.
WE MAY SEEM CRUEL, BUT PLEASE BELIEVE... WE ONLY WANT WHAT'S BEST FOR YOU.
AND RIGHT NOW, THE ACADEMY IS IT.
YOU WILL HAVE OTHER EXPERIENCES, GREATER EXPERIENCES.
YOU WILL SEE THINGS THE PEOPLE WINNING THE TOURNAMENT COULD ONLY IMAGINE.
I PROMISE YOU THIS.
THERE IS A GREATER WORLD AWAITING YOU, MY SON.
NOW LET'S JUST GET YOU THERE.

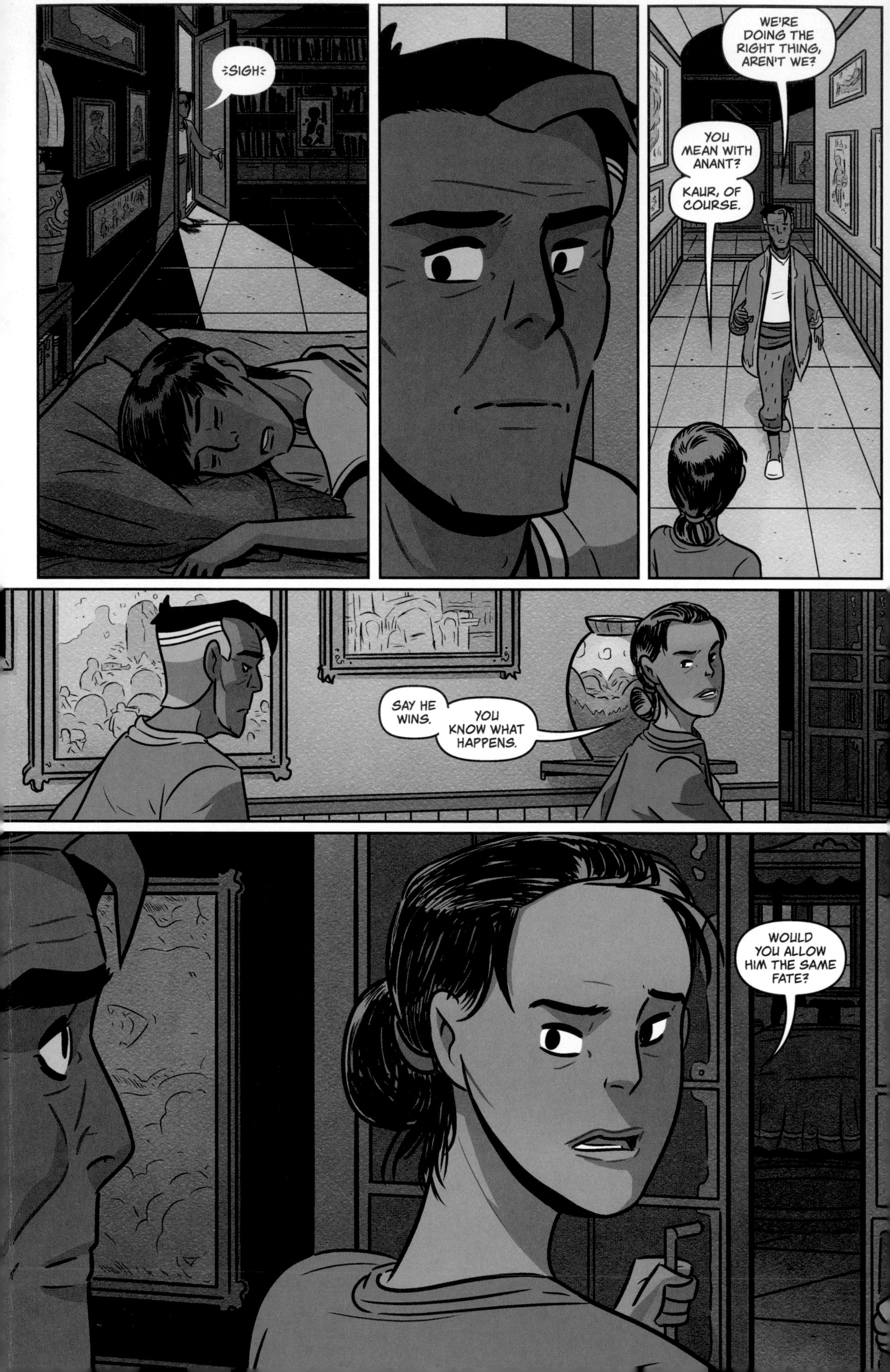

=SIGH=
WE'RE DOING THE RIGHT THING, AREN'T WE?
YOU MEAN WITH ANANT?
KAUR, OF COURSE.
SAY HE WINS.
YOU KNOW WHAT HAPPENS.
WOULD YOU ALLOW HIM THE SAME FATE?

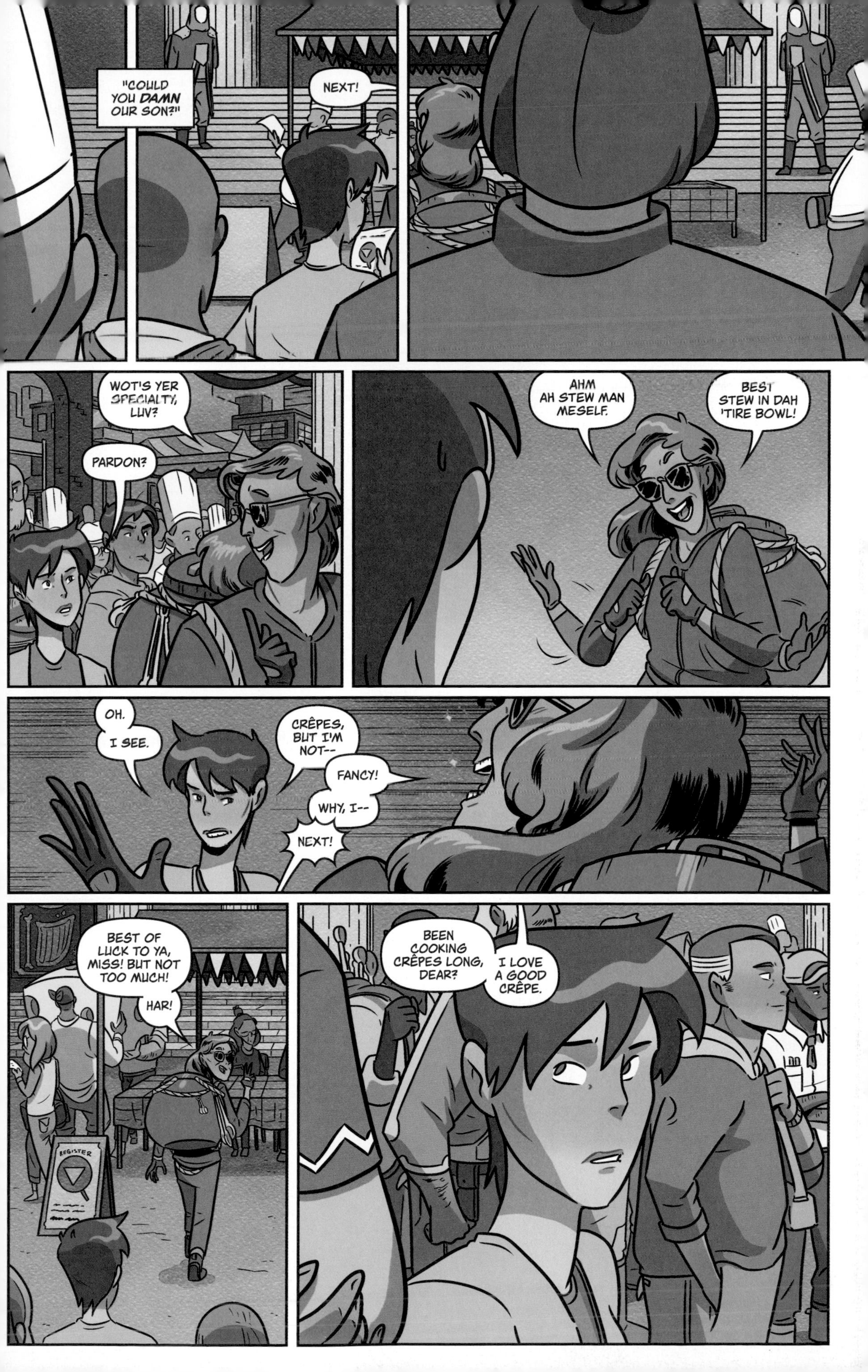
"COULD YOU *DAMN* OUR SON?!"
NEXT!
WOT'S YER SPECIALTY, LUV?
PARDON?
AHM AH STEW MAN MESELF.
BEST STEW IN DAH 'TIRE BOWL!
OH.
I SEE.
CRÊPES, BUT I'M NOT--
FANCY!
WHY, I--
NEXT!
BEST OF LUCK TO YA, MISS! BUT NOT TOO MUCH!
HAR!
REGISTER
BEEN COOKING CRÊPES LONG, DEAR?
I LOVE A GOOD CRÊPE.

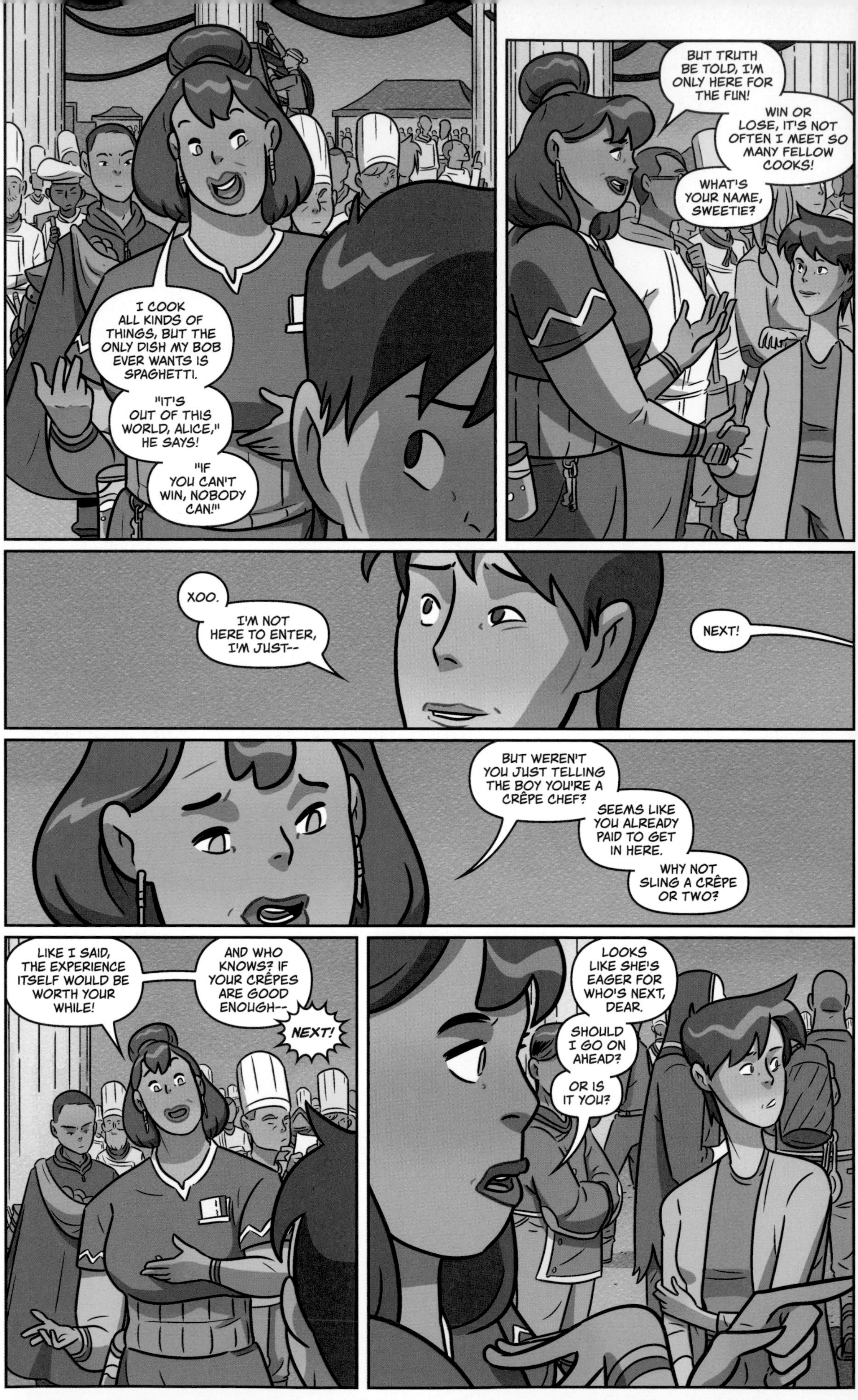
I COOK ALL KINDS OF THINGS, BUT THE ONLY DISH MY BOB EVER WANTS IS SPAGHETTI.
"IT'S OUT OF THIS WORLD, ALICE," HE SAYS!
"IF YOU CAN'T WIN, NOBODY CAN!"
BUT TRUTH BE TOLD, I'M ONLY HERE FOR THE FUN!
WIN OR LOSE, IT'S NOT OFTEN I MEET SO MANY FELLOW COOKS!
WHAT'S YOUR NAME, SWEETIE?
XOO.
I'M NOT HERE TO ENTER, I'M JUST--
NEXT!
BUT WEREN'T YOU JUST TELLING THE BOY YOU'RE A CRÊPE CHEF?
SEEMS LIKE YOU ALREADY PAID TO GET IN HERE.
WHY NOT SLING A CRÊPE OR TWO?
LIKE I SAID, THE EXPERIENCE ITSELF WOULD BE WORTH YOUR WHILE!
AND WHO KNOWS? IF YOUR CRÊPES ARE GOOD ENOUGH--
NEXT!
LOOKS LIKE SHE'S EAGER FOR WHO'S NEXT, DEAR.
SHOULD I GO ON AHEAD?
OR IS IT YOU?

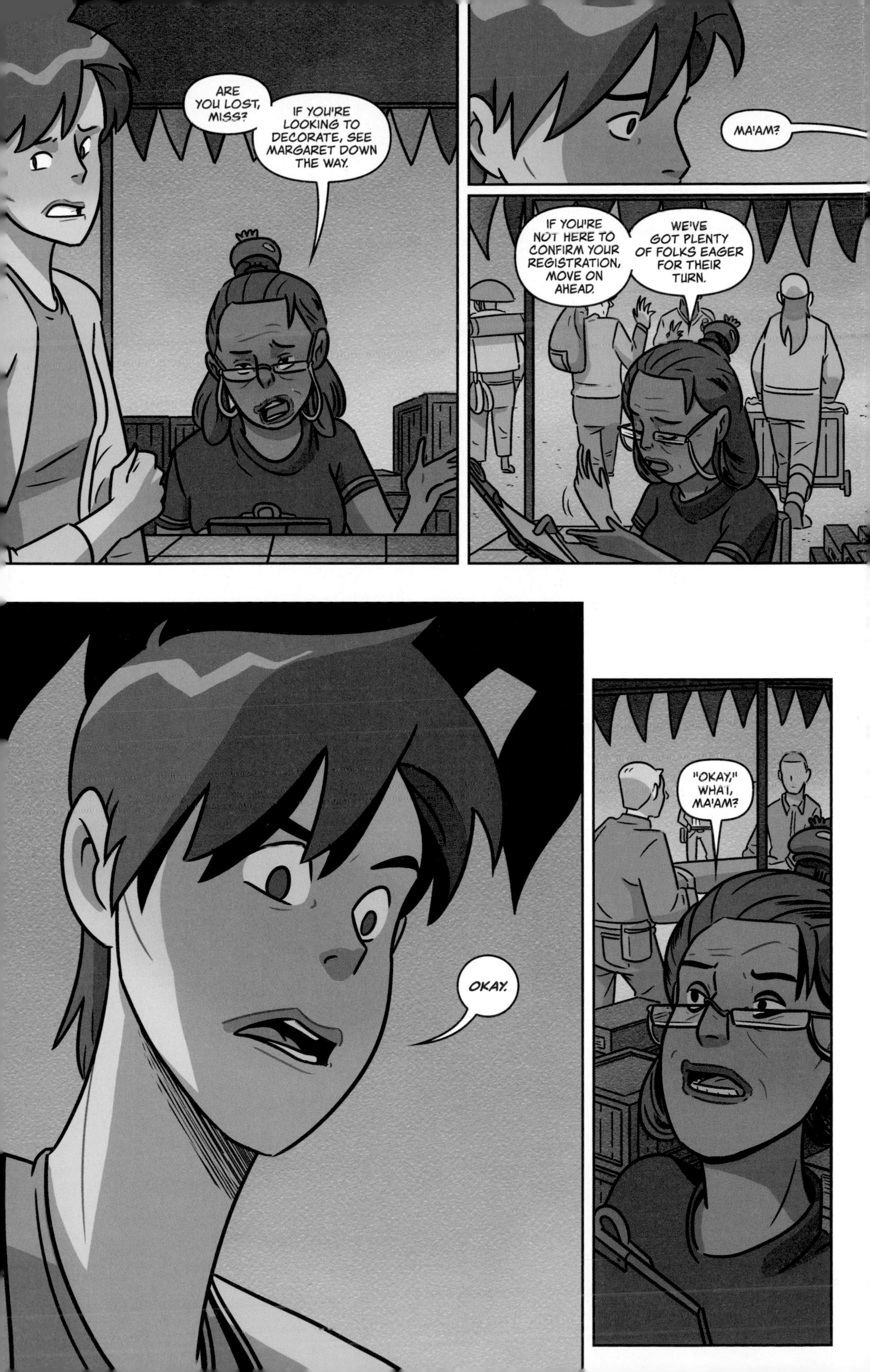
ARE YOU LOST, MISS?
IF YOU'RE LOOKING TO DECORATE, SEE MARGARET DOWN THE WAY.
MA'AM?
IF YOU'RE NOT HERE TO CONFIRM YOUR REGISTRATION, MOVE ON AHEAD.
WE'VE GOT PLENTY OF FOLKS EAGER FOR THEIR TURN.
OKAY.
"OKAY," WHAT, MA'AM?

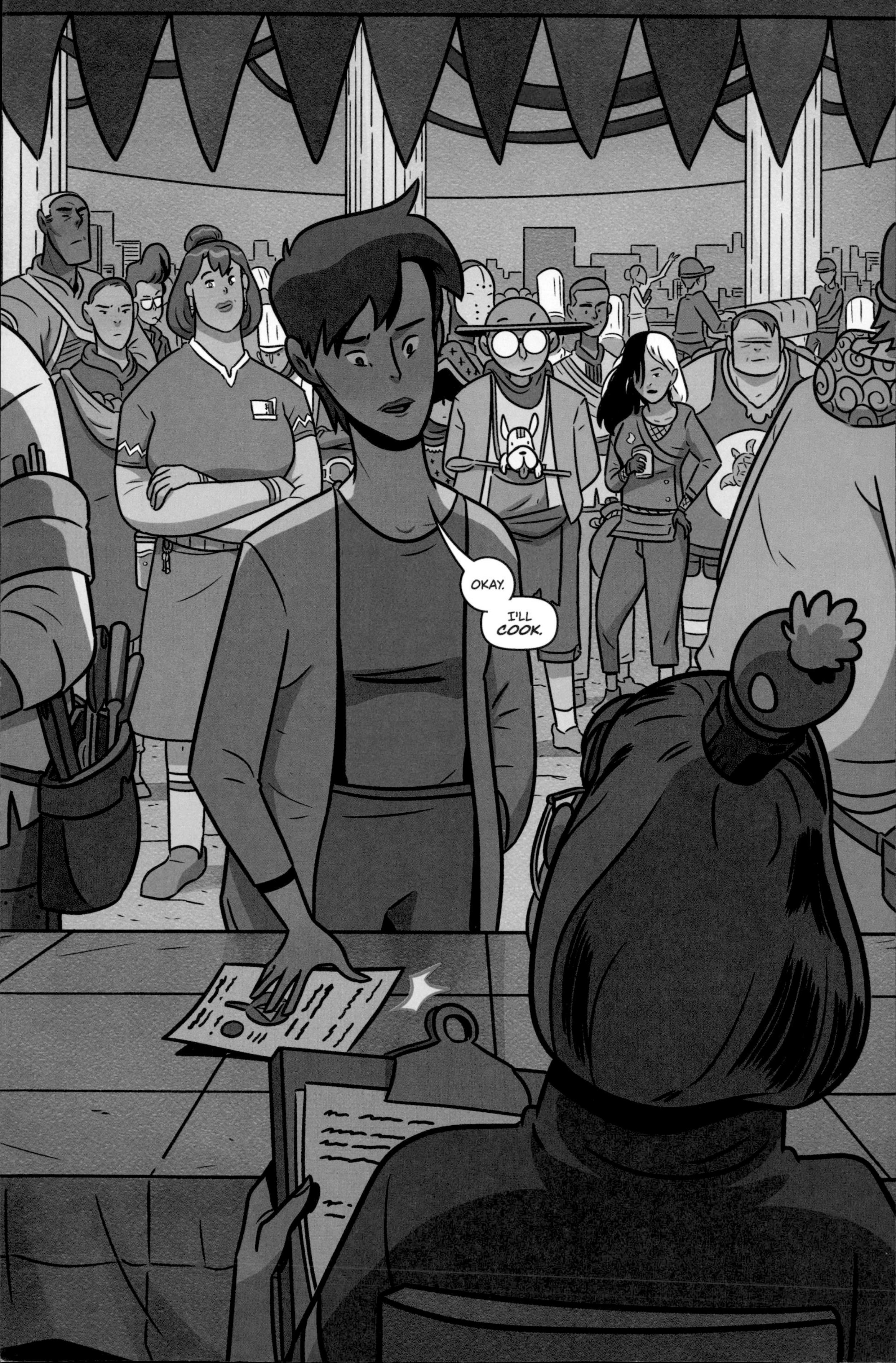
OKAY.
I'LL COOK.

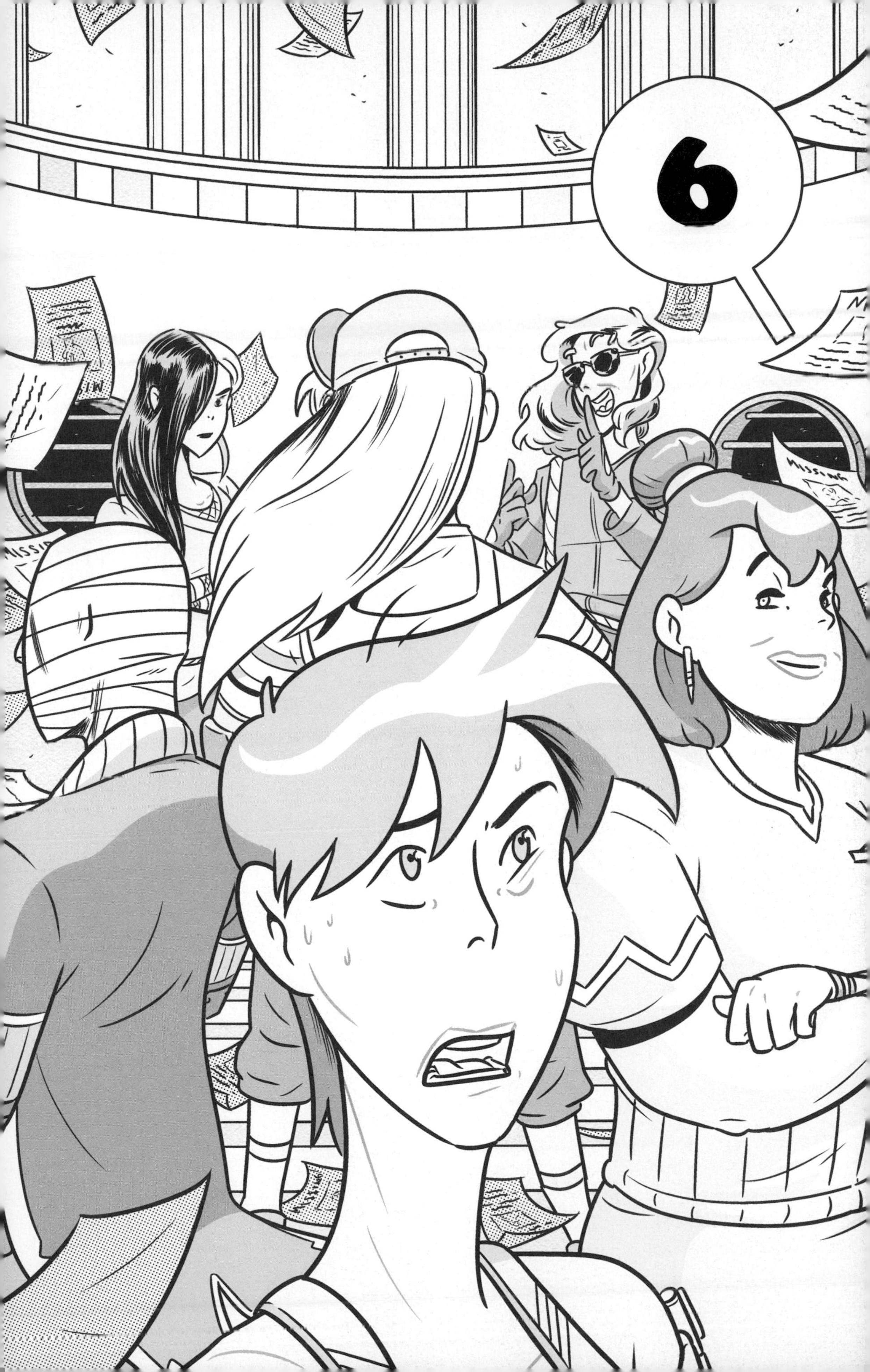
6

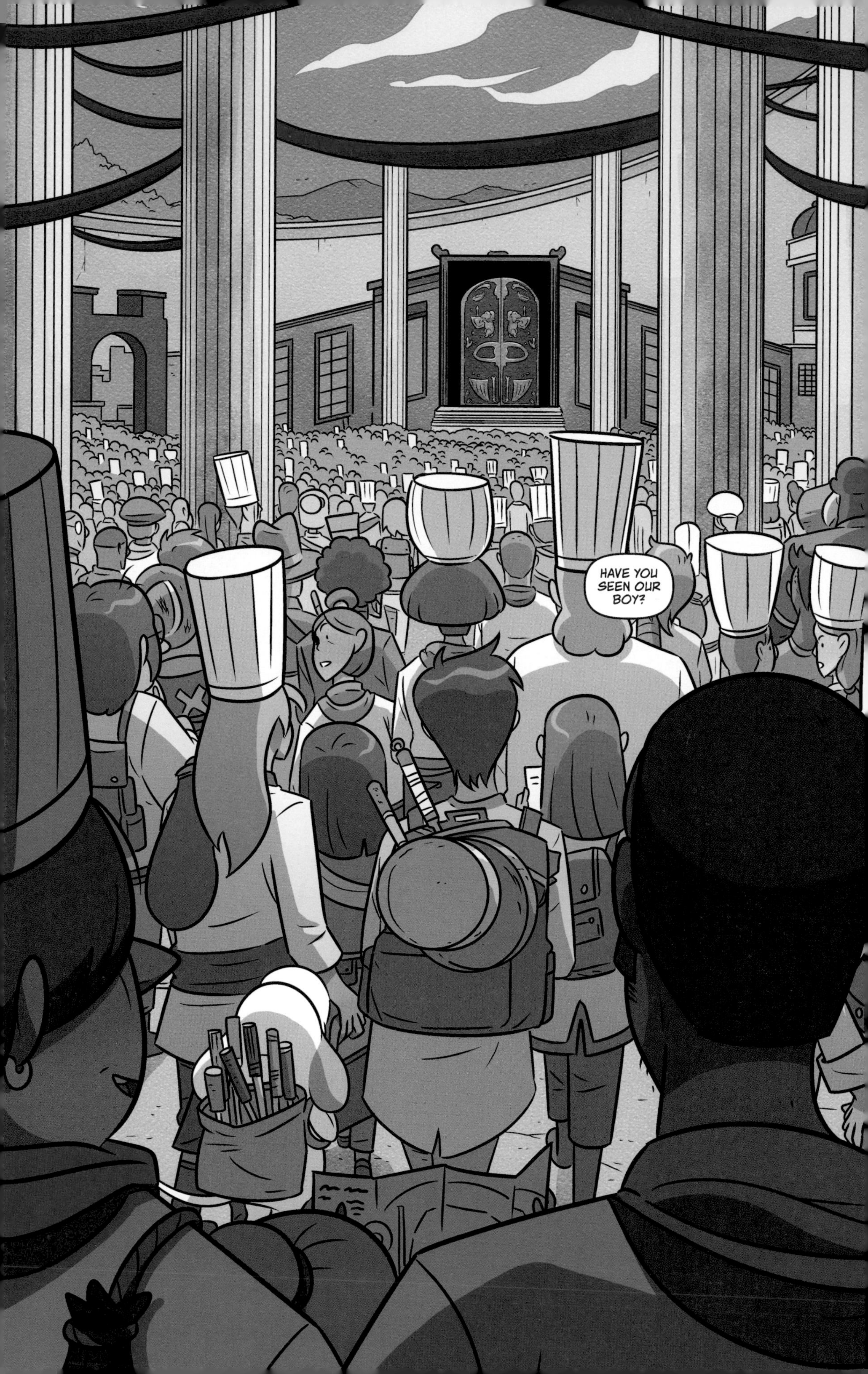
HAVE YOU SEEN OUR BOY?

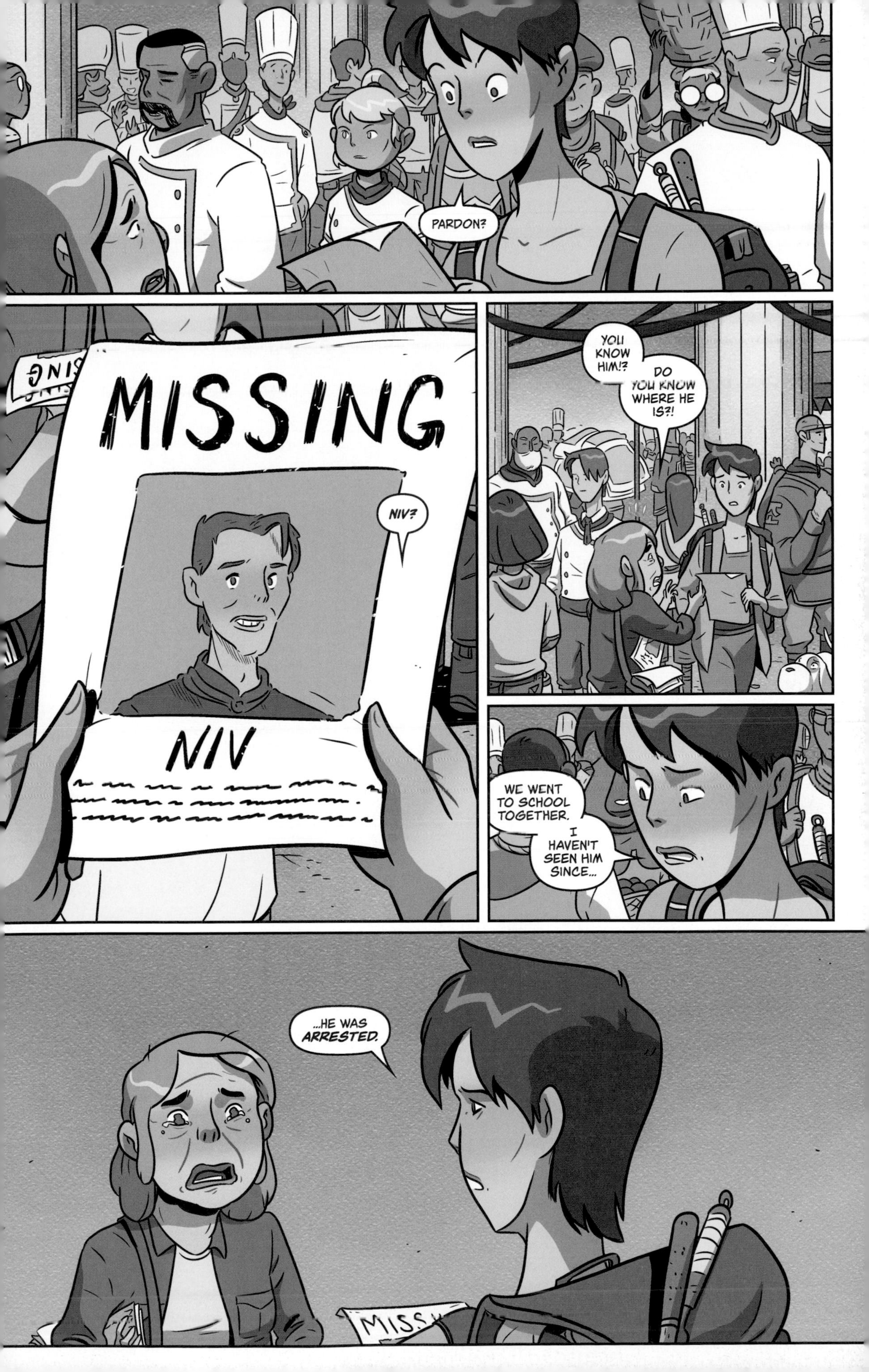
PARDON?
MISSING
NIV
NIV?
YOU KNOW HIM!?
DO YOU KNOW WHERE HE IS?!
WE WENT TO SCHOOL TOGETHER.
I HAVEN'T SEEN HIM SINCE...
...HE WAS ARRESTED.
MISS

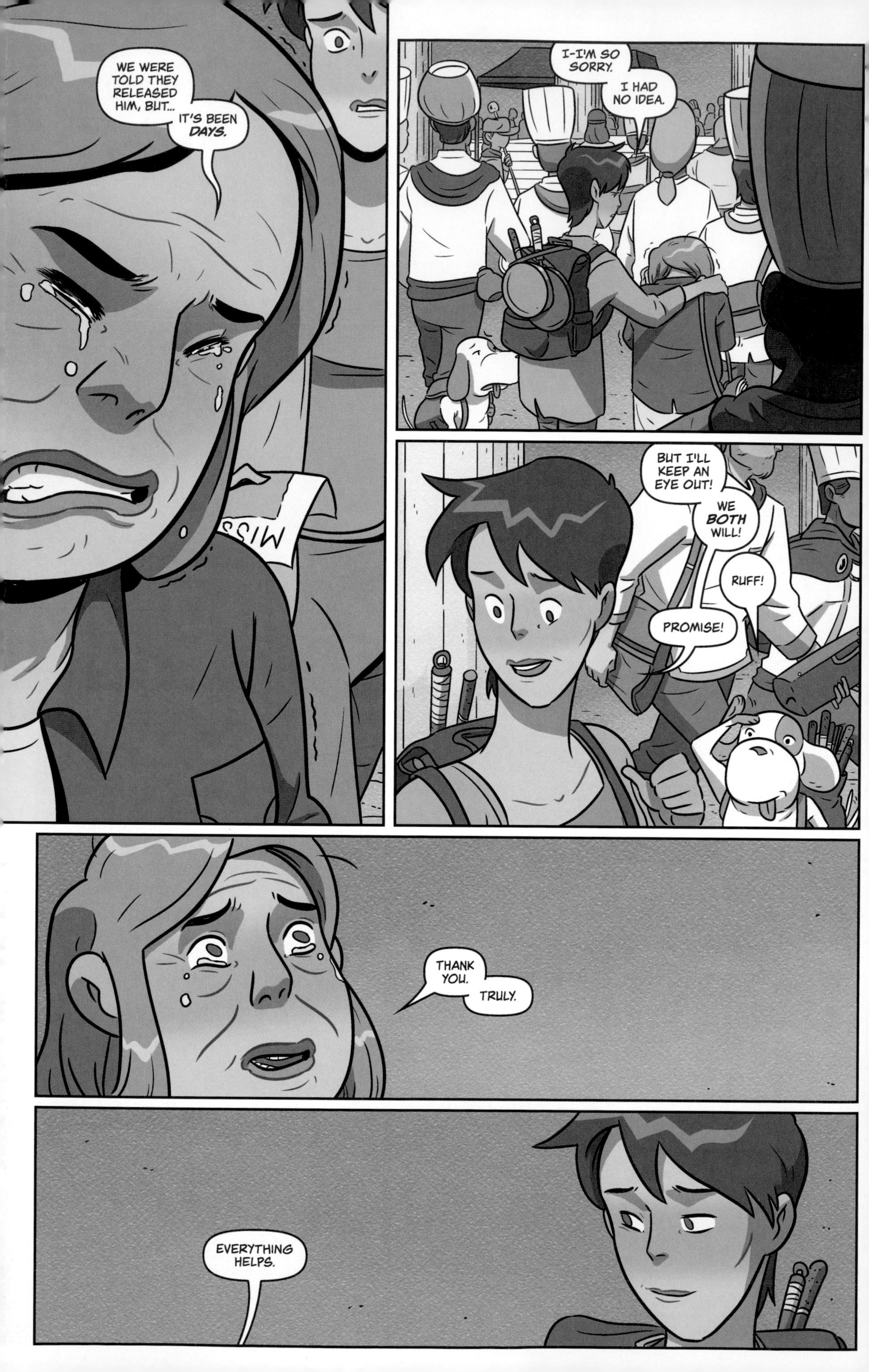
WE WERE TOLD THEY RELEASED HIM, BUT...
IT'S BEEN *DAYS.*
I-I'M SO SORRY.
I HAD NO IDEA.
MISS
BUT I'LL KEEP AN EYE OUT!
WE *BOTH* WILL!
RUFF!
PROMISE!
THANK YOU.
TRULY.
EVERYTHING HELPS.

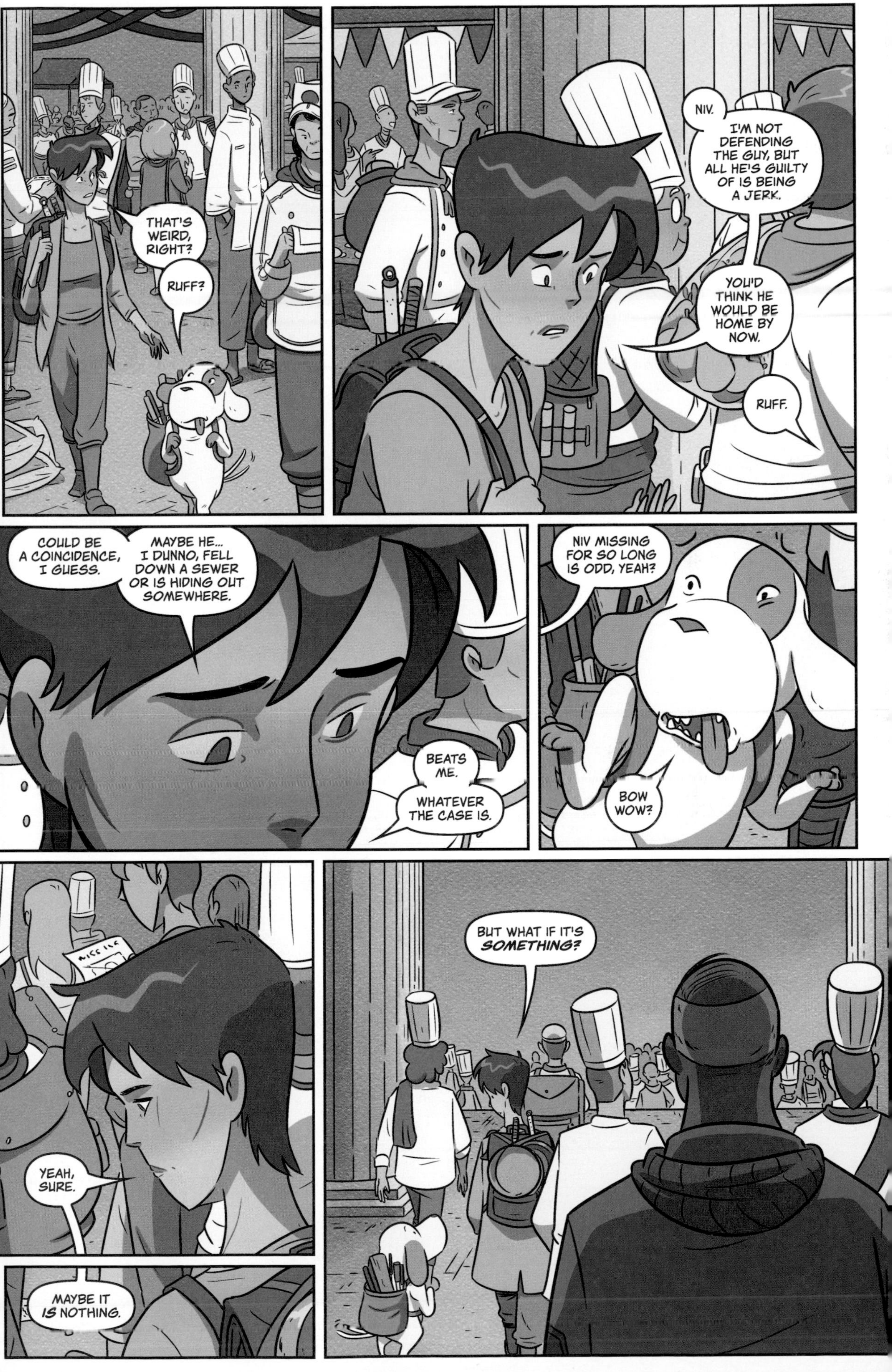
THAT'S WEIRD, RIGHT?
RUFF?
NIV.
I'M NOT DEFENDING THE GUY, BUT ALL HE'S GUILTY OF IS BEING A JERK.
YOU'D THINK HE WOULD BE HOME BY NOW.
RUFF.
COULD BE A COINCIDENCE, I GUESS.
MAYBE HE... I DUNNO, FELL DOWN A SEWER OR IS HIDING OUT SOMEWHERE.
BEATS ME.
WHATEVER THE CASE IS.
NIV MISSING FOR SO LONG IS ODD, YEAH?
BOW WOW?
YEAH, SURE.
MAYBE IT *IS* NOTHING.
BUT WHAT IF IT'S *SOMETHING?*

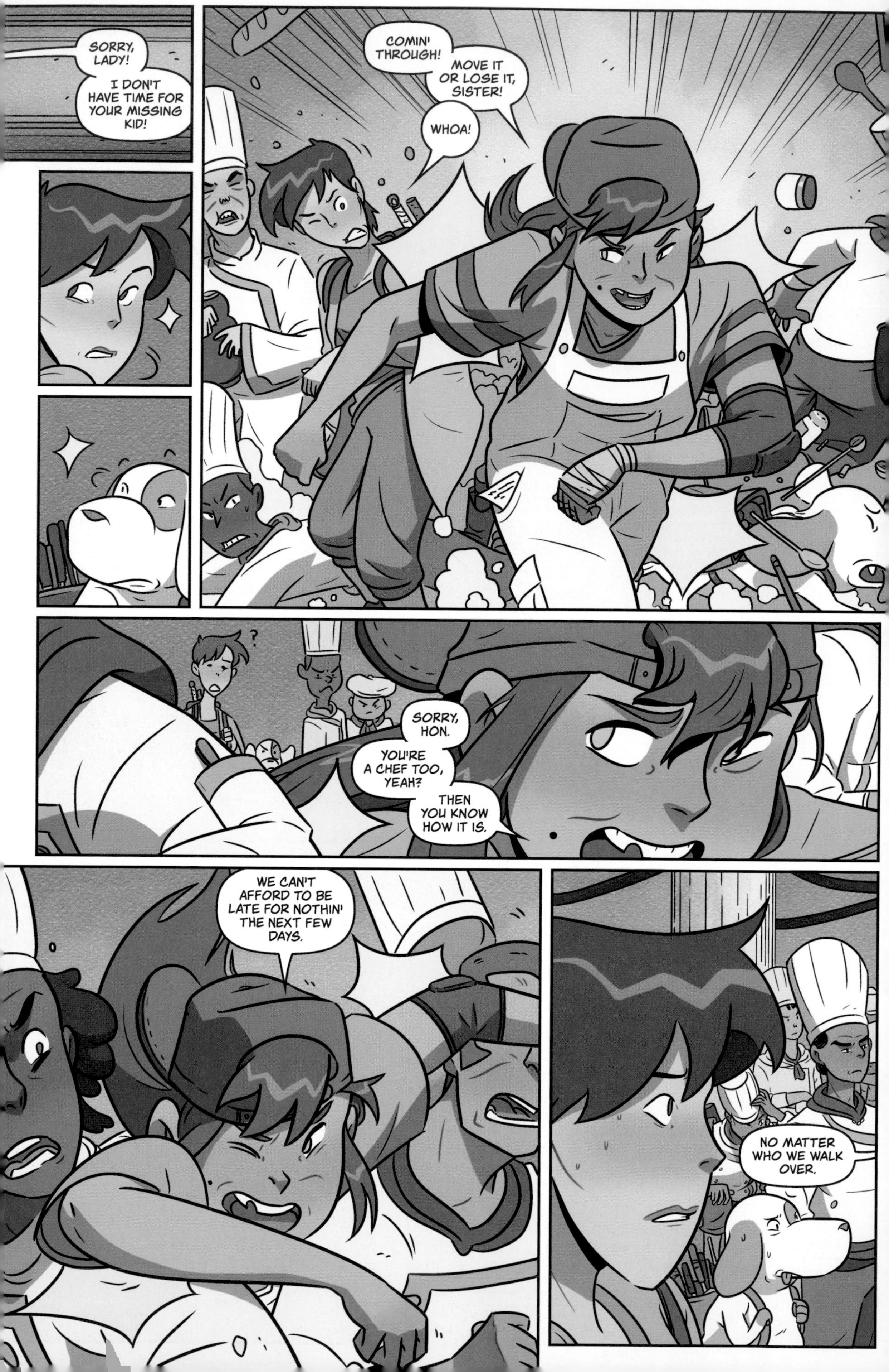
SORRY, LADY!
I DON'T HAVE TIME FOR YOUR MISSING KID!
COMIN' THROUGH!
MOVE IT OR LOSE IT, SISTER!
WHOA!
SORRY, HON.
YOU'RE A CHEF TOO, YEAH?
THEN YOU KNOW HOW IT IS.
WE CAN'T AFFORD TO BE LATE FOR NOTHIN' THE NEXT FEW DAYS.
NO MATTER WHO WE WALK OVER.

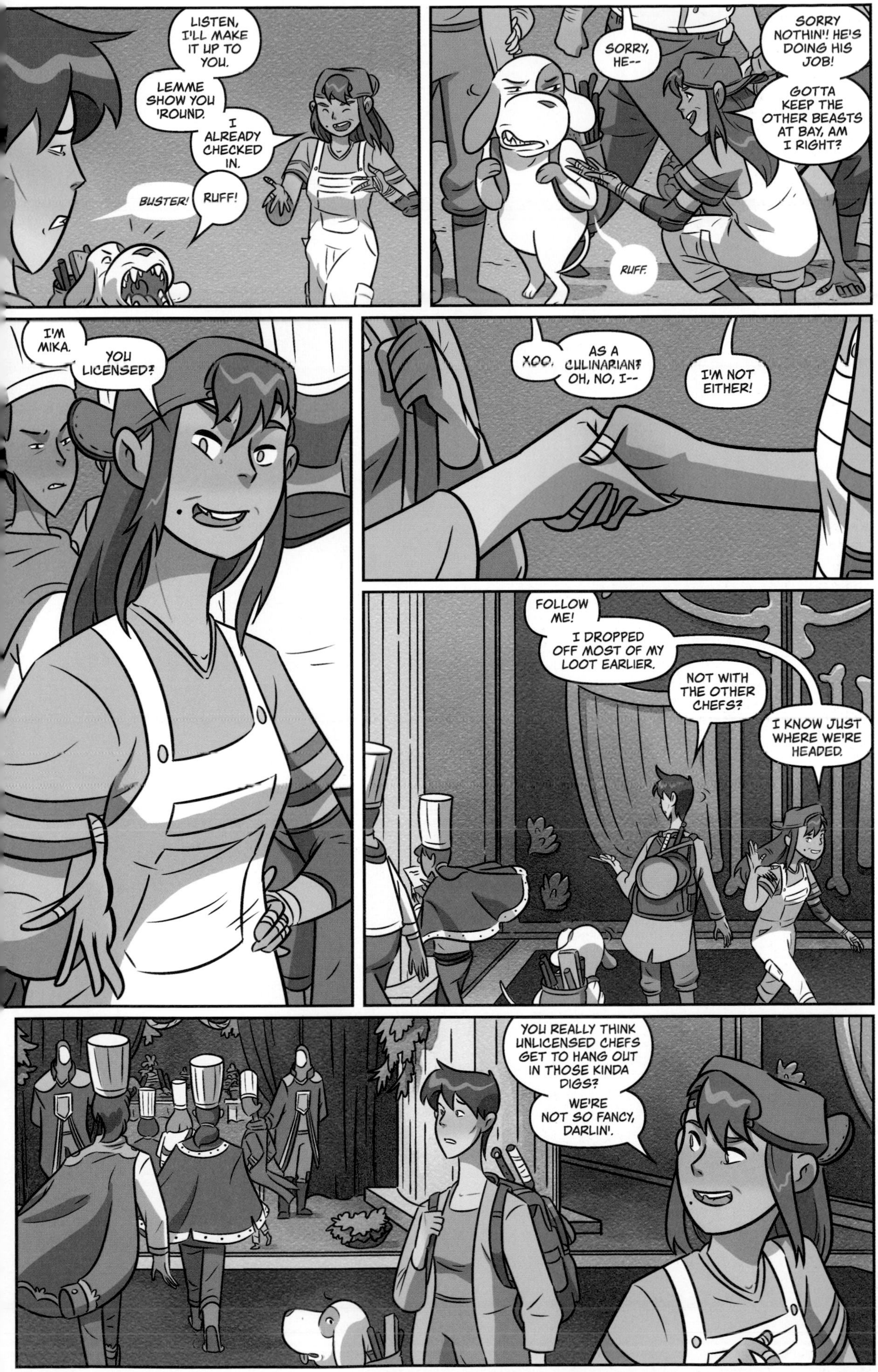

LISTEN, I'LL MAKE IT UP TO YOU.
LEMME SHOW YOU 'ROUND.
I ALREADY CHECKED IN.
BUSTER!
RUFF!
SORRY, HE--
SORRY NOTHIN'! HE'S DOING HIS JOB!
GOTTA KEEP THE OTHER BEASTS AT BAY, AM I RIGHT?
RUFF.
I'M MIKA.
YOU LICENSED?
YOU.
AS A CULINARIAN? OH, NO, I--
I'M NOT EITHER!
FOLLOW ME!
I DROPPED OFF MOST OF MY LOOT EARLIER.
NOT WITH THE OTHER CHEFS?
I KNOW JUST WHERE WE'RE HEADED.
YOU REALLY THINK UNLICENSED CHEFS GET TO HANG OUT IN THOSE KINDA DIGS?
WE'RE NOT SO FANCY, DARLIN'.

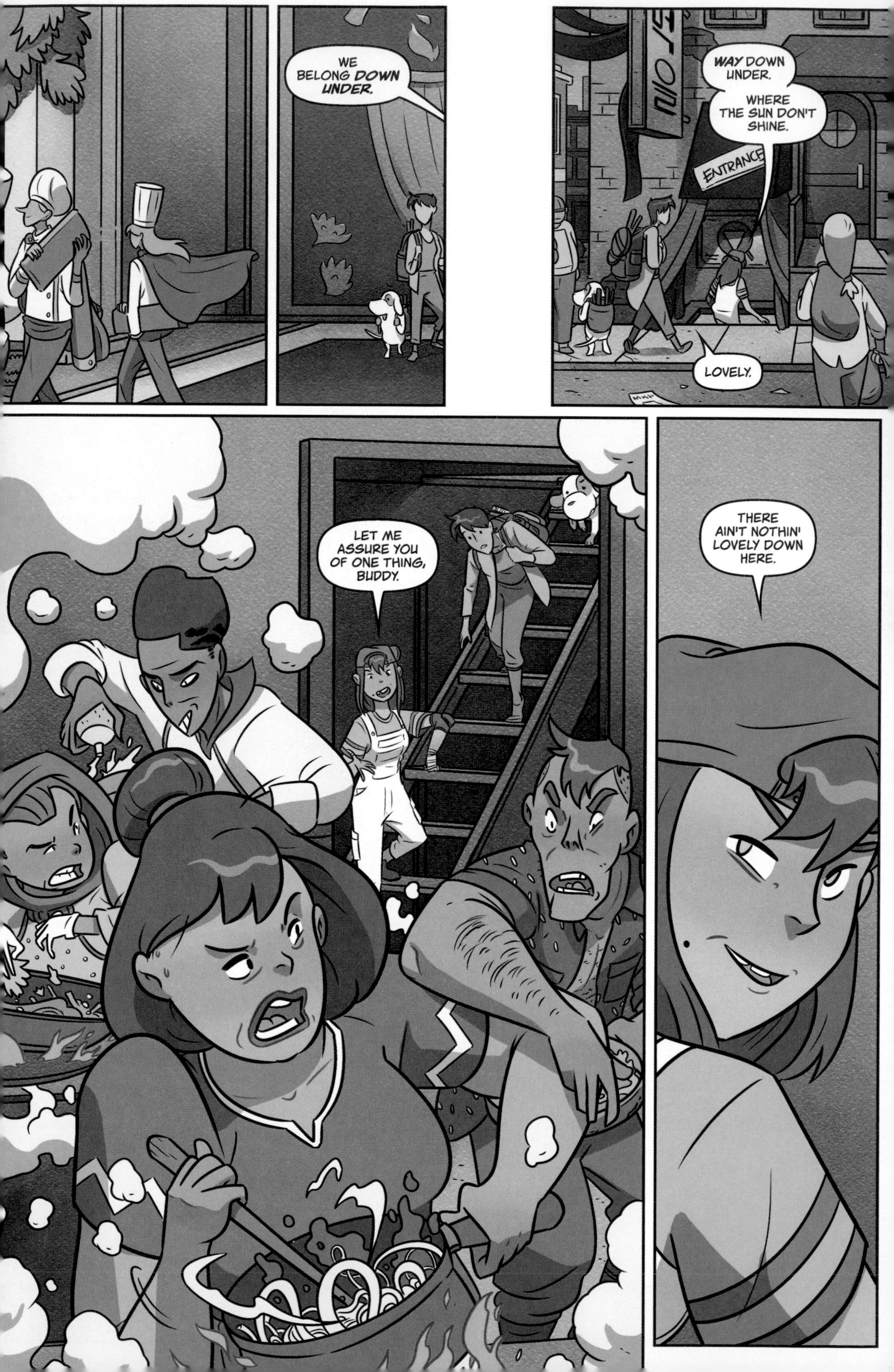

WE BELONG **DOWN UNDER.**
WAY DOWN UNDER.
WHERE THE SUN DON'T SHINE.
ENTRANCE
LOVELY.
LET ME ASSURE YOU OF ONE THING, BUDDY.
THERE AIN'T NOTHIN' LOVELY DOWN HERE.

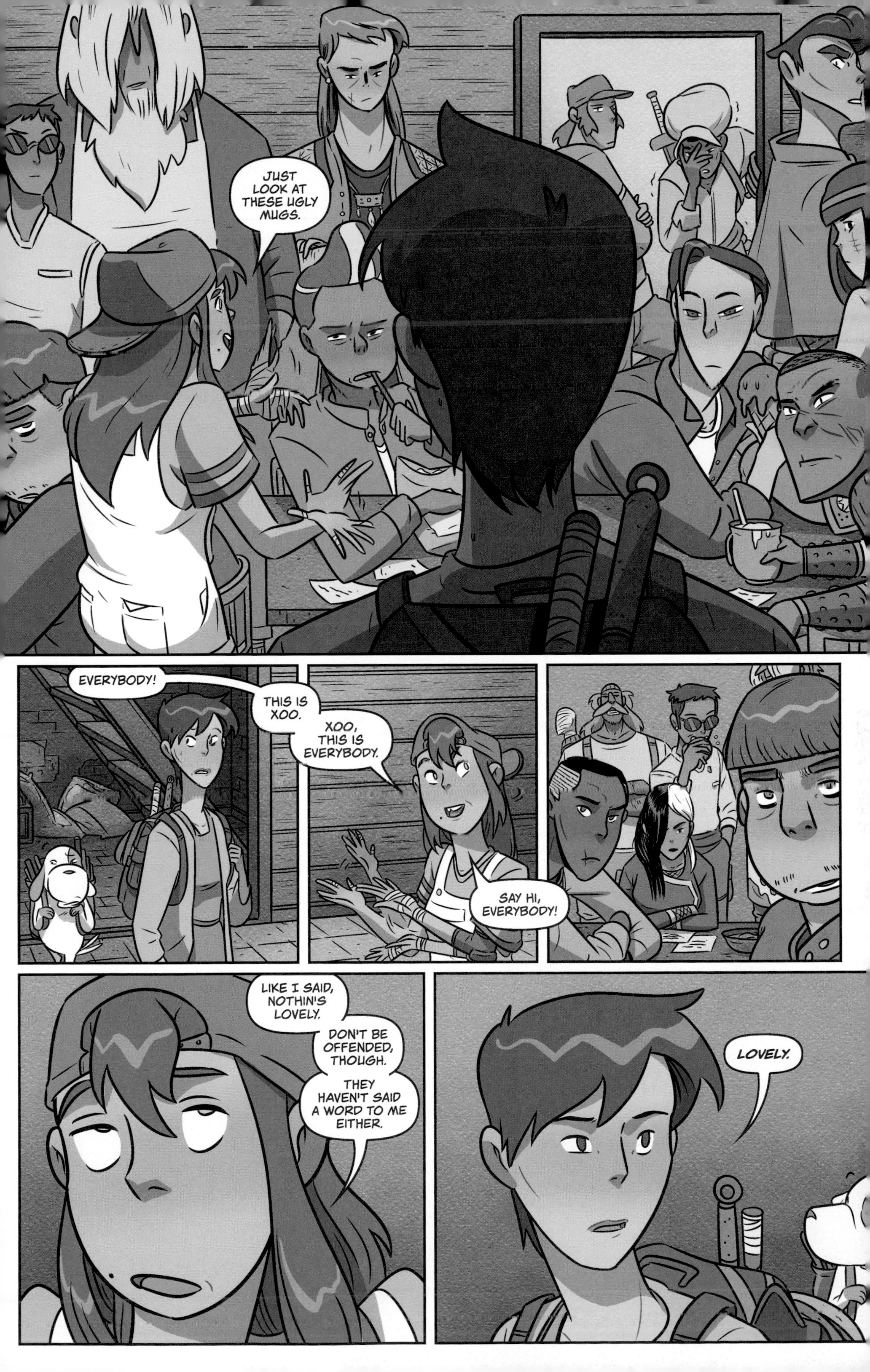
JUST LOOK AT THESE UGLY MUGS.
EVERYBODY!
THIS IS XOO.
XOO, THIS IS EVERYBODY.
SAY HI, EVERYBODY!
LIKE I SAID, NOTHIN'S LOVELY.
DON'T BE OFFENDED, THOUGH.
THEY HAVEN'T SAID A WORD TO ME EITHER.
LOVELY.

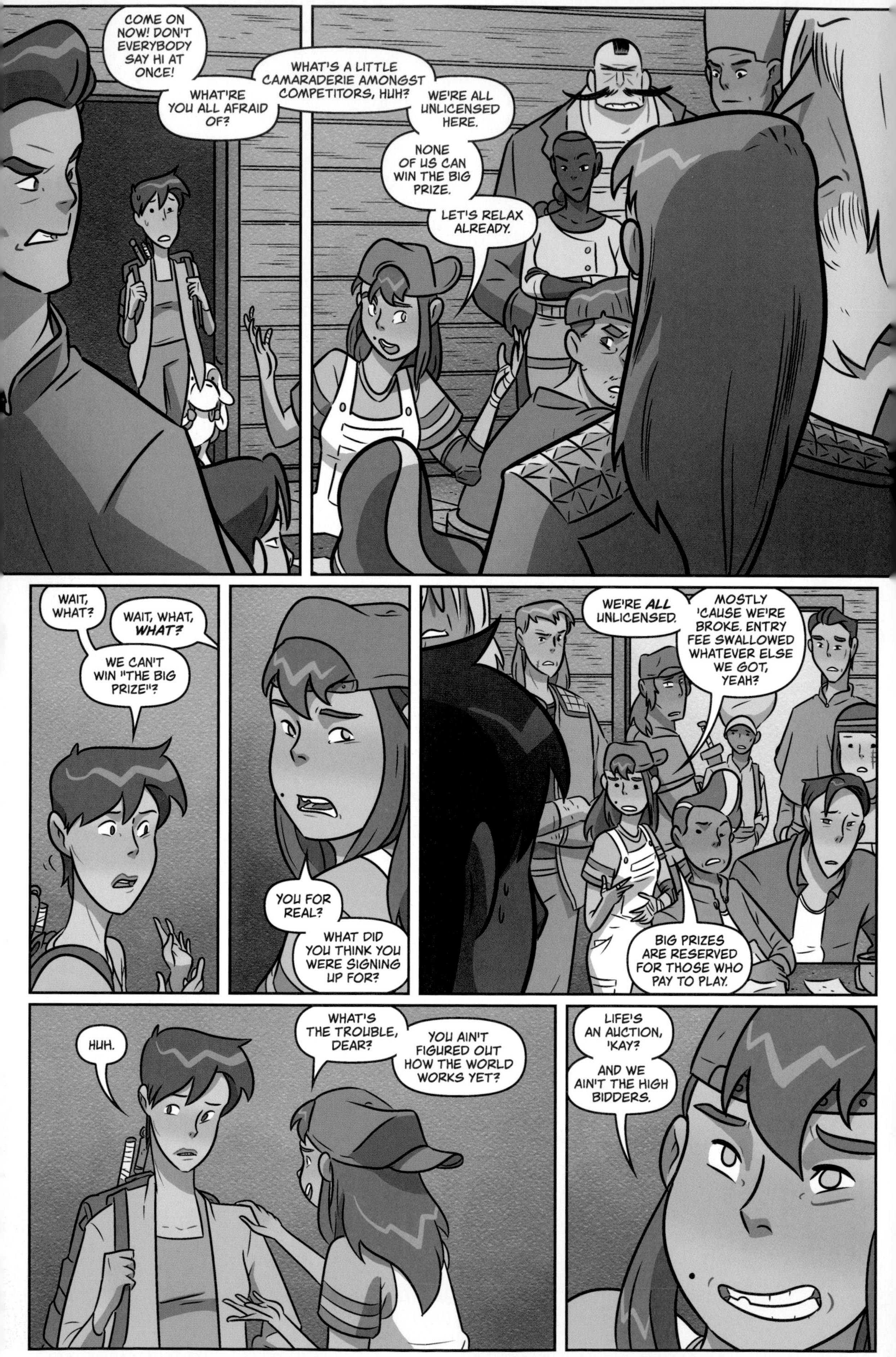

COME ON NOW! DON'T EVERYBODY SAY HI AT ONCE!
WHAT'RE YOU ALL AFRAID OF?
WHAT'S A LITTLE CAMARADERIE AMONGST COMPETITORS, HUH?
WE'RE ALL UNLICENSED HERE.
NONE OF US CAN WIN THE BIG PRIZE.
LET'S RELAX ALREADY.
WAIT, WHAT?
WAIT, WHAT, WHAT?
WE CAN'T WIN "THE BIG PRIZE"?
YOU FOR REAL?
WHAT DID YOU THINK YOU WERE SIGNING UP FOR?
WE'RE ALL UNLICENSED.
MOSTLY 'CAUSE WE'RE BROKE. ENTRY FEE SWALLOWED WHATEVER ELSE WE GOT, YEAH?
BIG PRIZES ARE RESERVED FOR THOSE WHO PAY TO PLAY.
HUH.
WHAT'S THE TROUBLE, DEAR?
YOU AIN'T FIGURED OUT HOW THE WORLD WORKS YET?
LIFE'S AN AUCTION, 'KAY?
AND WE AIN'T THE HIGH BIDDERS.

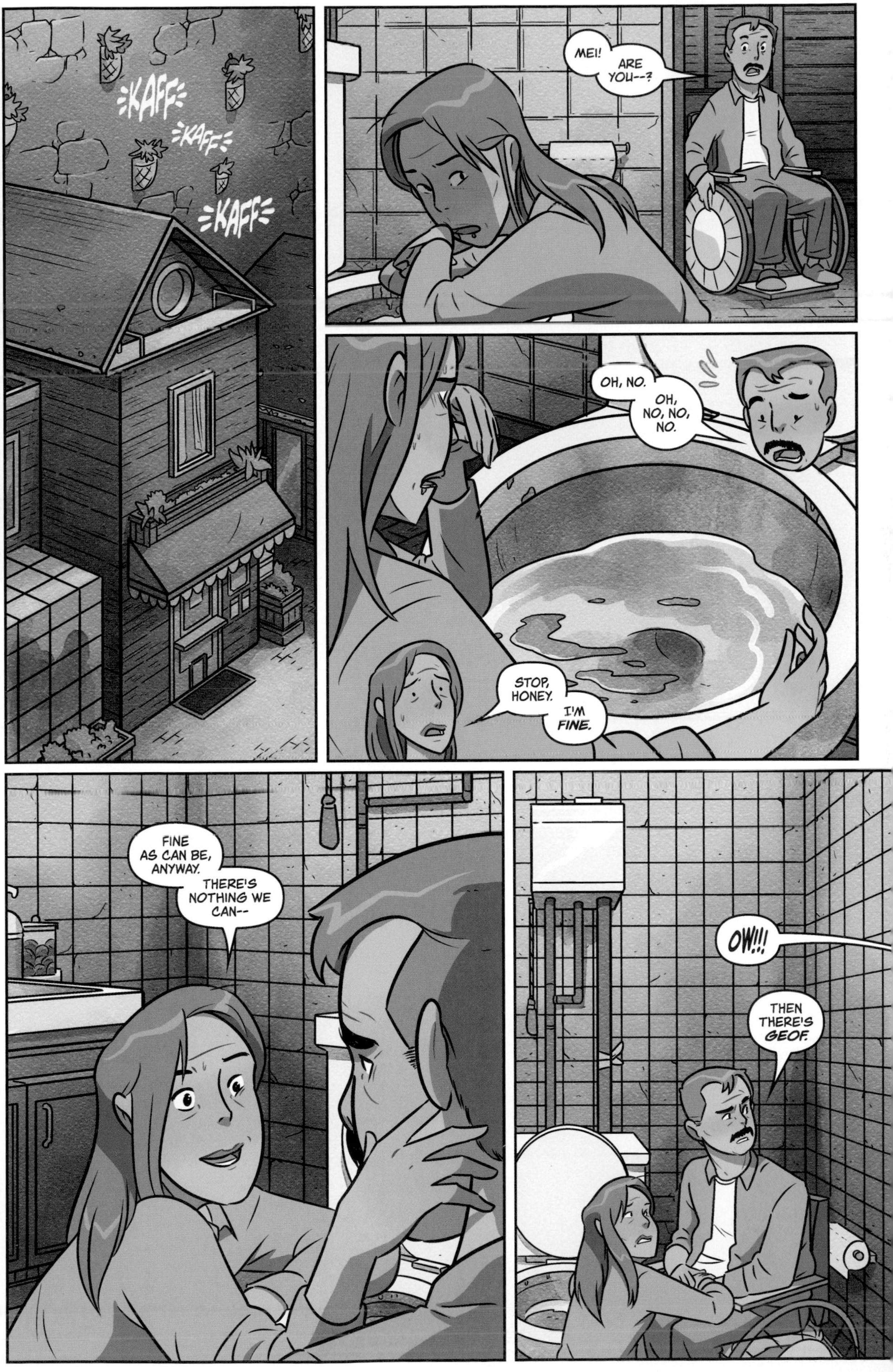
KAFF
KAFF
KAFF
MEI! ARE YOU--?
OH, NO.
OH, NO, NO, NO.
STOP, HONEY.
I'M *FINE.*
FINE AS CAN BE, ANYWAY.
THERE'S NOTHING WE CAN--
OW!!!
THEN THERE'S *GEOF.*

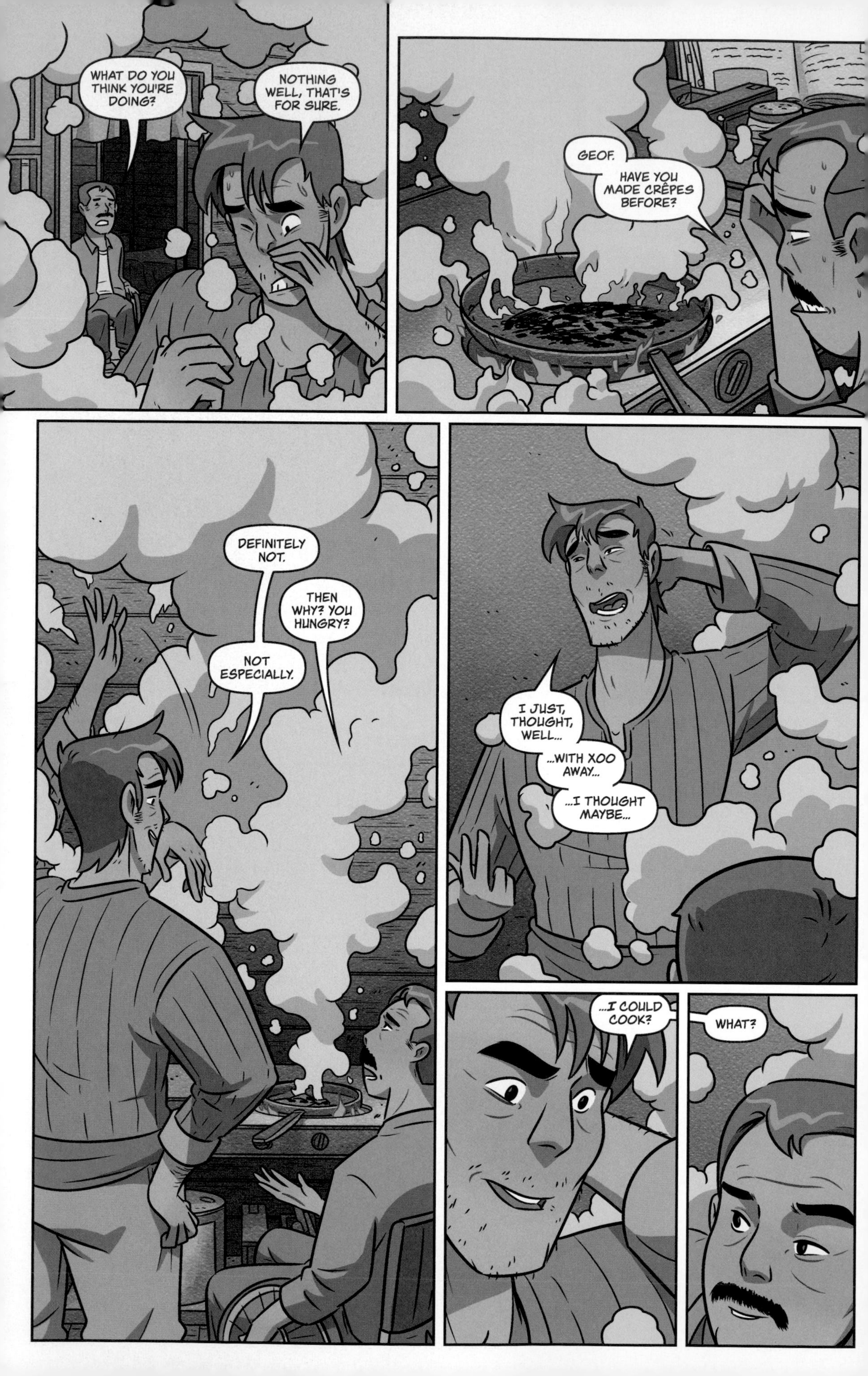
WHAT DO YOU THINK YOU'RE DOING?
NOTHING WELL, THAT'S FOR SURE.
GEOF.
HAVE YOU MADE CRÊPES BEFORE?
DEFINITELY NOT.
THEN WHY? YOU HUNGRY?
NOT ESPECIALLY.
I JUST, THOUGHT, WELL...
...WITH XOO AWAY...
...I THOUGHT MAYBE...
...I COULD COOK?
WHAT?

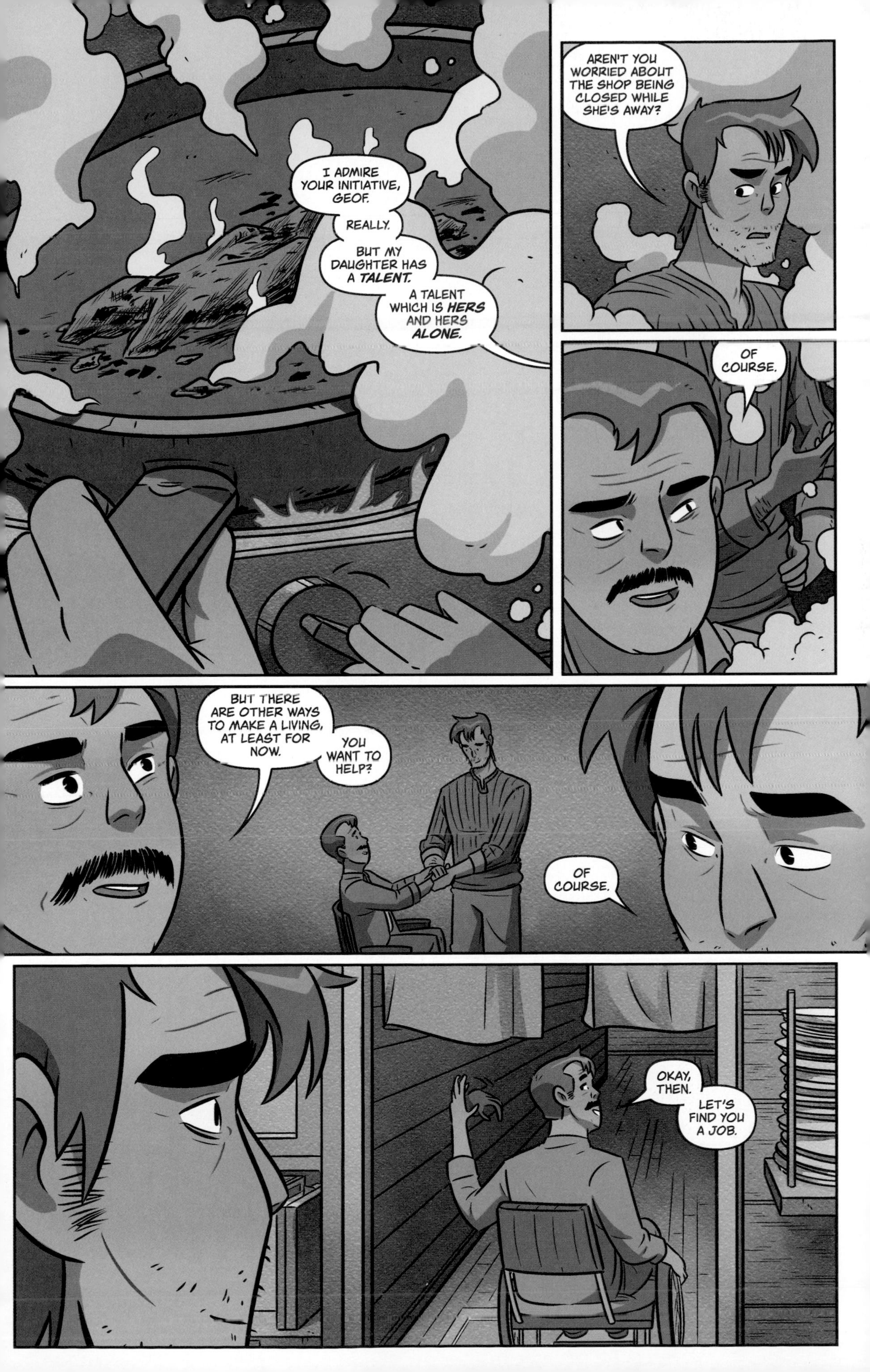
I ADMIRE YOUR INITIATIVE, GEOF.
REALLY.
BUT MY DAUGHTER HAS A *TALENT.*
A TALENT WHICH IS *HERS* AND HERS *ALONE.*
AREN'T YOU WORRIED ABOUT THE SHOP BEING CLOSED WHILE SHE'S AWAY?
OF COURSE.
BUT THERE ARE OTHER WAYS TO MAKE A LIVING, AT LEAST FOR NOW.
YOU WANT TO HELP?
OF COURSE.
OKAY, THEN.
LET'S FIND YOU A JOB.

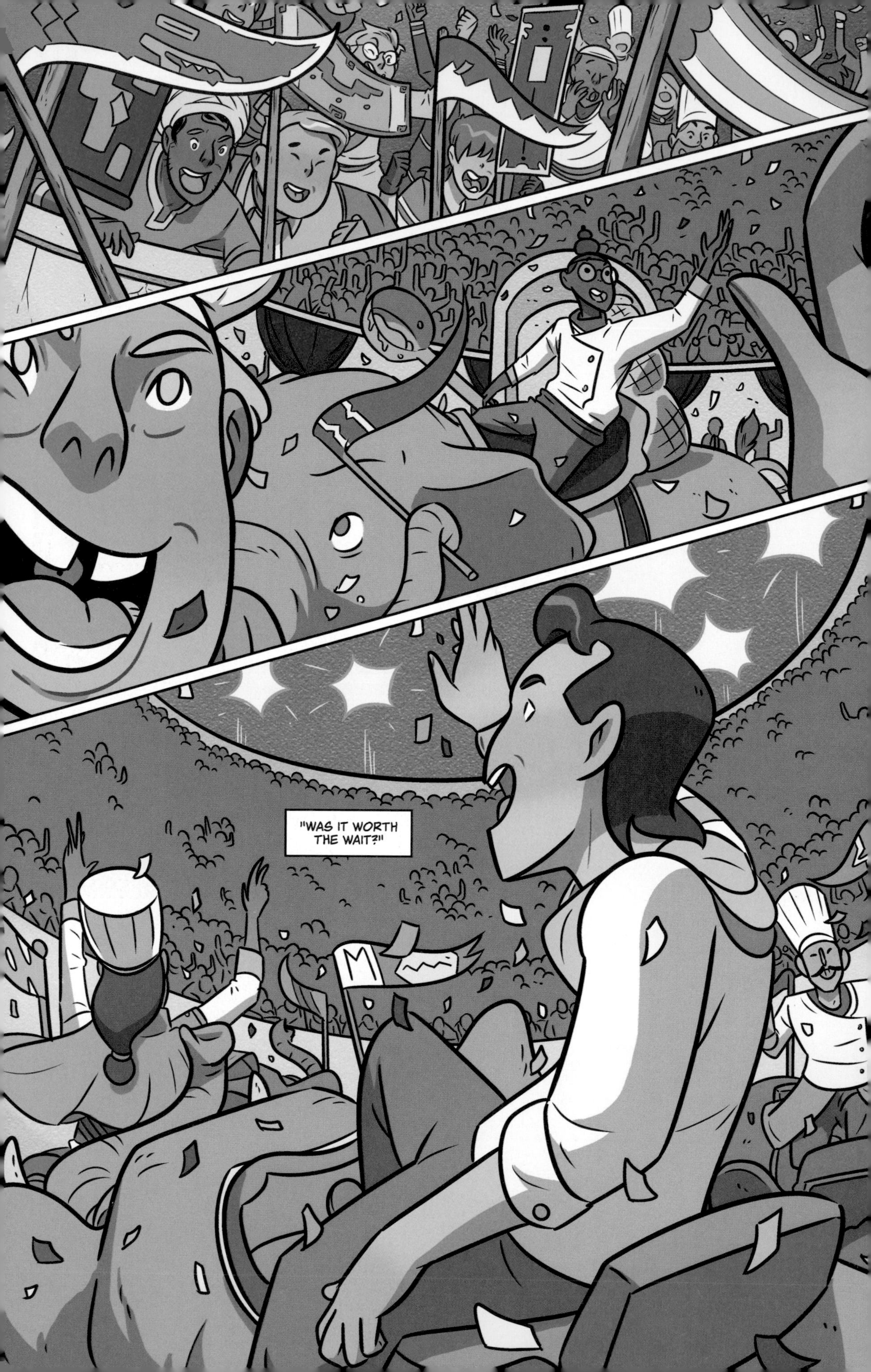
"WAS IT WORTH THE WAIT?"

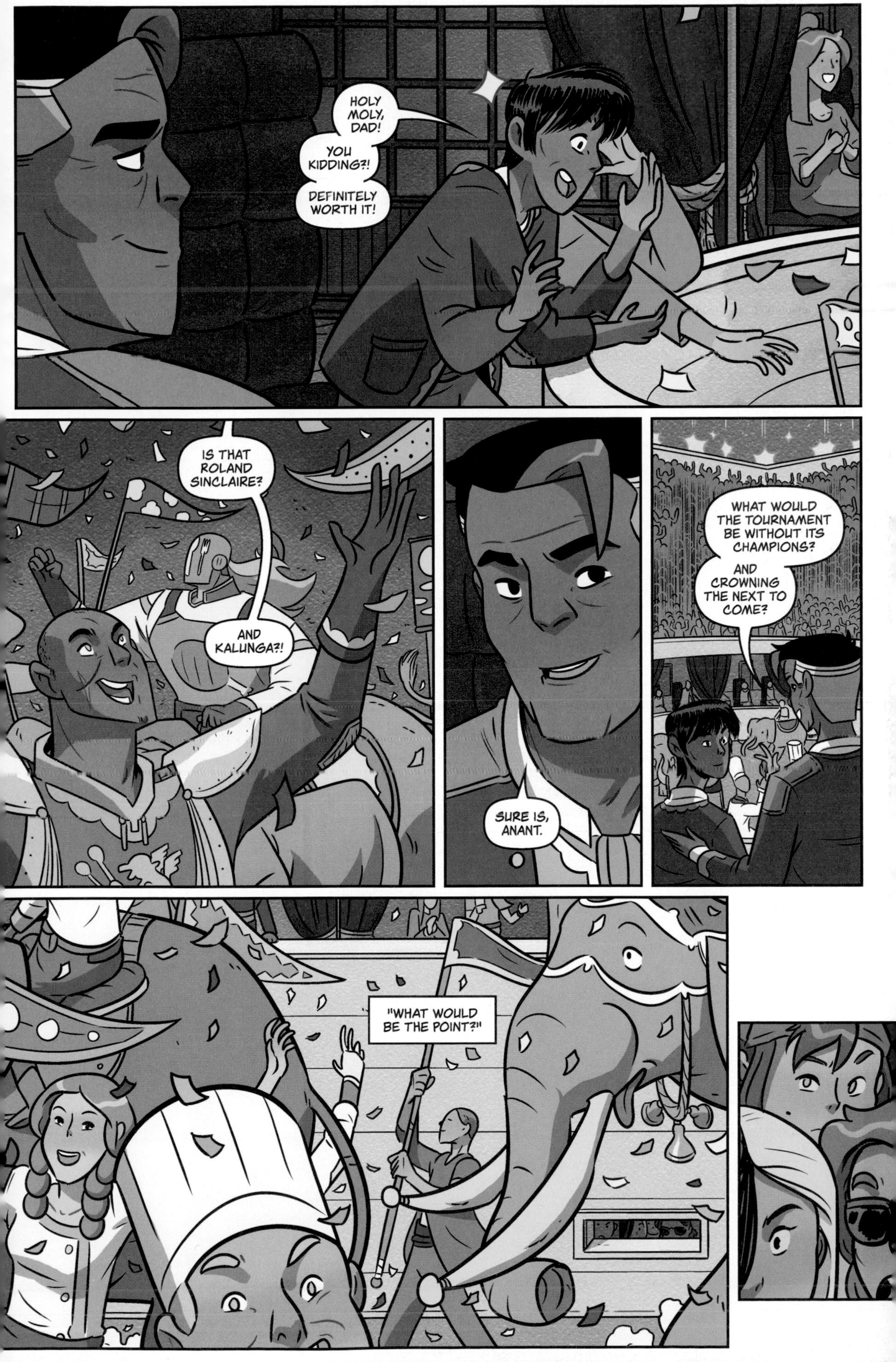
HOLY MOLY, DAD!
YOU KIDDING?!
DEFINITELY WORTH IT!
IS THAT ROLAND SINCLAIRE?
AND KALUNGA?!
SURE IS, ANANT.
WHAT WOULD THE TOURNAMENT BE WITHOUT ITS CHAMPIONS?
AND CROWNING THE NEXT TO COME?
"WHAT WOULD BE THE POINT?"

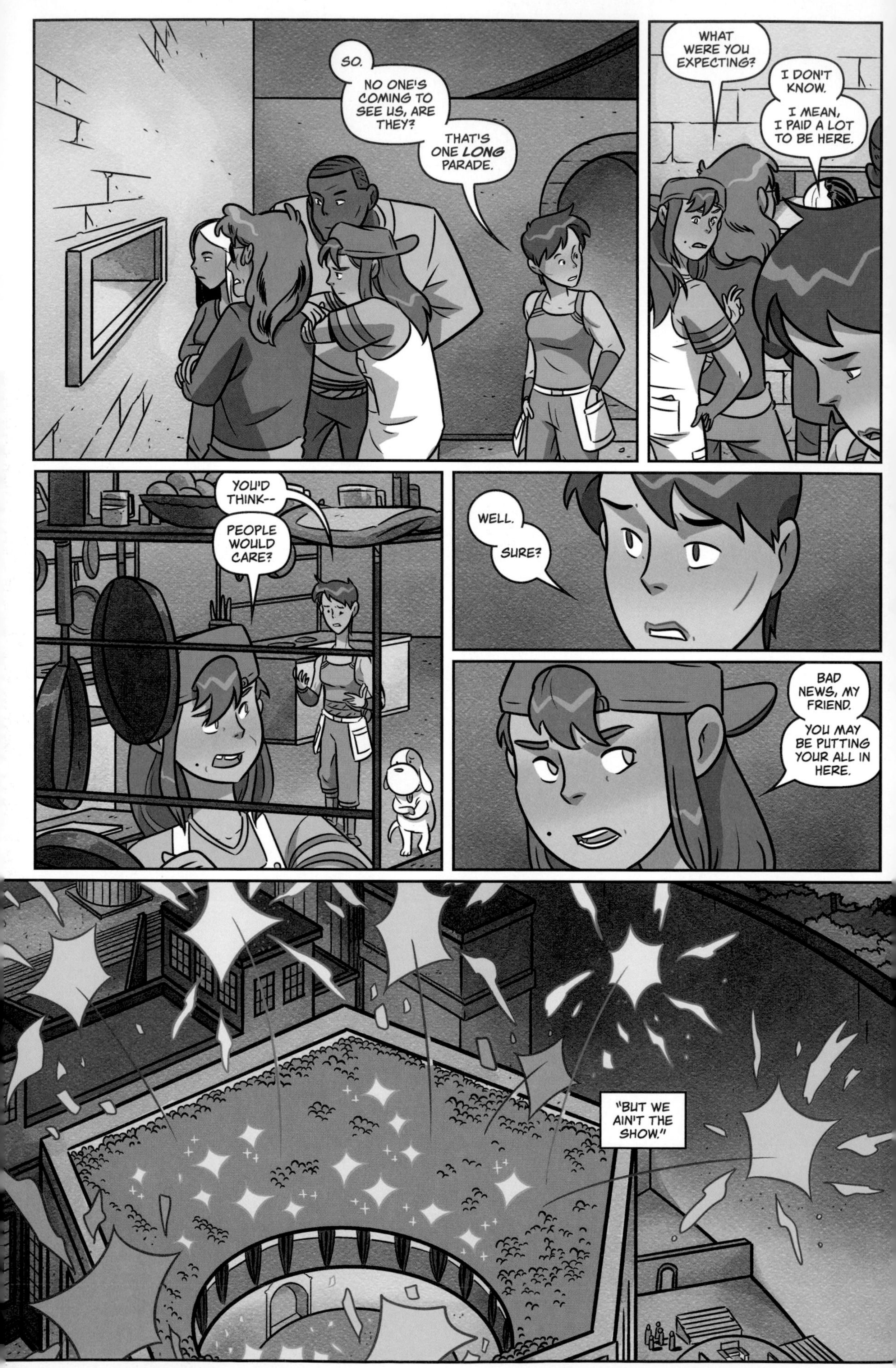
SO.
NO ONE'S COMING TO SEE US, ARE THEY?
THAT'S ONE LONG PARADE.
WHAT WERE YOU EXPECTING?
I DON'T KNOW.
I MEAN, I PAID A LOT TO BE HERE.
YOU'D THINK--
PEOPLE WOULD CARE?
WELL.
SURE?
BAD NEWS, MY FRIEND.
YOU MAY BE PUTTING YOUR ALL IN HERE.
"BUT WE AIN'T THE SHOW."

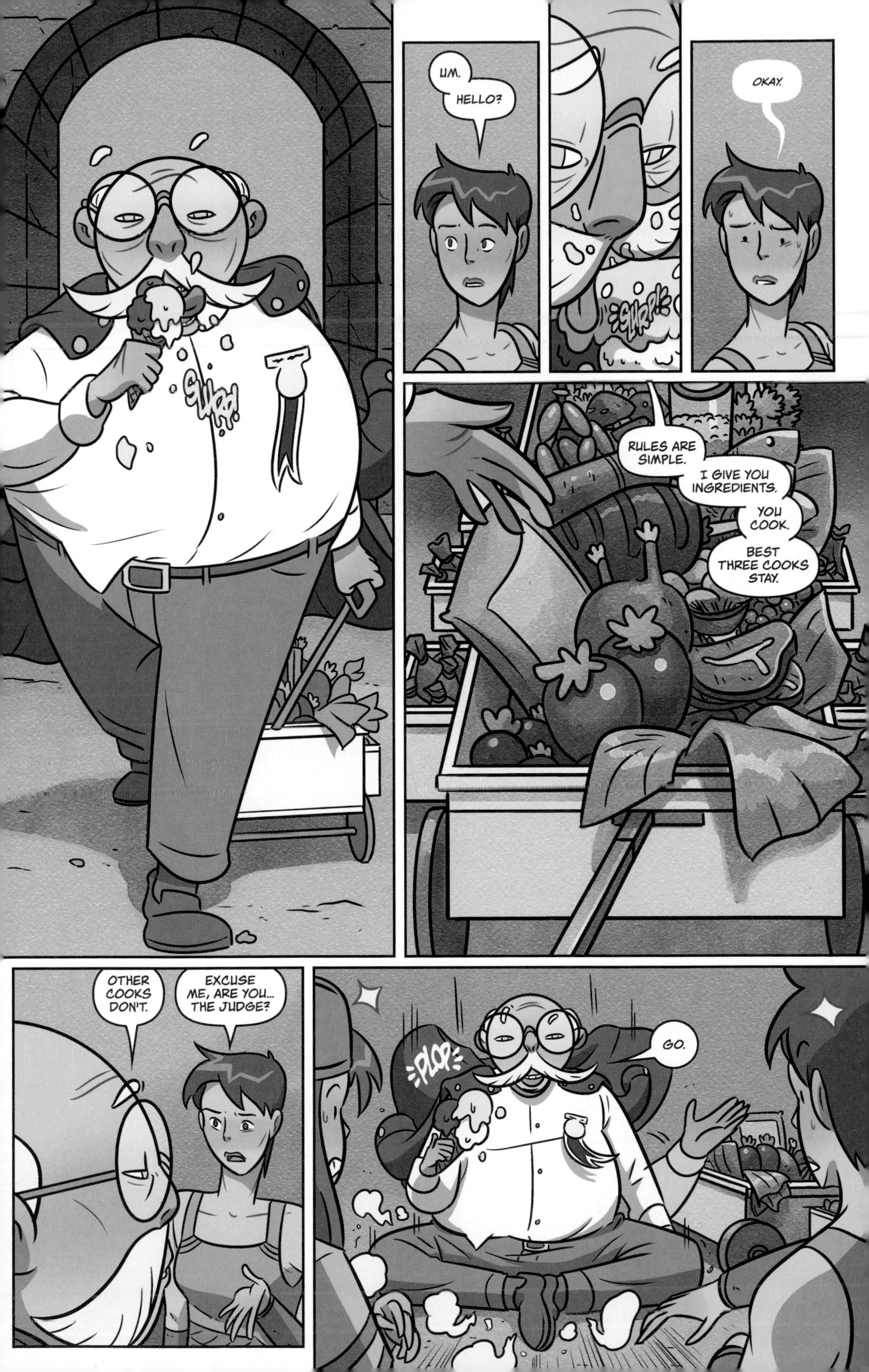
SLURP!
UM.
HELLO?
SLURP!
OKAY.
RULES ARE SIMPLE.
I GIVE YOU INGREDIENTS.
YOU COOK.
BEST THREE COOKS STAY.
OTHER COOKS DON'T.
EXCUSE ME, ARE YOU... THE JUDGE?
PLOP
GO.

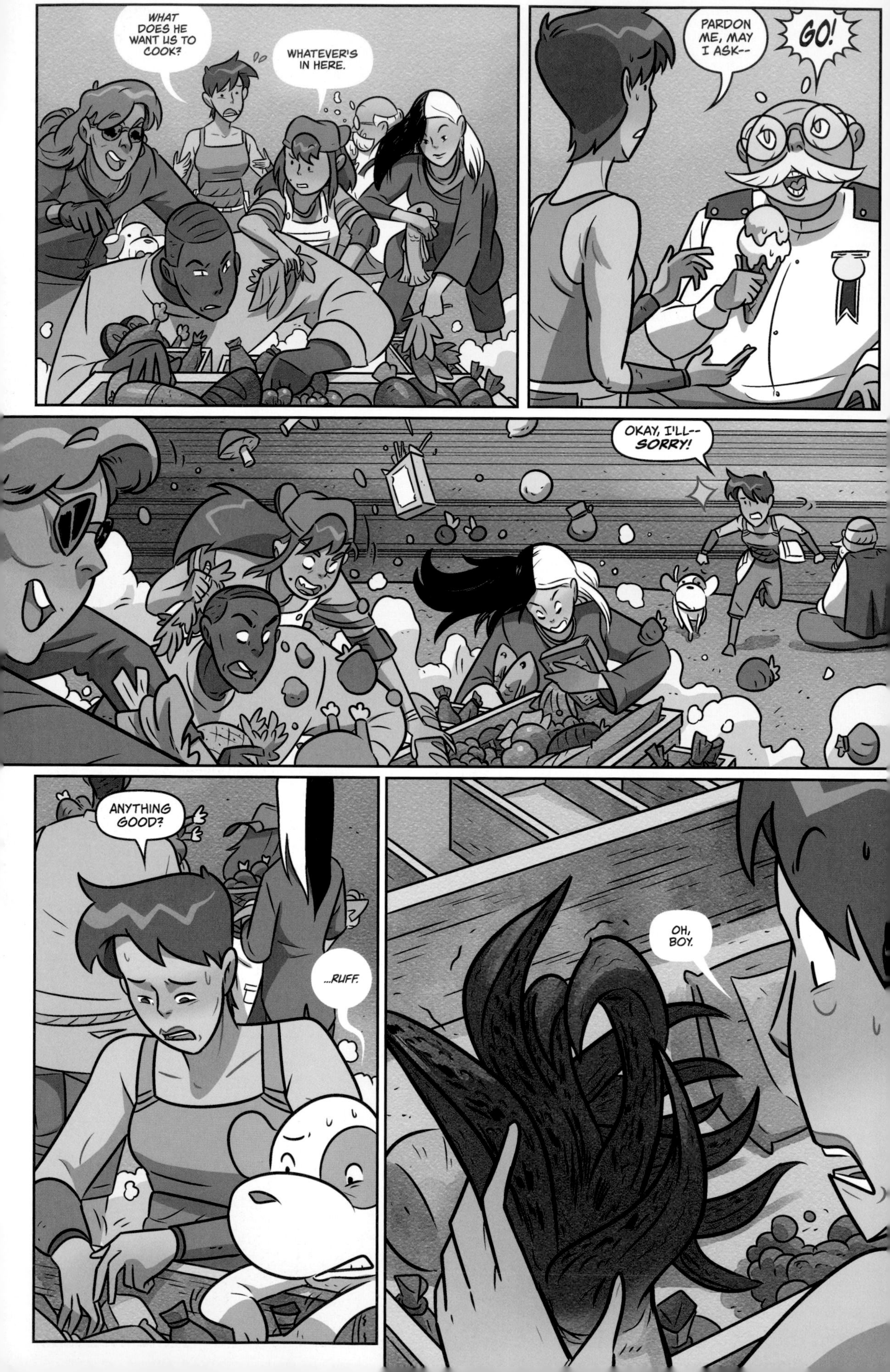

WHAT DOES HE WANT US TO COOK?
WHATEVER'S IN HERE.
PARDON ME, MAY I ASK--
GO!
OKAY, I'LL-- SORRY!
ANYTHING GOOD?
...RUFF.
OH, BOY.

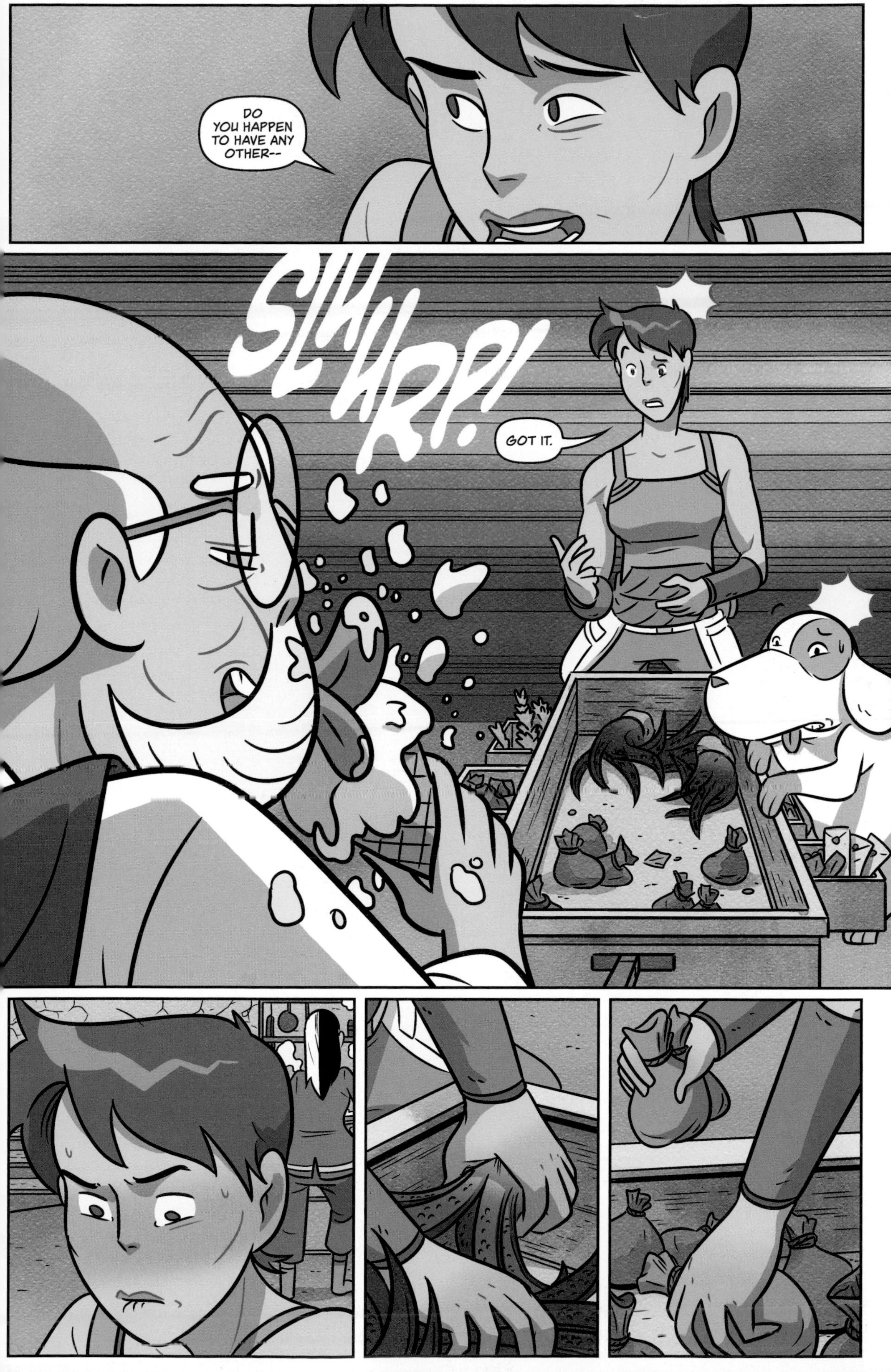
DO YOU HAPPEN TO HAVE ANY OTHER--
SLLLURP!
GOT IT.

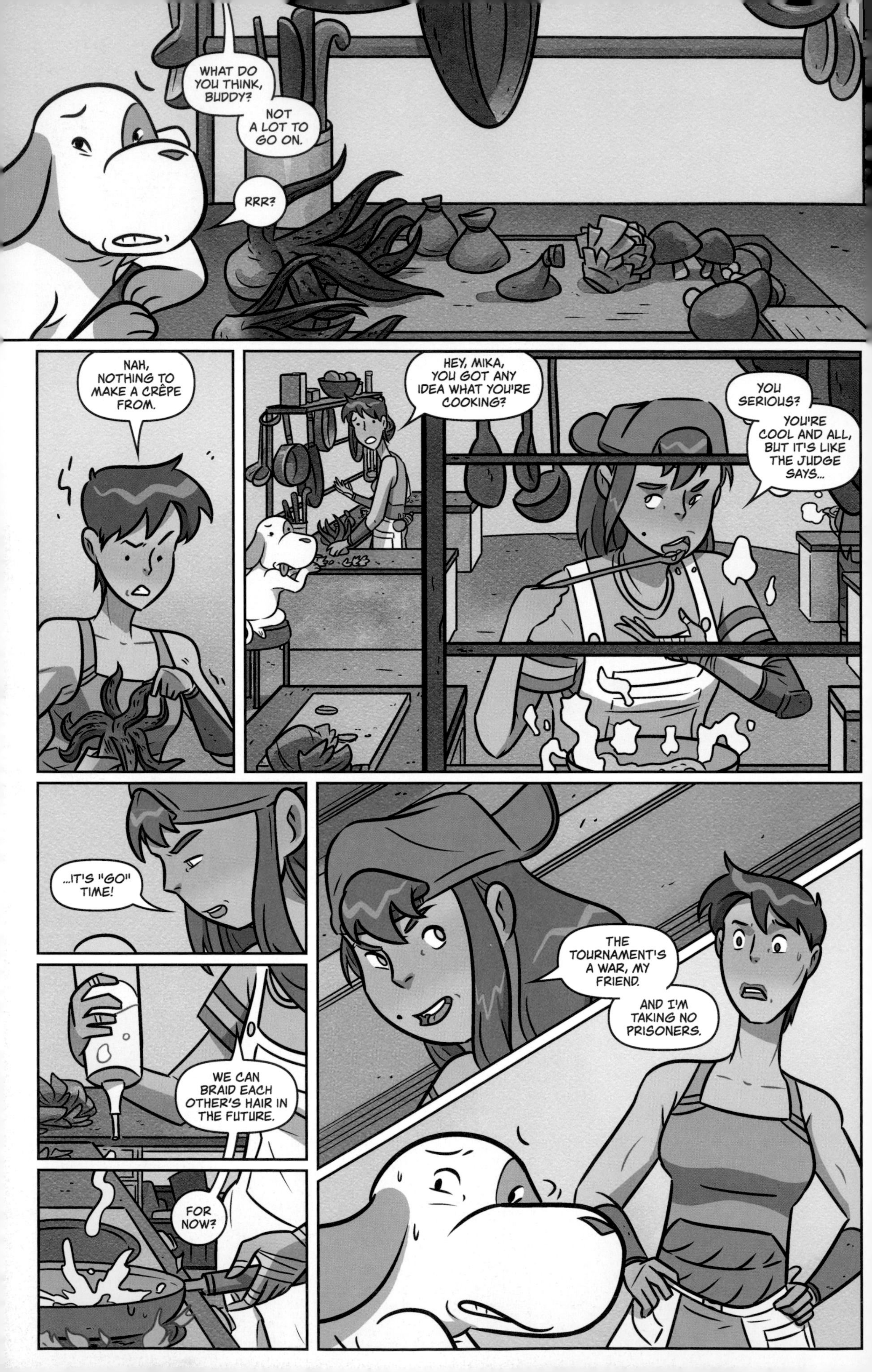
WHAT DO YOU THINK, BUDDY?
NOT A LOT TO GO ON.
RRR?
NAH, NOTHING TO MAKE A CRÊPE FROM.
HEY, MIKA, YOU GOT ANY IDEA WHAT YOU'RE COOKING?
YOU SERIOUS?
YOU'RE COOL AND ALL, BUT IT'S LIKE THE JUDGE SAYS...
...IT'S "GO" TIME!
WE CAN BRAID EACH OTHER'S HAIR IN THE FUTURE.
FOR NOW?
THE TOURNAMENT'S A WAR, MY FRIEND.
AND I'M TAKING NO PRISONERS.

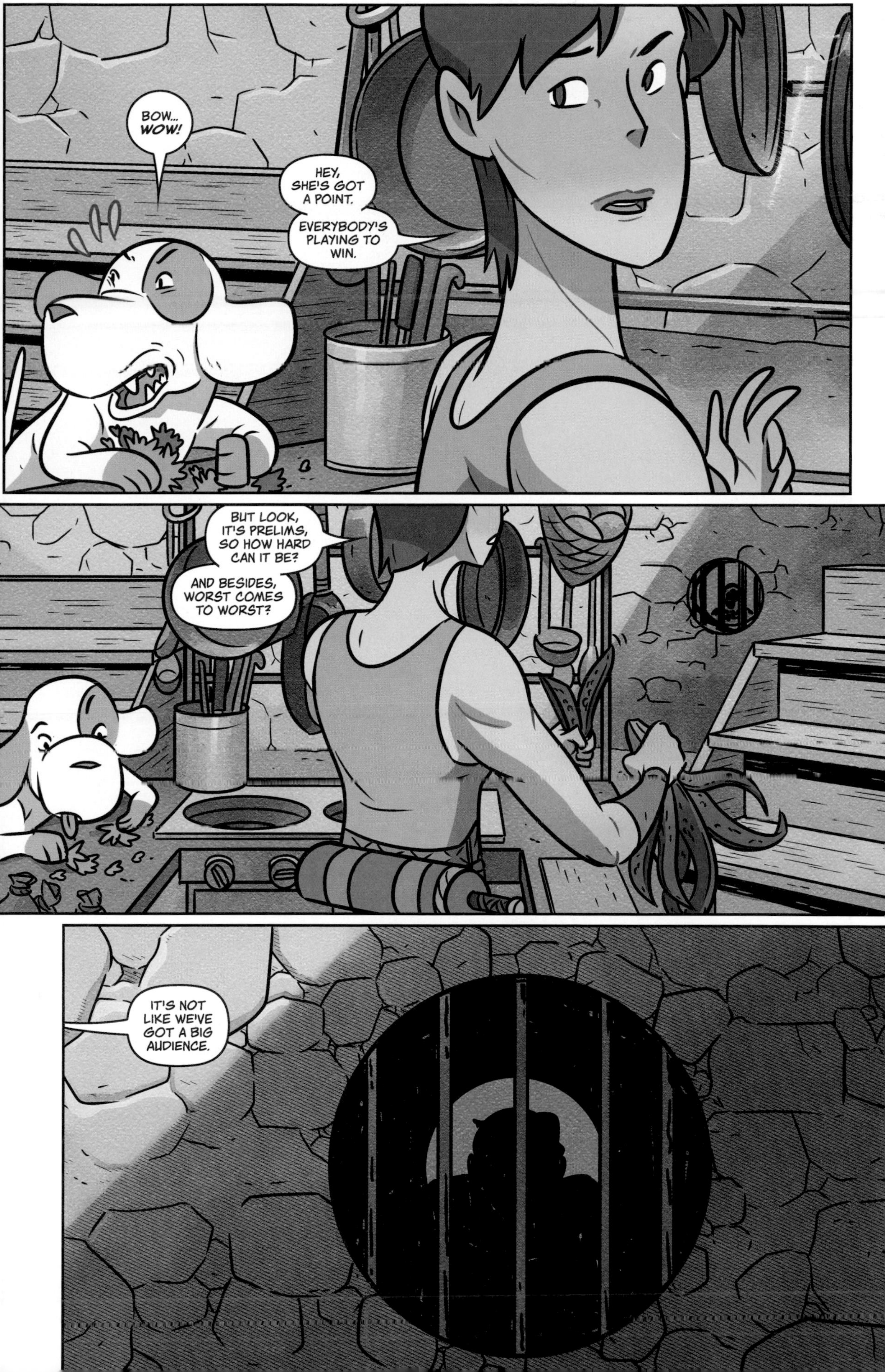
BOW... WOW!
HEY, SHE'S GOT A POINT.
EVERYBODY'S PLAYING TO WIN.
BUT LOOK, IT'S PRELIMS, SO HOW HARD CAN IT BE?
AND BESIDES, WORST COMES TO WORST?
IT'S NOT LIKE WE'VE GOT A BIG AUDIENCE.

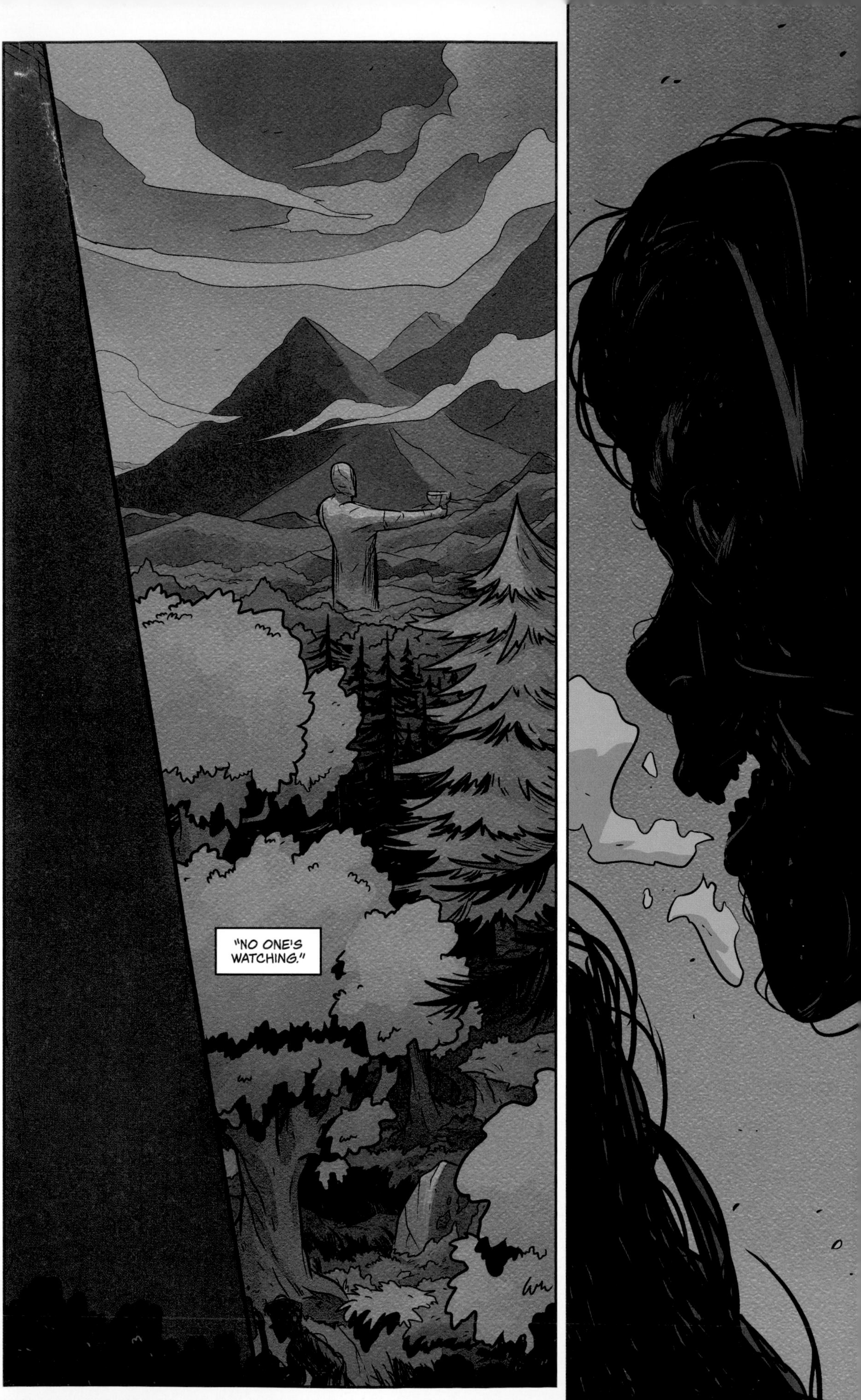
"NO ONE'S WATCHING."

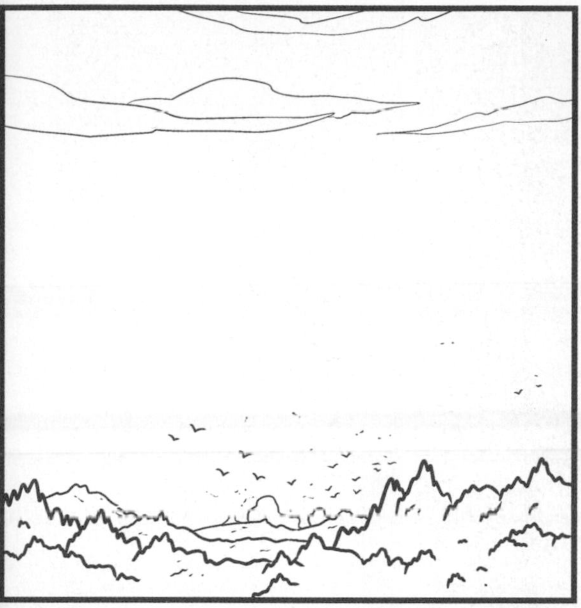

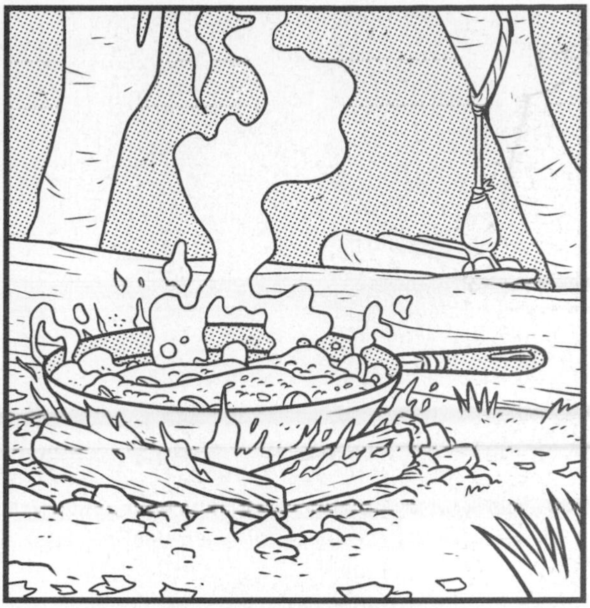

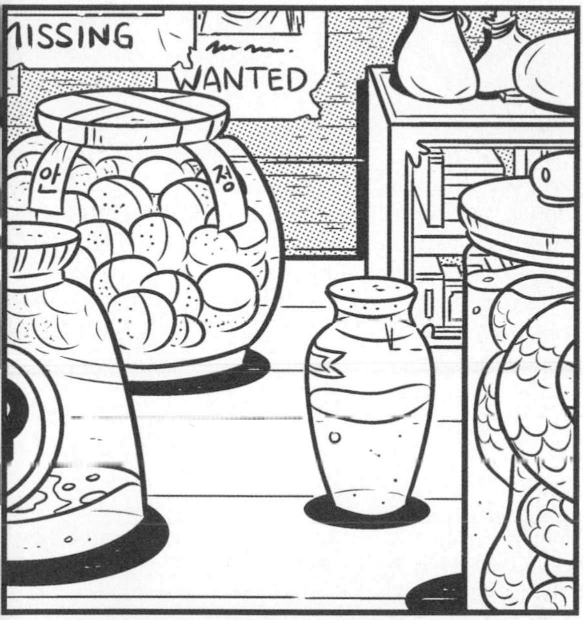
MISSING
WANTED
안
정

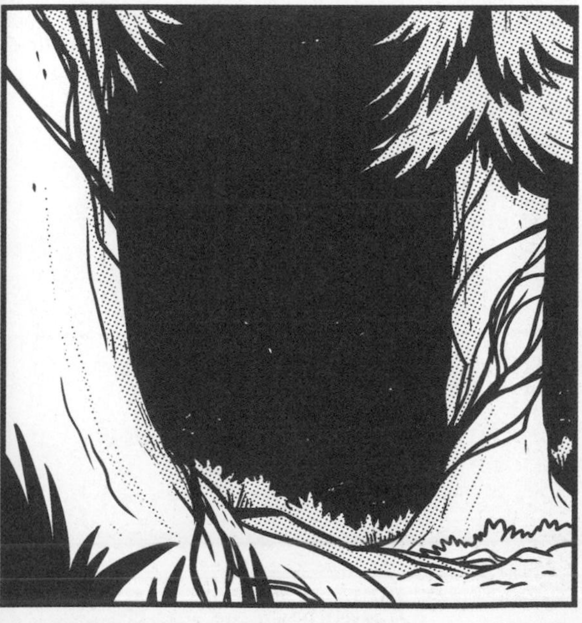

CRÊPES

by Ali Bouzari

Xoo isn't into precise recipes. Like playing jazz, her food revolves around improvisation on tasty themes rather than mindless repetition of something someone else created. A solid understanding of how her food works allows Xoo to pivot, adjusting to the chaos in her life and exploring delicious ideas as they come to her. Fancy academy students require perfect conditions to execute their fancy dishes. Xoo can whip up something delectable in the middle of a street fight. Here's a culinary street fighter's version of a classic crêepe recipe you can make at home:

INGREDIENTS:

1 cup flour

1 cup milk

2 eggs

DIRECTIONS:

1. Whisk everything together in a bowl.

2. Grease a nonstick pan on medium heat, pour in batter, swirl to coat the bottom of the pan, and pour excess batter back into bowl.

3. Let cook on medium heat for 15-30 seconds, until top side has just set.

4. Loosen one edge with a spatula, then pick the crepe up with your fingers and flip.

5. Cook 15-30 seconds until golden brown.

6. Stack, garnish, or add topping of your choice, and serve immediately. Or stack, cover in plastic, and refrigerate for later.

7. Go on fantastical adventures and star in a comic series that some might call an instant classic.

Crêpes aren't fussy. There's no danger of overmixing because the batter is so dilute that gluten has a hard time forming the tough, knotted networks that you'd find in over-worked cake batter. Crêpes don't need hours of slow fermentation or resting like pizza dough, nor do they require any special equipment to make.

For sweet crêpes, add a handful of sugar to the batter, or top unsweetened crepes with honey, maple syrup, chocolate sauce, jam, or your sweetness source of choice. If you want to push crêpes into the savory world, add a pinch of salt to the batter and finish the crepes with cheese, roasted vegetables, smoky meats, miso, hot sauce, or your favorite pickle.

Vegan, lactose intolerant, or just too lazy to go buy milk and eggs? Coconut, soy, or almond milk will work great, as will any other dairy alternative. I've melted down a pint of vegan ice cream and added that straight to the batter in a pinch. You can even use water; just make up for some of the lost protein and fat by adding a teaspoon or two of butter, oil, nut butter, or even mashed avocado to the mix. This batter also works fine with gluten-free flour.

It's harder to not make crêpes than it is to make them.

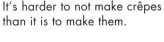

CULINARY TIME TRAVEL

by Ali Bouzari

Culinary schools pummel students with a barrage of techniques – frying, braising, fish butchering, dough laminating, sauce making, knife work, and dozens of other skills gleaned from the world's great cuisines. While all of these techniques are important, when I taught at a culinary school I focused my students on a deeper, more hallowed art: time travel.

Food is alive. Everything you will ever cook or eat contains millions of moving pieces that are constantly in flux. A pear, sitting undisturbed on a counter in an empty room, contains a humming clockwork of delicious gears that transform its taste, texture, aroma and color as they turn. A chef's job is to manipulate those gears to shepherd that pear through time – to speed it up, slow it down or pause it. Truly gifted chefs can even put it in reverse.

Heat is one of the most powerful levers we can pull to send food on a journey through time. With every ten degree Celsius increase in temperature, stuff happens twice as fast in our food. Have you ever noticed that old libraries smell faintly like maple syrup? As books (including this one) age, the backbone of woody carbs from which each page was made decomposes into small fragments, some of them identical to the microscopic crumbs that give maple syrup its spicy, earthy, caramel-y fragrance. At library temperature, however, the process takes about five decades.

Half a century is too long to wait for tomorrow's breakfast, so maple syrup makers use heat as a form of culinary time travel to fast-track the process. The mildly sweet, dilute water that seeps out of tapped maple trees doesn't have much aroma, but it does contain some of the same pulpy machinery that slowly churns out that syrupy aroma in paper books. Syrup makers use the heat of boiling kettles to supercharge that machinery, packing the magic of half a century into a few hours of scalding transformation.

Heat is the fire that drives food forward, and removing it helps to slow things down. Sushi chefs rely on thermally altered time to access the freshest products. We romanticize the idea of fresh fish eaten the same day it was caught. Sure, that might work for rockfish caught five hundred feet from the shore, but most sashimi-grade tuna are caught several days' journey out at sea. Even when refrigerated, the delicate oils in fatty tuna disintegrate quickly into fishy funk within a couple of days, which means that most deep-sea fish would smell old and unappealing before they even reached the harbor. The secret to the freshest fish is a dip in time-arresting liquid nitrogen. When fishermen plunge freshly caught fish into a deep freeze hundreds of degrees colder than the coldest part of your home freezer, the gears that turn below the surface grind to a halt, buying us time to get that fish from boat to plate in pristine condition.

To drive food backwards in time, chefs need help from the inside. Enzymes are a tiny protein labor force that live and work inside the cells of every living thing, building things up and breaking them back down in an endless cycle of growth and decay. As a sweet potato grows and winter approaches, the plant funnels hard-earned sugar into a botanical vault of starch to set food aside for spring. Sweet potatoes contain enzymes for reversing that process to transform starch back into sugar. Baking sweet potatoes slowly (starting them in a cold rather than preheated oven) encourages those enzymes to go wild, allowing chefs to travel backwards from starch to sugar to sweeten sweet potatoes with the sands of time.

Everything we do in the kitchen creates ripples that push and pull our food through time. Stirring a pot speeds the transfer of heat to your pasta, chilling a vinaigrette keeps oil and vinegar united for a few extra minutes, and adding sugar to jam helps to stall the slow onslaught of microbial hordes that would otherwise cause it to spoil.

There are limits to culinary time travel, and food's natural arc of growth and decay inevitably overrides any fiddling on our end. If we learn to recognize that arc and anticipate its path, however, we can do some incredibly tasty things in the meantime.

PROCESS SKETCHES

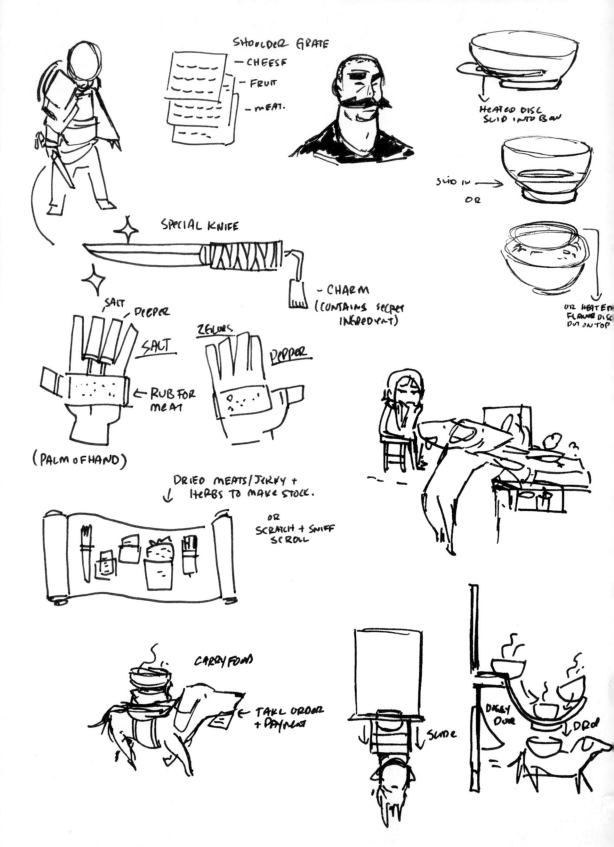